Polaris: Emperor of Nan Rong

Book One of the Series

San An

散安

Kang Lang

抗浪

ISBN-13: 978-0-9966338-0-2

Titles in the Series:
Polaris: Emperor of Nan Rong
Polaris: Empress of Ning
Polaris: The Demon General and the General Practitioner
Polaris Special: Dui's True Ending
Polaris: The Curse of Ice Blue Eyes

Polaris: Emperor of Nan Rong

By Lenne Penry

Polaris: Emperor of Nan Rong

Chapter 1: A Chance Meeting

"To the east, the elder star lies." A familiar tune bursts as I walk down the dirt road. It is late afternoon and the sun's vigor isn't as oppressive as it had been earlier so, I decided to return home. What a great day it was for fishing! I caught three large catfish! This should last for the rest of the week.

"The younger's name is Bao Lai! Pft! Ha-ha! What was that? That was way too shrill!"

Singing at the top of my lungs to test my terrible skills for the sheer fun has become a habit of sort, to stave off silence. It's a good thing no one's around to witness my embarrassment, or so I thought.

Without warning, the ground begins shaking and a few stones beside my feet jump as though scattered on a beating drum. When I look up, two horses are galloping hither at full speed. The men atop are clad in heavy armors decorated with unmistakable colors of the imperial army. What could soldiers possibly be doing in this secluded little area? Every succeeding, rapid thump of horses' hoofs peppering the road gives evidence that the fleeting thought is inconsequential. The men see me, I know they do, but there is no sign of them yielding. This little road is barely enough for them to ride side-by-side as they are. There is no room for me, too. They are going to run over me!

Every second they near, panic escalates. Without thinking, I dart for a gully to be out of their way. As luck would have it, my foot slips and I fall onto a thick thornbush. My precious fish are covered in dirt and my clothes and flesh are cut by the jagged thorns. Small amounts of blood begin trickling from my arms and back. Such as it is, I at least had my life.

The horses fly by where I previously stood on the road. Those men undoubtedly would have trampled me without a second thought. There is no remorse from them; not even a slight apology. But then, what could anyone expect from imperial soldiers? They cower before their lords and treat everyone else their doormats.

Naturally, temper gives into fury. Climbing out from the gully, words begin gushing without discretion. "I'm so sorry to be in your ways, my lords! I just thought men wearing imperial colors are supposed to protect the people, not run them over!"

The horse on the right comes to a halt, followed by the one on the left. The men whip around their steeds. I can feel blood draining from my face. I never speak when I should and always do when I shouldn't, I realize that, but it is too late. Retreat seems an obvious choice. Yet, they have horses, how can I outrun them? Then again, why should I run? I've done nothing wrong.

The two mumble a few words to one another and then advance. The one on the right, the man who stopped after having heard my charges, dismounts and approaches first. He is tall and his eyes are sharp and cold. Even so, I can't help but notice the hazel colors of his irises and the long majestic silver hair. What an unnatural combination! He appears more of a demon from an old silk scroll than a man; and maybe, he is. That scowl on his face is sending chills down my spine. I'm not inclined to believe myself a coward. Still, it takes clenching both hands just to keep from shaking.

The odd man scans me over, every inch from the top of my head down to my toes. Then, like a beast, sniffs the air around me as if searching for something. His strange actions fill me with dread, but also restlessness. The sun is on the verge of setting. I need to go home. Whatever fear overtaking me is pushed back by sheer obstinacy. My lips part; yet, I do not have the chance. The galloping of another horse down the dirt road startles me to turn as another armored man rides forthwith. Unlike the others, his light suit is common and bland, without their intricate, expensive embellishments. I assume he must be of lower ranking. The brown mare stops abruptly and the rider jumps off.

"I'm sorry, Generals! I got lost! You both were riding so fast, I couldn't keep up!" The young man gasps for air, though I wonder why, since the mare had been sprinting and not him.

"If you can't keep up, then you shouldn't have come." The sinister, demon-like man replies. "And, if you are going to be a burden, I will kill you."

13

The young man winces, before embarrassment sweeps over. I don't think that was an empty threat considering the feral expression crossing the older man.

"I'm sorry, General Hu. I'll try harder." The young man mutters through a low bow.

Since his arrival, I've been gawking at the newcomer. He appears particularly childish. I didn't think the army is so desperate that it needed such young recruits. Then again, what do I know about warfare? When the young man finally notices my silent intrusion, he flusters, kneels down, and then bows deeply onto the ground.

"Your Highness! I didn't see you there! I'm so sorry! Generals, you've found our lord at last! Thank goodness!"

"He is? Where?" I spin around, only to meet my shadow. The phantom he addressed isn't there, but a demon suddenly flies past me.

"Get up, you idiot!" General Hu growls furiously.

"I don't under—" The young man is forcibly pulled to his feet before he can finish.

"Do you have any idea what you've just done? Give me a reason not to kill you right here and now!" Immediately upon his outburst, Hu unsheathes the sword latched to his hip. Gold engravings on the blade reflect the setting sun, turning the fearsome thing blood red.

"Hold on there! What's your problem?" Jerking the young man back, I step in between the confrontation. "He didn't do anything. What's wrong with you?"

"Stay out of this!"

"How is anyone supposed to stand idle when you threaten a boy for no reason? Bully someone your own size!"

"You've got a big mouth for a little girl."

"And you've got a pretty big skull for someone with no brain."

Where did that come from? Insulting strangers isn't a habit of mine. That slipped out naturally as if I were bickering with an old friend. The old man often said trouble followed my temper.

"Why you—!"

Resentment boils within his gaze. I have no doubt that if he were inclined, would cut through me to slay the young man. General Hu's grip around the sword tightens and the surrounding heavy feeling heightens. I really thought he would strike. Just as the end seems near, a hard voice terminates the scene.

"That's enough, Bai Hu. Qing Hai meant no harm. Anyone could have made such an easy mistake. Had you let insults go, we wouldn't be in this mess." The man who rode on the left horse had watched the event without interest, but now he thinks it's necessary to intervene.

As he comes closer, his tall figure and broad shoulders tower over me. Black raven-colored hair, encompassing the strong face and stern jaw, flutters in the gentle wind. Kind eyes, as blue as night skies, though distant as they are, seem to study me with great care. Never in my life have I met men such as these. The capital must be another world comprised of fantastic people so very different from commoners elsewhere.

"Qing Hai, don't be so impulsive," continues he.

Qing Hai smiles weakly and bows to both men. By the by, he glances at me from the corners of his eyes, though I don't understand why.

"You, girl. Why are you dressed as a man?" The one with blue eyes inquires.

"What do you mean, *girl*?!'" Qing Hai flusters terribly while turning completely to face me.

"Answer!" General Hu pushes on.

Well, that's a silly question. "It's none of your business," is how I want to rebut. Actually, there are a number of reasons, but I won't be bullied into admission.

"Because men's clothes are more comfortable," is my indolent reply.

"Sarcasm, is it? Or, do you think you're funny, girl?" General Hu growls. "Maybe, you are. I see a complete fool standing before me and the only usefulness for a fool is to die and make room for others."

"I expected as much from imperial soldiers. You want to harass the common—to boast whatever little power you have? Go for it, but do it in your own time! I've got places to go and things to do."

Turning around, I start away when Hu grabs my collar. "Where do you think you're going? Do you think we'd let you leave after this?"

"She's a woman, General! You can't just manhandle her that way!"

"A woman who knows too damn much! We have to kill her! There is no choice! Don't you agree, Yue?" Hu turns to the other man, but the one with blue eyes I thought to be kind, simply shrugs.

"I don't know anything!"

As I attempt to pull away, Hu's grip tightens. A hefty jerk from his meaty paw slams me against the heavy armor. It feels nothing short of hitting a wall. My back is now bruised and bloodied.

"Leave her alone!" Hai reaches for me but Hu knocks him to the ground.

"I told you, I don't know what you're talking about!" Turning around for one final effort, a fist slams across

Hu's face with every bit of strength I can muster. Slowly, the hold on my collar loosens. The General rubs his face absently.

"That really hurts," Hu remarks flatly.

I can't tell whether he is mocking me. That doesn't matter. I've backed far enough from him that another escape could be attempted. Should I fail, he'll kill me for sure. Then again, could I reason with him instead? Maybe an act of faith by not running would be more prudent. My mind races but I only have seconds to decide.

Before resolve can form, my feet decide for me. Hu reaches out and misses by a hair's breadth. Wind whips across my cheek and tousles unkempt hair, drowning Hu's incessant cursing and the surge of voices trailing behind. After an indeterminable span of time, I stumble and fall to the ground. My chest and legs are burning in tandem. Quickly, I crawl over to a nearby bush and lie still to recover.

Soon as the thought of escape resumes, Hai suddenly picks me up from the shrub. I never heard him approached.

"Ack! C-Calm down! Please, Miss! Stop flailing!"

"Let go!"

Despite my voice and body trembling erratically, his pleading, apologetic stare hold more anxiety. The rounded eyes and boyish face peering down remind me that he's just a child. Hai has no interest in my death. He's in as much trouble as I am, if not more. My reply is a short nod and then, he puts me down.

"Are you going to let me go?"

"I-I can't do that. I'm good at tracking. He'll know I'm lying if I say otherwise. Listen, I won't let him harm you. You have to believe in me. General Yue won't allow him to kill you in cold blood."

Hope rising in my chest is dashed away sorely; replaced by exasperation. "Are you kidding me? General Yue couldn't care less what happens to me! He just shrugged when Hu said he'd kill me! And you... Hu would have killed you if it hadn't been for him! You can't even protect yourself. How can you protect me?"

Hai's gaze lowers. Though I didn't mean to, it's obvious I wounded his pride. A short pause ensues and then Hai looks up and gives a brief smile.

"General Hu's not all that bad. It's just... it was my fault. I said something I shouldn't have and he's only trying to protect the country."

"How is killing me going to protect the country? I'm not the emperor of Ning!"

"There's no time to explain. You'll just have to believe me. I won't let him hurt you." Hai extends a friendly hand. By the ardent expression of kindness in his eyes, it's palpable that he will do everything to protect me; though, his ambitions may be too much for his skills.

Running is pointless. He's found me after all and he can do so again. Even if Hai were to let me go, General Hu might slay him for failing and I don't want that on my conscience.

Chapter 1 – 2

"Took you long enough, kid." General Hu mutters gruffly as he sees us emerging from the woods. As we come near the two men, Qing Hai moves in front of me whilst keeping the right hand cradling mine behind his back. He squeezes tightly to reassure everything is well. When he speaks, the hardened tone is completely unexpected.

"She is willing to cooperate. There is no need for violence. I will not stand by and allow you to harm a civilian when no crimes have been committed."

"You dare speak to me like that, Recruit? Pass basic training and you think you're tough?   You're lucky you're Minister San An's nephew or I'd take your head."

Qing Hai does not respond. Even though his back is to me, I can feel strong defiance in his stance. Following a long pause, Hu lets out a sarcastic laugh. "All this for a woman you thought was a man a moment ago? Fine. Whatever. Yue and I decided not to kill her after all. She could be useful to us; at least, she better be if she wants to live."

"Useful how?!" Hai's grip tautens.

"Don't be such a pervert. I wasn't implying anything depraved. I like my women to look like women and I definitely don't need to coerce anyone. Bring her along. We'll let San An deal with her."

21

"My-My uncle? What does he have to do with this?"

"The sun is setting. Don't waste any more time." Hu turns around and remounts the ironclad steed. Yue does the same. They start for the road ahead at a slow trot. Hai gradually lets out a heavy sigh. It's obvious he was more frightened than I was during the exchange.

"Let's go. My uncle won't let anything happen to you. I promise." Hai throws a smile over his shoulder. I'm inclined to believe him, simply because I don't have a choice.

Chapter 2: A Missing Monarch

Well into the dark night, hoofs steadily pound against the ground, stopping only a time shortly before daybreak, and then continue again. My body and mind are exhausted; mostly, I'm anxious of what lies ahead. Why must I meet Minister San An in the capital and how can I be a threat to our country's security for dressing as a man? I want to ask, but Hai had said nothing of import for both of us to be in trouble. If he does tell me something useful, I am certain General Hu will end us.

In the late afternoon, we finally reach An's massive gates. The bustling capital is beyond anything my imaginations can dream. Beautiful buildings, beautiful people, and beautiful things all crowd together in this magnificent place of commerce. Each wondrous sight, exotic scent, and cheerful tone sends my heart fluttering from elation. At the same time, fatigue wreaks havoc and all I want to do is collapse.

"Just a little farther," Qing Hai whispers encouragingly. If it weren't for him sitting behind keeping me upright, I would have fallen off the horse long ago. His amiability is greatly appreciated. All the same, I hate these imperial soldiers. They brought me into this chaos, of which I don't want any part.

Eventually, we near the massive palace jutting above every surrounding structure. The wealth of a nation is clearly displayed for all to see. The breathtaking scene seems surreal. Charmed by magnificence, a smile begins curling over my lips, which then abruptly dissipates when General Hu turns about.

"We're going through the back entrance," he snaps. His eyes are as sharp as knives. For whatever reason, he is vexed again.

After a while, the back entrance comes into view. General Yue goes inside to fetch the Minister while the remaining two stand guard. I don't know why they bother. I have nowhere to go. At least, I have no way of returning home. I don't even know which way home is. My sense of direction has always been terrible.

Feet shuffle and sway to keep awake while stress and lack of sleep are slowly pulling away consciousness. Qing Hai pats my shoulder and smiles. I do my best to return the gesture. All the same, my vision is reeling. I can barely see straight. In time, another man dressed in beautiful silk exits with General Yue. As he sees me, charming brown eyes grow wide. His face is the last thing I remember before losing all consciousness.

Chapter 2 – 2

A large decorated room finely furnished with polished, dark-colored wood furniture. Windowpanes, wall panels, and arched doorways are exquisitely embellished by unmatched intricate patterns. Surrounding me on this massive bed are silk sheets the color of honey so luxuriously soft that by comparison, rose petals are no less than jagged thorns.

Sitting up, I rub my head absently but fatigue suddenly surges, and then I fall back, caught by two large, fluffy feather pillows. For a moment, I thought I must be dreaming, until *his* voice shakes me to be on alert.

"Boo!" He's glaring at me from the sofa by the closed windows. What madness is this? His hair is no longer silver. It is dark brown. The long locks hang loosely toward his waist. Upon construing my confusion, Hu laughs.

"I'm not a hundred years old. There's no reason why my hair should all be grey. Makes me look like a demon though, doesn't it?" He grins and his fangs can clearly be seen.

"You are a demon." I roll my eyes.

He returns another laugh. "Glad you liked my costume. It makes people in battle so very afraid of me. Anyway, after all I did to frighten you, it was the

Minister who made you faint? That's a big insult to the Demon General."

He sounds like he's joking around but that seems out of character for him. If he had held a sword over the bed and tried to stab me, it would be more believable.

"Is that why you're here? Do you want an apology?"

He smirks, though there is something strange in the response I can't quite understand.

"Our guest needs sustenance and rest after the previous ordeal. Would you mind sending Jin in here for me, Demon General?"

The voice that abruptly enters our conversation belongs to Minister San An. For a quick moment, he turns to me with a slight smile, before refocusing attention to Hu. The younger man grumbles incoherently; though, ultimately complies and leaves the room.

Wasting no time, Minister San An sits on the edge of the bed and raises the back of his hand to examine my forehead. He is in his thirties, I surmise, rather too young and handsome than I had imagined a minister would be. Dark coal black hair draping down his shoulders swing gently when he reaches for my wrist. "Remain still and let me check your pulse."

I figure, I have no choice. Since the Demon General takes orders from him, then Minister San An is not a man to be reckoned with. After a minute or so, he frowns.

"I'm afraid your pulse is rather weak. Please, allow Jin to tend to you. Inform him should you need anything. I know you must be very confused but I—no, your country—needs a great favor from you. Later, I will explain everything and I hope you will consider the matter. For now, I must return to court for the assembly. Please, excuse me."

I haven't the chance to say anything when he parts from the room as swiftly as he had entered. I will not lie, I am enjoying the pampering and attention of such handsome men; the Demon General included. Whatever it is the Minister will ask of me, I don't think I will deny him, especially since I am, after all, being held hostage. Going against the wishes of the imperial court could easily be viewed as treason.

As I ponder San An's unspoken request, a young man in his twenties enters the room with a tray of food and tea.

"Oh, hello."

He ignores me until the tray is on the side table. The young man, knitting his brows, carefully studies my face. "I can't believe it. You look just like him."

"Just like who?"

"His Highness," he replies.

The answer to the ordeal is so obvious, I can't believe how slow I am. Qing Hai mistook me for our emperor when he thought the Generals had found him. It must be that His Highness is missing. This is not something known throughout the land. Why should it? Once Ning become aware of the situation, war would come to our borders immediately. This is the reason Hu wanted my demise and also the reason I was brought to the capital.

"Do you understand now?"

I bite my lip and nod.

"Good. I advise that you agree to this, but I also want you to know that this is not something to be taken lightly. This is not a chance to be pampered. This is an opportunity to protect your country. If you do not play the part wholeheartedly and are exposed, you will be executed for impersonating His Highness. Even though the idea was not yours, no one will stand behind you. The council will deny all connections to this plot. Worse, if it is discovered that His Highness is missing, our land will suffer not only from external political strife, but internal. The vast number of nobles vying for his authority is endless. They will stop at nothing until one is left to claim the throne. I know this is a lot of pressure. That is why I am here to assist you in any way I can. My name is Shu Jin. I go by Jin. I am His Highness's personal attendant."

"I am... Bao Lai. I-It's nice to meet you."

This is not news I want to hear. I need to flawlessly impersonate the most important person in the country or everyone could die? What nonsense! Aggravation surges but it only makes me lightheaded. I fall back onto the bed.

"Are you all right?" Jin rushes over and puts his arms around me. This is a little friendlier than expected from someone I'd just met.

"Isn't it inappropriate for you to touch His Highness this way?"

A startled expression bursts in exchange for my weak laughter. Then, he smiles. "Yes. I'm sorry, Your Highness."

Jin moves away, fetches the tray of food, and places it in front of me. Before exiting, he turns around once more. "Oh, I had forgotten. General Bai Hu and Qing Hai asked for permission to visit you. I advise only speaking to one of them since you need rest and they tend to draw out conversations whenever they are together."

"What would His Highness do?"

"He would not meet with either. His Highness He Pi is selective of his acquaintances. Should I send them both away?"

"Yes, send them both away." If I am to play my role as I should, I cannot do anything His Highness, He Pi, wouldn't. Even if it means offending a few people, I will have to get used to it.

Chapter 3: Someone Special

When the moon is high overhead, the door creaks open and Minister San An enters. He smiles sweetly whilst giving an amiable glance. Unintentionally, slight color creeps over my face.

"I did not mean to disturb at such late hours, but I've received word that you've considered the task."

"I don't truly have a choice."

"Perhaps, not *truly*, but there are other choices. By that, I mean if you appear a fool at court, the truth will be known and you will not have to pretend very long."

"Of course not, I would just be executed." My sardonic answer is accompanied by a tepid wave into the air.

The Minister smiles again and then I become embarrassed for my brash response.

"I know you feel trapped but I am not cruel. I cannot permit you to leave because you know the truth and yet, I don't think an unwilling person would be of use to us. We can always continue the ruse we have been using for some time now, while our men search for His Majesty. After careful deliberation, I've come to a single conclusion that will relieve you from this deception and also preserve your life."

My posture stiffens. The Minister draws close and leans down to face level. "The only way is to have you watched over by one of us."

"I don't understand. You're all watching me."

"Yes, well, perhaps at a closer level." He looks away for a quick moment. A delicate hint of uncertainty enters the expression; dissipating as quickly as it comes. Turning back, he smiles. "You may enter the Circle at the Peony Palace or you can simply wed one of us and become the responsibility of whomever you choose."

He has to be joking. Become a consort to the missing emperor or marry a random person? Either path would certainly keep me from having to impersonate His Highness and allow my life to be spared, but they are far from what I'd expected. I stand frozen in place; my face as crimson as the sash around San An's waist. The reaction must amuse him, because the Minister laughs.

"Was that too sudden? I will permit you some time to think things over. There's no need for an immediate answer. One is required come sunrise. I hope you will consider these alternatives if truly, you do not wish to take part in our political ploy."

"I don't understand. Why must these be the alternatives? I could stay as a servant to one of you or just tend to the gardens. I am not very bad at tending to gardens."

31

"I'm afraid these boys won't take their duties seriously were they to watch over a servant. But a wife... a man will be inclined to give all his attention to his wife and therefore, will ensure both your safety and honesty from allowing another soul to know our secret."

So, it is all a matter of trust and I am not viewed as trustworthy, is that it?

"It's not that I do not trust you," San An answers my mental inquiry. "I cannot say the same of the others. Once you leave these grounds, one or more might attempt to take your life."

There's truth to his reasonings—bizarre as they are. I have no idea which path to take. As I contemplate the choices, he continues.

"And, should you choose me, I will ensure for you a life without hardship. You will never be in want of anything. I am not your first choice, perhaps. I am not young and handsome, but as I am not as young as these boys, I am also not as foolhardy. They can love and hate on a whim. I will undoubtedly love you with every part of me until I draw my last breath. So please, do consider things carefully."

If I flush any deeper, my head would turn into a tomato! What is he talking about? He's gorgeous! And yes, he is older than the others, but there is something dignified and mature with this age. Ack! What am I saying? I have no interest in this! I just want to go home and eat my fish and water my garden.

I turn elsewhere and try to think of anything and everything to distract from the moment. When San An places a hand on my shoulder, I jump back.

"Do I frighten you?" Slight pain crosses within the tone.

"N-No! I... just... I don't understand! Yesterday, your boys thought I was a man and I know I'm not half as pretty compared to the women I saw strolling around the markets. I can't even imagine how beautiful the women in the Circle are! You, sir, can do a lot better!" I fold my arms and keep my head down, embarrassed by my own outburst.

"Conceivably, you are not the most beautiful woman, but beauty is only part of the equation. You have all of our attentions and that makes you special. Everyone wants to claim someone special."

Inexplicable resentment begins creeping over my psyche. My eyes dart to his face. "A prize, is that it? Because I resemble His Highness, that makes me special? You want to win me because it inflates your ego? If that's the case, then I'm sorry to say you don't understand what love is, Minister!"

Taking a seat near the window, I scratch my head irritably. I thought he would be angry. Instead, San An laughs. A smile reappears.

"No, I'm afraid you don't understand what love is." He replies. "To find someone special is ordinary inclination. It is natural to be able to discern between beauty and ugliness, intelligence and stupidity, and yes, even common and rare. Love simply means to care for, so how can caring for someone I find special means that my love is less than any man who loves for beauty, intellect, or even money? Love is love, no matter the reason. If love needs to be based on any particular reason, then I think that is too mechanical."

My head tilts due confusion. I don't know how to argue with that and my own ignorance just draws me deeper into a void. I want to reply but nothing will come. Following the painful ensuing silence, San An relieves a sigh.

"Forgive me, I did not mean to grieve you. I only wanted to speak my mind, for I fear regret will consume me if I did not at least try. You are entitled to your opinions. I merely hope you will not think too poorly of me for having caused your anxiety."

"N-No. I don't think poorly of you at all! It's just that you don't even know me. I could very well drive you mad." My attempt to chuckle off the tension is met with his simple smile.

"What if I say that you already have?" The sheepish tone comes forth and then, he quickly glances away.

"I don't understand."

"That you don't understand makes me admire you even more."

San An reaches out; though, before his fingers graze my cheek, he withdraws. My heart immediately flutters and my face feels warm. Following a span of silent contemplation, a soft chuckle breaks from his pale rose lips.

"It's late and you need rest. Let us end here for now. I look forward to speaking with you again. Please, don't hesitate to call for me should you require anything. It is my desire to fulfill all your wishes." The Minister bows gracefully before taking his leave.

My eyes widened during our exchange and even now that he's left, I can't seem to force them back to the original position. I'm so confused! What was all that about? Did he just seriously propose to me? The image of his smiling face is engraved into my mind. The more I struggle to push it away, the more it comes flooding back.

Around him, I feel inferior in every way, and for some reason, it makes my heart race. The intellect and guidance of an older man, is that what I need most? What am I thinking?!

Vigorously shaking my head, I stuff my face in my hands. Sometime later, I fall asleep in distress and before I know it, Jin comes into the room and wakes me to prepare for the dreadful event.

Chapter 4: The Path to my Future

Around noon, the men assemble in the chamber and after a brief conversation, my decision is requested. Before me stand the Generals Zhen Yue and Bai Hu, Qing Hai, and Minister San An. Yue is indifferent, so he looks off elsewhere, while Hai is terribly embarrassed with his eyes to the ground. Hu smirks at me but I don't understand why. Finally, San An smiles sweetly with hopes in his eyes.

The idea of imposing upon uninterested parties bothers me. I'm certain Zhen Yue, Bai Hu, and Qing Hai would object even if I were so bold. As for joining the Circle, it's unthinkable. Not only have I no desire to become a courtesan, the thought of being a prisoner in painted cells brings angst. I don't know the right answer, but as I glance from one to the next, the choice is obvious after all.

"I want to become He Pi. I want to help maintain peace for Nan Rong until His Highness is found."

"You are willing to risk your life and the lives of the people? Are you certain you can play the part?"

"Yes, Minister. I will become He Pi no matter what."

"Very well." San An replies. "Jin, she is your charge. Amongst current parties, you are most acquainted with His Highness. Teach Bao Lai his mannerisms, his speech, and aspects of his mind. Should she fail, the country may fall with her."

He is not determined to scare me. San An is merely reinforcing the risk. Despite having made my choice, I'm still nervous.

Jin bows deeply while the others exit the room. Aside from the Minister, I doubt I can associate very much with them from now on. For some reason, that makes me a little sad even though our encounter in prior days had caused much distress.

Once we are alone, Jin nears and leans down to face level.

"What are you doing?"

Jin grabs my arm when my feet toggle back.

"Hold still. You look like him, but not perfectly. He spends most of his time inside and I can tell that you do not. No, this won't do. Stay here."

Jin abruptly parts from the room, leaving me to shuffle irritably, until curiosity gets the better of me, and then I'm left perusing the room for clues of the man I must become. Ah, who am I kidding? I have no idea where to begin. Thankfully, Jin walks through the door and throws a set of clothes on the bed along with a box made from redwood. It's beautifully carved with images of lotuses and water lilies on every panel.

"First, you must mirror his image. Then, you must walk and sit as he does to at least endure the assemblies. Lastly, and only when compelled, should you speak and make decrees on the council's behalf. Come, sit here for me." Jin points to a chair in front of the vanity while opening the redwood box to remove a set of powders. Once I settle, he begins painting. The unfamiliar scent of powder is making my nose twitch.

"Tell me about him." The quick attempt to distract Jin is more so in part, to distract myself. "What should I know about He Pi?"

"His Highness speaks very little during assemblies. He finds them boring. That will be to your advantage. However, he sits with great posture, which you do not have. Control your breathing to remain still. Later, I will teach you the proper pose. He is also a very intelligent man despite masking his talents through childishness."

"He is childish?"

"Ostensibly. He shirks going to assemblies whenever he can, teases every woman in the Circle, and inveterately vexes his ministers through sarcasms. He'd sleep until noon, if I would let him, and tends to sneak out of the palace at night to wander about."

I can't believe this. Who knew our country was led by a man so... "Irresponsible! How irresponsible! How could *he* have taken the throne over anyone else? Why even bother searching for someone that irresponsible?"

Jin frowns at the uncouth outburst. I withdraw. Sighing deeply, he slowly resumes the task and applies another layer of powder to my face.

"Irresponsible, yes, but he is a good leader. He is brilliant even if he is lazy. He is powerful even if he is small in stature. He is always aware even if he seems absentminded. I was not worried at first, but when he did not return after two days, the Prime Minister sent men to search for him. He's never gone for more than a day at most."

"How long has it been since he's left?"

"Over a month. The ministers told the court that he is away at the Summer Palace. More and more, they can see through the ruse. His Highness tends to stay solely in the capital now. The Summer Palace has been sitting bare for years. The plan is to next tell the court that His Highness is unwell to buy additional time, but that excuse will just bring more questions with his prolonged absence. You are our only hope, you see. However, you must remember that this position may not be temporary. If he is never found, you must live his life for the rest of your days, but without his freedom. The ministers will direct you to carry out their will. You will simply be a puppet. Do you understand?"

I nod. Since stepping foot into the capital, I have been a puppet without freewill. I can accept that if it means peace. However, should war come and the people look to me for He Pi's intellect and guidance, then all will be lost. Not to mention that although the ministers are one for now, who can say they will not eventually struggle for control over me? I need for everyone to believe I am He Pi, so that should anyone challenges my authority, I will have the support of the court.

"Tell me more. How does he normally speak? What does he like or dislike?"

"He rarely speaks to most people aside from me. I have been his servant since we were both children. To me, he is always cheerful and sometimes, even playful. To others—except to women, I suppose—when he does speak, does so with little fervor. You can even say his speech is somewhat indolent. He likes women and wearing disguises when he leaves the palace. He dislikes... pretty much everything else."

"So, he's a lecher? Great! A sarcastic, indolent lecher who likes to play dress up!"

Jin laughs when I roll my eyes. "Well, a lecher in performance. He actually never does a lecherous thing."

"What do you mean? He... pretends to be a lecher?"

"He doesn't trust women; hence, His Highness flirts with any he'd meet. If the woman is disgusted by his advances, then he thinks she is trustworthy."

"How so?"

"Though it's flawed logic, he decided that decent women without ulterior motives would not suffer lecherous men; even when the man is royalty. In any case, since His Highness is interested in every woman, he gives off the sense that he's not interested in anyone at all. Those who can take the hint shy from him. The others, frankly, are wasting their time."

"So, he's not interested in marriage? That is a relief."

"I would not jump to conclusions. He is engaged."

"I don't understand. Didn't you just say he's not interested in anyone?"

"An emperor must marry. That is a duty he must oblige. To keep from civil war, he must provide an heir."

"Then, what am I supposed to do about that?" I shuffle uneasily. Jin signals for me to remain still.

"Don't worry. He's been engaged since he was sixteen and has yet to marry. He's twenty-two now and not a step closer toward anything finite. I understand his dilemma. It's one of the few illogical things he actually ever does."

"And what is his dilemma? Maybe, I should not pry into a stranger's business, but since I must become him, then I need to know how he thinks."

Perhaps Jin doesn't want to tell me for fear of betraying his master, because he pauses for a long moment before complying.

"He was not first in line for the throne. His mother was not empress. She was a consort. She fought hard to secure his position and it was upon the late emperor's deathbed that His Majesty He Pi was declared the new heir. Empress Pai retaliated. This caused great battles at court for many years between all the women whose children had claims to the bloodline. Factions upon factions formed. Everyone thought civil war was near until, finally, things settled when a mystic was called to court and it was proclaimed that divine right belonged to the child with the Mark of Heaven on his shoulder. His Majesty, of course, was the only one."

"Mark of Heaven?"

"He has a red dragon-shaped birthmark on his left shoulder. That is something we will also need to prepare. Now then, I think you finally have his complexion."

The first thought that comes to mind when I look in the mirror is that He Pi needs to go outside more. How ivory his skin must be for this many layers of powder to portray! I think he may have appeared more of a woman than me.

"Now, for his garb. Take off your robe."

The moment those words leave his mouth, we both flush profusely. I may look just like their man but I'm definitely not one. Even though I'm sure he doesn't want to see whatever is under my robe any more than I want to show him, Jin fights with himself and repeats the request.

"I can't do that. Anyway, why can't I just dress myself?"

"His Majesty only appears in court after I dress him and every little detail counts. He likes his clothes a certain way but can never do it himself."

"I'm not half as helpless as His Majesty!"

"You agreed to this: to do whatever is necessary to become His Highness. Have you changed your mind?"

"N-No. But I... Promise me, you won't laugh."

"I would never..." Jin begins glancing over before deciding against imprudence. The awkward gaze averts to the wall.

Oh, thank goodness! I nearly keeled over from embarrassment upon disrobing. Luckily, there are bandages wrapped all over my upper body. Who could have done this? Certainly, it wasn't Jin since he's blushing ear-to-ear just from staring at the wall. The Demon General was in the room when I woke. The thought of this possibility makes me shudder; though, I can't imagine it was Bai Hu either.

"You're hurt! Who did this to you?" Sudden resentment sparks in Jin's voice like that of a provoked mother hen.

"It's a long story. Half of it was my fault. Not as bad as it looks. Whoever bandaged me exaggerated the severity."

Although his brows are still knit tightly, the subject subsides. Jin then drapes the gold robe around my body. Immediately, he frowns. His Majesty has a flat chest, as he should. I do not.

"This is not possible," he mutters. "Can't just... No, that won't do."

"Well, if you tie the robe loosely, maybe they won't show."

"We can't give the notion that anything's changed. Would you be willing to possibly... remove... No, what am I saying?!"

Jin turns away again. As much as I want to help, is he seriously suggesting that I remove my breasts? That is not what I agreed to! But, I did say I would help and I always strive to keep my words. I mean, if I am to impersonate He Pi, possibly, for the rest of my days, I have no need for such things. On the other hand, if he returns tomorrow, then all would be for naught.

No, I don't want to! Shaking my head, I start to tell Jin that I can't do that but he's already formed another idea. Taking a large sash off the bed, he binds my chest.

"Allow me to try this alternative. It will hurt you. I'm sorry. Bear with me."

"Ngh!"

Though it would not flatten, the sash compressing my chest is enough to hide the majority of the area that needs to be hidden. The compression is painful; more so, it is difficult to breathe. I'm becoming lightheaded.

"You're wobbling. What's wrong?"

"I... *Oomph!*" One misstep from my staggering legs sends me stumbling headfirst into Jin's arms.

"Hey, are you okay? Stay awake!" Jin places me on the bed and removes the sash as consciousness begins seeping away. I hear him call my name but I can't comply.

Chapter 5: Second Proposal

"What's the meaning of this?!"

"Awake already? How do you feel?"

Is he joking? When I opened my eyes, Jin's face was inches away. I immediately darted off the bed and woke him in the process. Through it all, he still has the gall to answer casually against my shaking finger.

Slowly rising, Jin runs fingers through his dark, let down hair. The long strands hang loosely around the handsome features of his face. Naturally exuding grace and charming airs, Jin is more deserving of playing the emperor than the servant.

"Come back to bed. You're obviously still tired. Rest for today and we'll try again tomorrow."

"Try what exactly?!"

"Try preparing for your role. Look, I'm not that type of person, okay? You fell unconscious. I stayed to ensure you were safe and then I fell asleep, too. I'm sorry. I shouldn't have been so rough with the execution. I'll be gentler next time."

"What *are* you talking about?!"

"I am talking about binding your... particular area. Do you have such poor views of me that you interpret everything I say and do to be dishonorable?"

I have no idea what happened. I was unconscious after all. Then again, he is so exquisite and I am nothing to be desired. There is no reason he would ever…

"No, I'm sorry."

"Come back to bed and rest." He pats the area adjacent. I don't want to continuously offend him so, I hesitantly comply. Jin moves off and starts for the door just as I lie down.

"I'll bring your breakfast in a bit. Don't overdo things or you'll start bleeding again."

What does he mean by, "*again*?" I was merely punctured by thorns and those small wounds should have sealed by now. After disrobing, I examine the fabric to find small specks of blood scattered over the fine silk. When he had tightened that sash around me, the cuts must have reopened. What a shame. This robe is probably worth more money than I'll ever have.

A few moments later, Jin returns with a silver tray and after placing it on the table, moves toward a dresser and retrieves a small box.

"Turn around. Let's change your bandages."

"It's not that bad. I think I'm better off without it."

"Then, at least let me apply this balm on your wounds. Save your stubbornness for the ministers, Your Highness." His tone is somewhat teasing. I don't want to argue either way.

Jin removes the bandages and applies the balm once my back is turned to him. The cold sensation makes me jump and suddenly, soft chuckles erupt from behind.

"You're quite the sadist," I scoff.

"Yes, I know." He replies coolly.

What an answer! I twist around to return a quip, but words can't form in the midst of Jin's burning cheeks provoking my own. His expression is one of fright.

Something is definitely off. Jin's looked away and the room is suddenly becoming chillier. I reach to pull the robe tighter and instead, clutch at nothing. Oh, dear heavens! There are no more bandages covering what should be covered, and the robe is on the other side of the bed.

"I'm sorry!" Nearly slamming my head against the bed frame, I dive under the sheets. All I hear in response are retreating footsteps.

Obviously, there is nothing about me that deserves to be viewed fondly, but his reaction is a little harsher than expected. A teasing remark here or there; even a snide one would have been better than to have simply fled. What else could I expect? I was mistaken for His Highness. I was mistaken for a man.

Chapter 5 – 2

San An comes around noon and brings a new tray of food. It is unlike the Minister to serve anyone. He must have come on Jin's behalf. I wonder whether anything was exchanged between them regarding my shameful display. As usual, San An smiles tenderly.

He sits on a side of bed and touches my forehead. "I hope you don't mind. I heard you are not well. This is my fault. I should have personally taken you into my care instead of leaving you in the hands of a boy."

"I'm not sick. Please, don't worry about me."

"Perhaps, physically, you are well. Something inside troubles you, am I wrong?"

His tone is so friendly and calming; I want to tell him everything.

"Well, it's just... I don't know if I can do this. I want to, but wanting to do something and being able to do it, are two very different aspects."

"It is still early. You can change your mind. No one will be angry. I just hope you'll consider my offer, if you do."

The touch of San An's fingers gently stroking my hair makes me impulsively recoil. Why is he acting this way? No one as wonderfully handsome and sweet as the Minister should think so much of me; even if his

49

reason is not one I find flattering. Though, I could do a lot worse than be married to him. More like, even in my wildest dreams I couldn't imagine marriage to someone this incredible! Who am I kidding? If I had any other face, he would not look at me twice. I feel as though I'm cheating to win his attention through means I cannot control and therefore, I don't deserve his affection.

"Thank you for your support and kindness, Minister. I will stay the course."

"I see. I am glad you have convictions, even though it means I will be denied my ambitions."

Through dejection, San An smiles cordially. My conscience is writhing from tumult. He's been so thoughtful. However, without the right words to ease glumness, the room defaults to awkward silence. A warm sensation unexpectedly touches my hand. Instinctually, I jump.

"Do I make you uncomfortable?"

His soft, but firm hand is covering mine. Self-consciousness is billowing from realization that my skin is rough and worn. I want to pull away for this reason, but if it means he'll take it as a slight, I probably shouldn't. Without my reply, his thumb begins smoothing over the coarse skin. Immediately, my hand jerks back.

"S-Sorry!" So much for not wanting to slight him. My face is burning from embarrassment.

"Why must you apologize? I am the one who has offended you. Forgive me."

The Minister stands up and I feel terrible for being so uncouth. How it happened is unbeknownst to me; my hands are holding onto his sleeve. I don't know which of us is more surprised by my brazenness.

"You did not offend me. Please, I'm sorry. I'm just not used to..."

An incoherent mumble veils the last words of excuse. Taking no offense, San An resumes my side. The Minister gently picks up my coarse hand and flips it over to survey my palm.

"Would you like me to tell your fortune?"

"You can do that?"

"Are you surprised? Not every man who becomes a minister is all noses."

"I didn't mean *that.*"

"I know," he chuckles. "Shall I begin?"

"Please."

"To be fair, someone taught this to me very long ago. I can't vouch for my memory after all this time. In any case, here is your life line." His finger slowly traces along a crevice on my palm. The ticklish sensation sends my heart shooting like a rocket.

"This one represents wealth and this one represents intellect." His finger runs over the two lines. Each time, my breathing shifts.

"Now, give me your other hand."

"What's different about this hand?" I put out my left palm.

"These are the same lines, but for your soul mate."

"So, the person with these matching lines on his right hand is my soul mate?"

"That is what I was told," San An laughs. "I've yet to meet anyone successful in finding their counterpart through this method. In my opinion, hands should be held, not examined, and fingers should be used to feel, not just touch." His fingers run from my palm to my wrist and then, flipping my hand over, he brings it toward his pretty lips.

"Minister!"

He pauses. "You need not be so formal. San An is just fine."

"San An..."

"Yes, Your Highness?"

"Don't take this the wrong way, but I'm very embarrassed right now." My hand withdraws.

"For what reasons could you be embarrassed?"

"Don't tell me that you didn't notice how rough my hands are."

"Is that the only reason?" San An chuckles mirthfully. "I favor your hands because they belong to you. How they appear matter little to me."

"Well, I'd rather keep them hidden all the same." Folding both arms across my waist to keep the rough things shielded, the sound of his soft chuckles merely causes further embarrassment. Am I that amusing?

"If you insist, Your Highness. I did manage to read something else off your palm. Would you like me to tell you?"

"Sure."

"Very well. Your fate is intertwined with someone who has a place within this palace."

"And is that person you, San An?"

He takes little notice of my sarcasm or my frown.

"Fortunes are meant to guide. The rest is entirely up to you, Your Highness."

We stare at one another for a short moment. He sounded so serious, I couldn't do else but laugh. Without taking offense, San An returns my sentiment. After a few more pleasantries, he quits the room.

As I unfold my arms, memories of his touch make me blush. Why do I keep feeling so worked up when he's near? Secretly, I enjoy his consideration. I do wonder whether his attention toward me has any connections to his feelings toward His Majesty. However, that is something I have no right to ask. I should relinquish the subject for now.

Chapter 6: A Test of Intuition

In the evening, Jin came to the room and hastily shuffled together the contents of the empty trays. Without acknowledging me, he quietly left the room. I understand the offense he must feel. There was no point to make him face me. In truth, I couldn't look at him either.

Late at night when the moon is overhead, I lie awake and wonder if my convictions, as San An called them, are right. Every stupid mistake I've made has led up to this point. What if, by continuing to make these mistakes, I will cause suffering for others? How could I impersonate an emperor? What was I thinking? I can't even fit his clothes. How am I to fit his shoes? In my heart of hearts, I believe this to be the right course even though the very idea is preposterous.

Argh! I can't take this! I'm so tired but my eyes are wide-open! Vexation torments me and my heart is beating wildly out of my chest. As I sit up and bury my head in my hands, an unsettling feeling suddenly weighs down. I can't stay in this room any longer—this room that doesn't belong to me. I'm wearing clothes that aren't mine, breathing in air from this fine palace that never should enter my peasant lungs, whilst pretending to be someone regal. I can't do it! I have to leave!

Hallways after hallways and nothing's changed. I've been traversing through this endless maze for the past ten minutes. There should be a flight of stairs, an exit to a balcony... anything! Oh, dear heavens. What was I thinking? I'm lost. If someone sees me with His Majesty's face and not his body, the ruse would be for naught.

Where is He Pi's chamber? Logically, I should retrace my steps and return to the same hall from whence I came. Right. That's what I'll do.

Just my luck! Upon arriving at the end of the corridor, the path diverges. Another choice is before me and another chance for mistake. Then again, what if I am doing the right thing even though I do not know it? I want intuition to take over and prove the validity of my resolve. Should I go right or left?

Go right (Continue to page 57)

Go left (Continue to page 60)

Chapter 6 – 2

I decide to go right. Just as I reach the end of the corridor, Jin comes around the corner. At the sight of me, he becomes livid.

"What are you doing out here? Did anyone see you?"

Before I can reply, he grabs my wrist and pulls me down many hallways until we reach His Highness's chamber. Upon opening the door, Jin flings me inside and I stumble to the ground. However harsh is his reaction, I know that he saved my life.

"No one saw me." An answer chokes out. "I couldn't sleep so I... I don't know what I thought. I just wanted some air."

"Do you know what would have happened had someone else caught you?" His voice is as cold as ice. "You cannot leave this room until you appear his exact replica. Otherwise... otherwise, they'll have you executed." Jin kneels down behind me as his voice trails away.

"I know. I shouldn't have been rash. But maybe, I shouldn't be here. Maybe, I should just join the Circle so I don't cause more trouble."

One stupid mistake after another. It's one dumb mistake after another only to accomplish nothing in the end!

I turn back to apologize. However, slight tears misting over Jin's light brown eyes put me off guard.

"I won't leave again without your permission, I promise. Don't be sad. No one saw me. I can still be useful, if you think I should stay."

Jin bites his lips and stares for a long moment. Suddenly, his arms fly around my shoulders. "If they execute you, I don't... I don't want to think about that! I don't want you to die!"

Jin's grip tightens as his arms shake. I don't understand the reason for his reaction. Why is he so protective when he barely knows me? Is it just his disposition to be caring? He'd spent his entire life guarding He Pi, who is now lost. Maybe, he doesn't want to lose me, too, because of this face. I am his He Pi returned. He must be lamenting for his friend through me. Jin doesn't want He Pi to die; neither, do I. I hope that he will come back and free everyone from this bondage of secrets they all have to carry. As I return the embrace, hot tears wet my shoulders.

"It's okay, he'll come back. I know he will. He has to!" In saying so, my own mouth quivers and tears flow down my face.

I don't personally know He Pi, but I understand how important he is to everyone—not just for what he is, but also for who he is as a person. I can't replace him. If I can make Jin happy by being a surrogate friend, I want to at least try.

Jin draws back and places a warm hand on my face. He brushes away a few tears and smiles, though it is rather sad.

"I know he will. All the same, you must not be reckless."

I nod and there is nothing more that needs to be exchanged between us.

Continue to page 61

Chapter 6 – 3

I decide to go left. Just as I near the end of the hall, a guard spots me and believes I am an intruder. My attempt to flee fails. When the ministers are called for, I am sent to gaol. San An and Jin push for leniency but the council would not hear it. No one else defends me, as was expected. The other ministers have long decided that the moment I become a threat to their credibility, the only choice is to dispose of me.

At the next assembly, I am sentenced to death for treason; the charge fitted for anyone who impersonates His Highness. By noon, I am executed before the assembly.

The End.

Chapter 7: His Highness's Shoes

When he comes the next day, Jin is friendlier and more importantly, he appears a little happier, too. Before I can greet him, a small bouquet of three flowers wrapped in colored-paper is presented. The blooms are exceeding large and fragranced.

"I apologize. You must endure living solely in this room for a while longer. Hopefully, these peonies can remind you of the outdoors and bring a little cheer to your day."

No one's ever given me flowers before. Considering all the troubles I've caused him, he's too kind. Slowly, heat rises to my face as the bouquet is cradled close to my chest. An odd elation wells inside while an unruly smile forces its way to my mouth.

"They're beautiful. Thank you, Jin!"

Jin nods. After placing the pile of clothes on the bed, he begins dressing me. The ordeal from prior day that caused tension between us was useful after all. He's already seen underneath my robe. There is no reason to be shy about it now. Well, I say that, but we're both still as red as tomatoes.

Jin loosely binds my chest and states that contrary to the gold robe, a black one would help shade upper curves. I have no sense of fashion, so I have no objection.

"Enter the assembly from behind the throne; never the side. Sit straight but don't puff out your chest. We can practice later. Don't look at anyone directly but still, keep your head up. Don't grab the arms of the seat; do curve your fingers around them." He throws the list of things I must do into the air. Jin had given this much thought. I must not fail him.

When the many pieces of clothing find their places on my body, I turn to the mirror and nearly fall back. I do not recognize my reflection and that is a good thing, I suppose.

"Not bad at all. Besides from your complexion and height, you can easily pass for him now."

"My height? His Majesty can't be that much taller, can he? Especially, since Qing Hai mistook me for him."

"Yes, well, he's only a little bit taller than you. Most people wouldn't notice. I do. I'll have to adjust the shoes. Go on, walk around the room. Let's see your posture."

I nod and step forward. As I do, nearly fall on my face. He catches me, though, I can't erase utter flooding embarrassment.

"I can't fit his shoes," I sigh.

"Don't be so hard on yourself. The first step is always the most difficult."

"No, I mean, I can't fit his shoes!" The shoe slips off when I raise my foot. His feet are almost twice the size of mine.

"Another adjustment. Good. Best we find them now than later. Take the shoes off and try again."

I do as he say and then stroll across the floor. My movement is rigid and slow.

"Why are you walking like that?" Jin chuckles. "Regal doesn't equate to rigidity."

"That's not it at all! His robes are so long, I'm just trying to keep from falling."

Jin surveys me for a moment, then comes close and puts his right arm around my waist. His left hand grabs onto my left hand.

"Come. I'll hold you so you won't fall. Follow my pace. Too fast... too slow... just like that... you're slanting, stand up straight."

Before I know it, we've gone on like this for an hour or two. There's a gentle air about Jin that makes me feel so safe. His arm around me, his hand in mine—I don't want Jin to let go. It's a strange thought; or perhaps, rational. More and more, I will come to depend on Jin for the rest of my days until He Pi returns—if he ever will.

In any case, I'm glad to have his guidance and support.

Chapter 8: Age behind Innocence

In the afternoon, Jin brings my meal and takes away the shoes for modifications. I don't want him to wait on me but he insists keeping his duties. Although he's only giving me attention because of these duties, I enjoy it all the same. Still, I know nothing of Jin and how he came to be an attendant. I only know he has pride in his post and that no one else could do more for He Pi.

As I lean back in the chair, a loud sigh fills the room. What great meals Jin always brings! He Pi and I must have the same taste or maybe, he has much better taste than me. I ate too much and have nowhere to go. For fear of becoming sluggish, I start from the chair and practice walking. Without Jin to hold me, I stumble about and trip over the loose robe. Then, as expected, fall flat on my face right near the door.

"Ouch." I'm useless without him. Depression takes over and I decide to just lie here for the time.

"The floor is no place for an emperor to sleep." A familiar voice calls for my attention. Minister San An, smiling by the threshold, gazes down. How he comes and goes without me noticing is somewhat frightening.

"S-San An!"

I sit up and attempt to regain what little composure I could. San An kneels down, takes my chin in his hand,

and then slowly closes the distance between our faces. Nerves freeze me in place.

"I cannot believe it. You are his spitting image. For a moment, I thought he had returned." A soft laugh accompanies the smile.

"Everyone thinks we look alike, anyway," I mutter.

"Perhaps, though some of us are not foolish enough to believe you *are* him. Jin has outdone himself."

"Y-Yes. Yes, he has. Jin is very meticulous and accomplished in all aspects of his duties."

San An chuckles. "That's quite the compliment. I'm sure you've grown fond of him over these past few days?"

A frown falls over my mouth. Suddenly feeling defensive, I want to tell him that it's none of his business; though, I manage to hold my tongue. When I do not respond, he continues. "I hope you realize it would be foolish to pursue a relationship outside of master and servant between you and Jin. Should His Highness be found, Jin will simply resume his usual duties and you will be returned to your home. Jin cannot go with you and you cannot stay with him."

"Jin and I are just friends. At least, I'd like to think we have become friends."

"Just friends? One would reason that after displaying your bare body to Jin day after day, friendship would be the last thing on either of your minds. Were you a child, I would otherwise consider. Though your face is youthful, I see a mature soul through those eyes. You are a woman with a girl's disposition. Nothing is more deceiving than age behind innocence."

A momentarily glance into his gaze sends chills over me. Where has the former gentle expression gone? He sounds so callous and distant; his demeanor is almost unrecognizable.

"What are you accusing me of?"

"Don't misunderstand. I am not accusing you of anything. You seem confused and lost; drowning in thoughts you've yet to comprehend. It is natural for a woman, who's oblivious to the idea of love, to fall deeply for a man who tends to her needs daily; who has seen every part of her and returns for more. I only implore that you will consider the consequences of your actions in jeopardizing the country's safety when you decide to chase after the selfish desire of first love while impersonating His Highness."

It's true that I've never loved anyone and the idea is fascinating, but who is he to charge upon me impure expectations from Jin? I feel unclean just to hear him speak. Doubt disrupts my intention and resolve. My hands are balled into fists.

"Why are you so presumptuous to tell me how I should and shouldn't feel? I'm here for one reason and one reason only. That reason has nothing to do with building relationships with anyone! When this ordeal is over, I will leave. *Alone!*"

I have a short temper; that much is palpable. I'm also easily offended and easily embarrassed, which always make things worse. I grasp that this is not appropriate behaviors for He Pi, but I am still me for now. Even so, I know he meant no harm. San An never says a mean thing that is baseless. For that reason, his words cut even deeper. Then again, what can I do but just let it go?

"I'm sorry, Minister."

I thought he would lecture further or mock me in some way. Nothing of the sort happens. What does happen next makes me turn cold. My vision reels wildly around the room when San An encircles his arms tightly around my waist and places a warm, passionate kiss on my mouth. All the strength abruptly drains from my body. What on Earth is happening? Did I do something wrong again? I must have but... this hardly feels like punishment.

He must be testing me—to see if I would falter easily from a simple kiss. Yet, this is my first kiss. How can he carelessly steal away this special thing I can never have back! My head jerks away; his lips flutter to my neck.

"Stop testing me, Minister! I don't want to raise my hand against you, but if I must..." The words choke their way out. What's come over me? I can barely breathe.

"You are mistaken. I trust your resolve. It is mine that is dwindling."

His soft, seductive voice is lulling away my soul. The more I try to make sense of the situation, the more confusing everything becomes.

"I confessed my love and yet, you chose to become Jin's charge. He has the pleasure of tending to your needs; to know parts of you from which I am forbidden. Age behind innocence. I knew you would be my bane the first moment we met. I will be the person to jeopardize peace if I cannot find control, but your age behind innocence is robbing me of all composure!"

His lips make their way from my neck to my cheek, and then another kiss presses upon my mouth, taking my breath away. Never in my life has someone pursue me as fervently as San An. In reality... *no one* has ever pursued me, and I would be lying to say that I want to resist him. I've been strangely attracted to San An since we've met for reasons I cannot fathom. However, this is inappropriate in so many ways!

Pushing away San An, I stumble backward. "You don't know what you're saying, Minister! I'm not as innocent as you think!"

"You're not?"

He raises an eyebrow and heat inexplicably rushes to my face.

"What I mean is I'm not a child who can be easily distracted and swayed by kind words and sweet temptations. I know Jin is only looking after me because of his duties and you're right, I am an adult. I can take care of myself. I'm not hiding age behind anything. This is the real me. I'm childish because I'm ignorant—sometimes, borderline stupid—but that doesn't make me innocent!"

"You have never known a man's touch, have you?"

How can he ask a woman that without any discretion! My whole body is burning from embarrassment. I don't know whether it's more mortifying to tell him the truth or to lie. People my age should already know such things. Besides the fact that no one's ever wanted me, there are multitudes of other reasons why I'm behind. All I can do is look at the floor and hope for him to change the subject or for my heart to just stop and end my misery; whichever comes first.

Suddenly, he chuckles. My breathing ceases.

"That's about the reaction I expected. Age has nothing to do with innocence. It's all a matter of disposition. An experienced woman would become defensive when her claim to virtue is assaulted; an innocent one is embarrassed for still having it."

There's naught I can use to respond. It's not as though I can question his innocence! My eyes dart back and forth across the floor to search for relief. The sudden touch of his hand caressing my cheek throws me into rage.

"How dare you put your hands on me, Minister!"

Darting up, an angry glare directs back. I take my post as He Pi before someone who knows the ruse. "You have assaulted your monarch. We will allow the transgression this time. Next time, we shall not be so kind!"

San An draws back and smiles sweetly. The unaffected attitude turns me immobile. The Minister stands up, makes a low obeisance, and then leaves.

Once he is out of view, strength falters and my knees buckle. Why do I feel terrified of him? The idea is perplexing. In truth, San An has never caused me any harm and I believe he has my safety and best interest in mind. His recent strange behaviors I can only surmise alluded to jealousy. Still, the very idea of him now makes me shudder.

Chapter 9: A Servant Prince

For the past few weeks, endless days were spent with Jin, who tutored me in aspects of He Pi's personality, charms... or lack thereof, mannerisms, speech, and even his political mindset. I know nothing of politics while Jin seems to know as much about court matters as any minister. I can't tell whether progress was made, but he assured that I receive a passing grade. The true test, though, will be tomorrow when I must attend the assembly.

"Don't be afraid. Do exactly as you've just showed me and everything will be fine." Jin pats my shoulder while I slump down on the bed. "Just remember, posture is everything. The ministers have warned the court that His Highness has been ill. You won't be expected to sit very long or address them. And also, remember to remain seated until Minister San An approaches to assist you off the dais. He will shield your... particular area. Turn your back to the court immediately and then retreat slowly. Don't rush. Understood?"

I nod sharply. "I feel like an actor rehearsing for a stage performance."

"Yes, that is very accurate."

"I can do it," a soft mutter falls to reassure convictions.

Though I didn't think he heard me, Jin places a hand on my back. "Yes, you can, Bao Lai."

For a split second, I'm slightly confused as to whom he had addressed. I've almost forgotten that is my name. While returning a smile, I look up at his gentle face and sudden confidence overflows.

"Thank you, Jin."

"Are you hungry, yet? Should I fetch your dinner?"

"No. Please, sit with me a little longer. If you don't mind, Jin, could you tell me about yourself? Maybe it's too early to make presumptions but I feel we will be together for a very long time." I said something stupid again. My face turns crimson and I fluster like an idiot. "I-I meant *we* as in y-you and me—He Pi! Not... not the other me. I—"

"I knew what you meant," he replies. "You want to know how I came to be a servant? The simple answer is that my mother lost the fight against Consort Yi and Empress Pai."

"Your mother?"

"Yes, Consort En."

"What are you saying, He Pi is your... your brother?"

Jin nods as sadness creeps over his countenance. I'd always thought there was a regal air about him. Nothing suggests to me that he is a servant except for his claims. Jin looks away for a short moment to sort his thoughts and then continues.

"After Emperor Jin passed, the consorts and Empress Pai waged wars against one another. All of us children of the court were pushed and pulled like puppets on strings to carry out ambitions we could hardly grasp. Empress Pai staged a mass poisoning and was successful against all the consorts' remaining children, except for His Highness He Pi and me. My mother, then feared for my life, withdrew from the competition. However, Consort Yi retaliated with greater force. The enraged women, who lost their children, joined her faction. In the end, it was the mystic Wu Ling who resolved the conflict. To assuage the tension at court that would not subside, His Highness gave Prince San An the title of Prime Minister."

"S-S-San An? You mean he's... he was the crown prince?"

Jin nods. "Yes. Not only are they half brothers, they are also cousins. I imagine that was one of the reasons His Highness did not perish during Empress Pai's scheme. She spared her nephew believing her sister would step down, but Consort Yi was an ambitious woman."

"You are not a minister even though you should be a prince?" I ask because that seems a little unfair. Jin simply laughs.

"I have no desire to be minister or hold any political office. My mother grew ill near the end of the conflict. A short time later, I was left an orphan at court. With no one to back my political claims, His Highness did not see me as a threat, so he proposed that I become his personal advisor. I was sick of politics, sick of court, sick of people killing each other for something so meaningless, that I asked to be his personal attendant instead. So, don't feel sorry for me, Bao Lai. I'm not a servant by force. This is what I want: to be near my brothers, the only families I have left."

Sadness deepened when he spoke of his mother. There is no doubt that he loved her dearly and the memories of youth spent not in happiness, but in political wars, have taken its toll. I want to comfort Jin but what could I possibly say?

Eventually, Jin glances over and smiles. "I'm sorry. I didn't mean to be so depressing."

"What? No! It's not that at all! I was just thinking how wonderful of a brother you are to take such good care of He Pi. He sounds like a handful. You're older than him, aren't you? If I had younger siblings who are that unruly, I would beat their butts red!"

"I can't very well beat the emperor's butt red," Jin laughs.

"No, I guess you can't."

"What about you, Bao Lai? Tell me about you." He smiles charmingly as though burdened sadness was released. I think he is merely suppressing it.

"About me? Well, I... It's a little complicated."

"More complicated than being a servant prince?"

"Maybe not *that* complicated," I nudge him. "The truth is I don't really know who I am or where I came from. Ever since I was an infant, I've been living at a temple in the south. The old man—well, the priest— said I was dropped in front of the place without so much as a note. The old man—sorry, I kept calling him that because he hated it. The priest raised me because the nearby villages were poor and no one wanted another mouth to feed. I grew up as a student of the temple. Mostly, I just did meager chores.

I guess you can say I was a servant, too. They dressed me as a boy, so the other young men wouldn't feel awkward. Eventually, I came of age and the old man passed. The temple didn't want a female to interrupt their path to enlightenment. I left and well, wandered for a long time until I found an abandoned house near the village of Kou and made it my own. That was maybe a year ago? I'm bad with dates."

I glance over to see what Jin thinks. His brows are furrowing from outrage. Did I say something wrong again? My posture stiffens and my fingers twirl together nervously. Finally, he breaks the awkwardness by beating a fist against one of the bedposts.

"Path of enlightenment!" He scowls. "They want to reach enlightenment to end the sufferings of humanity, when right before them, a young woman in need is thrown out to fend for herself? Hypocrites!"

"It's—It's okay, Jin! I'm glad they threw me out. I would never have left if they hadn't. I wanted to but I lacked the nerves. Worked out in the end. Here I am a year later living in the palace as emperor and all, huh?"

He returns my humor with a glare.

"This life is not as grand as you think. You are in constant danger, not just from the court realizing the truth, but also from numerous political adversaries wishing to end your life. You cannot trust anyone. On top of that, you'll never be able to live as a normal woman with someone to care for you."

"I've never really been a woman to expect all those things."

"What do you mean?"

"I was raised as a boy and told to behave as a man so my presence didn't disturb the monks. I've never worn women's clothing and no one's ever truly treated me as such. I don't know what a normal woman's life is and for a long time, didn't know anything about life outside of temple. So, it's no big deal."

He doesn't know what to say to that. Everyone here sees me as a woman. I certainly don't think of myself as a man, but I don't ever think I am as a woman should be either. After leaving the temple, I shied from everyone my gender because I felt inferior. It is strange for me to actually pretend to be a man now, and yet, no one close to the situation views me as such.

In any case, I would be content to live the rest of my days here with Jin. San An's warnings abruptly shoot across my mind. A sharp pain wells in my chest. What am I saying? That's completely selfish! Who cares what I covet! I shouldn't be coveting anything! What about Jin? After all, he stayed at court to be near his brothers. If He Pi never returns, then why should he waste his life here?

A phantom itch is suddenly crawling over my arms; I can't keep from shuffling. "What about you, Jin? Don't you want to marry and have a family of your own?"

The question startles him. Eyes widen and his lips become half-parted. Following a moment of hesitation, he thoughtfully replies, "I've never considered the option. I've decided to devote my life to His Highness. I see no other path for me."

"But I'm... not him. I want for him to return as much as you do, but if he doesn't, you should at least think of the alternative."

Scoffing, long fingers run through his hair. "Yes, I'm sure women are very interested in a servant with nothing to his name. Realistically, I'm not fit to be anyone's husband."

Enraged by his self-degradation, I'm suddenly in front of him. "Are you kidding me? You're gorgeous, smart, and sweet! Any woman would be lucky to have you! How can you think that way?"

There is no response. He simply looks off elsewhere. I wonder whether there is more to his story. He hated court and thus, denied his birthrights and became a servant. And... he doesn't want to marry because he hates himself? No, that doesn't sound logical. Even if that were the case, would he deny any woman who pursues him? He keeps himself secluded, but why?

"You don't trust women, do you?" The accusation indiscreetly projects without comprehending how the thought formed.

Jin directs back a bewildered stare. His cheeks are burning from embarrassment, whilst frighten eyes broaden. He tries to deny but can't bring himself to rebuff. In the end, he says nothing at all.

"I understand. You were a puppet in others' ambitions. Women made your childhood a torment. You saw your siblings perished and attempts were made on your life. You are afraid history will repeat itself should another woman have control over you and use your claim to the throne against He Pi."

Maybe I sounded preachy, because his soft gaze suddenly becomes as sharp as knives.

"Don't presume to know me or how I feel! My mother was a good woman! She didn't deserve her titles stripped from her or the pain she had to endure during the conflict. Yes, she was a part of it, but she did it for me! No matter the heinous acts other women have accomplished, my mother was a good and virtuous woman who was pulled into a travesty that never should have happened!"

"I-I didn't mean to say anything poorly of your mother."

"Why wouldn't you? She took part and lost. For her failure, she was subjected to unbearable humiliation. Even after her death, they still shamed her! Women! The only things on your minds are power and pamper. Aside from my mother, I doubt anyone of you truly know what love is!"

His views finally brought to light; the resentment he feels toward all women is clear to me. I know he can discern the idea to be illogical, despite anger clouding his mind for reasons that *are* logical. It was because of this face that he had allowed me to come close, but since he hates the idea of me for being what I am, the best thing I can do for Jin is to keep distance. However, he is suffering. Retreat would be an act of cowardice. He's always been there to comfort me when I was unsure of myself.

Moving closer, my arms wrap around him. Surprised, Jin leans away. I draw him back.

"I am a woman. I am not your mother nor am I the women from court during your childhood. I have not proven myself to be worthy or vile; at least, I don't think I have. If I do cause you pain, chastise me. If I make you sad, then scold me. For the first time in my life, I feel happy and safe. It's all because of you, so I don't want you to hate me just because of my gender. I have no right to ask but I'm asking anyway. I don't know what love is; if ever I do, I promise I'll love you. I'll love you however you want me to; as a friend, a sister, a confidant. Maybe, I'll even make a good brother for you."

A weak smile forces its way over my lips. His expression is empty. Perhaps, it was too much to ask. He is merely my instructor. I've overstepped our boundaries and caused him more grief. Just as my hands leave his shoulders, Jin's arms encircle my body. I'm suddenly looking up from the bed into glistening unshed tears peering down. My heart is racing uncontrollably.

"Jin…"

"You can't just say something like that to me!" Such pain exerts to the surface. He speaks through gritted teeth in attempt to hold back the tumults.

"I don't understand."

"You can't just tell me you'll love me and expect me to keep composure!"

"I... won't do anything you don't want me to."

I didn't think my promise was inappropriate. Knowing me, I must have done something wrong. Bewildered and confused, the crimson face peering down fully reflects my sentiment. For a drawn moment, the room is silent except for the sounds of our hearts furiously beating in tandem.

Slowly, little by little, he leans down until our lips barely graze. Something keeps him and Jin withdraws.

"I'm sorry, Your Highness."

Jin abruptly leaves the room. I'm frozen in place.

He certainly behaves erratically. One moment, I think he hates me, and then the next, the opposite. At times, his moods shift on a whim. I wonder whether my actions confounded him or this is the true Jin. Regardless, my opinion of him will not change. In my eyes, he's one of the best people I've ever known. I respect and care for him deeply.

As I close my eyes to reflect his image, my heart begins racing once more. What's wrong with me? This is hardly turmoil I need on the day before appearing in front of the assembly. With San An there, it will take everything to retain control. This tension with Jin might really break my concentration.

Chapter 10: The Assembly

Jin was sterner than usual this morning when he came to dress me for the performance. I thought it best to leave conversations for later. At the moment, it's taking every last bit of composure to ignore San An's smiling face. The more he smiles, the more unsettling everything feels.

Arriving at the position, I wait for my cue. The orator calls out, "His Majesty, the Great He Pi, arrives at court!"

"His Majesty, the Great He Pi, may he reign for eternity!" The court responds in a reverberating echo while every member bows low to the ground.

Taking a deep breath, I walk from behind the large gold seat placed before the court. My back is straight and my hands are together. I march to the front of the throne and sit with posture. My gaze is directed ahead but not at anyone in particular. My hands circle the armrests but I do not grasp at them.

Below the dais is a sea of noblemen and others of import in their respective seats. Contrary to expectations, the assembly is held in open-air instead of an enclosure. Wouldn't they want to keep out prying eyes? I suppose this is simply a show. The council, comprising of He Pi, the ministers, and Prime Minister San An, actually creates policies and formulates decrees.

This assembly is to illustrate goodwill and resolve those issues not of great impacts to the country.

Jin instructed me to remain silent. No one else is speaking either. Awkwardness is making me want to shuffle. I almost did. Thankfully, Jin's preparations helped me catch foolishness in time.

After fifteen minutes of *utterly deafening* silence, San An steps forward. "His Highness has been ill and is still recovering. The court should allow his return to rest."

"His Majesty, the Great He Pi, may he reign for eternity!" The court repeats the previous display.

San An moves into position and I quickly turn my back to the assembly. After he escorts me from the stage, I sigh heavily knowing the performance is over.

"Very convincing, indeed." San An smiles amiably once we are inside.

"Thank you."

As I turn to leave, he calls out. "A moment of your time, Your Majesty. If you will escort me to the gardens."

I want to see the gardens, of course. I just don't want to see them with him. After knowing who he really is and after considering the perturbed behaviors he exhibited toward me, I lost all trust in him. When I hesitate, he pushes again.

"Please, I *insist*, Your Majesty."

I don't want to, but the cold tone that suddenly takes over his calm voice turns me into a coward. Heavy feet grudgingly swing around and follow him. The path we take is void of guards, which is to my benefit, since I can't help but shuffle uneasily. My eyes are everywhere except San An.

Finally, we reach the doorway that leads outside. Lost in amazement of this wondrously beautiful place, I didn't notice he had stopped and inadvertently, slam right into his back.

"I'm sorry!"

"You don't have to apologize, Your Majesty. Go on, enjoy the view. The gardens are not far away. I'm sure you need a bit of fresh air after being cooped up in that little room."

Little room? That room is bigger than my old house! He's right, though. I do enjoy the fresh air. Although, I don't want to drag out this encounter more than needed.

"No, please go on to the gardens. I will follow you."

San An slightly bows and continues. We pass several more picturesque archways until finely carved doors painted red and gold appears. The surrounding walls are a mixture of white and sand-colored stones arranged in impressive mosaics. Jutting from the enclosure are dense leaves I'd recognized anywhere. The peach garden is beautiful and it is massive!

Despite the impressive foreign sight, I'm suddenly stricken by nostalgia. When the old priest was alive and before age weakened his body and kept him bedridden, we used to venture up the nearby mountains during late summers to pick wild peaches. I spent those days climbing up and down tall trees, and then ran wildly beneath the shade; after which, the priest would call me over and flogged me for being too rowdy. In front of the other temple members, he never scolded my unladylike conduct since the subject of my gender was laboriously avoided by everyone. When we were alone, he made a point to teach me proper behaviors. I was annoyed by his lectures back then. Now, I understand the reason. He knew I could not live at the temple forever, and with all his efforts, tried to civilize me. If only I'd listened.

Stopping beneath the shade of a particular tree, San An searches the branches and picks one of the small fruits above. The presented token is nervously received. After which, I merely fumble the rounded fruit between my hands.

"These peach trees were specially sown by the request of my mother, Empress Pai." San An gazes lovingly at the charming flora above.

I look up. Why does he suddenly want to speak of this subject?

"Yes, I know Jin has told you of our past, that I am his brother and the former crown prince. Do you find it fair, Your Highness?"

"I don't know what you mean. Do I find it fair that Jin told me of your past?"

San An swiftly turns about. "Do you find it fair that the crown prince is not emperor when his brother has gone missing? I am the rightful heir. You have no claim to this throne; I hope you understand that."

Of course, I know that! However, I didn't know the Minister wanted the throne. I thought he was satisfied with his post. More so, wasn't it San An who suggested for me to become He Pi? Why didn't he just send me to the gallows in the first place? Actually, there's something else unsettling that just occurred to me.

"Is that why you wanted to marry me? To remove me from this ruse, so you claim authority?" Rage overtakes prudence and the peach in my hand is harshly thrown to the ground. San An's eyes glide toward the object and follow as it rolls away. He is offended.

"Pity. You do not appreciate the hard work of others. You only know how to throw away what isn't yours."

"Did you... Did you do something to He Pi?" Both hands clenched, I step forward.

"Don't be absurd," he glares back angrily. "He is my brother and I am his prime minister. I have almost every authority he has without the fear of others aspiring to take my life. His Highness has left me in the best possible position."

"Then why do you want to know whether it is fair that you are not emperor?"

"If He Pi never returns, then the country should not be in the hands of a stranger with no blood ties to the throne. Had you accepted my proposal, I would have made you empress; a true title, not one you pretend to hold."

"You want to marry a woman who resembles your brother? I think the throne is not the only thing you are aspiring for."

"And what is that supposed to mean?" He frowns.

"I wouldn't know," is my airy reply.

He tried to use me, to seduce me, and made me questioned my decency. He attempted to drive a wedge between Jin and me. Anger is enough to clear my mind of fear. Without allowing a response, I turn to leave. He rushes forward and seizes my wrist.

"I have not spoken all my thoughts, Your Highness. Please, *stay!*" With one swift motion of his hand, I slam hard against the ground. I sit there obediently not knowing why; the fear of him now winning over my rage.

"Do not think for a moment that my intentions toward you are anything but a man's desires for a woman. You resemble him, yes, but you are not him. I can tell the difference, if that's what you're asking. I am the eldest and yet, I must serve my younger brother.

Titles mean nothing. Respect is everything. He will never in his life respect me. You must, once you are mine."

What kind of sick twisted logic is that? He must have lost his mind! I don't know else to do except look away. Immediately, he pulls me closer.

"Everyone respects him—respects you—because his whore of a mother manipulated my father! My mother, the empress, lost to a harlot! She died in shame, for how could a woman feel any less to have scorned the affections of her husband? The things they said—the pain she endured—and all for what? That birthmark on his shoulder? That red blot of nothing!

Everyone knows the mystic was a fraud. Master Wu Ling died years prior to this man's arrival at court. To deter a civil war, they turned a blind eye to the truth and robbed my mother of her pride and respect! *My* pride and respect! And you, another fraud to claim what isn't yours. The other ministers would have it no other way. I am but one man in a position without absolute respect. There is naught I can do. And yet, if I didn't care for the country to break into war, would simply expose you for what you really are!"

San An grabs the collars of my robe and forcibly draws them open. My secret would have been revealed if not for Jin's sash. Frustration is eating at my core. I can't tolerate his madness any longer!

"Don't blame me for your wretched misery!"

In an attempt to pull free, my strength works against me and I fall flat on my back. Before I can fathom what had transpired, I look up and all I can see are his long fluttering lashes. What is happening? Something isn't right. I'm too numb to notice what had come to pass. Then, I feel it. His lips are firmly pressed against mine. I had inadvertently taken him down with me.

Pushing off San An, I struggle to my feet. However, he promptly gives reminder of my rumpled state. As I stop to fix the robe, San An moves in front.

"You needn't be in such a hurry to leave," he smiles sweetly. I shiver at the sight of that smile.

"What exactly do you want from me, Minister?! Respect? I respected you from the moment we met, but your actions have robbed every drop of it from me! I'm sorry that you are not emperor. That is not my fault! In the end, the title belonged to your father. Whomever he chose to give that right has the true claim. Your mother poisoned your brothers and sisters for the sake of respect! I do not know her, but I know that cruelty is! If you have done anything against your own brother for the sake of respect, then you don't deserve to rule!"

"You would talk about my mother!" San An grabs my arm and jerks me forward. His grip is so severe, I feel as if my bone is breaking. "Did you think no one tried to take *my* life? That Consort Yi and Consort En were without faults? Those two were the worst of the lot! One tried to burn me alive by setting fire to my residence. The other sent guards to slay me after the attempt at poison failed! My mother did what was necessary to protect me and ended the fighting. If it hadn't been for her, the wars at court would have lasted *much* longer with *even more* casualties, I assure you!"

I had no idea. I guess in political wars, no one is innocent. While they shared similar childhoods, San An is much different from Jin. His ambitions and hatred twisted everything about him to search for power and validation, while Jin turned into a recluse.

I still don't fully understand what he wants from me. At the moment, all I can think of is for Jin to retrieve me. I want to feel safe again. I don't know how to deal with this madness or if I can even break free from San An. One thing is true. Should I somehow manage to leave, I won't be able to do else except cower at the sight of him; more so than I already do. With whatever courage is left, I grab San An by the collar and draw his face closer. His eyes broaden for a moment and then resume their usual expression.

"Since I am the only thing standing in the way of your ambitions, then I give you every right to remove me. You're right! I have no blood ties to the throne and I am a fraud! Do whatever you must. I know you are a careful man. There's no reason you would walk about unarmed. No one is around. Kill He Pi and take what's yours!"

His eyes narrow and his lips purse. Maybe, he doesn't quite know what he wants after all. The long, excruciating moment seems to span eternity. Suddenly, the empty gaze arches upward and terror floods his countenance. San An embraces me while swinging around for us to exchange positions. Instantaneously, an arrow pierces through his shoulder. He lets out a pained groan.

"San An!" From behind his slumped shoulders, the assailant's blurred figure runs away. Panic takes hold and my body turns to ice.

"Run," he whispers. San An falls unconscious in my arms.

I don't want to leave him but his advice is best. Running back across the path, I scream for the guards. In moments, a horde of soldiers comes forthwith, including the three I met in prior days.

Generals Yue and Hu search for the attacker while Qing Hai and I rush to retrieve the Minister. Once we are inside, Jin comes with us to find the court physician.

Sharp phantom pains shoot through my chest when I glance at his face. This can't be happening. Why would he do that? Why would San An protect me? I'm nobody! It should have been me! I would trade anything for him to just wake up!

The physician forbids us from entering the infirmary, but I feel dread flows, the same dread I felt that day when the old man passed away. I don't care what San An did. I don't want him to die! He saved me—had attempted to save me so many times through his own coarse methods by having offered succeeding chances to leave this post. Whatever he said or did, I thought deep down he genuinely cares for me. He doesn't deserve such an end; an end meant for me.

Jin tries to calm my guilt but there is no way I can sit out here while who knows what is happening in there! Yet, I can't just storm in and make a scene. I still have this role to play. I don't know what to do but I need to decide now. I fight with myself and then decide to

Go inside (Continue to page 93)

Let the doctor do his work (Continue to page 100)

Chapter 10 – 2

I run inside and Jin follows suit.

"How is he? It's just an arrow wound! He should be fine, shouldn't he?!"

The court physician is startled. "Your Majesty! Please, forgive me. I don't know what more I can do."

"What is that supposed to mean?" The sight of San An lying still makes my heart drop. "Is he..."

"No, Your Majesty. He will soon unless an antidote can be found."

"Antidote? He was poisoned?" Strength leaves all of me in the instant that inconceivable idea takes form. Jin manages to catch me in his arms.

This can't be. San An had escaped all the terrors of his youth, all the claims made on his life, just to die now because of me. I refuse to allow that!

"No, you must save him! What are you sitting around for? I don't care what you do, you have to save him!" My fist slams against a nearby table; bitter tears can't be restrained.

"That won't solve anything, Your Majesty! Please, let the good doctor do his work."

Jin tries to pull me from the room. I push him away and rush toward San An. The physician is just going to watch him die. This should have been my death, not his! If he has to walk into the other world, I won't let him do it alone. The arrow is still on the tray nearby, dripping with his blood.

"Your Majesty, what have you done?!" Jin cries out as the tip punctures my palm.

The physician frantically approaches. I order him to desist.

"If he dies, I die. Get it? So, unless you want the death of an emperor on your hands, you will save him!"

My heart is racing. Pain is shooting up my arm. The poison is quickly taking effect. Breathing is becoming a chore. I've no choice but to lie down beside San An.

I can hear Jin telling me to stay, but I don't know how long I can keep from falling unconscious. Maybe, the end is nigh and thoughts are flying toward home. I suddenly recall following the old priest up the mountains when I was a child. An unbearable pain touched me when I ran off and climbed one of the tall trees. Even though the old man told me to stay close, I never listened. A strange plant nested up in the branches pricked my leg and then this same pain had taken over me then. The old man called it... what did he call it after he treated me... he called it...

"Sleeping nettle... Sleeping... nettle!"

Chapter 10 – 3

Perhaps I died; I am not certain. How can anyone be sure of reality when dreams sometimes feel more real than life? I was floating somewhere and speaking to someone. I think it was the old man. I miss him dearly. He was the only person in the world who truly cared for me; at least, before I came to this palace. Everyone here only wants me because of my resemblance to He Pi. Wherever he is, I hope he comes back. He never would have placed his brother in danger. I don't want anyone's life in my hands. I thought I could handle it but I was wrong. San An, please live. Please, San An, live!

Someone nudges my arm and impulsively, I sit up. A surge of pain ripples across my body. A groan escapes.

"I'm sorry. I didn't mean to… You were talking in your sleep. Are you all right?" Jin smiles wide through fatigue covering his brows.

"Where's San An?"

"He's fine. He's resting. You gave the court physician quite a scare." Jin's laughing; though, the expression is sad. "Lie down."

"No, I won't until I see San An!" Pushing off the bed, I try to walk. My lungs burn and then I fall back.

"I assure you, he's safe. Do you not trust me?"

"I trust you but I don't trust me. Am I awake?"

"San An means that much to you, does he?" Jin looks away. There lies a hint of jealousy in the tone.

"He saved me. How can I ignore that? He's your family! I don't want anyone to be sad because of me! That assassin... did they catch him?"

"No. He disappeared by the time the guards gave chase."

"He must have overheard... everything! He knows! He knows I'm not He Pi!" I failed on my debut. I put San An and the country in danger. How could I have been so reckless! A fist slams against a bedpost as tears stream down in torrents.

"We'll deal with things as they come," Jin reassures.

How can he still be so optimistic when nothing is certain? He makes me feel safe when I don't deserve it for this failure. San An was right. This pretense authority is nothing. Without He Pi, he should reign. He could save this country.

"Where are you going?"

Jin reaches out while I start from the bed. I shake him off but my legs give away and I fall to the floor.

"I'm going to give the former crown prince back his title. You don't want authority and He Pi is missing. San An had to suffer a monarch's tribulations; he should be rewarded as such. He can protect this land. I can't do it! I don't want anyone's death on my hands!"

The idea of crying is despicable. More and more, tears fall endlessly. I shove my head into my palms to hide the shame. Jin says nothing because there is nothing he can say. My weakness is clearly displayed to the man I wish to hide it from most.

Just when nerves are on the verge of consuming all of me, faintly, a familiar voice draws my soul from despair. San An, leaning against the doorway, is riddled with fatigue.

"That you don't want blood on your hands is a sign you are fit to wear He Pi's crown."

"San An! You shouldn't be up."

"She's right, Prime Minister. Please return to bed."

Though Jin addresses him by title, I can see he is worried for his brother. The older man gives a small smile. Then, stumbling through the door, he collapses in front of me.

"I'm alive. That is enough at the moment. Go fetch our dinners, Jin."

Even in this state, he is barking orders. I do not think it's very nice to treat his brother with such little regards. Perhaps, this is just their ways. Jin is not offended and seems glad to be useful. When only we remain, San An faces me.

"I heard of everything you did for me, Your Highness. You refuse to marry me, but you are willing to die for me? Quite the enigma." He chuckles, but pain soon puts an end to the endeavor.

"You're one to talk! You want to be emperor but you saved me. Why? I don't deserve kindness from you. Your ambitions would have been fulfilled through my death."

"I never had any intention of causing you harm," his brows furrow.

I offended him again and can't do else except blush in embarrassment at my own misguided accusations.

"Then, what do you want from me? If you want this throne, I will find some way to give it to you." I owe San An a great debt that can never be cleared.

"You know what I want," he replies airily. A crooked smile follows.

The insinuation makes my entirety bursts into flames. I can't believe he's willing to tease me at a time like this!

Embarrassment keeps me from responding. In due time, San An places a hand on my head.

"Don't do anything obtuse like that again... Your Highness."

"Same to you!"

Finally, I think we've come to an understanding. He sees me for who I am; not for the person I resemble. I understand him to be as confused and conflicted as Jin. He is not a bad person. Whatever it was that clouded his mind and caused his assaults against me in prior days dispersed. San An returned to his old self. Every notion that he had part in He Pi's disappearance is relinquished. This is enough to make me trust him; just not enough for me to desire being in his attention more than needed.

Continue to page 102

Chapter 10 – 4

Despite my guilt, the country's safety is more important. I must retain composure and keep this pose. Thus, instead of intruding, I fall to silent prayers for his safety.

In the end, San An lives and I couldn't be gladder. After several days in the infirmary, the Minister finally calls for me.

"San An, how do you feel?" I sit on the chair beside his bed.

"My state of affairs should not concern you."

His eyes are cold and distant and his demeanor is completely indifferent. Against my protest, San An slowly sits up.

"I shall make this quick. The assassin undoubtedly heard our conversation and realized you are an imposter. Therefore, your role as He Pi is rendered moot. I've instructed Jin to prepare a sum of gold for your services. Qing Hai will return you to your home."

"You're letting me go?" My heart aches for reasons I cannot construe. He's right, I'm not needed anymore. This is what I wanted, isn't it?

"I won't take anything from you, San An. You saved my life. I'm forever grateful."

"Don't be ridiculous. The arrow wasn't meant for you. Regardless, we are done here. Leave me."

San An returns to rest. Hesitantly, I part from the room. My mind and body are stricken by phantom pains. Why do I feel this way? Intuition tells me that I made a terrible mistake, but what was it?

"Bao Lai, are you ready?"

I look up to find Jin holding a small parcel. Though dejected, he continues.

"The Prime Minister—"

"I know, Jin. I can't accept any gifts. But, thank you, for everything. I hope someday we can meet again."

There's more Jin wants to say that can't take form. I leave the palace and return home.

For the rest of my days, I live as a recluse. I never amount to anything and I never serve any purpose. Each day, I feel utter regret but I don't know why. What mistake did I make? Was there another path I should have taken in life? I'll never know.

The End.

Chapter 11: Mu Dan

A few nights later, Jin and I are called to San An's quarters. When we arrive, Zhen Yue, Bai Hu, and Qing Hai are also present.

"Why have you summoned us, Prime Minister?"

My body hasn't fully recovered from the poison's effects. Making for a chair, I collapse in a thud. To my surprise, San An appears as though he was never injured. Of course, it's not like him to show weaknesses in front of others.

"Patience, Your Highness. Now that we have all gathered, General Yue has some good news to report."

Zhen Yue nods. Taking a step forward, he begins. "Qing Hai was able to trace the assailant's retreat for a short distance. We believe he headed east to Mount Fei Yang."

"That's great! Let's go capture him!"

I'm on my feet, excited by the prospect of bringing the person who'd injured San An to justice. Had the Minister perished, I could never forgive myself. However, the Minister shakes his head to signal that I shouldn't get my hopes up.

"We cannot enter Mount Fei Yang, Your Highness," San An explains. "Sending our soldiers there could be viewed as an act of aggression against Ning."

"They sent an assassin after us! Is that not an act of aggression?"

"We cannot prove that the assassin belongs to Ning or that he came on Emperor Yuan's orders. They will turn about and say Bei Ling instigated the offense or that we staged the ordeal to march on them."

"Then, what? Do we just let them get away with it?"

"No. We will send an emissary to speak with their representatives and ask permission to search Mount Fei Yang."

"Are you kidding me? We need to ask permission? Even should they agree, there's no way we'll find him! Unless..."

"Unless what? Spit it out already!" Bai Hu snaps crossly. No matter how I appear, he will never accept me as He Pi. In some ways, I appreciate that.

"Unless, the target joins the expedition to search for the assailant. Whoever wants He Pi dead won't waste the chance to correct his error. Let me go, too."

"Don't be stupid! You said the attacker knew you aren't His Highness. Why bother?"

"If our enemies knew, then why not just attack Nan Rong already?" This conversation feels out of my league. However, I'd already inserted myself, so I might as well continue.

Hu does not reply. The Demon General's grimace is so severe, I can feel it burning a hole through my head. San An smiles shortly and places a hand on Hu's shoulder. The younger man desists.

"You both have good points. It was through my carelessness that our secret was revealed. I will travel to Ning with General Yue and sort this out. If they truly know our ruse, then it will be obvious. Until then, remain calm on the matter. There's no reason for us to instigate a war over what ifs."

The last time San An protected me, he barely managed to survive, and now he wants to walk straight into Ning? Something is severely wrong with him! At the end of the day, he is the former crown prince and the prime minister while I am nobody. There's no reason for him to be placed in danger instead of me.

"No, I will go." Standing up, I slowly approach the group.

"You? You couldn't charm your way out of a wet paper bag!" Bai Hu smirks. "Let someone who doesn't appear a fool get this done. Besides, if they don't know you're a fake, then you'll really be in danger."

"Can't you be a little nicer to her?" Qing Hai interjects. I don't know why he feels compelled to defend me. I don't care what Hu says because I don't disagree. It was nice of Hai, anyway.

"When she is dressed as a woman, I'll treat her like one." Hu responds gruffly.

Hai protests and they go on for a few minutes about nothing. I now understand what Jin meant when he mentioned they always draw out conversations when they are together. This doesn't concern me at the moment. Ignoring the squabble, my attention refocuses on San An.

"Prime Minister, I will go with you."

"That is not possible."

Maybe he's forgotten I'm as stubborn as he is.

"*I'm going with you.*"

"Please, don't argue with the Minister." Jin reaches for my arm. I shake him off.

"You are the former crown prince. My first decree as He Pi is to restore your title. So, if you want to let this country fall to chaos by being reckless, then I hope you can live with yourself."

San An raises an eyebrow. I know I'm being an imbecile. I have no idea where this is going. From the corners of my eyes, I see Yue thinning his lips. He's disapproved of me from the very beginning. Strange enough, Hu is more than amused.

"That so? It was my idea to bring you to court. Don't I get a fancy title, too? Want to make me the Duke of Zhou?"   Hu nudges my arm while laughing boisterously.

"I'm demoting you!"

For my reply, I receive a grin.

"That's enough, Bao Lai."

By using my real name, Jin gives reminder that I have no authority. The bitter frown on his mouth makes me withdraw. I suppose there is no point arguing about this now. To persuade San An, it is better to be frank with him; alone and without all these interruptions. I'll visit him later when no one else is around.

Once things settle, Jin and I leave. He seems tense as we traverse the halls together. However, the tension is short-lived.

"Darling!"   Someone cries out from behind. Suddenly, a pair of arms flings around my neck and the noxious scent of blooms envelopes me.

"Who the hell...?"

My attempt to request for his assistance is thwarted; Jin is stricken by embarrassment. I turn back to face the assailant and the extremely beautiful woman before me appears vexed. Dressed in luxurious royal garbs, her face is flawlessly painted, her lashes are long and curly, and her brown hair sways airily, making the woven jewel and flower headdress tinkles with delight.

"Where have you been?" She scolds me. "Everyone said you left for the Summer Palace and then they said you were ill. I say that's impossible! You wouldn't go to the Summer Palace without me, would you?"

"Uh..." I stare at Jin but he's looked away. Is he blushing because of her? She's ten times the woman I could hope to be; all the same, I am always nervous around females. The feeling of inferiority is taking over me by the second and it's beginning to show on my face.

"What's wrong? Cat got your tongue?" She leans closer.

I step back. Nervousness is chipping away at composure; my voice suddenly increases in pitch. "Who-Who are you, again?"

"Excuse me?" She puts both hands on her hips and pouts. "Have you been consorting with other women again to have forgotten me? It's Mu Dan, your fiancée."

"My what?"

My eyes grow wide from terror, until I remember Jin's account. This is the woman to whom He Pi is engaged. Suddenly, I feel sorry for her. Should He Pi never return, she will be cheated of her nuptial. I am in no position to do anything about that. Anyhow, I have other things to worry about. Taking a step toward Jin, I feign fatigue.

"I'm sorry... dear. I'm not well. Can we talk later? Jin, please help me back to my room."

Jin complies and assists me down the hall. The stubborn woman can't take the hint. She starts after us and then walks beside me.

"Your voice sounds different. My poor darling, you really are sick! Let me tend to you."

When she puts out both hands, I press hard against Jin to escape her grasp. "No, no! I'll make you sick, too. Go back to the, the... wherever you just came from. Jin will take care of me."

"Where I came from? You're delirious! Jin, let me help you care for my beloved."

Jin doesn't reply. I don't understand why he refuses to help me! He just keeps on blushing. Clearly, she's beautiful, but to make Jin speechless is not something I expected. Is he nervous around women? He obviously doesn't trust them. Maybe, he is terrified of them, too. What am I saying? I'm a woman! He doesn't behave this way around me!

We arrive at my chamber. As soon as Jin and I slip inside, I immediately turn and lock the door before she has the chance to enter.

"What are you doing? Let me in!" She beats the door furiously.

"I'm tired! I'll talk to you later!"

My body still hurts. The encounter with this madwoman made it worse. A deep sigh escapes as I fall onto the bed. She is yelling something through the door. Whatever it is, I don't hear it. It's becoming difficult to stave off slumber.

Hours later when night descends, my eyes finally open. I think Jin must have already gone to bed. Usually, he'd wake me when I sleep too long. Today, he didn't. Was it because of *her*? It's pointless to feel jealousy, especially when she has no interest in him. Still, to have seen him behaved that way makes me uneasy. In my mind, Jin is claimed. He is mine! Perhaps, not in *that* way, but I see him belonging to me solely until He Pi returns. Then, I'd have to give him back. I don't know why I feel this way. I just do.

After an hour of feeling infuriated for no reason, I start from the room for San An's quarters. Crossing hall after hall, a familiar dread suddenly surges. I'm lost again. Where are San An's quarters? I thought Jin and I turned left here earlier or was that on the way back? Recalling our path, the memory of *her* previous intrusion suddenly enrages me. The nerve of that woman! I blame her for having been a distraction. This is the reason I can't remember where San An's quarters are located. That's not true; I'm naturally bad with directions. I still blame her!

Yet, standing still and being angry won't solve my dilemma. I just need to walk around until I find his quarters. First, I need to pick a path.

Chapter 11 – 2

I turn right and scuttle down the hall. Whilst peering around the corner at the next turn, an unsightly creature emerges a short distance away. Of all the luck! It's He Pi's fiancée. I hastily swing around to run back from whence I came before she can see me. Of course, it is too late. In mere seconds, her arms fling around my neck. As I stumble forward, she immediately pulls me into an embrace.

"Darling! Did you come looking for me?" She chirps happily.

"No, I did not!" My attempt to pull free is futile. Her grip is like iron shackles.

"What do you mean? Why are you avoiding me?" Mu Dan is wounded by my carelessness. I know I must feign He Pi's persona, but this is insufferable. Everything about her irritates me and I wonder what it was His Majesty saw in her.

"I'm… sorry." I mutter under my breath.

"I forgive you!" She hugs me again.

Well, that was easy! Obviously, the lecher and this crazy woman are perfect for one another.

"Listen… dear, I'm a little delirious right now. I need to speak to Minister San An. Do you know where his room is?"

"I thought you didn't like San An," she pouts. "Anyway, wouldn't you rather spend the night with me?"

All my nerves suddenly fire at once. Why my heart suddenly race because of *this woman,* I'll never know. "Well, it's important. Do me this favor just once."

"Why are you blushing?" She glares accusingly.

"I-I'm not. I'm sick. High, *high* fever... delirious!" A fake cough erupts. Using the excuse, I manage to pull free.

"My poor dear. Why don't you return to bed?"

"No, I need to do this. Please, help me."

Mu Dan stares directly into my eyes. Something in my words or expression startled her. I understand I am not behaving as she expects, but I don't think anyone really knows what He Pi would do in this situation except for He Pi. Slowly, a smile flows across painted lips. Linking our arms together, she drags me down the hall.

"You've never been so adorable, Your Highness!" She laughs happily.

"What is that supposed to mean?"

"Blushing and asking me for help. It's so unlike you!"

"Well, I *am* sick, you know. If I wasn't, I wouldn't."

"Liar," she frets.

We walk down several more corridors and then I realize that this is not right. We are nowhere near San An. Where is this crazy woman taking me? My arm withdraws but she holds on steadfast. I haven't felt strength like this since General Hu accosted me on the road.

"Where are we going?"

Disregarding my panic, Mu Dan continues. I think she enjoys this. Turn after turn, and then we are outside. In the dark of night, I can barely see her in front of me. Yet, Mu Dan walks as quickly and precisely within the path as though the sun is right above. I thought women of the Circle had to stay in the Peony Palace. She apparently knows every single inch of this massive place.

Intuition swiftly signals danger; more so, I'm irritated for too many other reasons. Agitated, I cry out, "Will you stop already?!"

Mu Dan abruptly complies and I lean down to catch my breath. My chest is heaving while she is unfazed. Turning around, her hands squeeze my arm. The grip feels like boulders crushing my bone.

"What are you doing? Let go, damn it!"

"You don't sound like you at all, Your Highness." Her blithe response is also somehow menacing. I can't see her face but perceptibly, a grimace is present.

"You dare disobey your lord? I said let go!" The authoritative approach backlashes. Air drains from my lungs when Mu Dan slams me ferociously against a nearby wall.

"What is my name, Your Highness?" She comes closer and speaks in a low tone.

"What? M-Mu Dan, obviously. What's the meaning of this?"

"My real name," the voice draws deeper. Is a completely different person standing there? She was my height moments ago; yet, I now feel someone tower over me. What does she mean by *real name*? I had no idea she existed until earlier today.

Obviously, she saw through my disguise. This is quite an overreaction. Should I just admit the entire thing? However, I can't trust her. She's standing here threatening me. How can I be sure she will keep my secret? Better for her to turn me in to the ministers and accept my fate than to imply the ministers and have them all, including San An, answer to the court for conspiracy. Mu Dan pushes the question again. Her grip is so severe, my arm is turning numb. I need to say something.

Lie (Continue to page 114)

Tell her the truth (Continue to page 116)

Chapter 11 – 3

"I told you, I'm sick. I can't remember anything! Let me rest and I'll tell you tomorrow!"

"Tell me my name or I'll break your arm," the tone draws even deeper.

"I don't... I don't know!"

"Why don't you know?"

Pain is slowly spreading. If she isn't going to break my arm, it wouldn't take much more for her to dislocate my shoulder. Who does she think she is, trying to pry an answer from me when she is hiding a secret of her own? My other hand is forming into a fist. I don't want to hit a woman but this may be my last choice. When her grip tightens, my decision is made.

"I don't care what your name is. If you're going to accuse me of something, then do it already!" My left arm swings across where her face should be; instead, my fist hits something more solid. I was right! She did grow taller. Reaching out into the darkness, I realize my fist connected with her chest. However, this is not a woman's chest to be sure.

"You're a *man*?!" The strident cry projects much louder than intended. From afar, the sound of shuffling footsteps nears us. The guards are making their rounds. My immediate reaction is to call out to them, but I can't. This *man* shoves his mouth over mine while pressing his body against me, choking all the air from my lungs. I struggle to push him off to no avail. He feels like a brick wall. And yet, if this person is really a man, should have the same weakness they all share.

My knee swiftly rams into his most sensitive area. Mu Dan groans and withdraws. His grip around my arm loosens. A hard fist slams against his face just for good measure and then I run toward the footsteps. They have long retreated. In the dark of night, the path is obscured. Honestly, I probably couldn't traverse this place in broad daylight.

My heart races and my lungs constrict. I haven't felt this fearful for my life since that day on the road. Why can't any of them, even the Demon General, be here now? I should call for help but if that madman catches me first, I'll be done for. Stumbling forward, I hit trees and pillars along the way and eventually slam into a wall. This is good. It is something to go by. Following the stone structure, I hope a door will soon appear.

However, time chisels at hope in the midst of the unending path. My breathing is growing more ragged. How much longer will it take for me to recover from the poison's damage? What a frivolous question! Unless I find help soon, I may not live long enough to worry about that. My body is shaking and I'm turning cold. Suddenly, footing is lost and the hard ground connects to my slumped body. This is it. I can't move a muscle. Consciousness is seeping away.

Continue to page 117

Chapter 11 – 4

I should tell Mu Dan the truth. She is He Pi's fiancée after all. Taking a deep breath, I admit to being a fake and carefully explain the situation.

"I see. This is a dangerous game you play." Mu Dan strokes my cheek and leans in closer. "It's too bad you're not trustworthy. If this is all it takes for you to reveal the Minister's ruse, you'll only end up causing trouble for Nan Rong."

"But, you're His Highness's fiancée! That's why I'm telling you!"

"It's a good thing *I* am his fiancée. Anyone else would sell this secret to many, many interested parties. His Highness needs a country to return to and you only serve to mitigate that certainty."

Without allowing a response, firm hands grasp at my throat. I can't breathe! All my attempts to retaliate are futile. The hold increases as time passes and eventually, life disperses before my eyes.

The End.

Chapter 12: That Bastard!

Waking up in my quarters, logic reasoned that the whole ordeal must have been a sordid dream. At least, I thought as such, until I push off the bed and shooting pain freezes me in place. Beneath the right sleeve is a large bruise running up and down almost the entire length of my arm. I poke at it and the pain makes me wince. It is completely swollen.

"That bastard!"

"Yes, I am a bastard. I apologize."

Oh, god. Who just said that? I turn about frantically and then notice someone by the window. There *she* sits. He appears the same as before, the same height as me, but I can't trust anything anymore.

"Who let you in here? Jin! Jin, where are you?!"

Mu Dan moves to the corner of the bed, all the while, glaring amusedly as I inch back, clutching at my arm.

"Don't bother. I told Jin to leave us be. We need to talk."

"Excuse me if I disagree! The last time we *talked*, you tried to break my arm! What did you say to him?"

"I said nothing and he told me the truth anyway. It's that simple. Frankly, had I wanted to break your arm, I would have. There's no need to try."

"You arrogant prick! Get out of my room!"

"*Quite the mouth on you!* I don't take orders from commoners. Besides, this is not your room. We can talk like civilized ladies or we can repeat last night's affair. That's up to you."

"Are you threatening me? Do they know your secret? You're no lady!"

"Neither are you," he smirks. "I liked you better last night when you were shy and adorable. Believe me, you'll want to be in my favor."

The nerve of this man! I've never met anyone so insufferable! If only the chair by the vanity were closer, I'd throw it at his head! I don't care what he wants to say. I don't want to be anywhere near him!

Quickly darting off the opposite side of the bed, I make for the door. He stands up and blocks the path. "Get out of my way!"

"I told you, I don't take orders from commoners." He grins. "Sit down and hear everything I have to say."

"I don't take orders from people who've injured me!"

"You *should* take orders from people who've injured you and who have no hesitation in doing so again."

The grin widens and I so badly want to hit him. However, upon raising my right arm, the pain becomes unbearable. I have to let it drop again. I'm in no state to fight him. Even at full recovery, he'd probably win.

Chapter 12: That Bastard!

"Jin! Jin! Shu Jin, where are you?"

There is no response from beyond the door.

"Are you deaf? I said he's not there. Sit down and listen."

That authoritative tone is intolerable! I can't do else at the moment but it isn't like me not to retaliate. Moving to the window, I stand still and ignore him.

"Well, that's very cute. Are you waiting for big brother to come save you? Jin will not return until after I leave, *Your Highness*. Don't believe me? We can be here all day."

He doesn't deserve a response. My eyes are locked on the closed panels. He can talk himself to sleep. I don't care. Time passes by in mind-numbing silence. Luckily, it seems he's grown tired of bothering me because Mu Dan hasn't said another word for the past thirty minutes. Good. I just need to find Jin and sort out this madness.

"What are you doing?!" Just as I turn, Mu Dan is at my heels. Putting out both arms, he locks my body into a tight embrace.

"Will you listen to me now?"

"No!"

"Well, that's too bad because I'm going to start talking and you're going to hear everything I have to say whether you want to or not." With that, his arms constrict, pressing our bodies into a single line. Mu Dan leans closer to my ear and begins. "Don't struggle. You're irritating me. I told Jin this is a conjugal visit. He's not coming back until I leave, understood?"

"You told him what?! D-D-Does he know you're—"

"No. He thinks I'm so pretty, he would do whatever I tell him. Men are easy to manipulate once you know how to hit the right spot. Women on the other hand, women like you, are too unpredictable."

"How long did it take for you to realize..."

"The first moment my arms flung around you, I knew. I spend all my time in the company of beautiful women at the Peony Palace. You think I can't tell an ugly one just because she's wearing men's clothes?"

My fidgeting ceases at the word, "ugly." I know I'm not pretty but I didn't think... and that must be the reason Jin does not behave so childishly near me. Still, it begs the question: he knows I am a woman, so why did Jin agree to this *conjugal* visit from He Pi's fiancée? More importantly, this *man* is He Pi's fiancée. Does His Majesty know?

"Yes, His Majesty knows my gender." Mu Dan answers my direct mental inquiry.

How did he do that? Only one other person has done that to me thus far and I want him to be here instead. I would gladly trade this man for San An in a heartbeat.

"I thought you were usurping his throne. Is he actually missing?" Mu Dan whispers.

"Yes. Did he say anything to you? Do you know where he went?"

"Don't ask silly questions. If I know where he is, I would fetch him. There *was* something he mentioned to me, though at the time, I did not think it relevant."

"What did he tell you?" Hope dash high; I jump a little.

"Calm down. I'll tell you in a minute. First, is there anything else you'd like to ask?"

"What? No! Tell me what he said!"

"You're being embraced by a beautiful man. Are you sure you don't have at least ten more questions for me? You may never be in a position like this again."

"Arrogant bastard! Just tell me already!"

Mu Dan chuckles softly while his warm breath tickles my ear. "All those years engaged to His Highness and I never had the chance to embrace him like this. Mainly, because we both prefer women. To have you in my arms now is quite a treat."

Damn it. Why am I blushing again? I hate Mu Dan! I hate that everybody keeps using me to exact whatever secret feelings they have for He Pi!

"I'm not him!"

"No. That is precisely the reason I can hold you this way. Be still for a moment and let me relish the thought."

"Are you crazy?"

"A little. Now, are you sure there's nothing you want to ask me? I'm willing to answer anything."

Honestly, I have a million questions but I don't want to drag this out. I decide to ask him one question and one question only so we can move on. What should I ask?

"Why are you engaged to He Pi?" (Continue to page 123)

"Why do you cross-dress?" (Continue to page 124)

"Who are you, really?" (Continue to page 125)

Chapter 12 – 2

"Why are you engaged to He Pi?"

This bothers me severely. Jin knows almost everything about his brother. This Mu Dan holds secrets no one can fathom.

He sighs softly and then leans closer. "Because he trusts me."

That is not what I wanted to hear. I need more details. He purposefully answered in such a manner that could easily lead to nine questions more. Not wanting to give him the satisfaction, I accept the incomplete answer.

Continue to page 126

Chapter 12 – 3

"Why do you cross-dress?"

He said he's interested in women, so it doesn't make sense for him to pretend being one.

He sighs softly and then leans closer. "It's easier this way to get close to women."

I don't even want to know what that means. I accept the befuddling answer.

Continue to page 126

Chapter 12 – 4

"Who are you, really?"

He sighs softly and then leans closer. "I'm the prettiest girl in your harem, Your Highness."

He giggles in my ear and I become enraged. Anyway, he's not going to tell me the truth and I don't want to give him the satisfaction by asking another question. I accept the impertinent answer.

Chapter 12 – 5

"Tell me everything he told you," I insist.

"That's all? Are you sure there's nothing else you want to know?"

"No!"

"Disappointing. Ah, I am a man of my word." He sighs again with a heavier air and holds me even tighter. "Here goes. His Highness questioned whether he is truly best for the country."

"*That's it*? *That's* your secret? Who doesn't feel that way when they're in charge? Even I've had my doubts and I'm not the real thing!"

"You don't understand He Pi. He's not a man with low self-esteem. That is to say, he never portrays himself as being pathetic to anyone. We were in his study drinking and well, liquor loosens tongues."

"He drinks?"

"Oh! I thought you didn't have any more questions for me! Liar!" Mu Dan laughs childishly.

"I don't. That was a question for me. Now, I've listened to what you had to say; so… get out of here."

"Just for that, I'll stay a while longer." The embrace sharpens and pain becomes unbearable.

"My arm hurts! Let go!"

My forehead rams against his painted face. He backs away, holds onto his nose, and then runs to the vanity. Over and over, Mu Dan continues surveying his reflection in the mirror.

"Look what you did! You almost injured my beautiful face!" Still holding onto his nose, Mu Dan turns to me wrathfully.

Shrugging, my body slumps to the ground. When I lift up the sleeve, it's apparent the color has deepened. Every touch feels like needles jabbing deep into my arm.

"I didn't think it was that bad." Mu Dan suddenly kneels in front and lifts up my injury.

"Stop! You're making it worse!"

"Be quiet for a moment," he waves a free hand at my face. "When Jin sees this, you'll tell him that you fell, right?"

"Why? Isn't he in love with you? Can't you just brush it off or tell him it's my fault?!"

Mu Dan smirks. Without another word, his long, bony index finger runs over the purple skin. The sensation is of a knife cutting through my flesh. I wince and draw back. He holds on steadfast.

"Don't be such a baby." He frowns. "Let me test something. Try not to scream."

"I think you've done enough! It'll heal if you'll leave me alone!"

"I wasn't really asking for permission."

With that crude response, he pushes my shoulder back with one hand and yanks my arm straight with the other. It feels as though he's ripped my arm completely off! Even if I wanted to scream, nothing could come out.

Pain puts me into shock and I fall over. For once, I want to lose consciousness, to be free from the torment, but it won't come. Every inch of me is paralyzed aside from my racing mind. Mu Dan is doing something to my arm.   The feeling is nothing short of repetitious stabbing. I think he is talking to me, but I don't hear a thing. Eventually, I just fall asleep from boredom.

Chapter 13: An Innocent Mistake

When sunlight pierces through the window, Jin wakes me from slumber. I lost an entire day all thanks to that *woman*. It's my ambition that should I ever see him again, to order his execution.

"Did you have fun with Mu Dan yesterday?" Jin smiles while placing a tray in front of me.

Immediately, sarcasm comes to mind but when I look up, see that he is genuine. I want to respond but my throat is sore. Instead, my head shakes violently.

"Oh? She said she had a very pleasant time with you."

I nearly spit out all the water I'd just drink. If by a pleasant time, he meant ripping my arm off, then sure! Speaking of my arm, I'm somehow using it freely. When I lift up the sleeve, only a slight discoloration near the elbow is present. It no longer hurts.

"Is something wrong with your arm?"

"Not anymore." There goes my evidence to hang him. "What exactly did she say to you, anyway? What did we do yesterday?"

"What do you mean? Weren't you there? She said you two spent the day discussing His Highness... something else about how soft he was to cuddle... I don't... I don't know." Jin flushes thoroughly.

Poor Jin. I don't have the heart to tell him the truth about Mu Dan. "Jin, did He Pi ever question his ability to rule over Nan Rong?"

"No, why?"

"Mu Dan said His Highness told him—her—that shortly before he left."

"You think he left because of doubt?" Jin settles beside me on the bed.

"I don't know. What if he did?"

"Then he will see how wrong he is and come back."

His words of optimism put me at ease. Yet, when I glance at his face, perceive that he is distant. As usual, Jin hides everything he feels.

"You don't have to lie to me, you know."

He looks over and smiles. "I'm not."

"You're doing it again. I'd rather you tell me that he won't come back; not because he can't, but because he doesn't want to. Then, at least, I think San An should be the one to restore stability."

Jin bites his lip and throws a hard gaze to the floor. "It's not that simple. Prime Minister San An can't take the throne."

"Why?"

"Because the country will erupt in civil war."

"That doesn't make sense. He has a legitimate claim."

"That may be, but old wounds haven't healed. Did you notice Master Yu's lack of effort in finding an antidote for him? If it hadn't been for you, he would have let the Prime Minister die."

I saw the court physician sat idle, but would he truly have just let San An die? How could he! I don't have a chance to ask when Jin continues.

"The court physician's sister was a consort to Emperor Jin. Both her son and daughter were poisoned by Empress Pai. You can see why he thought the end would be just for the Minister. I realized it when you barged in the room. And then, to see you lying there dying with him, I..." Jin's fists clench. Unshed tears glisten in his eyes.

"I'm fine." My hand moves to pat his arm. "Good thing I remembered sleeping nettle."

"What is sleeping nettle?" He returns curiously.

"The poison was sleeping nettle, wasn't it? I thought I screamed the answer to you."

"No," Jin replies through the blank expression. "After you fell down next to the Prime Minister, you were completely unconscious."

"Then, how did you find the antidote?"

The simple question is met with unexpected reactions. Jin looks at the ceiling, the door, and then the floor. He tries to ignore the subject. I can't let it go.

"Tell me!" Grabbing his arm, I give a light shake. He hesitates.

After a long moment, slowly and indecisively, Jin lets out a stifled sigh. "I... did something I'm not proud of."

"You know if you don't tell me, I'll just ask San An."

"Well, since that's the case, then I don't have a choice." A sad smile surfaces. "I threatened Master Yu. I said that if my brothers die, I would take the throne and well, it was a threat, you get the gist."

"Oh. Don't feel too bad. I sort of threatened him, too."

Jin neither notices my nervous chuckles nor shares my sentiment.

"I swore to myself to never covet power. At the time, power was the only thing to save you both. I was weak and foolish."

"But, it saved us. You didn't do anything wrong. I thought my actions saved San An when it was you all along."

Jin's head shakes. "I was willing to put my brother's life fully in Master Yu's care. He would have undoubtedly perished. Your impulsiveness forced my

132

hand. Without it, I would have been alone again. Thank you."

The sweet smile on his face makes me smile, too. It's just like him to be so modest!

"You don't have to thank me, Jin. So long as you're happy, that's all I want."

Picking up the crystal cup, I drain the remaining liquid. My throat is as dry as sandpaper from lack of sustenance in the previous day; all because of a certain *woman*. After setting down the cup, I push away the tray and lie down behind Jin.

"I'm still tired, sorry. Do we have assembly today?"

He doesn't respond, so the question is repeated. When he appears to be ignoring me, I nudge his back. "Hey, are you awake?"

What childish behaviors! Since he's chosen to snub me, I'm going back to sleep.

"Ahh," a quiet exhale escapes while my eyes close. Soon after, he stirs, and then they prop open in search of his figure. I don't have to look far. He's leaned over me. Our faces are inches apart. The unexpected sight throws my heart into furious palpitations, and then just as quickly, calms at the realization that this must be another instance of his erratic moods. I shouldn't take this seriously.

"Are you okay, Jin?"

"Do you... really care about my happiness?" His voice quakes. Jin is utterly apprehensive.

"Obviously."

"Don't joke!"

I shouldn't have rolled my eyes. He didn't take the blithe response in good stride. Color is creeping over his face and deepening as time passes.

"I'm not joking. Truly, I do. Why do you ask?"

"No reason. I'm just glad." A hint of delight sparkles within the gaze and then he smiles happily.

This is rather odd. After the encounter with Mu Dan, I realized I'm ugly. I am better off as a man, I suppose, and I thought Jin saw me as such. Or maybe, I'm overreaching in my assessment of his reaction and it doesn't really mean anything at all.

Reaching up, I pat his head and grin. He takes my hand between his own. His palm is warm and slightly trembling.

"I want to make you happy, too." He continues softly.

"What..."

Jin closes in and presses a warm kiss on my mouth. It isn't vulgar like Mu Dan's or seductive like San An's. It is loving and passionate. My heart throbs a new sensation that overwhelms from head to toe. Never in my life have I felt such a thing!

His hand slowly reaches for my face, but as his fingers touch my cheek, I remember whose visage I carry. Perplexity causes my momentary withdrawal. It's enough to inadvertently force him away.

"I'm sorry, I thought..." He stammers. Jin is hurt and confused.

"N-No! Don't apologize! It's just..."

I peer over at the mirror and see He Pi's face. With a sleeve of the long robe, I rub off some of the powder, and then hastily untie my hair and throw the crown on the side table. Maybe, Jin realized his folly or maybe, he realized my stupidity. Either way, when I reach out for his arm, Jin abruptly quits the room.

Chapter 14: Vainglorious

Jin doesn't return and I resolved that while he is sorting through his thoughts, it would be counterproductive to interfere. Hence, in the afternoon, I make another attempt to find San An's quarters. Surely, once I turn left at the junction this time, all will be well.

Of course, I should have known not to get my hopes up. Another impasse is presented after the turn. My choices have been terrible thus far. I can't decide which route to take. While leaning against a wall to contemplate the consequences, someone disrupts my thoughts.

"Are you lost, Your Highness?"

Believing it's *her*, panic strikes my nerve. I twist around, prepared to retaliate, yet before me is a gorgeous young man with emerald eyes and light brown hair. He's dressed in dark green clothes and holding a silk fan. Such noble airs float about him; I assume he must be someone of ranking.

"I-I-I... y-y-yes."

The young man is so utterly charming, I can't keep from stammering. For my ridiculous response, the stranger graces a boyish smile.

"You'll want to take a right here. His quarters are down that hall."

"Whose?"

"Prime Minister San An's," he answers casually.

"How did you..."

I can't finish the question since the answer is so obvious. Recollection of the pain he's caused me rushes in torrents. Quickly rounding the corner, I attempt to escape. What madness is this? He's already moved in front. It's as though he teleported, but that's impossible.

"How is your arm?" He taps the fan to my shoulder.

"Do you expect me to thank you after everything you've done?!"

"I do."

The smug response makes my blood boil. My anger must bring him happiness because he's grinning triumphantly.

"I don't have time for this! Get out of my way!"

Shoving Mu Dan aside, my objective is resumed, though he promptly calls out a warning. "There's no need for that. The Prime Minister has already left with the caravan. He left yesterday whilst you were busy sleeping in my embrace. And yes, we did cuddle after I fixed your arm. A woman doesn't work for free."

I can't believe it! San An put himself in danger to find the assailant who attacked me, and I didn't even have a chance to at least thank him before he left, all because of this *person* who seems to like tormenting me. The angrier I become, the happier he smiles.

How could He Pi be engaged to this jerk? Everyone spoke highly of His Highness. I'm beginning to question his sanity. Had he run away because of doubt just to leave the country on the verge of war, then I hate him for it. I want that if he doesn't return now, for him to never come back!

"What's the matter? Are you sad?" Mu Dan leans down until we're face level while making no attempts to hide his sarcasms.

My jaw grinds furiously. Ultimately, I decide to hurt him where he'd hurt most. Grabbing his cheeks with both hands, I yank them every which way. He flusters and hastily withdraws but my revenge had already been exacted. His cheeks are red and slightly bruised. Mu Dan drops the fan and holds onto his face.

"You evil, evil woman! What did you do?!" He screeches.

I shrug and wander back down the hall.

"Come back here! You have ruined a work of art! Do you hear me? A work of art! I will make you pay for this!" He keeps muttering something under his breath while running to find a mirror. I can't make out what it is.

Chapter 15: Kang Lang

The court grew restless in the passing weeks. I only attended the assemblies once since my arrival and that is not enough. They were told He Pi was ill and then were informed that he was injured. Naturally, the ministers pushed for another appearance lest the court believe His Highness had perished. Jin was against it but his words made little difference. Without Minister San An present to speak on my behalf, I panic at the prospect of needing to address the court.

Decidedly, the assembly will be today in the afternoon. Jin is dressing me for my role while I frantically play scenarios after scenarios in my mind. If anyone says this... then I should do that, and if not that... then this.

As usual, I look to Jin for reassurance. However, he's preoccupied and doesn't notice my pleading gaze. At the moment, his younger brother is missing and his older brother is off somewhere in Ning. We haven't heard any news since the caravan left. If I were in his position, I couldn't keep half of his composure.

When I finally give up the notion of binding his attention, ironically, Jin starts to speak. "Don't worry too much. Just do the exact same as last time and everything will be fine."

Why is he trying to bolster my confidence when he is obviously more troubled? It's what I wanted, but when he does reassure me, I only feel annoyed.

"You know that's not possible. San An is not here and the other ministers won't take part in my performance because they fear being tied to the ruse. Besides, everyone is aware of the recent assassination attempt and the measures Nan Rong has taken. They'll want answers."

Jin frowns. I'm making his attempt to calm me futile. More so, I've actually just stressed him further.

"I'm sorry, Jin. I'll do my best, I promise. I won't speak unless necessary and if I must, then I'll..."

I can't finish the thought. What am I supposed to do? I don't sound like He Pi. I can't attempt to copy his voice since we've never met. Not only that, I've yet managed to learn how to speak in the manner to which he was accustomed.

"Ah..." I said I would try my best to become His Highness. Instead, I've spent most of my time caught up in the chaos of his personal life. I feel like a failure.

Just when I think this will be my last day on Earth since the court will undoubtedly charge me for being a fraud, a familiar voice comes through the door. That *woman* returned.

"Darling!" He bursts into the room and embraces me. His arms feel no less than iron beams crushing my ribs. Jin flusters and turns away.

"I don't have time for this!"

Upon my outburst, Mu Dan releases his hold and tells Jin to leave. Once more, the latter complies without question. I take a few steps away from this crazy person. He glances over and smiles.

"Don't look so frightened. I'm not here to torment you. Not yet, anyway." The voice is his real voice—a complete mismatch from the disguise.

Twitching nervously, I retreat a little more. "What do you want?"

Mu Dan folds his arms and stands at a slight angle. "You're very rude! I came all this way to help you and this is how you speak to me?"

"Help me how?" Mirroring his stance, I frown.

"Get on with it. I don't have all day. You'll make me late for my chess games." Mu Dan replies languidly. The voice that came from him is different from any I've ever heard. A sudden smile covers his painted lips; his expression is one of victory.

"I-Is that He Pi's voice?"

"A perfect match, I assure you. I also know his personality well enough to pass for him. So, what do you say? Will you be my puppet?"

With Mu Dan providing He Pi's voice coupled with my physique, we'd be able to fool the court for another day. Soon as elation comes, hope is suddenly dampened by an uneasy thought. Could I really trust this person? Should he purposefully say something to propel his agenda forward—whatever that agenda's objective may be—I could not stop him without exposing my secret.

While I'm desperate at the moment, he's not the type of man who does anything without expecting payment. Maybe, it is better to rely on myself than to constantly seek help from others. Once more, he reads my thoughts.

"You're awful!" He scolds in the female voice. "I just want to help Your Highness however I can. You're my fiancé after all."

The word "*fiancé*" provokes another twitch from me. Once I rely on him, there will surely be a price. Nevertheless, he could guarantee the stability of this political structure until San An returns. On the other hand, this task is mine and I don't trust him. I don't want to be so pathetic that I need Mu Dan to save me from my own incompetence.

"Thank you for your offer. I will do this alone." A short bow and then I start for the door.

Mu Dan frowns. His arms fly around me. As I begin to protest, he sweetly interjects, "Good luck, darling!"

Giving a swift peck on my cheek, he then disappears down the hall.

What a strange and annoying person. Is he mocking me because I'm a woman or because I'm a commoner? I doubt he behaves this way toward He Pi. I just wonder whether is it due their gender or because he knows the consequences for expressing his feelings? Hmm. I suppose that curiosity is more suited for another day.

It's time for the assembly.

Chapter 15 – 2

The moment I lay eyes on him, I'm thoroughly stunned. I'd always thought he was handsome. In clothes befitting a prince, Jin is utterly sublime. However, he fidgets terribly upon noticing my silent intrusion. I guess he really hates the idea of being a court official after all. It just can't be helped. Without San An present, Jin must take his previous position. To appear before the court means he can't dress as a servant.

"His Majesty, the Great He Pi, may he reign for eternity!" The crowd responds to the orator's call while I enter the assembly in the previous rehearsed manner.

The familiar deafening silence returns and all eyes are on me. I'd hoped this display is enough to suffice the court's suspicions. Of course, that is hardly the case. An older man steps forthwith and the orator calls out, "Lord Po Sui of Hong Ran has the floor."

Breathing suddenly constricts, causing my arms to shake. Despite all my efforts to subdue the reaction, it is noticeable.

"Is His Majesty unwell?" Lord Po Sui gawks curiously.

My mind frantically weighs the outcomes of possible options. I can't form a resolve. This was a bad idea! I should have asked Mu Dan for help!

At the thought of Mu Dan, my mouth reflexively moves on its own. "Get on with it. I don't have all day. You'll make me late for my chess games."

The voice that bursts forth is not my own, nor is it He Pi's. It's a mixture of something strange. The attitude, however, is nearly a perfect match.

Lord Po Sui is taken aback. A crooked smile quickly follows. "Yes, Your Majesty. The court wishes you a speedy recovery. We know you are still recuperating from your previous injuries. Please accept our apologies for having pushed this appearance."

Lord Po Sui retreats following my nod of acknowledgement. Jin then crosses the dais to assist me while the orator and court calls out the usual phrases. Once we are alone behind closed doors, Jin bursts into laughter.

"What's so funny?"

"You," he answers coolly. *"You'll make me late for my chess games?"*

I rub my head shyly when he raises an eyebrow.

"Oh, Mu Dan taught me that."

"She's a good influence for you."

"The hell she is!" I should learn to control my temper. Jin is unaware of Mu Dan's sadistic side after all. "Never mind. It's better that we don't speak here."

Though he's thoroughly confused by my outburst, Jin nods and then follows me to He Pi's quarters.

When we enter the room, my agitation returns. Mu Dan is sitting on my bed, smiling as usual. At the sight of him, Jin abruptly leaves. I didn't even have the chance to fully gawk at my wonderfully handsome Jin yet! Once more, it is because of *this woman*.

Mu Dan claps his hands together and grins. "So, you owe me, don't you?"

"Owe you what? I don't owe you anything."

"You used my line. I told you, a woman doesn't work for free."

"You-You were at the assembly?"

"Of course! I wouldn't miss your performance for the world."

"Are you stalking me?"

"Obviously," he scoffs.

"Why?"

"Why else? I can't forget how adorable you were that night I nearly broke your arm."

At the mention of my arm, the pain momentarily returns. I look away while he starts from the bed.

Chapter 15: Kang Lang

"You can't imagine how cute you were; standing there with his face behaving so femininely. It's straight out of my fantasy!"

"You've been engaged for six years. I can't imagine you don't have the nerves to be forward with him."

"He and I are engaged because of a mutual agreement. Regardless of your opinion, I have no interests in men. Often though, I dreamt that one of us could switch gender. Alas, reality is disappointing. And then, you came along and won me over." Mu Dan draws nearer and I step back farther.

"Won you over? You harassed me! You think I want anything to do with you?!"

"And you harassed me. I guess we're even."

"I did no such thing!"

"No? You practically abused me; kicked me, punched me, and even bruised my beautiful face."

He keeps coming closer and like a fool, I keep moving back.

"That's because you started it!"

I don't know why I thought arguing with this crazy person would render merit. His face is purely delighted by amusement. Retreat continues until I suddenly trip on the hem of the long robe and tumble back onto the wall. Immediately, he is standing close, towering over me. How he keeps changing height is completely befuddling! Reaching out both arms, Mu Dan pushes against the wall and encloses me in between. I feel trapped inside a cell.

"Jin! Jin, come in here!"

"Why do you always ask for his help? I'm right here. Why not ask me?"

"I need his help to get away from *you*!"

"You can't just ask me?" He frowns.

What kind of nonsense is that? His impertinence makes me shake with rage but I know that any act of aggression would merely excite Mu Dan to continue. All because of this face! Memories of Jin's retreat haven't left me. This man must be just as confused. I quickly rub the powder off my face and remove His Majesty's crown. Long hair flows down my shoulders and I appear my gender.

"There! Do you see? I'm not He Pi! Your fantasy didn't come true, so leave me out of it!"

Mu Dan's expression grows severe. His eyes narrow and his lips thin into a line. I keep gawking at the door hoping for Jin to return. Of course, he doesn't. Mu Dan's right. All I do is rely on Jin for everything. I've never done anything for him. When he needed comfort, I thought letting him sort through this thoughts alone was best. I see now that it was selfish. Every time I feel troubled, including now, I keep expecting from him that which I've never given.

Slowly, my eyes meet Mu Dan's. He momentarily withdraws.

"What's wrong? Why are you sad?"

"I need to find Jin. Please, just leave me alone."

Pausing, he seemingly appears wounded.

"Do you really not like me?"

"I think it is you who do not like me. If you did, you would do as I ask."

A sudden burst of laughter erupts. His fingers forcibly run down my cheek. "You want me to be obedient to prove my affections? I didn't think you were that type of person!"

I don't know what type of person he is referring to but it couldn't be good. An angry glare is my single response.

"Tell you what, Your Highness. I'll be obedient from now on if you will fulfill your promise to marry me. After all, an empress can't disobey her lord."

"Quit mocking me!" I grab his fingers and throw them from my face.

"I'm not mocking you."

"Then, what the hell do you want?! I told you, I'm not He Pi! Why do you keep harassing me?"

Like a child being bullied, tears are welling. I know they're bound to fall in torrents and I don't want to give him the satisfaction. In a state of bewilderment, I do another foolish thing: I shove my face in his chest and sob. He initially falls back. Slowly, Mu Dan returns an embrace but it isn't the bone-crushing feeling I expected. His body is warm and his arms, comforting. I begin to forget why I'm even crying.

Coyly lifting my head to meet his gaze, I notice he's flushing more so than me.

"You're cheating," he chuckles nervously. "I can't bully a woman when she cries."

"I wasn't crying!"

"You are such a liar."

"So, you admit it! You're bullying me!"

"Obviously," he scoffs.

"Why?"

"Are you really that innocent at your age? It's because I'm in love with you."

His answer is so casual, it's as if he hadn't said anything at all. My cheeks are on fire and my heart skips a beat. What foolish reactions! By now, I should have learned not to take him seriously. I'm embarrassed for having believed him and even feeling a little excited by the prospect; however brief was the moment.

Rolling my eyes, I shove Mu Dan away.

"You're *hilarious*." As I start for the door, a heavy hand grabs my wrist.

"That's it? I told you I love you and this is how you treat me? Are you brushing me off? Are you rejecting me?" Pain crosses his expression; though mostly, he's just agitated.

"Do you think I'm stupid? You don't know who I am and I don't even know your real name! There's nothing about me to love except for the fact that I resemble your fiancé! That's hardly enough of a basis to place true affection!"

Mu Dan bites down on the lower lip while contemplating my frustration. Still, he is a stubborn sadist whose pride was challenged and thus, refuses to yield. The grip around my wrist tightens with his usual brute force. Pulling me into an embrace, his other arm chains around my back.

"I'm not lying!" He protests.

"I don't care!" I scream back.

Heat from his body rises tremendously and imprints onto my skin as though seeking to burn me. His rage is frightening. Still, I won't be intimidated. I don't know what love is but I don't love this person; this much I am certain. Despite his protest, whatever it is he feels must be misguided lust for He Pi. Every moment that passes, his grip becomes noticeably tighter while intense heat spreads to burn another part of me. Although I don't want to show more of my weaknesses, pain causes me to involuntarily wince.

"You're hurting me."

"Good! Then you know how I feel!"

A fervent kiss presses against my mouth. I try to turn away but his grip shackles me in place. A strange sensation of pain and pleasure passes through and then my body falls limp in his arms.

I hate him so much, but for whatever reason, I don't want him to release me. Confusion and frustration rise in tandem and threaten to drown me under their weights.

Chapter 15 – 3

"What is the meaning of this?!" A voice erupting with fury pierces the silent room, carrying a force which is only comparable to that of roaring thunder. Mu Dan quickly relinquishes his grip while I, pulling myself together from shock, stumble to regain control of my body.

Prime Minister San An steps inside and surveys the younger man. When he briefly glances at me, both displeasure and anguish cross the furrowed brows.

"I always knew something was insincere about you. I never would have guessed it was your gender. And here you are in His Highness's chamber assaulting *my charge*! I won't tolerate such a thing! Not even from his *fiancée*. You will be executed!" With that, San An prepares to retrieve the guards. Before he can move more than a few steps, I rush forward and grab onto his robe.

"Please, San An! He didn't mean any harm!"

San An's livid glare gradually fades to disgust. "Did you want him here, Your Highness?"

The Minister's tone is so bitter and cold that chills run down my spine. I don't want Mu Dan to be executed but I also fear his impulsive nature. I can't keep composure when he's near. How then, can I expect to maintain the ruse? This may be my only chance to be rid of Mu Dan. Yet, I cannot bring conscience to accept that.

"I asked him to tutor me. He knows His Highness as well as anyone. I made it through assembly today, didn't you hear? It was because of Mu Dan."

"And I suppose you were *repaying* him for his kindness?"

"No!"

"Then he accosted you!" The tone hardens. San An peers wrathfully in Mu Dan's direction.

"He was... It was my idea for us to role-play! We went a little far, I'm sorry!"

"You don't have to lie, Bao Lai." Mu Dan suddenly steps forth. I never told him my name. All the same, it's not surprising he knows more than he should.

"I *was* taking advantage of her, Minister." A sweet smile accompanies his admittance. "She's so tempting when she's angry, isn't she? *You* should know. I'm not the first man here who has forcibly put his hands on her."

Mu Dan grimaces. San An returns the gesture in full fervor. Just how much does Mu Dan know?

Leisurely, the younger man's expression relaxes. Both hands rise to signal surrender. "Well, do what you have to do, Minister. I am fully guilty of all charges."

Still scowling, San An carefully examines my expression and then shortly after, parts from the room. In believing that he is going to retrieve the guards, I give chase. Just as I do, Mu Dan grabs at my collar.

"I thought you didn't love me. Why do you care?" The tone is teasing but he's staring blankly at the wall.

"You idiot! Do you want to die?"

"Might as well, if it means I can't have you." He grins.

"Stop joking! Look, even if you do l-l-lo... meant what you said, that's no reason to be reckless! You only live once! Don't waste your life on something so useless!"

"You think love is useless? Typical idea from someone who has never been in love." Mu Dan scoffs while ruffling my hair. "If I weren't going to be executed, I'd teach you a thing or two about being a woman. You look like a kid!"

"Then, that makes you a pedophile!" I knock his hand away.

"Well, I can't be a pedophile since you're older than me."

How does he know my age? I've never told *anyone* outside of temple. Laughing at my dismay, he moves to the door.

"Where are you going?"

"To find the Minister. I'll save him the trip. Besides, I don't want you to shed tears for me. I'd rather walk to my death with fonder memories than you crying."

He smiles shortly then continues out the door. My chest tightens. I hated this idiot! I still do! Whether he lives or dies is not my business! I tell myself that but my body instinctively moves forward and reaches for his hair. Immediately, he shrieks and whips around.

"Don't mess with my hair! I don't want to meet the lord of the underworld looking unkempt!" Darting back inside the room, he makes for the vanity. "You evil woman! I think you pulled out a few strands! My beautiful hair!"

Mu Dan removes every pin and begins reassembling his locks. He's muttering something under his breath. Expletives, I imagine.

Strange, he is such a brute but when it comes to appearances, Mu Dan is as high-maintenance as a princess. The way he flusters amuses me. I inadvertently laugh.

"You think I'm funny, Your Highness?"

"Hilarious." I wonder how a man who cannot stand the sight of a few strands of hair falling is fine with the prospect of losing his head. "Listen, Mu Dan... or whoever you are, just leave the palace. I'll talk to San An once he returns."

"Leave the palace? *Me?* I'm too beautiful to be thrown into the filthy world of the common. I'd rather die!"

"You are really something, you know that!"

His attitude is vexing. I've never met anyone so disagreeable! At this point, I don't care anymore. Frankly, there were a few times I wanted to kill him myself. Shuffling angrily to the bed, my fingers reach up to rub my forehead. He's giving me a headache.

Following a short pause, I let out a heavy sigh and glance up. He's standing right in front of me. How did he move so fast? I never heard him stirred.

"What now? If you want to die, then go!"

"You're so *cold*," he pouts.

Damn it! I forgot to contain my frustration. With little effort, Mu Dan pushes me down and hovers atop.

"I'm going to die because of my love for you. Can't you at least reward me before I go?"

My first thought—a counterproductive one—is to yell his ears off. However, he likes it when I erupt with rage and he likes it when I'm shy. He wants that I am anything but neutral. The more I look into his eyes, the more I realize he can't feel satisfaction unless he holds power over another, or that he is incapable of feeling anything without going to the extremities. He mocks me because I am weak. He teases Jin to validate his narcissism. He couldn't overpower San An, so he challenged his authority the only way he knew how: by being impertinent.

My last resolve is to ignore him. Both eyes shut tightly.

"You've tried this before. Ignoring me doesn't work, remember?" His index finger taps my forehead sharply. For his effort, Mu Dan receives no reaction. He kisses me fervently but I manage to keep still. His hand then brushes against my face and then slowly, fingertips glide over my skin and descend toward my chest. I want to kill him but unless I'm actually going to do it, would solve nothing.

He doesn't really desire me, I know that. Mu Dan conveyed that I'm ugly. There's no reason for him to behave this way. The word "ugly" keeps echoing in my mind; spawning other thoughts that run in a repetitious loop. "I'm ugly. I might as well be a man. I am a man. I am He Pi."

Abruptly, his fingers stop their descent. Mu Dan whispers in my ear. "Who said you're ugly?"

"What?"

My eyes reopen to his perturbed expression. How does he keep reading my thoughts?

Mu Dan repeats the question while resentment manifests into a scowl over his painted mouth.

"You did."

"When?" He's taken aback. In moments, the memory comes to him and a small crooked smile appears. "Why don't you ever take me seriously when I'm actually being serious? I was just teasing you. You're such an imbecile."

"Yes, I know." My tone is flat and my expression is indolent; mirroring the true He Pi. Mu Dan pouts and then moves away. He lies down beside me for some time before a long sigh erupts.

"Kang Lang."

I glance over from the corners of my eyes. "What?"

"That's my real name. Don't ever call me that around other people. When we are alone, call me, 'Kang Lang.'"

"I thought you were going to die for the sake of my love. When will we ever be alone together again after this? Unless... you had no intentions of dying."

"Don't be sarcastic. I'm too beautiful to perish in such an ugly manner!"

"You knew San An wasn't going to fetch the guards?"

"I knew the Prime Minister would not do anything to upset you. I'm a little jealous. He is a fine gentleman."

"Are you... jealous of him or are you jealous of me?"

"Both," he laughs wryly. "I thought if I could persuade you to feel guilty enough, you'd give yourself to me, but you're so *cold.*" He moves off the bed and starts for the vanity.

"You're a real bastard, Kang Lang."

"I like it when you say my name. I'll have to make sure we are alone together more often from now on, Your Highness."

"I can only tolerate you in small doses."

"If you were any other woman, I'd punish you for that." He replies curtly. "I don't find you amusing anymore. Although, I'll tell you a secret, if you want."

"Do I *want* to hear this secret?"

He turns around and grins. "I should hope so. I know the identity of your elusive assailant."

Does he really? Before I even consider believing him, I'd already flown off the bed.

"Who?!"

A teasing smile and then he turns away. I shake his arm severely. "This is not a joke! Do you have any idea what San An and the others have been through? Whatever secrets you hold, you will tell me now!"

"So demanding! I know just about everything that goes on around here," he smirks proudly. "Collecting information, infiltrating bases, impersonations, assassinations, and so forth. That assassin and I used to serve the same lord."

While Kang Lang is genuincly beautiful, there hides something utterly dark underneath, that for a moment, he let slip across his eyes. It is eerily frightening. My breathing stalls just as I catch a glimpse. He quickly represses it. Finally, everything makes sense. This is the reason he's so strong, manipulative, and outright talented at his craft.

"Tell me!" I shake his arm again.

"A woman doesn't work for free!" He giggles in Mu Dan's voice.

"Is that what Kang Lang would say?"

Placing both hands squarely on my shoulders, he replies, "No, darling. Kang Lang would not answer anyone for anything. Mu Dan will answer to her lord under every circumstance."

"I don't understand. Would He Pi not eventually fulfill his engagement?"

"He Pi is not here, my dear. Besides, His Highness never had any intention of taking Mu Dan as his empress. Haven't you figured out by now the nature of our relationship?"

No, I haven't. Admitting that I don't understand anything is an understatement. "What must I do for Mu Dan to answer me without becoming her lord?"

"Don't ask to buy the merchandise when you're not willing to pay the price." He shakes his arm free. "I won't tell you a thing until I'm empress."

"Why is that title so important to you?"

"You have the emotional intelligence of a child! You'd never understand! Speak to me again when you've changed your mind."

Kang Lang frets and starts for the door. I yank him back.

"You're very forward tonight, Your Highness." Although his reply is playful, his voice is taut and cold. He's lost all interests.

"Please, just tell me. I don't have the authority to make you empress. You know that! I'm barely able to fool the court into believing my authority. How can I instill yours?"

"That is your problem, Your Highness, not mine."

I need to confirm whether Ning is preparing for war if indeed they know my secret. San An surely has news but I doubt he'd found anything at Mount Fei Yang. This is my chance to be useful. Yet, Mu Dan's proposal is preposterous! San An knows his secret. He would never allow it! Should I just promise Mu Dan whatever he wants?

Don't lie (Continue to page 163)

Make a false promise (Continue to page 164)

Chapter 15 – 4

I can't do it. I can't lie and make a false promise. He would see through it anyway. I'm the fool here, not him.

"I'll give you anything else but I can't promise you that."

Mu Dan jerks back his arm and leaves. I'm disappointed. However, it was presumptuous of me to think the Minister's efforts were for naught. San An would probably not want to receive me after that shameful display. I should search for his generals instead.

Continue to page 166

Chapter 15 – 5

"Fine! Help me! Once everything is settled and if He Pi does not return, I will marry you."

"That's a big *if*, isn't it? Should His Highness return, then I'd get nothing. If he doesn't, then I'd still lose him. Doesn't feel like a win."

"Should he return, how can I make you empress?"

"Don't be dense. Declare me empress now and secure my title. He Pi won't make a fuss to strip it from me."

"I can't do that."

"Of course not. You know full well there are no time constraints. He may return in a day or in ten years. Until there is proof he's perished, you are free from the arrangement. Given the lack of constraints, you're willing to agree to anything. How despicably deceptive of you!"

As expected, he saw through my ruse. I'm the fool here, not him. I cast down my gaze to hide my shame.

"I really like this side of you," Kang Lang whispers as an arm slips around my waist.

"Are you serious? My being deceptive excites you?"

"It's only because you're so transparent. What would you really do if I had agreed and there is proof

His Highness will never return? Would you really marry me?"

"I..." can't finish the sentence. I suppose a promise is a promise.

"You would, huh?"

How does he keep doing that! Maybe he's right. I am transparent.

"Tell you what, Your Highness. I'll take that deal. All you have to do is be willing to have our honeymoon tonight, after which, I'll tell you everything I know."

"What happens when he does return? I would be cheated in that case!"

"I suppose. Should he come back, I'll marry you anyway. See? No harm done." He grins sweetly. The boyish tone is exasperating.

"That's the stupidest thing I've ever heard!"

"Why? Your proposal isn't any better for me. One of us will be cheated either way. I hold what you need. Speak to me again when you're serious about making a deal."

Kang Lang darts from the room so swiftly, I can't catch him. I'm disappointed but it was presumptuous of me to think the Minister's efforts were for naught. San An would probably not want to receive me after that shameful display. I should search for his generals instead.

Chapter 16: An Emperor's Privilege

In the barracks, Qing Hai and Bai Hu are fussing near the archery range. They really fooled me before. From afar, they seem really close, almost like brothers.

"Oh, it's you!" Hai waves as I approach.

Hu smacks the younger man's arm and then stomps forward.

"What are you doing out here, *Your Majesty*?" Hu glares at Qing Hai as a mean of chiding him for being too informal toward He Pi.

"General. Hai. Have you any news from Ning?"

"Isn't that something to ask the Minister, *sire*?" Bai Hu folds his arms and puffs out his chest.

"I didn't want to disturb him. He's had a long trip."

The elder of the two knows I'm lying. Due to the other soldiers nearby, he has to feign respect for my authority. Though, he's not happy about it. Hai, on the other hand, is as innocent as ever.

"We weren't allowed to accompany the caravan," he begins. "Maybe you should talk to General Yue. Oh, never mind. He's already left for his rounds."

"Or *maybe,* you should talk to the Minister!"

Hu's tone is as sharp as his tongue. Obviously, should Bai Hu know anything, he'd never tell me. With a short nervous nod, I leave the barracks.

More than anything, I want to see San An. At the same time, I don't think I can face him. Have I done something wrong? Was it my fault Mu Dan tormented me? My mind keeps replaying Kang Lang's embraces and kisses. It is the same unsettling thing that occurred to me after San An's previous advances.

How it happened is unbeknownst to me. I'm suddenly in front of San An's quarters. I don't remember walking here, yet here I am. Why then, am I afraid to call for him? While I struggle to decide whether he should be disturbed, the door abruptly opens and San An signals for me to enter. I drag my feet and keep my head down; just waiting for him to scold me. I want that he would instead of looking so disappointed.

"I've been expecting you, Your Highness."

At the table, the Minister pours fragranced white peony tea into a pretty cup and carefully hands it to me.

"Thank you."

"No need to thank me. Although, I suppose I should apologize for having interrupted your affairs earlier."

My eyes lock onto his face but San An won't give acknowledgement. He's hurt and betrayed when there's no reason for him to feel this way. I thought after the ordeal in the garden, he came to his senses and saw me for what I really am: a stranger of little import.

"Prime Minister... San An. Have you brought favorable news from Ning?"

By trying to brush off the uncomfortable subject, I thought we can move forward. If there was more to say, he decided against it. San An nods slightly and places his cup on the table.

"Yes, I'm glad to report it doesn't appear Ning is aware of our ruse. Furthermore, when we entered Mount Fei Yang, we were able to capture some ruffians who revealed that the culprit did in fact impeded on their territories and killed several of their men. The assassin then fled and returned in the direction of Nan Rong. Specifically, toward An."

"He's here in this city?!" In shock, I spill tea on the pristine table. San An pulls a kerchief from his jacket and clears the mess before I can apologize.

"It's no trouble, Your Highness. You do not have to worry while I'm here. In any case, I've thought about the subject for some time on the return trip. It is practically unheard of for anyone to attack our grand fortress during the day. The peach garden is one of the safest areas in the palace. My thought is that whoever attacked us did not have to put much effort into infiltration. That is to say, I think the traitor is amongst us. Not only that, he could have easily poisoned us through other means. There was no need for such a direct method. He wanted to be followed to Ning."

"Why now and why implicate Ning?"

"I am sorry to say I do not know."

Logic points at Kang Lang. He said he knows the assassin. I wonder if he *is* the assassin. Yet, he had so many chances to be rid of me. All he's done was toyed with my emotions. Still, he's the manipulative type and I can't even begin to postulate his final objective. My mind drifts away as I contemplate the matter. In due time, San An places a comforting hand on my shoulder. The unexpected sensation causes me to jolt.

"You do not need to fear me," he remarks sadly.

"No... I was lost in thought. You surprised me."

"What were you thinking?"

Should I tell San An? I have no proof whether Kang Lang is the assassin or not, and bringing him into conversation might just push San An to send him to the gallows. I don't want innocent blood on my hands. Yet, should Kang Lang be guilty, he needs to pay for his crimes.

"Nothing. I've troubled you long enough, Prime Minister. Thank you for all your help."

After a short bow, I start for the door.

"Are you going back to him?"

The bitter words cut through me. A mixture of tumultuous emotions overwhelms my heart, causing my entirety to freeze in place.

"As I've conveyed before, in your role as He Pi, you cannot pursue a romantic relationship. Then, you had a choice. It is far too late for that now. The court has acknowledged you. An attempt was made on your life. You must take this seriously; if not for your country, then for yourself."

I would be lying to the Minister by saying I'm not leaving to find Kang Lang. Neither can I confirm his suspicions. He would misunderstand my actions. Instead, I leave without responding. However San An interprets that is entirely up to him.

Chapter 16 – 2

The Peony Palace was easier to find than expected. The edifice is directly to the right of the main palace. Yet, as strikingly beautiful as the structure may be, it brings great offense to the sense of smell. Heavy scents of blooms engulfed the area to such extremities that I immediately shoved a sleeve over my nose to filter the air. When I approached, two guards at the front bowed low and then exchanged meaningful looks. I didn't understand the reason until stepping inside.

There must be a thousand women in this place! Each lovelier than the next! The sight throws my heartbeat into variations. I feel like a brute standing in a field of flowers and inferiority is overtaking me once again.

"Wh-Whoa!" It doesn't take long until I grasp that jealousy is moot. Like a stampede, they all rush at once. Realizing my folly, I attempt to flee but many pairs of hands tug at my robe. Almost in unison, the women chatter in maddening shrill voices. My arms fly over my chest to protect from groping hands. The more I fight to leave, the farther I'm dragged away from the door.

"Why are you so shy, Your Majesty?" A woman shrieks in my ear.

"He's nervous like a little boy, it's so cute!" Another cry out.

"Stay a little longer. Don't you want to spend the night with me?"

"No, he's mine!"

"You already promised tonight to Minister Leung, he's mine!"

On and on this goes. My head is aching from the nonsense while my body is tugged back and forth like a leaf stuck in a typhoon. Hands instinctively ball into fists, but I can't just swing at any of them. Right before breaching my breaking point, the crowd around parts as an infuriated woman bursts through the lines.

"He's mine! Keep your hands off my fiancé!"

I've never been so glad to see Mu Dan in my life! He throws the other women aside like ragdolls and after wrapping our arms together, pulls me to his chamber. Once we are finally free, I breathe deeply and collapse onto the floor.

"How in the world did He Pi manage to survive these crazy women?"

"By becoming my fiancé." Mu Dan moves in front of his vanity and gasps. "Those harpies messed my hair out of place!"

While combing the tangles out of his long locks, he mumbles incoherently. The only word I catch repeatedly is, "harpies." His reaction amuses me, so I watch him for a time. The line between his genders blurs. I can't tell whether Mu Dan or Kang Lang is his real self.

Eventually, boredom sets in, and then my attention is captured by each expensive thing in the massive room. It's inconceivable that there are identical luxuries for each courtesan.

"It's such a waste."

"What is?" Mu Dan calls back.

"I'm glad he's not actually consorting with these women. All the same, it's taxpayers' money he's using to keep them here; well-clothed and well-fed."

"Well, that's an emperor's privilege. *Your* privilege. Marry Mu Dan and rid yourself of these harpies. You'll make the taxpayers very happy."

"You don't give up, do you?"

"Never!" Mu Dan leaves the vanity and sits before me. He pokes my face and then laughs. "Look at you, all afraid of those harpies! You make such a cute He Pi!"

"I took the trouble of coming here. Hear me out."

"Well, I'm listening, Your Highness. If you want answers, that's a different matter."

"Fine. Then, listen. I don't know who you are, Kang Lang, so I don't trust you, but I must rely on you because you hold the truth. The assassin who attacked me fled to Mount Fei Yang in order to implicate Ning. He then returned to Nan Rong. The council thinks he is amongst us. Since you are the only assassin I know, I naturally think it's you. Honestly, did you try to kill me? Maybe the better question is, did you kill He Pi?"

Contrary to expectation, Mu Dan is not offended. A steady smile stays on his face throughout my charges. He stares for a long moment and then pokes my face again.

"You're so silly! If I wanted to kill you, you'd be dead by now! San An was shot in the shoulder. My aim is not that bad. I would have pierced the arrow through his throat just to watch him choke on his own blood." He relishes the violent words as though recalling fond memories. "As for your last question—No, I did not kill my fiancé. He is precious to me. Not in any manner you would ever understand but I do cherish him."

"Then who is trying to implicate Ning? Tell me!" My fist inadvertently flies against the wall.

"For that answer, you will have to pay the price."

"Or I could just have San An torture the answer out of you!"

"Don't make me excited. I won't be able to sleep!" He laughs happily. An eager smile curls over the petal lips which then widens from my disgust. "It's getting dark, Your Highness. If you're not going to hand me over to be tortured, then we should go to bed."

He isn't going to cooperate after all. Still, I am satisfied with his response.

"Fine!"

Upon reaching for the door, I freeze when his firm hands squeeze my shoulders.

"You misunderstood me, Your Highness. I meant, *we* should go to bed."

"I know you're mocking me, Kang Lang, and it's hardly charming."

"Why did you come all the way here just to flaunt yourself in front of me and tempt me with the notions of torture and murder? Why not summoned me to the main palace?"

I had forgotten that in front of everyone apart from the council, I do have some authority. What a waste of time this was.

"That... was not my intent. I didn't want anyone to be suspicious."

"You mean, you didn't want the *Prime Minister* to be suspicious. I thought you desired Jin. Increasingly, I think you favor San An. Although, since you've come all this way for me, I must have won you over."

His tone suddenly makes me shiver from dread. While I shrink back, he sends a sultry and seductive whisper into my ear. "It'll be fun. I promise to make you feel *so much pain* that you can't ever forget me."

175

My response of twisting away is met with vociferous giggles. I want to pound his face in but that would just excite him. Instead, I take the friendly approach. Turning around, I clutch at his arm.

"Escort me back to the entrance. I'll send flowers to Mu Dan and make the harpies jealous."

He contemplates for a short moment and then smiles smugly. "You finally understand this barter system. Don't send me lilies. I want roses, orchids, and peonies."

"Yes, yes! Any flower you want!"

The door opens and my *fiancée* parades me through the crowd of women. Regardless of Kang Lang's sentiment, Mu Dan is happy.

Chapter 17: First Love

"It's not safe to wander here, Your Highness."

Almost a week has passed since Jin's spoken to me. We've been in each other's company from time to time while he fulfilled usual duties; not much has been exchanged. After our previous awkward encounter, he withdrew emotionally. Perhaps, he's still not forgiven my foolishness. There were so many things I could have done to better our relationship but I fell short.

"Jin. I didn't know there's assembly today."

"There isn't. Why are you in the peach garden? Have you forgotten everything that transpired? "

"I'm just looking for clues. The assassin won't likely return here."

"The generals have combed through this area. Anything of import has been taken into account. Please, go back inside. It's not safe for you to be in the open like this."

"Jin... What if I told you I may have a way to find the assassin?"

"We're not using you as bait." Jin reaches for my hand.

I refuse to move. "You misunderstand me."

Pausing, his full attention thrusts upon me. I'm unsure whether this burden should be placed on his shoulders. Whatever I tell him will undoubtedly be transferred to San An and I can only guess *his* reactions. Doubts cease my convictions. As always, Jin is reassuring.

"You don't have to hide anything from me. I'll keep your secrets. My duties are to look after you. I can't execute them fully unless you trust me."

"You're the one person I never want to keep secrets from, Jin. I don't want this to trouble you, so try not to overreact. Mu Dan is actually Kang Lang, a former assassin."

I expected for Jin to become alarmed. He doesn't bat an eye.

"I know," is his calm reply.

"You know? How do you know?"

"Despite Mu Dan's opinions, I am the closest person to His Highness. Mu Dan did not do this."

"May I ask why you always retreat when he's near? Are you enamored with him?"

"Don't be ridiculous." Although he denies the attraction, his attention is forced away. Colors ever so lightly appear over his cheeks. "I shy from him because he is a man. It's unnerving to see another man look so..."

"So... beautiful?   I thought I was the only one unnerved. Wait, you knew Mu Dan is a man. Why did you leave me alone with him?"

"He said you wanted to learn more about His Highness and he would teach you how to be a woman. You mentioned that you didn't know what it meant to be one since you've never worn women's clothing.   I thought since he's experienced, Mu Dan could be a good influence for you. Why are you frowning, is something the matter?"

"If by teaching me to be a woman, you mean he can put his hands all over me, then sure!" I don't know what brought me to confess. Or, am I only complaining?

Jin becomes startled and then another indescribable expression takes over. I hate the idea of keeping secrets from him.   I want him to know my lips *have* been stained by the kiss of another man, despite having been repulsed by the grotesque act. Why this matters to me is perplexing.

Jin's eyes gradually darken. The expression turns to pure outrage. His hands clench tightly into fists and his entirety trembles. What have I done? I didn't intend for him to become upset.

"Jin—"

"Don't worry, Your Highness. He will pay for this. Kang Lang will never bother you again!"

"What? N-No, Jin, that's not important."

"How is it not important?! Am I supposed to be complacent knowing another man's put his hands on you?!"

I've never heard his voice raised this way. I don't know what he's implying or whether he is implying anything at all. Shock turns me immobile.

Immediately, the countenance on his crimson face turns wrathful. I lunge forward when he turns to leave and grasp at whatever I can; only to fall on my face.

"Jin, stop! He knows the assassin's identity!"

Pausing, Jin tilts his head in my direction. A brief moment of contemplation ensues and then without hesitation, he continues on the path.

I have to stop him. Once he removes Kang Lang, our only source of information will be relinquished. I have to do something. Anything!

Chapter 17 – 2

"Jin! Please don't leave! I love you!"

The words erupt from my mouth before I can grasp the idea. I've spent much time with Kang Lang, albeit not through my device, and the only thing I've learned through it all is that I don't want anyone else but Jin. Kang Lang confuses me. I can't lie and say in some ways I wasn't drawn to him, but I don't want him. Minister San An is severely kind to me, but I don't love him either. The one person who's been on my mind since the day I became He Pi, is Jin.

I wanted to be his friend and failed miserably. I hate the idea of him affected by another. I hated Mu Dan for this reason. I couldn't care less how anyone else sees me, but I'd hoped for Jin to eventually see me as a woman. Never in my life have I ever cared about being a woman until I met him.

What's given me the most pain lately is the sight of him walking away. Every time he leaves my side, I feel lonely. I kept it inside because I thought he'd never accept me. To see him so enraged just now signals that perhaps my desires are not farfetched after all.

Slowly, Jin turns around. The anger within him subsides; yet, he appears sad. For a long time, silence washes between us.

What does he see when he look upon me now? He can't possibly see a woman. Perhaps, I was wrong. Jin's merely upset because I'm his charge. It's not because of jealousy. He's just overprotective.

The blank expression makes me anxious. I feel as though my heart will burst if he does not answer soon. Then, as a bird flittering from one of the trees above disrupts the serenity, Jin turns his back to me.

"You should go inside, Your Highness. It's not safe here."

Jin retreats from the scene. All that remains is the deafening silence of loneliness. A searing pain penetrates my heart and I can't breathe. Despair pulls me under while dreaded cold sweeps over every part of my soul.

Chapter 18: A Confession

A week passes by without any trace of Jin. Another servant comes and goes with my daily meals but I have no appetite. My heart is crushed and my mind is in shambles. Whatever happens outside of this chamber does not concern me. I don't even know why I'm still here.

Late one morning, San An comes to my side. Upon seeing his face, I begin to wonder the path not taken. One man finds me special, another lusts after me from delusions, and another treats me with disregard. Why of the three, am I in love with the man who won't accept me?

At the sight of my disheveled hair, wrinkled clothes, tearstained face, and defeated disposition, the Minister locks the door so that no one else may enter. "What has happened? Why has Jin allowed you to fall to this state? If the servants see you this way, it will be cause for alarm."

Sluggishly, I attempt to move off the bed. I haven't slept in days; my body slumps to the floor. San An nears and kneels in front. He checks my pulse while fine brows knit sharply.

"I intended for you to attend assembly today but you are in no condition. What has happened to your convictions to become He Pi?"

183

Unsure whether I am actually awake at the moment, a blank stare returns the Minister's concern. San An frowns, but then decides against chastising me. Instead, he pulls a kerchief from his jacket to wipe my face. Slowly, a long sigh casts out.

"I will send for Jin. You must make yourself presentable. Ning's emissary will come to us next week and we need this meeting to go well."

As I look into his eyes, all I see is disappointment. He tasked me with protecting the country and I haven't done a thing. I've let emotions ran wild, behaved foolishly, and made all the wrong choices. I was too enamored with the idea of being treated as a woman; I forgot who I am as a person. I hate breaking promises no matter the obstacle.

San An begins moving away. My hands quickly reach for his arm. Shaking my head, a low and hoarse tone escapes. "No, don't send for Jin."

"It must be terribly painful to see him, but I can assure you, it is less painful to see the person who's broken your heart than to never see *that person* again." He implies he knows the feeling well.

"I will not fail you, Minister. Please, just let Jin have his space."

Following a drawn silence, San An makes an obeisance and leaves. I pull onto the bed and look at the mirror from across the room. What an ugly sight. I have tarnished the image of He Pi. Due to Mu Dan's speculations, I believed His Highness ran away. If he didn't, his legacy shouldn't suffer because of my lack of control. As long as I must play the part, anywhere I am present is just another stage. Until the curtain closes, my heart should not be opened.

At the moment, all I can do is sleep to recover strength. When I wake, I'll do whatever it takes to become He Pi.

Chapter 18 – 2

Two days later, San An escorts me to assembly. It's palpable the court is restless from my delayed absence. Thus, before long, a man in purple and silver garbs moves to the middle of the floor.

"Governor Gui Xing of Ting Heng has the floor," the orator announces. The elder man bows, shuffles his sleeves, and then moves closer toward the front.

"Your Highness, we hope you are well. As representative of the eastern Hong Ran City borders, your servant requests information pertaining to the recent assault. Is Nan Rong in danger of a Ning invasion? The court is aware that the recent assassination attempt involved Mount Fei Yang but we have not been informed of Ning's response."

San An readily steps forthwith on my behalf. I raise a hand to stop him. In front of the court, he cannot challenge me.

"Governor, we are under advisement that Ning was not involved in the assassination attempt. The assailant has not been found but our generals are doing their best to bring our enemy to justice. Ning will send an emissary to Nan Rong within the next week. We will discuss our future relations then; as always, with the idea of peace in mind."

Gui Xing bows but does not return to his seat. I know exactly the reason he's troubled.

"Pardon my intrusion. Have you recovered, Your Majesty? Your voice is different and you don't seem your usual self."

"We have been ill these many months, and then to have suffered through the attempted assassination... it has affected us in more ways than expected. Rest assured. Regardless of how we may change on the outside, at heart, Nan Rong is our primary concern."

The elder man bows low and retreats to his seat. I can't imagine that his curiosity was satisfied.

"Censure Zhuo of Ling Ling has the floor." The announcement follows as another man moves to the middle. He is portly, bearded, and is adorned in a gold robe that could rival the ones in He Pi's wardrobe.

"Your Highness. Your servant Zhuo has come on behalf of Ling Ling to request funds for a construction project. Many fields were added in the past year and it is imperative to expand our irrigation systems. Ling Ling has long been a key territory in providing the imperial army with provisions. We wish to continue our support."

I know nothing of finance and can't bluff a decent answer. It sounds like a good idea and naturally, I want to approve. However, I'm not certain. When I do not provide an immediate response, San An interjects, "His

Highness has been in recovery and has not the chance to review the tax reports. Please allow me to assist."

With my gesture of approval, San An steps forward. "Censure Zhuo, from the May reports, Ling Ling surely has collected enough taxes to implement this expansion, does it not?"

The Censure shifts uneasily while keeping attention to San An. "Prime Minister, indeed we have collected a large sum of taxes. However, the recent increase in cost of construction materials and the amount of labor we must employ is too great. I am afraid Ling Ling will not have much in reserve for emergencies should we take on this task."

"Ling Ling is undeniably known for its massive fields; yet, on the last survey His Highness conducted, there were few suitable pieces of land available for expansion. The cost of extending the irrigation system to these areas is minute. Certainly, the price is nothing compared to the summer home Your Grace purchased in Lu only a few days after collecting the May taxes. If there is disagreement, unquestionably, the court will not refuse sending one of our ministers to audit the records."

Censure Zhuo flusters and withdraws the request. He bows and starts for his seat. However, I am dissatisfied with the solution.

"Prime Minister. We want Ling Ling to expand their irrigation systems to all the new fields."

San An looks over but does not dare retort. The Censure, upon hearing my orders, eagerly turns back. "Your servant is ever grateful, Your Highness!"

"You misunderstand us, Censure Zhuo. We want Ling Ling to expand the irrigation system using the collected taxes from May. In two months, we will send a minister to review the progress and should it be found that the task has not been completed due to lack of funds, we will consider the proposal after a thorough audit of Ling Ling's finances and everyone who has ties to its oversight."

San An bows. "His Highness has decreed, so it will be done."

Censure Zhuo turns pallid. He staggers back to his seat in the same manner a prisoner would to the gallows.

While gazing at the sea of nobles gathered, I wonder how San An is able to recall aspects of each territory under Nan Rong. He truly is amazing. I am glad he's at my side.

No one else moves to the floor. Hence, San An calls for assembly to dismiss. I sigh in relief when we are back in the halls.

"You gave me quite a fright," the Minister chuckles.

"I apologize. In order to be successful at this task you have entrusted me, I must practice. You cannot speak on my behalf perpetually without raising suspicions." Determined to keep this new composure wherever I go, my response is perfunctory. San An simply frowns.

He wants to say more but fear of prying eyes keep him. San An signals for me to follow. Once we enter his quarters, I take to the tea table and he joins after locking the doors.

"Do you intend to become His Highness in all regards?" The Minister removes his cap and runs long fingers through the smooth hair.

"Yes. I know I cannot mimic his personality or his voice, but if I can convince the court he has changed, then perhaps it is enough."

"Perhaps. I saw doubt rose in many faces today. None were displeased by your *policy*. Well, except Censure Zhuo."

"You really saved me. I would have given him the funds without question. That would have been a mistake."

"He Pi would have been more generous."

"Oh?"

"He would have provide the funds and audit the ledgers on the same day. His Highness has quite the sense of humor." San An speaks fondly of He Pi even while covering it with sarcasm. No matter how their pasts affected them, I feel these three brothers deeply care for one another.

"San An, has progress been made in finding the assassin?"

The Minister shakes his head whilst casting a gaze to the table. "I'm afraid not. I am also fully aware of the offer Kang Lang has made. That is why I asked if you intend to become His Highness in all regards."

Is he really suggesting for He Pi to marry Mu Dan? Though I glance into his eyes for an answer, the Minister refuses to acknowledge me. After a short pause, San An continues.

"The country needs an heir. Truly, it is fortunate that He Pi's betrothed is a man. With your compliance, he's promised full disclosure of his knowledge."

"But, San An, neither Kang Lang nor I were born of noble blood. Why would you want another fraud to take what's yours?"

A sad smile falls over his lips. San An stares repentantly. "I never meant to say those words to you. They were spoken out of anger. I suppose I never apologized for my behaviors in the peach garden."

"You didn't say anything that was incorrect. Why can't I just declare you crown prince and then abdicate?"

"Nan Rong will never see me as emperor. Whatever are my ambitions, they cannot be."

Just when I thought resolve was formed, this path is placed before me. If I marry Kang Lang and establish an heir, the future seems secure. But, does that mean there is no hope the real He Pi will return? Once more, San An reads me like an open book.

"At this point, the chances of His Highness returning are slim. It is pointless to procrastinate our duties more than needed."

"Let's say I marry Kang Lang; it would be wrong for our child to ascend the throne. Your child, San An, should be the rightful heir. Have you... Have you never considered anyone from the Circle?"

Abruptly, he turns away and for the first time ever, I see San An blush. It is rather endearing. The Minister remains silent, though vaguely, his breathing changes. I can't believe he's nervous! The sight of his innocence makes my heart jump.

"You, too, San An?"

"I, too, am what?" He responds softly as embarrassment deepens.

"You're shy around beautiful women and you are surrounded by them! I think I understand why you, too, feel so comfortable with me."

"You're mistaken. I am not comfortable near you because you are deficient in any manner. It is because I feel you are genuine. You don't need powders to create a mask or perfumes to cover the stench of deceit. You don't need beautiful clothes to hide the ugliness inside. That is how I feel and I'm sure Jin doesn't disagree."

Colors burn my cheeks. It is quite the compliment even though I don't deserve it. Especially, since I'm wearing He Pi's mask. For the most part, San An is considerate of me, but why did he have to bring up Jin's name? My mind race to retrieve everything I can recall of him and suddenly, the pain in my chest returns.

"I shouldn't have mentioned him," San An offers an apology through rising concern.

"No. I must exert better self-control. All the same, I can't marry Kang Lang. I have every expectation He Pi will return. Until then, if you don't mind, please prepare me for the meeting with Ning's emissary. I also want to learn of court matters when you have the time."

San An nods in agreement. I thank him and return to my quarters.

Chapter 18 – 3

Upon entering the room, my back presses against the door and then slowly, my failing body slides to the floor. I wasn't nervous during the assembly. Now that it is over, hindsight begins critiquing every little thing I should have said and done. I don't think I fooled anyone. Maybe the only reason no one accused me of being a fake was lack of proof... for now.

Closing my eyes, all I see is the crowd of noblemen and politicians looking up at the dais. So many people can cause my demise with one little word of doubt. A deep sigh erupts and then my head tilts against the door.

"You shouldn't be so hard on yourself. I thought you did well."

He was there all along. How did I not see him? Kang Lang is sitting on my bed, dressed in the manner I had only seen once before; wearing the clothes of his gender. He comes toward me, and for once, I don't feel intimidated.

"You were at the assembly again, Kang Lang?"

"I never miss any of your performances, Your Highness. You nearly gave San An a heart attack. He was so precious!"

"Don't make of fun of San An!"

Kang Lang shrugs. "Just when I've fallen out of love with you, the Minister thinks it's a good idea for us to wed and provide an heir, no less. I won't lie. You do excite me in such a manner that I'll make it very painful for you."

He strokes my cheek and receives no reaction. Leaving his side, I settle onto the seat by the window, remove He Pi's crown, and throw it to the floor.

"I have no intentions of staying. Your fiancé will return and then I'll take my leave. However, so long as I'm still here, I am He Pi and you *will know your place.*"

Initially, he finds my grimace amusing. The expression soon turns indolent.

"Hmph. Since you don't plan to stay, then there's no need for me to torment you. It would be a waste of time to drill discipline into you; my efforts would be in vain." He throws up both hands and then walks to the chair in front of the vanity. "Of course, you know this means I won't give you the assassin's identity."

"Yes, I know. I have faith in San An and the generals. I'll be glad when another attempt is made on my life. This time, they'll catch him for sure."

"You *want* to be attacked again? No wonder I'm so attracted to you. You're such a masochist!"

"Hardly. I just want answers more than anything."

"Uh-huh. Should you happen to perish, to find your killer, the Minister would tear the world asunder!" Kang Lang's grin carries a hint of irony. I think he's jealous.

"You overestimate my influences, Kang Lang."

"On the contrary, it is you who is blind to your influences. If I were you, I'd flaunt myself in front of San An more often, hoping for a reaction. You only need one overreaction to have him eternally bound to you. You'll be set for life."

How can he say that so casually? Is that something a woman should do? I'm shocked that he's telling me this when he's standing there as a man. I'm beginning to think Mu Dan is attracted to He Pi, and Kang Lang might be infatuated with San An.

"It's a good thing you're not me or you'd embarrass us both. Anyhow, *you* are more than welcome to flaunt yourself in front of him. I'm not that type of person."

"No, you've grown dull." Kang Lang pouts through the sulking stare. Suddenly, he leaves without another word. Could it be? I'm glad he finally sees me as He Pi.

Chapter 18 – 4

San An came to fetch me early in the morning and I've been in his study for an indeterminable span of time. His initial lessons comprised of etiquettes, basic political repartees, expected questions from the emissary, and appropriate reactions to take. My head is swimming! It's intimidating to think just how much more there is to learn. There's hardly any room left in my head. All I can do is attempt to shove more knowledge in, though at this point, it seems futile. As always, he understands my opinion even though I've not said a word.

"I apologize, Your Highness. I've kept you too long. It seems we've missed lunch."

"It's fine. I appreciate everything you've done for me and everything you continue to do. Anyhow, I'm not hungry."

"Well, I'm rather famished. Will you mind stopping here and joining me for repast?"

"Not at all."

Of course, I want to stop! My head is throbbing but I didn't want to make a fuss.

"I'll send for our meals. Feel free to rest on the sofa."

With that, he shuffles the notes we've been reviewing and steps outside. I collapse on the sofa and then smack my forehead several times to dull the pain. Did I actually retain anything from today? I feel like a dolt. At temple, my master always scolded me for skipping studies. When I did attend, I always yawned so excessively that the monks became infuriated. Now that I recall my childish past, I realize He Pi and I are very much alike. A crooked smile begins forming over my mouth just as San An reenters the room.

"You do not need to be formal, Your Highness. Lie back down. I will wake you when the meals come."

"No, I'm fine. Aren't you tired, San An? I'm not an easy person to teach, I know that. Maybe *you* should rest for a while."

Chuckling, San An sits down beside me. "You are far better than His Majesty. He kept falling asleep during our lessons, so much so, that I had to remove all the furniture and taught while standing. Then, he merely fell asleep against the wall."

"You-You taught He Pi?" Everyone commended He Pi's mind. Was it really due to San An's handiwork after all?

"Why are you surprised? He took the throne at a young age, before having received formal training an heir apparent should. I may have despised him at the time, but it was and always will be my duties to ensure he can become a successful ruler. And, he has. I'd thought everything went in one ear and out the other. It turns out he's hardly the person on the inside that he works so diligently to portray in the exterior."

"You speak fondly of He Pi. Sometimes, I think you are cold toward Jin. Is it because He Pi is also your cousin?"

San An quickly tilts his head toward my gaze. I still can't read him.

"You think I am cold toward Jin? He doesn't want to be treated as a prince. He wants to be a servant. I was against him taking such a low post but that was his decision. In any case, I do not favor one brother over the other. They both have their charms and their deficiencies. It's true that in our youths we hated one another, but blood can't despise blood in the end. And yet, I'm afraid after everything our parents have accomplished to place us in the current situation, our bloodline will end this generation."

"What... do you mean? Isn't Qing Hai your nephew?"

San An shakes his head. "He is within my household but we are not related. That is a story for another time. His Highness never had any intention for marriage and Jin is against the idea that he deserves to be happy; although, he's probably frightened of the prospect more than anything. He's the type to banish the world and yet, with a word from... a certain someone, may change his mind."

A certain someone. Does he mean me? Can't be. I told Jin that I loved him and he rejected me. Even though he didn't say the words, it was thoroughly clear. Pain wells in my chest and my nose burns, signaling incoming tears.

"I'm sorry. I did not mean to upset you."

San An wraps an arm around my shoulders. No matter the stupid things I say and do, San An is always forgiving. He never runs from me and I don't think he'd ever reject me. Kang Lang's words are ringing truer. All I need is an overreaction from San An to make him mine forever.

His bloodline will end unless he can provide an heir. His brothers have no interests in marriage. I don't want to think what's insinuated, but the thought keeps pushing itself into my head. I feel like a terrible person... I am a terrible person! I can't just toy with San An's emotions because I feel dejected. It isn't right! He's too good for me! Even were I to fall for San An, I don't deserve him!

"Why are you so quiet?" His soothing breath falls on my forehead as he speaks. I was too busy thinking of not doing something stupid, I didn't realize I had already done it. When did I lean over and put my head on San An's shoulder?

His arm tightens and draws closer as I attempt to lean away. Sudden warmth floods through my being when his soft lips caress my temple. The same sensation as when he last kissed me fill every inch of my body, though this time, the echoing impression is a thousand times stronger. Everything about him has always been so incredibly seductive. Recently, there is something sweet and loving in his nature I can't quite decipher. My body becomes paralyzed. I can't move away and yet, my voice won't come. This is wrong. I need to do something!

Oh, thank goodness! A servant announces at the door and the Minister withdraws. Relief and pain flood at once. What's happening? My face is hot simply from looking at him. Am I really that fickle?

San An places the tray on the table and calls me over. Nervously, I approach the seat across. As we sit down together, light clinking sounds begin throbbing from overhead. It's raining.

"Is it too warm in here? Should we move to another room with a window?"

"No, I don't think it's hot."

"Why is your face red?"

"My-My face?"

The Minister smiles softly. He's making fun of me!

"I must have stood up too fast."

My pointless denial goes unchallenged. Soon, silence creeps over the room while we eat. San An's glancing at me but I'm too embarrassed to lift up my head. My heart won't stop racing. Am I flaunting myself in front of him? Do I feel guilty or excited for having caught his attention once more? A lump suddenly forms in my throat. I choke and cough up whatever I was eating. What a grotesque sight it must be! Thoroughly taken by embarrassment, I cover my face with a napkin.

"Are you all right?" An unexpected gentle hand strokes my back.

Inching my eyes upward from the napkin, I peer at San An, who's kneeled beside the chair. He seems so concerned. I can't imagine he still sees me in that manner. I've been at court long enough that my presence is hardly special anymore. Why then, is he so sweet? I've done nothing to earn his regards. The nicer he is, the angrier I feel.

"I'm fine! Thank you!" The thwarting outburst forces me to my feet. San An seizes my hand before I can flee.

"Have I done something to upset you?"

"No."

"Then, why are you upset?"

My anger is baseless! He's offended, so I must reply.

Chapter 18 – 5

I thought of lying to San An but he doesn't warrant my disrespect.

"Prime Minister, I... I can't stand it! I can't stand you being so nice to me! It makes me feel guilty and confused and all sorts of other things! None of which makes any sense!"

"Then, what must I do?"

"It's not as though I want you to hate me, but you don't have to be so nice to me. I'm nothing special, you know that!"

"I see. You still believe that I do not see you as you are, Bao Lai? I was mistaken to have proposed for the absurd reasons I've mentioned. Trust me when I say I'll forever be ashamed for my past transgressions. Hopefully, you'll come to forgive me, even if I never will."

"Are you saying... you're nice to me because you feel guilty? Please don't. I've forgiven you for everything and I hope you will forgive me for all of my transgressions, too!"

San An's head gently shakes. "I hold no grudges against you. If I am being too polite, it is not by design. I suppose a man can't truly control how boorishly he behaves sometimes."

"But, you're not behaving boorishly. You're behaving as though you're…"

"As though I'm what?"

My face is burning again. First, I insult him and now I'm on the verge of injuring him. I should have just lied! Standing here dumbfounded, I can't finish the sentence. San An finishes it for me.

"As though I'm… in love with you?"

I nearly fall over from just hearing it. Everything feels cold except for my scorching cheeks. My heart is racing so fast, I can't keep still.

"Maybe, it's because… I am."

I think my heart just stopped. My eyes are bulging from my head. Elation and sadness are welling in tandem. What about San An? Why am I so damn selfish? Maybe, I've always known and it didn't need to be said. I've forced it from him. There's no reneging it now!

Turning slowly to meet San An, I can only see the side of his face. He's looked away. How terrible he must feel; far worse than how I felt from confessing to Jin. In San An's case, rejection was expected. San An let pride falter just to satisfy me.

"Very… funny."

"Please don't patronize me. I'd rather you reject me than disregard my admission."

He retains usual composure; though, it's obvious I've hurt him. His hand slowly releases mine while my body is not listening to my mind again! On impulse, my hand wraps around his falling fingers. San An is bewildered and so am I. What am I doing? My feet are moving toward him. I've lost all control!

As I'm on the verge of doing something worse, San An gently shakes free. "Excuse me for having been so bold. Despite my affections, you are now He Pi. If I lose myself worshipping you, we'll chance being discovered and you'll be in danger. Forgive me."

He smiles sadly and parts from the room.

What just happened? Did he just reject me? I can't breathe. Everything in me is shivering from anguish.

San An, what did I just do? If you hate me now, I can't object. Conscience is drowning under despair. No one is left by my side. Kang Lang, Jin, San An... Is this the loneliness of becoming He Pi?

Chapter 18 – 6

For the remainder of the day, I lie in my room and listen to the falling rain. This is the first time it's rained since my arrival. Tempestuous waves lash against the palace and tempt sleep to take away distress. I couldn't be wider-awake. If I had kept my mouth shut, I would be in his study having pleasant chats and reviewing notes, instead of lying here feeling like a failure.

Why did I hurt San An? I'm not *that* oblivious to claim I didn't know how he felt. At first, his attention was flattering, then somewhat frightening, and now I'm just conflicted. I do like spending time with him. I like conversing with him. More and more, I come to see him as he really is: a kind and gentle person. What have I given in return for his gentle kindness? I insulted him, wounded his ego, carelessly flaunted in front of him, and worst of all, nearly caused his death.

Memories of that day still torment me. The assailant knew I was not He Pi. Why did he attack me? Was it really to implicate Ning? He could have achieved the same without using poison on the arrow. Why attempt to kill me when he was aware that I'm nobody? I'm nobody... but San An protected me. I can't stop witnessing the Minister's expression when the arrow pierced him. Even in that state, he was worried for my safety. For everything I said to him just moments prior, I feel guilty even now.

Had he perished... I don't want to think about that! But I keep seeing the arrow in his shoulder! Why? Why won't my mind let it go? Is it because it... pierced his shoulder? San An is much taller than me. The angle from which the arrow was released was too high to have struck me. Additionally, this assassin served the same lord as Kang Lang. There's no way his aim is that bad! It wasn't me the assassin targeted. It was San An!

This revelation makes little difference unless the assailant can be found. At least, it's a start.

"Minister!"

Startled, San An jolts up when I storm into his chamber unannounced. He's done it to me so many times, I figured this was the norm. Yet, he is displeased.

"San An! The assassin wasn't after me. He was after you!"

"Yes, I'm aware." He sits up and brushes the loose hair from his face.

"What do you mean, you're aware?"

"The angle of the arrow was too high to have connected with you. The poison itself wasn't very potent either. Provided the great certainty of success from striking at that range, a more lethal poison could have been used. The wound, if anything, was more cause for concern than the venom."

"How can you say that? My insides were on fire! I could hardly breathe for a long time after. You were poisoned much longer than I was, but you showed no signs of the afflictions. You're too strong, San An."

The expression grows distant. Though his eyes are on my face, he doesn't see me. Gradually, his lips press into a line.

"You say the poison caused you that much pain just from being in your system for so little amount of time?"

"Yes. Are you saying that you didn't feel any of it? I don't understand."

"You weren't in the room when the arrow was pulled from me, correct?"

"No, I ran in afterwards. The court physician wasn't doing anything, so I became angry and well, you already know."

"I see." San An moves off the bed and makes for the door.

"Where are you going?"

"Trust me for now. I will return later. Thank you for coming to speak with me. You've been a great help."

"Help with what? I didn't do anything."

The Minister gives a short smile and then leaves. As much as I want to run after San An, I should do as he asked. Now that I have a reason to stay awake, my body feels drained. The rain echoes noisily and tempts me to slumber. Maybe, I'll just close my eyes for a moment until he returns. There's no sofa in this room. Hopefully, he won't mind lending his bed for a little while.

As I lie down, something comforting strikes the senses. Intoxicating scents suddenly drifts from the bed sheets and pillows. I move a little closer to where San An was lying and close my eyes to enjoy the traces of warmth that he left behind. Five minutes. I'll wake up in five minutes.

Chapter 19: An Emotional Ruler

The door clicks open. Lazily, I sit up and rub my head just as San An quietly enters the room. He's completely exhausted. Outside, the rain had stopped and birds are chirping happily. How long have I been asleep?

"I'm sorry, San An, I didn't mean to overstay. You should get some rest and I'll come back later."

Deafening silence floods the room. I lift my head to engage the Minister who's staring back in disbelief. His face is lit crimson.

"What's wrong? Do I have drool on my face?"

Laughing softly, I tilt down to wipe my mouth with a sleeve. As I do, the ghastly sight catches me off guard. Oh, dear god! I must have rolled about the bed in my sleep and inadvertently loosened the robe; exposing more skin than he needs to see. How do I keep coming into these uncomfortable situations with him! Quickly wrapping the collars tight, I crouch into a ball. No matter how much I want to apologize, embarrassment keeps me from succeeding.

"Why did you sleep here?" The Minister, directing his attention to the wall, begins coyly.

"You said you would come back."

"I did not say when. I would gladly have come to you, instead."

I'm an idiot! I thought he meant he would return in an hour or two. It was not an invitation to stay and chat.

"I-I'm sorry."

"Since you are here, I might as well tell you this now. I've spoken with the council and we've decided to put Master Yu to death."

"You've what?" I couldn't have heard him correctly. "San An, did you just say...?"

"Yes."

Nodding firmly, the Minister opens the window to let the cool morning breezes enter. Guilt causes panic to flow. I'm cold all over. What's happened? Did I cause Master Yu his life? Yet, San An is a kind person. How can he speak of taking someone's life so easily?

"I do not want to upset you, but it's better to hear this now from me than through gossips from others."

"Why? How can you do such a cruel thing?!"

Anger surges to push shock aside. I rush to tug at San An's sleeve. He closes the window to keep out prying eyes and then turns to me. Apathy veils his countenance.

"You believe I am cruel? There was a reason you suffered far worse than me. You were poisoned by sleeping nettle. I was not."

"I-I don't understand. The arrow went through you and you *were* poisoned. How could we not have been poisoned by the same thing?"

"The physician dipped the arrow with the more potent substance hoping to exploit the opportunity without raising suspicion. The original poison on the arrow is easily treatable. Had I perished from such a simple thing, he would have been brought to trial. With sleeping nettle, as long as he appears to have done all he could, he can claim to be faultless. He must have hesitated just before you rushed in."

"What are you saying? Master Yu is in league with the assassin?"

"No. He is not. He is a simple opportunist. By trying to kill me, he almost killed you and that is unforgivable."

"But *I* punctured myself with that arrow. He didn't! He might have contemplated the idea but there was no action. That's not a reason to end his life! You *will* call off his execution!"

I have no clout to speak to the Minister this way. My authoritative tone must have irked him. The apathy he used to hide emotions quickly fades to displeasure. "You would rather he killed me first before seeking justice?"

"N-No, of course not! I never want you in danger! It's just... if he was going to poison you, wouldn't he have, long before I interfered? I agree he should be punished for plotting whatever he had in mind. Punishment should not be as severe as death."

"I'm afraid reality is harsh. The council has enough troubles to handle. We don't need a traitor to create more strife. You are to reign as He Pi. You need to view this position from the logical perspective, not the emotional. A logical ruler can often be mistaken for a tyrant, but an emotional one is likely to let chaos ensue. Master Yu is not the type of man to feel indebted when he is forgiven. He is the type of man to be angered by the condescension of forgiveness and ultimately, will seek other methods for his vengeance. His fury is against me, not you. His blood will not be on your hands. It will be on mine."

"No, San An. It will not be on yours. The moment he plotted your demise, he took the risk. I am glad that he failed and if he failed because of me, then his blood is on my hands. I disagree with the council; I believe in you. If you think this is right, then I apologize for questioning your judgment. Even knowing that he will perish through my fault, I wouldn't have changed a thing. There was nothing I wanted more at the time than for your safety. If I had to dispose of him then for that to happen, I wouldn't have hesitated."

"You care for me that much, Your Highness?" There hints a touch of pathos in his tone; though, truly, I think it is sarcasm.

"You are a dear friend to me, Minister. You've saved my life in more ways than you'll ever know. I am not ungrateful."

"But you think I am cruel?"

"No. I apologize for the accusation. You are not cruel. If anything, I think you are too emotional."

Turning away, he starts for the bed. Fatigue on his brow has only deepened. I shouldn't bother him much longer. After a short obeisance, I part from his chamber and make my way to the Peony Palace.

Chapter 20: An Ugly Realization

The guard sent to fetch Mu Dan from inside the Circle was rather startled from my order. I don't think I've seen anyone so happy since coming to the capital. His face was red when he went inside and three times as crimson when he exited. The first word that comes to mind, of course, is pervert.

Without needing an explanation, Mu Dan grabs my arm and leisurely parades across the large common room while ensuring that all the harpies see us. If only they knew the truth about Kang Lang, he would be in much trouble.

"So, you've come to me at last, have you?" Kang Lang puts a finger on my chin. I brush him aside and move farther into the room. It's become more decorated since my last visit.

"I'm here for business. I want to ask about Master Yu."

"The only business you should have with a beautiful woman is anything but boring questions, Your Highness."

"Really? I thought the only business a beautiful woman should have is to protect her own honor, not push for it to be taken."

"Are you insulting me?" Mu Dan grins.

"Seriously. Will you tell me? I will send flowers again."

"I don't want flowers. I want something better."

"Whatever you want that's reasonable, I will accommodate."

"I am nothing if not reasonable!" Mu Dan pulls me toward a table set with two chairs and takes the seat across. He's excited, which doesn't bode well for me.

Planting both cheeks in his hands, Mu Dan leans onto the table. "Well? How may I help you, darling?"

"I understand Master Yu has a grudge against the Minister. Would he be willing to go as far as taking his life?"

"Yes."

"Let's say he did attempt something and was then pardoned. Do you think he'd continue with vengeance?"

"Yes."

"Could you answer in more detail than just, 'yes?'"

"Yes." A grin accompanies the short reply.

My blood pressure is elevating at the same rate that composure is dwindling. As long as I can keep from emotional extremities, I should be safe from his capricious taunts. He's not making this easy.

"Will you just tell me everything you know?"

"I know a lot of things, darling. You'll want to be more specific."

Kang Lang can discern my exact intention and yet, he's chosen to waste my time. I don't have a choice. The words are forced through gritted teeth. "Will you tell me everything you know regarding Master Yu's role in the assassination attempt?"

"Well, what's there to say? He dipped the arrow in sleeping nettle after pulling it from the Minister and you poked yourself with it. Willing to die for him, huh? Are you sure you're in love with Jin? He's left you alone for some time now and San An is *fighting* to control himself."

"Stay on topic. Would Master Yu seek to end San An's life once he is freed?"

"Yes, he would. That is my honest opinion. Though, who knows what Master Yu is capable of except for Master Yu?"

I'm satisfied with knowing that San An will be rid of a threat. At the same time, I'm saddened by the idea of Master Yu's demise. Is there no other way?

"No, there isn't." Mu Dan answers my mental question directly. "Is that all you came to ask me?"

"No. Tell me why the assassin targeted San An instead of me."

"Oh, but you know the price for that answer."

"*That* price is reserved for the assailant's identity. I want to know the reason he targeted San An."

"But that would lead you to the answer. I'll want something else on top of that which you've already promised."

"As long as it's reasonable."

"Of course, of course. Do you agree?"

"Whatever you want."

"Good girl. He targeted San An because the Minister stole his lover."

"What...! Kang-Kang Lang, are you serious?!"

"No." Mu Dan pulls a sleeve over his painted mouth and giggles obnoxiously.

"You bastard! Quit messing around and be serious!"

"This *is* serious! You should see how pale you look! I think someone's in love with San An!"

"You better tell me now or I'll have them throw you out of the Circle!"

"Calm down! The answer is obvious. The assassin just wanted to implicate Ning. There was no reason to target you. You're just a puppet. The council couldn't care less about your life. Now, San An... that's a different matter. Although, from what I've seen, the intent was not to take his life but to taunt Nan Rong into attacking

Ning. With San An out of the picture and His Highness missing, civil war might erupt. Ning would be irrelevant at that point."

"Why would civil war in Nan Rong be a bad thing for our enemy?"

"Are you that dense? Because your *enemy* doesn't want Nan Rong."

"They want... Ning?"

"Bingo! It's about time!"

"But, the assailant came back to Nan Rong. Who in Nan Rong wants Ning?"

"Figure it out in your own time. You owe me and I want my payments now."

"Fine. Brief the servants and I'll send over whatever you request."

I start for the door. He moves to bar the path.

"Don't be so naïve. You know what I want." Mu Dan pokes my forehead tersely.

"No, I'm dense. I really don't. Write it down and send it over. I have better things to do right now." My attempts to navigate past him fail. His arms fly around me with the usual bone-crushing fervor.

"I keep falling out of love with you and then you come to taunt me with his cute face. Now I find out you're in love with San An. I'm so jealous, all I want to do is punish you."

"I said you can have whatever you want as long as it's *reasonable*."

"This *is* reasonable!"

"Not by my standard. The standard was not agreed upon, but I have always implied it to be mine, and you willingly answered me."

"You speak so *seriously* like the Minister but your tone reminds me of He Pi. Just... too... adorable!" Kang Lang grins and leans closer. When I show no reaction—no intent to withdraw—he stops.

"You're hopeless," he mutters while releasing me. "I don't want a wallflower. I want a bloom bursting with fiery flames or even just a blushing rose."

Sighing, he settles on the bed and begins playing with his hair. "Oh, well. Since I have no interest in claiming you, I might as well ask for something else. I've told you my secrets; now, tell me yours."

"I don't have anything worth telling."

"Liar. Tell me the truth and I'll relinquish the debt. Lie to me and I'll punish you. Come, sit with me."

This feels like a trap. What truths does he want to hear? I really don't have anything interesting to confess. Though, I guess I don't have a choice.

"Don't be shy! There we go! It's not the first time we're in bed together. Come closer so I can see your face." The enraptured man drags me farther onto the bed. "See, isn't this nice?"

"I thought you've fallen out of love with me."

"Don't glare! Just because I'm not in love with you doesn't mean I want to stop hurting you."

"So it's mental torture, is it?   All my secrets exposed?"

"That's right!   I'll be gentle this time around, I promise."

Grinning happily, Kang Lang grabs my chin and forces our gazes together. I can't help but glance away from the awkwardness.

"We haven't started. What are you trying to hide?"

"I'm not hiding anything."

"Then look at me."

Slowly and grudgingly, I comply. He smiles at my obedience. I want to poke his eyes out.

"First question—"

"How many questions in total?"

"As many as I want. I ask and you answer. It's that simple. So, first question, are you in love with San An?"

Embarrassment overwhelms me and my gaze tarries away. Kang Lang tightens the grip on my chin.

"What does that have to do with anything?"

"We've been over this. *I ask* and you answer."

"I—I don't know."

"I don't like that answer. *Yes or no*?"

I don't really know. I'm certainly attracted to San An and I want to be near him, but is that love or something else? Anyway, what difference does it make? Is Kang Lang baiting me into something? My heart's racing for no logical reason whatsoever.

"I told you, I don't know!" Knocking his hand away, I move back.

Kang Lang is disgruntled; though, only moments after, he erupts in giggles. "It's as good as a, 'yes!' How does it feel to flaunt in front of San An after admitting to Jin your affections? What would Jin say if he knew how unfaithful you are?"

It's not as though I haven't thought about my emotional disgrace. To have it shoved in my face so blatantly makes me feel a hundred times worse. This bastard just wants to see me miserable. Tears are misting over my field of vision but I won't give him the satisfaction!

"Jin rejected me! You seem to know everything about me; you must know that, too. I didn't flaunt in front of anyone!"

"Jin never outright rejected you. You just assumed. San An comes to lend a comforting shoulder and suddenly, your loyalty shifts. Tell me, do you think you're trustworthy?"

"I..."

"Certainly, you must know yourself. Are you capable of loyalty?"

Despite his playful tone, my resolve is being torn to shreds. For a drawn moment, shame keeps my head down, so I didn't notice how close he's come. With one slight shove, Kang Lang knocks me down and moves on top.

"What the hell are you doing?!"

Kang Lang foils my attempt at rolling away and locks me in place. "Answer the question."

"Why?!"

"I'm curious. I want to know what kind of woman you really are."

"You've already formed your opinion of me! This is pointless!"

"I'm giving you a chance to redeem yourself. Don't struggle. You can't hope to win, so you might as well play along."

"I don't know!"

"You *don't know* whether you're capable of loyalty? That's certainly terrible. The Minister trusts you so much and all you'll do is hurt him, won't you?"

"No, I won't hurt San An!"

"No? But you already have. Surely, you noticed that his heart shattered when he caught us kissing. Did it feel good?"

"How is hurting San An ever a good thing? And I didn't kiss you, bastard, you kissed me!"

"You weren't struggling very hard, were you? Anyway, what I meant was did it feel good when I kissed you?"

"No!"

"You're lying."

"Conceited ass! No one wants to taste your vile lips!"

"I told you not to lie or I'd punish you." Kang Lang grabs my fingers and squeezes them tightly in his palms. The force feels nothing short of pincers crushing every bone. It took all I had to keep from giving the reaction he wanted.

"Disappointing. Tell me the truth or I will break all your fingers."

"Why does it matter?!" My elbow strikes at his face. Kang Lang leans back and out of range. I couldn't even graze him.

"So violent!" He chuckles. "I like honesty. That's all. Tell me, did it feel good?"

My chest heaves as tears flow. Slowly, a pathetic confession parts in a desperate whisper. "Yes."

"Did you want me to stop?"

"No."

"Were you ever attracted to me?"

"Y-Yes."

"Have I ever excited you?"

"Yes!" The answer came through gritted teeth. I feel as though I'd just been slapped.

Kang Lang smiles victoriously. Then, resting his forehead on top of mine, he whispers, "Do you want me to take you?"

"What? No! You idiot! Get off me or I'll tell all the harpies that you're a man!"

Mu Dan quickly falls back and giggles. His female voice replies, "Who, me? A man? No one would believe you!"

"Are we done here, you egotistical bastard?" My fingers won't stop throbbing. A few turned purple.

"One last question and it's for your own good. Honestly, do you think you're trustworthy? You've already admitted that I excite you. Might as well tell the truth."

"No." My lowered head mutters the wretched response.

I can't be trustworthy. I have feelings for both Jin and San An, which means I have no loyalty. Since I was attracted to Kang Lang due to his advances, then I can't trust myself. I'm too emotional, as San An said. It makes me a terrible person.

"You're not a terrible person," Kang Lang replies while standing up to stretch. "If you can admit your faults, then you're better off than most people. Don't deny your feelings. Just because you love Jin doesn't make your affections for San An less valid. Be honest with both; then, you'll still be trustworthy."

"Why do you care anyway?"

"Because you are He Pi. I give advice when he's conflicted. Simply because you've taken his post doesn't mean Mu Dan's duties have been relinquished."

"And I suppose you push His Majesty onto your bed and bruise his fingers, too?"

"Of course not. He would have just told me the truth. You'll thank me sooner or later."

"I highly doubt that! Anyway, we're even."

"For now. You're a little dense, so you'll need my council again. Next time, we'll get a bit more physical. I *know* how much that excites you."

The insufferable person continues grinning. My humiliation satisfied him; Kang Lang offers his arm and takes me outside.

Chapter 21: Ask and You Shall Receive

After everything I've done to injure San An, he came the next day to resume my lessons. His composure is retained though with great certainty, he's concealing the pain I've caused. I wonder whether Kang Lang's accusations are true. Am I in love with San An? I don't know what to think anymore.

"Shall we stop for today?" San An leans back in the chair and runs fingers through his hair.

"No, not unless you're tired."

"You seem distracted. Surely, the fault is mine?"

"N-No. You're right, I am distracted but for other reasons. Kang Lang said the assassin wanted to implicate Ning so that Nan Rong will host the attack. He thinks it's because the perpetrator wants Ning."

"The council has considered that possibility; however, there's little evidence to suggest a true intent. Ning must have thought the same; hence, their emissary will come to us within the week. We must show them that we are honest and that Nan Rong did not stage the event for our benefit. Should everything go well, we may be able to gain an ally for the difficulties ahead."

"The fact that the assailant returned to Nan Rong implies we are at fault. Will they actually believe us?"

"The assailant wants fingers to point both ways. If we do not attack Ning, then perhaps Ning will take up arms against us. Kang Lang's assessment is not wrong but he's approaching this from the assassin's point of view. In truth, the assassin is insignificant. We must find his lord to quash the true threat."

"Kang Lang said they served the same lord."

"I would not put too much thought upon his words. Kang Lang served many lords. This assailant is no different. His current allegiance could be with any number of factions."

"What must I do? I feel helpless, San An. I don't think I've done anything right so far and I continue to be an impasse the longer I remain ignorant."

The corner of his mouth lifts a small fraction. San An places a warm hand on my shoulder. "That is my fault. I wanted to protect you but you deserve to know the truth. After the last assembly, I've come to realize that you are able to wield knowledge effectively. For the time, you must prepare for Ning's emissary. Afterwards, I will speak with the council and have you included in our meetings."

"Thank you!" I'm so elated by the notion of being useful that I smile unrestrained. In my heart, I hope Jin will be proud of me. The thought of him restores my composure. Shyly, I glance up at San An. "May I ask something else of you, Prime Minister?"

"Anything, Your Highness."

"Have you seen Shu Jin recently? I can understand that he doesn't want to see me. I would just like to know that he's well."

"I thought he would have told you that he was leaving for Xiong. That is to say, he's already left."

Did I do this? Did I make him leave? I feel horrible for having run Jin out of his own home.

"Don't be alarmed." San An reaches for my hand. "He's only gone to visit his mother's home to pay obeisance to his ancestors. He often leaves this time of year. He'll return soon."

"Oh. Thank you, San An. That's reassuring."

Although he simply nods, San An is wounded by my careless regards for Jin. I don't understand the Prime Minister's reason for loving me. It's probably not a good idea to ask, though, if I knew the reason, I may be able to dispel whatever misconceptions he has of my worth.

Ask him (Continue to page 231)

Don't ask him (Continue to page 234)

Chapter 21 – 2

"San An, please don't be angry. I have no desire to hurt you. I just truly want to know."

The Prime Minister's hand withdraws. The expression clearly shows that he understands my curiosity. For a moment, he is aggrieved. Usual poise is regained and then he continues humoring me.

"Your Highness does not believe my affections to be genuine, I take it?"

"I don't doubt that you favor me, Minister. I want to know the reason. I do not dare think I am deserving of your friendship and attention, and I certainly don't deserve your affection."

"Only because you believe my affections are misguided, am I wrong?"

"No," the word falls in a soft whisper. My head hangs in shame for lying.

"I suppose I've left you wanting of answers from the first moment we've met. It's no secret I *was* misguided to desire someone special, even though I despised your resemblance to him all the same.

After the event in the peach garden, knowing that you were willing to sacrifice your life for me, I finally came to see you as Bao Lai. Regret consumed me for having misjudged you. I thought you had agreed to the task simply for the lavished life. That couldn't be true when you recklessly put yourself in danger for my sake. No one's ever cared enough for me to do as you had.

All my life, I never truly knew loyalty. Those who stood beside me often expected the favor returned; whether that advantage was material, authority, or merely intellectual exploitation. It was that selfless act of yours which removed the veil over my eyes—the veil which kept me from seeing anything in the fairer gender except ambition and deception, as I've come to experience them.

Ultimately, I did not sincerely love you until I woke in the infirmary and saw you lying beside me. Then, I viewed you through lucid eyes. Then, I knew I could not live without you. If you had died, I would have gladly followed."

He pauses to catch his breath or maybe to finalize his resolve, and then pushes on. "Call it fate or chance that we met. Whatever the reason, I've come to love you dearly, Bao Lai. Every day that I cannot look upon you as my own, I feel another piece of me fade away. Despite the pain that ails my soul, I will not push you to accept me. I want you to be happy and safe. As long as I draw breath, I will ensure this future for you."

San An said all he could before composure dwindles, and then he rises to pace near the door. I had no idea his affections ran so deep. Tears fall down my face though I do not realize it until they drip onto my hand. My heart is stricken with pain. Every part of me wants to hold him in my arms. I know I cannot. If I behave rashly simply because of his affections for me whilst I'm unsure of my affections for anyone, I'd only hurt him.

"Thank you for your honesty, San An. I wish for your happiness and safety as well. I'll never believe I can deserve your affection but I am glad to have you by my side."

"Then I shall stay by your side until the very end." San An bows deeply.

In the days that follow, all my time is spent in his company. There's something comforting and sweet in the air that surrounds him. I feel that each day we grow closer as friends and confidants. Despite his affections for me, San An remains the perfect gentleman. I've decided to resume my path and let go of every notion of love until peace is once more certain for Nan Rong.

Continue to page 235

Chapter 21 – 3

No, it's a bad idea to ask. Even I know that. San An's hand eventually retracts and we continue lessons until dinner comes around.

In the days that follow, all my time is spent in his company. There's something comforting and sweet in the air that surrounds him. I feel that each day we grow closer as friends and confidants. Despite his affections for me, San An remains the perfect gentleman. I've decided to resume my path and let go of every notion of love until peace is once more certain for Nan Rong.

Chapter 22: Han Bei

Han Bei, Lord of Ren Liu and Grand General of Ning, came to Nan Rong this morning with a large caravan. I haven't seen a man this effeminate since Kang Lang. The latter only appears very feminine while portraying Mu Dan. Han Bei is sublimely beautiful. Even so, the stories I've heard from San An imply that Lord Han Bei is a force to be reckoned with.

After the initial greetings, we moved to the peony garden for tea. Guards line the path to ensure our safety; though, safety is not the most disconcerting aspect at the moment. Perhaps, it is my imaginations. Although this man is very friendly; at times, his eyes seemingly sharpen when glancing in my direction. Each time I turn to meet his gaze, he's already looked away. I wonder if he knows I'm not He Pi.

Folding the silver and black robe neatly, Han Bei takes the middle seat. He smiles graciously at San An; yet, disregards me. Then, taking the cup of tea, he raises a toast. "To the health and wellness of His Highness. May he reign over Nan Rong for a thousand years."

What kind words indeed; though, they would have been kinder had he directed them at me. The toast was seemingly raised for San An, which wouldn't bother me if there was certainty he was ignorant of my deception.

"To peace between our lands. May we always be able to enjoy the simple pleasure of tea with our great friends from the East." At my reply, Han Bei makes a slight nod. A corner of his mouth curls into a smirk.

After draining the cups, another round is poured, and then prepared conversations are rehearsed. Around noon, the main topic finally emerges. The first to speak of this matter is Han Bei.

"Ning has not come to Nan Rong for many decades. This reunion is truly long overdue. It is regrettable we must meet under these circumstances."

"Yes, truly regrettable. However, we are grateful for Ning's continuing support during the trials placed before Nan Rong." San An answers courteously.

Han Bei returns a short bow. "I was surprised to hear the assailant entered Ning. The last report was of him leaving Mount Fei Yang for the southern capital, is that correct? Has there been progress made?"

"I'm afraid we've nothing further to report. At this time, the identity of the instigator is yet to be evident."

"That is lamentable, indeed. Ning wishes for peace to remain between our two lands no matter who has the claim to fault. Although such aggressive actions are unlike Ning's usual peaceful approach, it has brought Nan Rong to our borders once more in arms and ultimately, a bond is formed. We should all be grateful for that."

I've been silently listening to them converse for some time now, as San An instructed, but those last words from Han Bei suddenly irk me. He's blatantly being sarcastic and the air of condescension he leisurely employs forces my jaw to clench. Glancing over at San An, I can see a smile present but it is empty. This Han Bei has the gall to offend Nan Rong in front of my most trusted advisor. I need to let it go but frustration deem otherwise.

"With Ning's past policy of invasion without cause, Prime Minister San An graciously entered the tiger's den on our behalf in search of the assassin. It is inopportune that the culprit points fingers at both our countries. Surely, as men of peaceful virtues, we will not be swayed to hostility and become puppets of others' agenda."

Since Han Bei has my direct attention, I cannot see San An's reaction. Though, I can easily surmise his opinions. The emissary, to the contrary, smiles amusedly. He gives a short nod and then conversations become livelier regarding more pleasing topics.

Chapter 22 – 2

To my surprise, during our time alone to discuss the events of the day, San An did not scold me. More so, he hid all notions of his true thoughts. I left his company and returned to the halls. As I take the path leading to my quarters, a familiar face wandering about gives me pause.

"Lord Han Bei. You have not retired for the night. Is everything to your satisfaction?"

Han Bei bows and beckons me outside. I'd barely made it past conversations earlier, so I don't think it's a good idea to speak with him alone. Instinctively, my head turns about in search of an excuse.

Han Bei chuckles sarcastically. "It's merely an informal conversation, Your Highness. You needn't search for the Prime Minister."

He saw right through me. I'm embarrassed for being so weak and useless on my own, and to have it clearly displayed in front of Ning's emissary is unforgivable. Without recourse, I lead him to the gardens. The moon overhead is bright on this night. The wind is mild. I thought the weather suitable for conversations at our previous table but Han Bei shakes his head.

"Perhaps, deeper into the garden where we can have a bit more privacy. There are some things the guards do not need to hear."

"What things would those be?"

"I came as Ning's emissary; not as their enforcer. You do not need to fear me, Your Highness." The sarcastic smirk widens and I become more frustrated. What can I do except play along for now? Thus, I follow him farther inside to a part where tall trees are abundant and the moon above becomes a slight shadow.

"This is far enough." Han Bei remarks while turning toward me.

"What is it you want to discuss, Lord Han Bei?"

"So very to the point, sire. You remind me of someone I knew from long ago."

"This is all you have to say?" The last time I was out in the dark, Mu Dan nearly broke my arm. Nerves involuntarily force curtness. I really should attempt civility.

"Patience, sire." His voice is constantly melodious and sarcastic; thus, his intentions are unreadable. "I merely wanted to express that I was rather impressed by you earlier."

"How so?"

"In Ning, there are rumors that the Prime Minister has the true authority in the Southland and He Pi is his puppet. You've proven that thought to be incorrect with your outburst earlier—uncouth, as it was—and shown me that you are deserving of respect."

"Oh. Then, allow me to apologize for my outburst. I didn't mean to offend."

"I was not offended. I slighted your elder brother and you slighted me in return. As far as things go, we are equal."

My elder brother? I suppose he means San An. I was afraid he'd seen through my disguise but that doesn't appear to be the case. With anxiety dwindling, I can finally let out a sigh of relief.

"Well, I'm glad we were able to find common grounds. Let us return inside."

As I turn to leave, strong arms slip around my waist. The sensation of warm lips pressing against the base of my neck makes me jump. Han Bei suddenly chuckles softly in my ear.

"Forgive me for being so forward, Your Highness. I've done all I can to hold back my passion. I can't quite suppress this any longer. Your reaction just now makes me want you even more."

The cool sensation of his breath turns my constricting lungs to ice. Panic overrides composure; I turn to push him away. Han Bei's hold fastens.

"What-What are you doing? We're both men!"

"And? Have you never a male lover, Your Highness? You've not taken a wife all these years; not even a consort. If you're waiting for the right person, I am much better than any woman."

His caressing lips tickle my neck and once more, I jump. Though as I try, it is impossible to break free. His arms are no less than iron shackles keeping me in place.

"It's not what you think! I'm not attracted to men! I love wo-women."

"Your voice betrays you, sire. As do your eyes. Your livid stare earlier warranted my attention and your nervous demeanor just now warrants my passion. I can feel your pulse *racing* at my touch. Do you deny it?"

"L-Look, even if I were ever to consider... we can't marry!"

"Who said anything about marriage? It's intolerable for two men to marry in this age. Frankly, I'm merely interested in becoming your lover. Although, it's very adorable you would jump to the idea of marriage first."

His seductive chuckles make me quiver. I want to tell the truth but that is not possible. Unlike the encounter with Mu Dan, I can't just hit an emissary from Ning. There's nothing my brutish tendencies can solve. Everything must be resolved through my weak words.

"Lord Han Bei, I'm flattered by your advances, really. But I-I'm engaged and I take promises seriously."

"Since when is a monarch limited to one lover? Your father had over fifty consorts outside of Empress Pai."

"That-That is the reason I must have only one lover. I do not want the past to repeat itself. The last wars at court nearly tore apart Nan Rong."

"I am a man. We cannot have a child together for you to worry about such frivolous things."

"That may be, but I take my vows seriously. I will not lie with another."

For a long moment, Han Bei considers my sentiment. I nearly keel over from holding my breath. Slowly, his arms release me.

"Your virtues are those of a virgin female, Your Highness. You light my soul aflame! It is regrettable we could not meet sooner, but I will respect your principles."

I hope he cannot see me in the dark; else, my crimson face would give away the truth. It's inappropriate for anyone to behave this way toward He Pi. Was this to test me or was he entirely serious? If there is a chance that I made another blunder, this must be reported to San An. Though, I don't know whether I should. It might make him jealous or it might just make him laugh at me.

"Why are you stalling, sire? Have you reconsidered?"

"N-No. After you, Lord Han Bei."

Chapter 22 – 3

After parting with Han Bei, I storm through the halls and make my way to San An. Why does every man want me when I am He Pi; yet, no one would even look at me as Bao Lai? I'm so confused, I can't even see straight!

Soon as San An opens the door, I clamber inside, fall on the bed, and bury my face in his pillow.

"What is the matter, Your Highness?"

Letting out an angry groan, my fists beat furiously against the bed like a child in tantrum. "I think I made another mistake, San An!"

"What do you mean?" San An locks the door and sits on the edge of the bed.

Keeping my face in the pillow, the sordid event is replayed. When he doesn't reply, my head turns to gauge his thoughts. The Minister's expression is blank.

"San An, are you angry?"

"No." His answer is too succinct. I don't believe him.

"I'm really sorry! I shouldn't have gone outside with him!"

San An looks down and brushes loose hair from my eyes. "It was not your fault. I would have done the same in your position. No one could have guessed *that* was the reason he kept gawking at you earlier."

"You-You noticed that, too?" I dart up and grab his arm.

"Yes. I thought perhaps he saw through your disguise but it appears he was too enamored with your face to have looked farther down."

"Farther... down?" My head feels hot. Falling back, my face buries into the pillow. "It's not *my* face. It's He Pi's face. Everyone's in love with him!"

"Well, I would not go that far. You may have his face but not his personality. Clearly, your feminine wiles are more potent than you think."

"Are you making fun of me?"

Even though San An turned away, there is a distinct smile on his face. "Not at all, Your Highness. I doubt Lord Han Bei would have been quite as brazen with the real He Pi."

"What am I supposed to do? I can't look him in the eyes anymore after *that!* You don't think he was testing me, do you?"

"No, he tested you during the earlier exchange. There's no need for that now. I would advise that you behave more pleasantly toward him until he returns to Ning."

"What? You want me to get cozy with him? That doesn't sound like you at all, San An!"

"Yes, I do hate the idea of other men putting their hands on you. When it's a man who has no aspirations for your female self, I don't seem to mind as much."

His smile widens. I think San An's on the verge of laughing. I can't believe he's so cruel!

Protest (Continue to page 246)

Leave (Continue to page 249)

Chapter 22 – 4

Again, I start up and grab San An's arm.

"It's not funny! Whether Han Bei thinks I'm a man or not, it was completely embarrassing!"

The more I protest, the more the Minister's smile becomes a grin.

"F-Fine! So because he thinks I'm a man, I should just let him touch me however he wants, is that it?"

As I storm off the bed, San An seizes my wrist. One light tug and then I fall into his lap. My heart is beating so rapidly that my whole body blushes.

"W-What are you doing, San An?"

Without reply, his smooth lips press across my fingertips. His free arm encircles me and suddenly, it becomes difficult to keep my breathing steady.

"I was only joking, San An. You know I would never... don't be jealous." My hand moves away from his kisses. His lips flutter to my cheek.

"S-San An. That tickles!"

Sudden playfulness in his demeanor is completely baffling. He must truly be jealous. The thought makes me glad, which in turn riles a sense of guilt. I try pulling away but a firm hand lands on my cheek and draws our gazes together.

"Han Bei is not the first nor will he be the last man to desire you. I couldn't care less for his reasons. I can't stand the thought of another man touching you. You may never return my affections. I still want you to know that."

I do return his adoration in some ways. I just can't bring myself to say it. If I can't give San An all of my affections, then offering anything would simply be mockery. Confusion and tumult build within; my heart is on the verge of bursting.

San An leans down and presses a loving kiss against my mouth. Stress abruptly dissipates to another sensation. I feel as though I'm floating in some faraway heaven. I don't want him to stop. With every stroke of his lips, I fall a little deeper into his embrace.

His touch, his kiss, and even his intoxicating cologne seduce me into a trance from which I cannot wake. All my will relinquishes to his whims. I don't recall how long we've been locked in each other's warmth. When he finally withdraws, I'm left utterly breathless.

I'm so happy to be with him. I don't want to leave his side. And yet, elation is quickly banished when he turns away.

"I'm sorry, Your Highness. I shouldn't let jealousy cloud judgment. This is not the time to let emotions run rampant. Perhaps, when the ordeal is over and He Pi returns, and if you are willing to accept me, I want you to join my family."

He smiles softly at the recollection of each condition that must be fulfilled for us to be together. That he still wants me to become his wife makes me happy even though inside, guilt is billowing in torrents.

I love Jin. Despite not having returned San An's kisses, this is unforgivable. I want San An, but my lack of loyalty for him solely is unforgivable, too. Whatever exultation comes to me, I feel remorse in treble.

Continue to page 251

Chapter 22 – 5

Since he'd rather mock me, I might as well leave! As I storm off the bed, San An seizes my wrist. One light tug and then I fall into his lap. My heart is beating so rapidly that my whole body blushes.

"W-What are you doing, San An?"

Without reply, his smooth lips press across my fingertips. His free arm encircles me and suddenly, it becomes difficult to keep my breathing steady.

"Are you jealous?" My hand moves away from his kisses. His lips flutter to my cheek.

"S-San An. That tickles!"

Sudden playfulness in his demeanor is completely baffling. He must truly be jealous. The thought makes me glad, which in turn riles a sense of guilt. I try pulling away but a firm hand lands on my cheek and draws our gazes together.

"Han Bei is not the first nor will he be the last man to desire you. I couldn't care less for his reasons. I can't stand the thought of another man touching you. You may never return my affections. I still want you to know that."

I do return his adoration in some ways. I just can't bring myself to say it. If I can't give San An all of my affections, then offering anything would simply be mockery. Confusion and tumult build within; my heart is on the verge of bursting.

However, it was my decision to leave. I came to be reassured that Han Bei was not testing me. Since that is the case, I must not flaunt myself in front of San An. He's breaking from usual composure and I'd only hurt him unless I'm willing to offer everything.

"I'll be careful, San An. I promise."

The Minister sighs and slowly releases me.

Without his warmth surrounding me, the room feels dreary and cold. Bidding San An goodnight, I leave his chamber with heaviness settling over my heart. There's more I wish I could have said. I feel the same was also true for San An.

Chapter 23: Invasion from the North

In the morning, San An, Han Bei, and I gather in the peach garden. The fruits dangling lovingly from the branches above are much larger now than I recall. Despite the charming scene, this garden only brings bad memories. This is where San An was injured, where Jin rejected me, and where now, Han Bei is glancing seductively in my direction. With all my efforts, I attempt to keep composure but it's not easy.

"I have heard of this magnificent structure. Even in Ning, there are tales of Empress Pai's great garden monument." Han Bei begins. "Is it true that Her Highness requested for construction to be completed by the day of your birth, Prime Minister?"

I had no idea. I thought San An loved this garden because of his mother. I did not know it was a symbol of her love for him. No wonder he comes here often.

"Yes, that is correct." San An replies. Reminiscence glazes over his eyes.

"It is unfortunate that the son of an empress, the eldest child of the former Emperor Jin, is not the monarch of this country when the Southland follows a patriarchal system. In Ning, this befuddles us. We've always believed the right of succession is due the eldest daughter."

"Ning's order of succession is to the daughter?" The words leave my mouth without discretion. He Pi should know that! Immediately, my burning face turn away to hide the outburst.

Nevertheless, Han Bei graciously explains the reason. "Yes, Your Highness. We are a matriarchal society and it makes every sense. One cannot ever be entirely sure whether one's daughter-in-law is presenting a child from one's bloodline. One can always be sure that one's own daughter is presenting a true heir to one's line."

"I-I see." I like that idea. It does make sense.

"There have been claims that His Highness He Pi is not truly Emperor Jin's child, while indisputably, the Prime Minister is indeed his son. How strange it is that the former crown prince is not emperor."

San An's brows crinkle from displeasure. Han Bei is clearly trying to irk him with the sore subject. Strange. If he has any regard for me, why insult my *elder brother*?

"Nan Rong is in the best hand possible, Lord Han Bei. Previous titles are meaningless when the current authority is capable of leading the country to peace. Such as it is, Emperor Yuan is without heirs. With his previous ascension to power, Ning's matriarchal system was disrupted. I hope the future bolds well for the East with such troubling revelations."

Han Bei smiles wider; though, from my point of view, it appears more of a grimace.

"Indeed, it is troubling. Our late Empress Dong Xing left one son to our great nation. It is true he is without heirs but given his age, Emperor Yuan has a long road ahead to prepare. Rest assured that any woman to receive his regards is certainly not spoiled."

When I heard of Emperor Yuan, I imagined him to be a scruffy old codger. It seems he's rather young. Is every country currently led by youths? Before I can contemplate, San An continues.

"I recall rumors of court wars in Ning similar to the chaos in Nan Rong. Empress Dong Xing was not the only child of Empress Piao, was she?"

"Such things happened so long ago; no one can be sure whether her younger sister survived the conflict or whether she ever existed at all. We, too, look to current capable authority to lead our country to peace."

The two men smile in tandem and gracefully bow. I feel like a fool for not contributing to conversations but I don't know what to say. Ning believes He Pi is just a puppet. I suppose it's still better than thinking Nan Rong is without someone as adept as San An to lead.

Just as the day is seemingly going by smoothly, a messenger rushes into the garden and calls San An to council. Without further pleasantries, the Minister makes a short obeisance and withdraws. I knew being in this peach garden never bring any good news!

Han Bei's presence is keeping me from running after San An. The emissary is little bothered by the disruption.

"Well, it appears it's just us again, sire."

I tremble slightly at the sound of his melodious voice. Forcing a smile, I continue leading the stroll.

"I'm sure everything will be fine, Lord Han Bei."

"You don't have to reassure me, sire. Any urgent matter in Nan Rong will have little impact on Ning. Perhaps, it may even be to our favor."

"What are you implying? Does Ning plan to invade Nan Rong?" Turning around sharply, my hands ball into fists.

"Given the opportunity, one never knows what one is capable of," his lips purse. "At the moment, you are behaving like a child. Given this opportunity, I'm not sure what I'm capable of."

I don't understand his insinuation but I'm unnerved.

"You blush so easily, sire, even when I've not said anything overzealous. Surely, you must know that if you are within my favor, I can easily secure Ning's alliance with Nan Rong."

Everything about him reminds me of Mu Dan. He's simply a more controlled version of that crazy person. Although, is he really implying that once I make him my lover, he'll forge an alliance between our countries? If only he knew the contents under my robe; he'd take it all back.

"I don't care for coercion, Lord Han Bei."

"Neither do I, sire."

"To be within your favor for an alliance, you do not think it coercion?"

"I'm offering an incentive."

"And I told you that I cannot."

"You cannot what, sire?"

"I cannot make you my lover!" In my state of agitation, I fall into his trap of humor. My face turns bright red as he bursts into laughter.

"I never said taking me as your lover would put you in my favor, sire. It's odd that you would presume *that* above all else. Would you like to continue our conversation from previous night?"

"N-No. My apologies!"

This man must be near my age, but I feel so far behind him, he's right to think of me as a child. Despite keeping silent on the subject, certainly, Han Bei can tell I'm no emperor. For all my attempts to play this role properly, I still default to my old self. What a miserable failure!

His thin finger reaches for my chin and lifts up my gaze. The smile across his face is as seductive as the expression in his eyes. How can people like him be so frightening when they've not a sword in their hands? It must take as much mettle to be a politician as it does to be a soldier; if not more. A soldier's mistake can cost many lives. A politician's mistake can destroy a country. I'm not fit for either role. I'm just a peasant in royal garb on the verge of bringing chaos to Nan Rong.

"S-Stop!"

Han Bei, whose lips were closing in, abruptly desists. "You will resist me, sire?"

"I told you, I cannot. Other men might find your advances irresistible but I have my duties. I'm sorry." Pulling away, I rub my face.

Han Bei falls silent. Following a long pause, he chuckles. "What type of person do you make me out to be, sire? I do not advance on every man I meet."

"I... did not mean that!"

"Yes, you did. In all honesty, this is the first time I've ever attempted to seduce a male. It's rather surprising since I've never considered the possibility until we met. And then, all I want to do is make you mine. You do not believe me? I can understand. I just find you much more interesting than the usual females of the court.

You're not a woman, obviously, but there's something feminine and juvenile in your nature I find endearing. You can even say, I find it *exotic*."

His hand strokes my cheek and I cringe just a little. I understand this attraction now. As He Pi, I must appear highly androgynous and that can be appealing. As Bao Lai, I'm just a boring woman. Still, I'd rather find favor in him by playing along than have him disengage from talks of an alliance.

Clearing my throat, I avert from the awkwardness and take to the path again.

"An alliance between our lands will be beneficial, Lord Han Bei. It's no secret Ning has the largest army out of the five countries. However, Nan Rong is well versed in warfare and our generals and council can best the greatest of foes. Furthermore, the southern region is rich with minerals and our fields can easily supply enough for two armies. In recent years, Bei Ling, Ye, and Feng Jia have had eyes on both of our territories. It is best we stand together than to remain divided and conquered."

I struggle to throw together everything I could remember. The rant is deficient compared to the notes San An provided. Han Bei smiles as we walk abreast; though, he remains unreadable.

Once we turn a corner in the path, the emissary glances down. "You have rehearsed well, sire. Forgive me for not taking you seriously prior. You appear very young but now I see you are mature, indeed. Might I ask for your age?"

Oh, goodness! My eyes nearly bulged out of my head. I should know the answer to this! Jin told me, didn't he? He Pi was engaged to Mu Dan from the age of sixteen and now he is...

"Twenty-two." I reply.

"Oh? I was sure you are twenty-three. Was your birthday not only a few weeks ago? Our records must be wrong."

He's testing me! If He Pi's birthday was a few weeks ago, then why did no one mention it? Surely, for an emperor's birthday, even a false one, a celebration would have been called to order.

"N-No, I am still twenty-two."

"Well, then my apologies, sire. Our records truly are incorrect. When is your birthday?"

His records are not wrong. He knows the exact answer. I was too focused on the studies of difficult subjects, I never asked basic questions. My palms are sweaty and a lump is forming in my throat.

"Well, I... do not want to tell you."

"Why is that, sire?"

"I despise the topic of my birth. The stains of the past cannot divest. It was my father's decree for me to succeed the throne that nearly caused a civil war, and it took the Mark of Heaven on my shoulder to solidify my claims. My life, my youth—from the moment I drew breath from my birth—none of these were by my design. So, let us not go any further into discussing my past."

I think the bluffed answer was decent. It must have been, since Han Bei has fallen silent. Still, all I can do is hold my breath until his next wave of interrogation.

A strong wind unexpectedly rushes past, carrying a chill that is peculiar for this season. I withdraw momentarily to shield from the gust but as composure is regained, realize the emissary's moved in front and wrapped his arms around me.

"Lord Han Bei. I am fine, thank you."

"Such a tormented soul you must hide under your childish demeanor, Your Highness." Han Bei gazes down with troubled eyes. I try to step back but his hold becomes stronger. "Relinquish your engagement and let me stay by your side. I will protect you from every sorrow and erase all the anguish you've carried these many years."

Is he serious or is he mocking me? This feels uncomfortable. I'd only meant to discharge the interrogation; not push him to... whatever this is.

"Lord Han Bei, I'm fine. Really."

"You do not have to bury your pain, sire! Let me carry them for you!"

"No, I'm fine! Really!" The more I push him away, the stronger his grip becomes. If he presses himself any closer, he might feel the bounded rises of my chest.

"Darling!" A shriek echoes through the garden as the crazy *woman* puts his arms around my neck and tears me away from Han Bei. I can't believe how glad I am to hear his voice!

"I've been looking everywhere for you! I've been so lonely!" Mu Dan pouts while clinging onto my arm.

"I'm-I'm sorry, dear. I've been busy."

Lord Han Bei flusters momentarily but the colors that rise to his face dissipate as quickly as they come. The emissary bows in Mu Dan's direction. The latter shirks the gesture and keeps his back to the former.

"I don't want excuses, darling! Come inside with me!"

"I-I can't. Please, Lord Han Bei, let me introduce my betrothed, Lady Mu Dan. Mu Dan, this is Lord Han Bei of Ning."

Upon hearing the emissary's name, Mu Dan loses composure and buries his painted face in my shoulder.

"What are you doing?" The whisper I send into his ear goes unanswered.

"It's a pleasure to meet you, my lady. Please, forgive me for keeping His Highness away so long."

Mu Dan shakes his head but never shows his face to Han Bei. Turning toward the palace, he drags me along against my protest.

Abruptly, Han Bei exclaims, "You haven't changed a bit, Kang Lang!"

Mu Dan stops in his track. I turn from one to the next. The resemblance is definitely there.

"You two know each other?"

"Neither have you, brother." Kang Lang replies coldly in his real voice.

What on Earth did he just say?

Twisting about, Kang Lang grimaces at the older man. Han Bei's expression is of pure condescension.

"So, this is where you've been hiding after your miserable failure. Sire, by your lack of surprise, surely, you knew his gender?"

"I-I... Yes, I knew."

"And you would prefer *him* over *me*?" Han Bei moves closer and jerks me away from Mu Dan. The younger man's grip is still around my wrist.

"Find your own lover, Han! He Pi is mine! Since when are you interested in men anyway?"

"I can ask you the same thing, *little brother.* Cross-dressing all of those years has finally turned you into a woman, has it?"

They keep tugging me back and forth. I don't know how to react to this madness. I feel as though I'll be ripped apart.

"S-S-Stop it, you two!"

"Look what you've done! You've upset my fiancé!" Mu Dan kisses my cheek in his attempt to drag me away but Han Bei is easily stronger and draws me into an embrace.

"Just what do you think that will accomplish? He loves me and we're engaged. He Pi will never surrender his Mu Dan! Isn't that right, darling?"

Between these two crazy people, I obviously choose Kang Lang. At least, I'm a little more used to his insanity.

"That-That's right. I am engaged to Mu Dan. I'm sorry, Lord Han Bei."

"Just give me one night to change your mind," a sultry whisper flows into my ear.

My face bursts with fervent heat. I reach out and furiously grab onto Kang Lang.

"Stop pushing yourself in his favor! His Highness doesn't want anything to do with you, ugly troll!"

"Who are you calling ugly, you cross-dressing toad!"

Everything is so utterly confusing. I can't tell which gender anyone is anymore! Maybe there's hardly any difference in the first place. That doesn't matter. I don't care about these two. Where is San An?

As though he heard my cries, San An appears a little down the path. I call out his name and run to his side.

"Help me!"

San An does not find the scene amusing. My whispered plea is met by troubled eyes.

"Your Highness, please come with me. You as well, Lord Han Bei."

I look over my shoulder to see the two brothers standing near.

"What about me?" Kang Lang frowns.

San An nods. "Perhaps, you can be of some use."

The Minister leads the way and the three of us promptly follow.

Chapter 23 – 2

In the war room, the two generals and Qing Hai, along with a few ministers are gathered at a round table. Once we take our seats, San An briefs the situation.

"An attempt on Emperor Cai Pai's life was made. The culprit fled to our Mount Chou. We have confidence that this is the same assassin we are searching for."

Cai Pai is the child emperor of Bei Ling, whose territories border north of Nan Rong. Mount Chou is near this border. The assassin meant to implicate the Southland.

"Furthermore, Bei Ling has crossed into Nan Rong without discretion in search of this assassin. We cannot allow this invasion without retaliation, but we must be careful not to incite a war."

"Why does everything keep pointing back to Nan Rong? We are not behind this!"

"Well, duh." Bai Hu mutters. He and the others are gawking at me for stating the obvious.

"I see," Han Bei cuts in. "I came to Nan Rong to build amity. Since the plot to have our two lands wage war has failed, the ploy now takes to Bei Ling. This is worrying. If Nan Rong is taken, Ning will not be far behind. Your Highness, I will give my full support in this investigation and have Ning prepare reinforcements should matters worsen."

Han Bei bows and I return the gesture. "Thank you, Lord Han Bei. As you've stated, we must stand together; not just for the security of our countries but also for our people."

"What do we do about Bei Ling?" Minister Li Shen continues the discussion.

"Generals Yue and Hu will attempt to subdue Bei Ling's advance. I will go and speak to their leaders. Hopefully, there are men of sense amongst them. Otherwise, we will quash their forces as necessary."

San An is willing to put himself in danger again. He's the prime minister. As far as I can tell, he's just as important as He Pi. Why is he so willing to chance his life when all the other men in minister robes just sit around and offer no real efforts? At the thought of San An in danger, sharp pains come over me. I don't want him in peril.

"San An, I should go instead. You are needed here should things go awry. You must direct the court. Besides, Bei Ling would undoubtedly be more willing to meet with Nan Rong's emperor."

San An is displeased. With Han Bei in the room, he cannot speak his mind. I know he's worried for me. More so, I don't have his dignified air to command respect. Bei Ling would never take me seriously no matter which titles I throw at them.

"You must stay in the capital, Your Highness. I cannot allow for you to be in danger."

"And I cannot allow for *you* to be in danger!"

San An breaths heavily but does not contend. In his place, Han Bei offers a solution. "Your courage and ardent affection for your elder brother move me, sire. Allow me to assist the Prime Minister at Mount Chou. I will protect him with all my abilities."

I don't doubt Han Bei's strength. Kang Lang is one of the strongest men I know and Han Bei is easily stronger. However, I care for San An too deeply just to watch him leave again.

During my hesitation, Mu Dan places a reassuring hand on my shoulder. "Lord Han Bei is Ning's Grand General. Have faith in him, Your Highness."

The young man impresses unspoken thoughts through a hard stare. From him, doubt is finally lifted. I need to trust Han Bei. Mostly, I need to trust San An.

"Thank you, Lord Han Bei. I'm putting my brother's life in your hands."

Han Bei bows low. After the details are decided, everyone leaves for their post while I wander down the halls, dumbfounded. Once again, I find myself of little use.

Chapter 23 – 3

"He'll be fine," Kang Lang taps my shoulder when he comes up.

"Yes. I trust San An and I also trust Han Bei."

"Then why are you so distressed?"

"The usual," a wry laugh bursts. "I'm useless as usual. I haven't done a thing since I've arrived except parade about in He Pi's clothes and cause trouble for the council. I keep thinking I can become His Highness but I really can't. I fail as Bao Lai. Why should I succeed as He Pi?"

Useless tears can't be contained. Kang Lang, letting out an exhale, offers a tight embrace.

"Don't be an imbecile. No one expects for you to really become His Highness. Anyway, you've gained Ning's alliance. That is no small task. Han Bei covers his nature with derision. He's actually a complete stiff. I've never seen him so accommodating before. Had he met the real He Pi, Han Bei would have returned to Ning and let Nan Rong fall where it may. It's Bao Lai who's kept him."

"He thinks I'm He Pi and he's helping for all the wrong reasons."

Laughing loudly, Kang Lang kisses the top of my head. "You and your reasons! Can't you just accept things as they are without giving into reasons? Who cares why Han Bei wants to help? If he's willing to risk his life to make you happy, then you should let him!"

"He's your brother. How can you say that?"

"He's never been a brother to me a day in my life. Then, he comes here and tries to steal you away. The nerve of that cad!" Kang Lang, grinning impishly, pinches my cheeks.

"Ack! Knock it off! Anyhow, I was thinking of pointing him your way. It's just too bad you're both brothers."

"You thought what?!" Kang Lang gasps deeply from offense. "I can do much better than Han Bei! In any case, you know I like women!"

"So you say, but I *know* you have a crush on San An."

While the blushing youth is stunned in place, I move away. Kang Lang lunges forward and slides an arm around my waist.

"Everyone has a crush on San An. That doesn't mean anything!"

The more his frown deepens, the more my laughter can't be contained. Letting out an aggravated sigh, Kang Lang decides against taking offense and joins in. Since he's in a good mood, I should attempt to pry for answers again.

"Things are becoming dire. Will you please tell me the identity of the assassin? This is important."

"Nope. A deal's a deal."

"You said the assassin served the same lord as you and you're from Ning. Does that mean Ning has something to do with this?"

"Not telling you a thing, darling."

"If you won't cooperate, I can always disengage from Mu Dan and take Han Bei as my lover."

"For your own safety, I would advise against that. He's ruined many girls' reputations; sometimes, several in one night. He's nowhere close to the gentleman that I am."

"Gentleman? *You*? You're as gentle as a bed of nails!"

"A bed of nails is still gentler than a bed of broken glasses."

He's really serious. Kang Lang's proud grin doesn't hold a hint of sarcasm. He truly does have pride in being a *gentleman*. Considering everything he's put me through, I can't stomach the idea.

"Ugh! I give up! You're both just... terrible!"

Shoving away the ridiculous man, I storm down the corridor.

Chapter 24: Bei Ling's Revenge

Dinner is laid on the massive table in all the grand fashions befitting a celebration. Sadly, I'm the only one present. I guess no one told the chefs that our guest of honor left for Mount Chou. It's impossible to eat everything alone. I summoned for Kang Lang a while ago. I hope he's not still mad about earlier. Why is he so late? The food's growing cold.

The wonderful wafting scents and enticing presentations are making my stomach growl. It would be rude to eat before he arrives. All I can do for now is sip a bit of wine from the crystal cup. Wait, did I ask for wine? Only tea was brought yesterday.

Just as the cup leaves my lips, Mu Dan wanders in, pouting. I stand up to greet him and immediately land on the floor. What's happening? I can't breathe. Everything is shaking uncontrollably. I can't move my limbs!

"Your Highness! Your Highness!" Kang Lang's screaming echoes somewhere in the darkness. The muffled tone comes and goes until I can hear nothing at all.

Chapter 24 – 2

My head aches and my body feels heavy. One sip of wine couldn't have possibly put me in the infirmary, unless... there was more in the cup than wine. How could I have been so stupid! San An would never allow alcohol at the table. He's against clouded minds in front of the emissary. On the other hand, if I was poisoned, then why am I not dead? Maybe the wine was stronger than I thought. Anyway, I can't think straight with this heaviness pulling me under. All I want to do is fall asleep.

Click.

Hmm? What was that? Just when my eyelids begin drooping, the door gently slides open. A woman cautiously slips inside; her movement, fluid and gentle. It's a good thing I'm facing the door; otherwise, I never would have noticed her.

That's odd. I don't recognize this person. She can't possibly be a servant. The stranger, tall and voluptuous, is as beautiful as He Pi's courtesans. Come to think of it, I might have seen her in the Peony Palace.

"Who... are you?" There really must have been more than wine in that cup. It hurts to breathe.

"Oh, you're still alive." The strange sighs disappointedly. "I feared as much. Mu Dan doesn't know when to stop her meddling. Honestly, I didn't want you to suffer, Highness. Forgive me."

"What...?"

The stranger stares back apologetically; that's the utmost compassion I'll receive. A hidden blade swiftly slips from beneath the long sleeve and glistens as cold metal reflects candlelight in the dimly lit room. The chill of dread rushes over me. No matter how I wriggle, my body won't respond.

"Kang Lang! San An! Somebody!" My chest is burning. It's so hard to breathe! No one can hear me. This really is the end!

She raises the blade and immediately brings it down. Just as my eyes close to prepare for the impact, a sharp groan suddenly precedes a heavy slump.

Upon witnessing the scene, my blood runs cold. The assailant's eyes are wide open, but the light of life has faded from once bright amethyst stars. She crossed the veil before her body touched the ground. Crimson rivers flow from the open wound on the side of her neck. More and more, blood pool around the still body. Standing over the slumped figure, looking down, is the owner of the bloodied hairpin.

Long hair hangs loosely around the stern countenance. The gaze directed at the dead courtesan is so terrifyingly chilling, it makes me quiver. Aside from my labored breathing, the room is deafeningly silent.

For a prolonged pause, my savior remains over the still body. Then, slowly, the frown on his face curls into a vicious smile. Mu Dan closes his eyes and deeply inhales the scent of blood from the hairpin that left a gaping hole in the assailant's neck. Warmth colors over his cheeks. Mu Dan is entranced in pure ecstasy.

Once pleasure grows dull, he looks to me and like a hunter stalking cornered prey, slowly nears the bed. Across the face peering down lies an expression mixed of bewilderment, pleasure, and lust. The person behind those eyes is unrecognizable.

Throwing down the hairpin, Kang Lang kneels beside the bed. Shock and fear form lumps in my throat. I'm neither able to utter a sound, nor do I know the right words to say.

Without warning, his mouth covers mine with such fervent force that I can't catch my breath. His right hand forcibly glides from my face to my neck and then descends toward my chest; his fingers ruthlessly digging into my flesh. His left hand reaches for my throat and begins squeezing. Pressure builds each passing second. I can't move and I can't scream. I can hardly even breathe.

What's wrong with him? I know he's a sadist but this is inconceivable. The kill excited him to such a level that he's lost all control. This isn't my Kang Lang! I miss the teasing bully I've come to abide! I need to stop him before Kang Lang crosses a line from which we can't return!

Chapter 24 – 3

I have to snap him out of it! I can't move or talk. I'll just have to hurt him using the only part still under my control. My lips part and his tongue slips inside. Immediately, sharp teeth clamp down.

"Mphmf!" Kang Lang withdraws from shock, though only for a fraction.

"Stop, Kang Lang! S-Stop!"

The man who usually does as he pleases—whenever he pleases—without regards for others, unexpectedly pauses at my behest. Darkened emerald eyes bear directly into mine. I hastily stare back, pleading for him to return to his senses. The agonizingly long moment lapses with no end in sight. I'm scared to breathe lest that alone becomes provocation.

"Kang Lang... please."

Twitching eyes suddenly blinks several times. As though awoken from a dream, emerald stars gradually brighten from their state of daze. Then, as if nothing happened, Kang Lang laughs boisterously while squeezing the breast still in his hand.

"You bastard! What the hell are you doing? Don't touch me!"

"You called for me, didn't you? I see the poison hasn't completely washed from your system. There's so much I can do to you in this state."

The cheeky grin makes my blood boil. I'm just glad he's back to his old self. Kang Lang is a jerk. I prefer him this way. I don't want to see him lose himself again.

"Are you all right, Kang Lang?"

"I don't know what you're talking about," he shrugs.

"Right. Who is that woman, anyway?" It's sad to see human life slip away. Someone will miss her terribly. "Did you really have to kill her? Couldn't you have knocked her unconscious?"

"I saved your life. Don't tell me how to do my job!" Kang Lang glances back, but his gaze quickly averts. Light blushes are rising to his cheeks. He's trying very hard to keep from becoming excited.

I need to distract him from the bloody scene. However, before a word is uttered, a young man with messy hair steps into the room and nearly falls over from shock.

"Oh, my goodness! What happened here?!" He cries.

Unlike the young man, his older counterpart walks into the room and merely shakes his head at the gruesome sight, as though he'd grown accustomed to bloodshed. I can't believe my eyes. It's Master Yu. San An spared him after all!

"Master Dui, get a hold of yourself! Come tend to His Highness. He still can't move!" Mu Dan snaps.

The young physician tiptoes carefully to my bedside while avoiding the pools of blood. Master Yu, on the other hand, ignores everyone and composedly fetches a box from the cupboard to prepare another draught.

"It's very fortunate that Lady Mu Dan brought you just in time, Your Highness. Else, you would have been done for." Master Dui remarks.

"Don't say stupid things like that so casually!" Mu Dan snarls. "His Highness is not allowed to die! Do you understand me? You'll do everything to keep him safe or I'll pile your corpse on top of that bitch's once I'm done with you!"

"It's okay, Mu Dan. Why are you so agitated?"

Mu Dan turns away to keep from engaging me. He's been acting strangely. I'm worried for him. Before I could say another word, Kang Lang immediately quits the room.

Chapter 25: Kang Lang's Confession

I dreamt of Jin and then San An. I miss them both but I know that in the end, I'll only come to injure them. No matter what Jin says, he cares for me. No matter what I say, San An will love me. I've finally known love so I should feel happy. Yet, all I see in the days ahead is pain. I will hurt one of them, if not both, and they'll in turn hurt me, somehow. What exactly did I dream about? I don't truly remember. I just feel so alone.

"Mhmm..."

What is this warm sensation on my lips? Am I still dreaming? With much effort, both eyes spring wide open to a disagreeable sight. I'm locked in an embrace while familiar lips tickle my mouth.

"What are you doing?!"

Pushing the intruder away, I dart up.

"You were crying, what was I supposed to do? Anyway, you can move again. That's somewhat disappointing."

Kang Lang, in his male role, is lying beside me, grinning. Picking up a pillow, I bring it down against his face. He rolls away, laughing obnoxiously.

"Bastard!"

"I never get tired of hearing that. You should use that as our term of endearment after we're married."

"I'm not marrying you!"

He catches the pillow thrown at his face with ease. "After everything we did last night, you'll have to now. I've already claimed you. San An won't be interested anymore."

"You did what?!" Rage and pain give rise to temper. I've shoved Kang Lang against the wall before realizing we've left the bed.

Boisterous laughter grows; Kang Lang throws both hands in the air. "I'm kidding! Do you think you'd be able to walk right now if you spent the night with me?"

"Stop mocking me, damn it!" I'm so relieved but my chest won't stop heaving. "Stay away from me!"

"I saved your life. Can't you be a little more grateful?"

"If I have to feel grateful for you saving my life, then I wish that you hadn't!"

Moving to a bedpost, an arm reaches out for support. My heart can't take this. Every day, it's something to strain the organ further. After bouts of deep breaths, I can finally feel at ease. At once, two arms glide around my body and pull me into an embrace.

"Stop teasing me. It's not funny!" His hands won't budge when I slap them.

"I'm not." He whispers softly in a rather stern tone.

"What do you want, Kang Lang?"

"I want to stay by your side and protect you from now on." His lips touch my hair ever so lightly.

"Are you seriously quoting Han Bei?"

"Don't mention that idiot! I'm being honest!"

"Why? I'm not He Pi!" I thought he's moved past this façade I play.

"I know. I want to protect *you*, Bao Lai. I don't want to be Mu Dan anymore. I want you to accept me as Kang Lang."

"Well, won't He Pi be disappointed that I stole his fiancée!" Turning around, my palm smacks against his forehead. He grabs my hand and begins kissing my wrist. "That tickles! Stop! What are you scheming now?"

"I told you. I'm in love with you."

"You also said you've fallen out of it."

"I changed my mind," he smiles warmly. Delicate tenderness in the soft stare is entirely foreign. I didn't know he could be this way. Deep down, I fear whatever he might say next. As I attempt to change the subject, a thumb presses against my lips.

"I spent so much time wanting to hurt you; I never realized it pains me to think I can be without you. The thought of you dying... even close to it... burdens me with a sadness you can't fathom. You must know I've spent much of my life as a killer. There isn't a life I'm not willing to take. I find extreme pleasure in causing death and pain. Sometimes, I think they are the only things to make me feel alive.

But I can't bear to see you that way. Do you understand? If you had died yesterday, I would have ripped this palace apart. Had it been any other woman on that bed, I would have taken her until I was satisfied. I would have tortured her until I took her life, too.

Last night, that frightened expression on your face—the fear and terror I saw in your eyes when you caught a glimmer of what lies within me—I never want to see you so distraught again. I know you cannot love someone who exists just to slaughter. That's why... I don't want to be that person anymore. Love me. I will change if you can learn to accept me."

This is his love confession? Chills run through my center just hearing the words. Knowing he's capable of every horrendous thought, I can't even look at him. How twisted is his soul under that perfect shell? The touch of his hands makes me shiver from dread.

"Don't look away. This is the real me. I'm showing you my soul. Don't reject me. I don't know what I'll do... No, I won't hurt you anymore."

Kang Lang lifts up my chin and captures my gaze within his emerald stars. He removes every trace of concealment and allows me into his soul. It's so dark and wrathful like a swirling void; I feel sucked into the abyss.

"I love you, Bao Lai. Let me protect you from now on. Let my love for you absolve me from my sins."

Though he whispers the words softly, I feel them bear deeply into the very core of me. My will is wholly stripped away. Steadily, he reaches down and drains the air from my lungs with a loving kiss. Gentle, soft lips slowly descend toward my neck. No matter how tempting and passionate he is, I only see one face in my mind. As obscured as the image may be, I can't conceive that it's his.

"I'm sorry, Kang Lang. I don't love you." The mechanical words break whatever hold he has over me.

Kang Lang stares back in disbelief, until resentment abruptly creeps over his entirety.

"Why? What does San An or Jin have that I don't? Title? Wealth? Power? I have all those things in Ning! I will make every single wish of yours come true. I'm willing to throw away my soul if I must! I'm offering you every part of me! So, what is it? What must I give for you to even just consider me?" His stare hardens and his teeth grind. It must be my imagination; he's on the verge of tears. I've never seen him so human.

"It's not any of those things. I don't care about that."

"Then, what is it? Am I not handsome? Talented? Charming? Have I not saved your life? I've saved you more times than you know! This was not the first attempt on your life, nor will it be the last. I've killed for you and suffered for you! And what is there to show for it? Your derision? Insults? Abandonment? Jin left you and San An has done the same. I'm here! I'll always be here for you! Why is that not good enough?"

I understand his frustration but I must tell him the truth. "Thank you for letting me see the real you. I'm frightened but I'm not afraid of you. I accept you as you are but I don't love you. I can't lie and say things I do not feel. You *are* always by my side and I do care for you."

"Care for me? You would lie so blatantly? I'm not daft! I see the way you look at Mu Dan. You think I'm a sideshow; someone you can use for information and then disregard whenever it amuses you. I hate you for your callous selfishness and I hate you for using me! Mostly, I just hate myself for expecting someone as judgmental as you to understand what love is."

My head hangs in silence. He's right. I was too busy judging Mu Dan that I never stopped to consider Kang Lang. It wasn't for his cross-dressing. It's because he's always teasing me in the most inappropriate ways. I never thought he was trying to tell me something else. I formulated that Mu Dan is sadistic and my first reaction was to flee. I've only ever sought him for council and nothing more; that was when it was convenient for me. And, there's no doubt he speaks the truth, that he saved me many times before. I feel so ashamed! I can't ever make it up to him and any attempt now to rectify this guilt would be disdainful.

Tears well but I can't let them fall. He's the one who has been injured. He's the only one who deserves to cry.

Kang Lang scoffs harshly and releases me. I grab onto his arm when he moves away.

"I'm sorry," tears keep choking back the words. "I'm so sorry! Please, just be my friend. I still want us to be close. Please don't leave, Kang Lang!"

The hard stare gazing back is laced with disgust. Without another word, his arm jerks away and Kang Lang storms from the room.

Why is this happening? Why would he love me when he's seen the truth of my nature—a nature I did not even realize? I'm presumptuous, judgmental, and self-centered. Ever since I became He Pi, I've lost a part of me that was Bao Lai. My master didn't raise an ingrate. I've taken Kang Lang, Jin, and San An for granted and I'm never there for them. This is why I am alone and why I'll always be alone.

Chapter 26: An Apology

A week later, the caravan returns with an unfamiliar face peaking from the crowd. This dark-haired, bronzed skin, burly man who towers above everyone is introduced as the infamous bandit chief of Mount Chou, Wen Meng. He kneels as I approach.

"Please don't be on ceremony," I raise up Wen Meng.

"You are too kind, Your Highness."

There's a fierce manner in his disposition and I can feel his massive strength just from standing nearby. Yet, he is also friendly in an unassuming way. Wen Meng's an ordinary person without the usual noble airs to which I've grown accustomed, and it puts me at ease. Although, he is a bandit, so I best remain vigilant.

"Come inside. You must all be very tired. Make yourselves comfortable."

The returning caravan and Wen Meng enter the main palace where servants and other council members immediately come to attend our guests. San An tugs at my sleeve, so during an opportune moment, we slip away. Upon entering private quarters, the Minister rubs his shoulders while taking a seat on the bed. I've never seen him so fatigued.

"Allow me, San An." After locking the doors, I move behind the Minister and attempt to unknot the tight muscles on his shoulders and back.

"You really needn't bother, Highness." Glancing over his shoulder, he smiles.

"It's no bother. You would do the same for me."

"If you insist. Thank you." San An sighs deeply and runs a hand over his tired face. "As you know, Wen Meng and his bandits have decided to ally with the imperial army. Apparently, the one who attacked Cai Pai retreated into his territory. Wen Meng was able to injure the assassin; unfortunately, he managed to escape. Wen Meng caught a glimpse of the assailant's uncovered face and we've made some progress."

"What of Bei Ling?"

"By their council's order, Bei Ling's generals marched into Nan Rong. I feared as much. Cai Pai is still a child. He can't comprehend politics enough to make his own decisions. I'm just glad we could meet men with sense and were able to negotiate an interim retreat while we search for the instigators."

"Interim retreat? Meaning, they will return?"

"Yes. We must find the party behind this plot quickly before Bei Ling orders a full march. It is fortunate that Lord Han Bei has taken a shine to you. For now, we don't have to concern ourselves with Ning."

"San An... I have something to tell you. Please don't overreact."

The Minister gives his full attention. "What troubles you, Your Highness?"

"You'll hear this from the council later. Maybe, it's better to hear it now. Shortly after you left, an attempt was made on my life. Kang Lang saved me and—"

"Tell me the person responsible!" Frustration and wrath pour from his expression. San An takes to his feet. I've never heard so much fury in his voice.

"Please calm down!"

"How can I remain calm when the woman I love was in danger?"

Happiness swells from hearing that he still loves me. I just can't stand to see him so distressed.

"She's dead."

"She? Who sent her?"

"The report states that she's from Bei Ling. She's been in the Circle for almost five years. Wait, where are you going? San An!"

I reach for his sleeve but it slips through my fingers. He storms from the room without another word. By the time I scramble after him into the hallway, there's no trace of San An. He's moved so fast, I can't tell where he's gone. I should have known his reaction! I should have held onto him tighter!

Chapter 26 - 2

Where could San An have gone? He's not in this corridor or the last ten. There are too many; I've yet to search them all.

"San An, where are you? Ack!" As I round a corner, someone does the same. The interloper, flustering, reaches for my wrist to keep me from landing on my behind.

Kang Lang, adamant to retain his male persona, forces a grin. "Watch where you're going, silly girl!"

I didn't expect him to forgive me so soon. It's wonderful that he's cheerful again but guilt reminds me of my shame and I can't look him in the face. "Kang Lang, are you all right?"

"I'm not made of glass," he taps my head with the fan. "Where are you off to in such a hurry?"

"I was briefing San An on the assassination attempt and he stormed off. Have you seen him?" Oh, no. I'm using Kang Lang again. I'm such a terrible person! "N-never mind, I'll find him. Sorry for running into you!"

"That was reckless of you! Why would you tell him that without tying him up first? It's pretty obvious he'd run to the Peony Palace."

"Oh. I see. Thank you, Kang Lang."

"Hold on there!"

When I shyly scuttle by, he jerks back my collar.

"You can reject me, but don't go chasing after other men too quickly. We still have to talk."

"Talk, right now?"

"Yes, *right now!*"

He pulls me into one of the empty rooms nearby. After closing the door, Kang Lang turns back and frowns. "Why do you keep looking at the floor? Do you hate me that much?"

"No!" I glance up to see his perfect grin.

"Keep your chin up. I don't like talking to your hair."

I do as he asks; though, my attention keeps darting everywhere except for his face. Kang Lang lets out a frustrated sigh and pinches my cheeks. My eyes are beginning to water. I still can't look straight.

"You are so stubborn," he grumbles. Releasing my cheeks, a hand cups around my breast. Impulsively, a fist flies at his arm.

"You bastard! What's wrong with you?!"

The jerk turns beet-red and guffaws obnoxiously.

"I'm-I'm sorry."

"Damn! You really hit hard!" He tersely rubs the right arm. "Anyway, why are you apologizing?"

I feel so guilty; I can't bring myself to answer. Awkward silence fills the room. Kang Lang drapes both arms over my shoulders.

"I'm sorry. I didn't mean to say all those things before. I... just lost control of my emotions. I won't do it again."

"Why are *you* apologizing? I'm the one who's sorry! You didn't say a wrong thing, Kang Lang! I can't make it up to you! Why do you even want to waste your time with me?"

With my face buried in his chest, both arms wrap around him as though we haven't seen each other in years. Unbeknownst to me how it happened, this crazy person has become my friend. Even if I'm a terrible person who doesn't deserve his attention, I just want him to forgive me.

His gentle hand slowly strokes my head. "Hey, if San An came in now, he'd get the wrong idea, right? Cheer up. I'm not mad and you're not a terrible person."

"How do you keep reading my mind?"

"Because you're simple," he sticks out his tongue. "No more crying! I hate tears!"

"But, you're a sadist."

"So? It takes all kinds. Unless you can cry blood, knock it off." He gives me one big squeeze and then moves away.

"I'm really sorry, Kang Lang."

"Why? I bullied you. It was natural to despise me. Just because I pointed out a few of your flaws, suddenly, we should be girlfriends?" He giggles. "What happened to you? You used to question all my motives. You've become really gullible, you know that? At this rate, I might be able to guilt you into all sorts of fun things."

"I'm still sorry."

"Stop it already! If you truly want my forgiveness, then come to my chamber tonight. Otherwise, I don't want to hear it. Thwarted by a fake He Pi! I never thought this to be my downfall!" He clicks his tongue and frowns. "I've decided to stay by your side and protect you from now on, whether you like it or not. Until this conflict is over and His Highness returns, you can count on me."

"Why?"

"*Why*? I think the phrase you're looking for is, '*thank you!*'"

"Well, of course, thank you! But why?"

"Are you hard of hearing? How many times do I have to confess my love for you to finally understand?"

"But… why?"

"It's like talking to a wall!" Kang Lang pokes my forehead and starts for the door.

"Where are you going?"

"To find San An. I have *such a crush* on him! I might just steal him away from you."

"I'm willing to share if he doesn't mind."

"Oh? All three of us together? I like this side of you!" He cackles loudly and continues out the door.

It's wonderful to see him happy and laughing as usual. Obviously, Kang Lang's masking much his real feelings. I do want him to find happiness. Hopefully, someday soon, he will be smiling ardently at someone deserving of his devotion.

Chapter 27: Unfaithful Woman

San An comes out of the Peony Palace just as we arrive. One glance at Mu Dan's male counterpart, he frowns.

"This is not the place to discuss private matters." Without giving room for contentions, the Minister takes the lead to his quarters.

Once behind locked doors, Kang Lang holds my hand and saunters to the tea table. Then, pulling a chair severely close to mine, he takes the seat next to me. San An, appearing particularly miffed, quietly takes the seat across the table from us.

"What were you doing at the Peony Palace, San An?" I nervously begin.

"I've disbanded the Circle. This is no time to have untrustworthy people amongst us. Even now, I truly don't know where all loyalties lie."

"Did you hear that, Bao Lai? The Minister did exactly as you wanted."

"What do you mean?" San An stares in dismay.

"My dearest Bao Lai thought the Circle was a waste of taxpayers' money. She wanted to do away with it from the beginning."

Kang Lang, grinning, squeezes my shoulders. Is he flaunting his affections for me in front of San An hoping for an overreaction? That is to say, is he trying to push me into San An's favor even more? With the Minister near, embarrassment controls my composure and I can't bring myself to scold Kang Lang. However, blood is rushing to my face. It seems San An may be misconstruing my reaction.

"Well... that is true. I do think it's a waste."

Kang Lang grins and gives a quick peck on my temple. "She's so frugal, isn't she, Minister?"

"Yes, she is rational. You are not. Why are you happy, Kang Lang? Without the Circle, you have no place here."

San An is becoming angry. I also think he's being a little mean. "Mu Dan is still He Pi's fiancée. Really, he can stay."

"I see. If he makes you happy, Your Highness, I will not object."

Makes me happy? I don't want to slight Kang Lang when he's only trying to help, but I can't let San An feel dejected either. As I begin to explain, my *friend* leans over and cuts off the attempt with his lips. Furiously, I push back, but his weight continuously bears down, rendering all my efforts moot. Only when the sound of a door slamming against the frame reverberates throughout the room does Kang Lang finally move away. San An left and I feel miserable.

"What is your problem?! Why did you do that?!"

293

A barrage of punches frantically assaults his arm. He pulls back, laughing. "Ow, ow, ow! Stop! Do you know how hard you hit? I think you bruised me!"

"What exactly were you trying to do?!"

"I was trying to make San An *so* jealous, he'll come begging to spend the night with you. You should be thanking me."

"Like hell I should! I don't want him to do that! Not to mention the obvious fact that he probably hates me now for not breaking your face in!"

"You don't know anything about men, do you?"

"I know enough!" That's a terrible comeback. I have no idea what that even means.

Kang Lang holds onto his stomach and bursts into delirious laughter.

"Knock it off! Quit acting like an idiot! I'm going to find San An."

I've only taken a few steps toward the door before Kang Lang tugs at my collar.

"Let him steam for a while. It'll get that much more heated when he comes by later."

"Will you stop?! I'd rather he feels nothing for me than for him to be unhappy!"

"Why?"

"Because I lo…"

My heart skips a beat and then my face burns.

"Because you what? Lo…ath him? Or lo…ve him?"

"Shut up."

"It makes me sad to see you 'lo' another man. Can't I have a little fun once in a while?"

"Stop being so damn inappropriate!"

"Nope!"

What a jerk! The more vexation takes me, the wider he grins with that perfect innocent, boyish grin. Kang Lang just wants to be near because he likes to make me miserable.

"Yes, I love it when you're miserable."

"Stop reading my mind!"

"I would if you'd stop screaming your thoughts at me through your silly expressions. Anyway, sit down. I have something to tell you."

"Do I even want to hear it?"

"Of course, darling. I'll tell you who the assassin is."

"You-You will?"

"Yes, but only if you promise not to go chasing after San An for the rest of today."

"F-Fine."

"Good girl. Come now, sit."

"I'm not your dog!"

"You *are* my pet." He smiles smugly.

I want to hit him again but now is not the time to falter to temper. I'll save my wrath for later.

"Good girl!" He grins as I comply. "Okay, here goes. The assassin's name is Ying. He's famous for having two different colored eyes; one blue and one brown. We trained under the same master in Ning. That was a long time ago. Recently, he's been serving Su Jian."

"Who is Su Jian?"

"This information is news to me. Ying is not an easy man to find. He's killed countless veteran trackers. My source had a difficult time staying concealed until recently. Anyhow, this is news I wanted to tell the Minister. It just became *so* amusing to taunt him, I couldn't help myself. According to my source, Su Jian is from Bei Ling and somehow has ties to the Minister."

"We need to tell San An."

"No, you promised."

"But this is important!"

"Not really. Ying was injured by Wen Meng. He won't be doing anything for a while and Su Jian isn't going anywhere. Since you can't run after San An, want to have some fun with me?"

"What kind of fun?"

"Don't make that face. I'm going to do for you what I did for His Majesty. We're going to play dress up and then take a stroll around the market."

"You mean, leave the palace? I don't know if I can do that."

"You can *do anything* so long as no one finds out, silly! Don't you trust me?"

I think I finally understand their relationship. Kang Lang is He Pi's confidant; the latter probably trusts this man with his life. I would, too. It does sound fun and I'm tired of treading up and down these same halls every day. If I cannot speak to San An, I'd rather spend time with Kang Lang outside than stay and chance running into Lord Han Bei. The thought of the emissary's busy hands make me shudder.

"Okay, as long as no one finds out."

Chapter 27 – 2

Not long after waiting in my chamber as Kang Lang instructed, the latter bursts in with a pile of clothes and a wooden box filled with makeup and accessories. He throws the heavy load onto the bed. I've never seen him so excited.

"Pick whichever you like. The pink one with the lotus print is pretty, don't you think?"

"I hate pink. Why did you only bring women's clothing?"

"Did you forget which gender you are?"

"No, but I've never worn women's clothes. It would feel weird."

"Weird? It's *weirder* that you've never worn the clothes of your gender. Here, put the pink one on."

"I told you, I hate pink! I wouldn't know how to put it on anyway!"

"Oh? Then take your clothes off and I'll dress you," he grins impishly.

"Did you really expect me to answer favorably?"

"Yes. You are my doll for today."

Petulantly, I snatch the items from his hand. Behind the changing screen, the articles are examined. He's always worn courtesan robes and this one is no different. Besides from slipping my head through the neck hole and arms through the sleeves, where do all these other pieces go? While I fumble with the sashes and cords, Kang Lang calls to me.

"Just come on out. I'll help with the rest."

How does he know? Was he spying on me? I run from behind the screen to find him lazing on the bed.

"What's with that face?" Kang Lang starts to his feet. I have no response. If he did peek, Kang Lang wouldn't have seen anything too graphic anyway.

After piecing everything together, he removes the powder from my face and paints a new mask.

"There, that's done. Time to do your hair. Go sit by the vanity."

"Whoa!" I nearly fall back from looking into the mirror. This mask on my face is vastly different from He Pi's. For once, I look my gender and yet, I can't recognize my own reflection.

Kang Lang leans over my shoulder and teasingly whispers, "Who's that pretty girl?"

"You?" I frown.

He giggles vociferously. "Well, of course me! This time, also you! Sit still and let me style your hair."

"Is all of this necessary? We're only going out for a little while."

"So? I can only be seen with a pretty girl. It's bad for my reputation otherwise."

"You have a reputation outside of the palace?"

"Don't ask silly questions. Now sit still. Your hair's a mess."

Kang Lang takes down my hair and combs through several knots. I feel embarrassed for being so unkempt.

"Well, it's hard to set the crown properly. Without Jin, I'm pretty useless."

"Jin again? You're better off with San An. Well, you're best with me but if I must concede, then at least let me lose to San An."

"You don't like Jin?"

"I don't like men who chose to serve and who are too afraid to pursue their desires. That's not how real men should behave."

"Hey, don't insult Jin! I think he's smart, kind, and sweet! In other words, he's wonderful!"

"He's also a scared little boy with mommy issues. Well, I guess they all have mommy issues, even He Pi. Jin's so much of a frightened pup; I find him vexing. What? I'm telling you how I feel. Don't scowl or you'll ruin your makeup."

"Not every man needs to be brash when it comes to love. You think putting your hands all over someone is a sign of affection but Jin's not like that."

"Well, what better ways to convey desire than putting my hands all over someone's body? Even a blind person can't misinterpret that."

"Sometimes, you can be really insufferable, Kang Lang."

"That means I'm sufferable all the other times then."

He looks in the mirror and grins. My blood pressure is rising again.

"You're such a jerk. Why are you He Pi's fiancée? Well, actually, why do you even cross-dress?"

Kang Lang shrugs. "Because it's fun."

"You won't tell me?"

"If you really want to know, I'll tell you, but I expect something in return."

"Figures. I fear to ask."

"It's simple really. The next time Han Bei puts his hands on you, punch his ugly face as hard as you can and tell him Kang Lang is the greatest lover in the world, he can't ever come close. Oh, and then knee him where you kneed me."

"I... can't do that."

"Why?"

"He is Ning's emissary!"

"So?"

"What do you mean, 'so?!' Why do you hate him?"

"I'll tell you once you promise."

"What if I only do one of the three? Will you tell me?"

"Well, I suppose that's fine. I hope you choose the last option."

What choice do I have? He smiles happily and then settles into position. "Here comes my sob story. Get ready. Ning has a matriarchal society. Han Bei and I are the only children in our family. Since he's the firstborn, he's always gotten everything. My parents love him. Sometimes, I think they regret not having drowned me when I was still a babe. That's why I cross-dress. I thought if I appear the daughter they wanted, I wouldn't be cast aside and my parents would accept me."

"Are you serious? Kang Lang, that's horrible! How could your parents treat you with such little regards?"

"No, I'm not serious."

His swift response is accompanied by a blank expression. He continues fixing my hair without looking up as though nothing had transpired. After allowing Kang Lang a short moment to redeem his nonsense, which is met without success, my fist slams against the vanity.

"Are you going to tell me or not?!"

"Calm down! It's not my fault you're so gullible! Stop making that face. It is true that Han Bei was favored in every way possible and I was not. At the age of five, I was sent off to training. Shortly after, I advanced to the top of the class and was moved over to the assassination and infiltration regiment where my skills could best serve. That was where others like me were taught, well, everything necessary to go anywhere and do anything."

"Top of the class? Ning has schools to train children for such things?"

"Ning is a vicious country. Do not think that because the law is under a matriarchal structure that there is little threat. There's a reason Ning's army is so massive. It's because pawns like me are groomed early. If you are a male, expect to become a soldier. If you are a female, prepare to become a wife and mother as soon as your fourteenth birthday. With its large force, Ning can easily bully others to retrieve whatever resources are needed to fuel its war system."

"That's horrendous! Is there no freedom at all?"

"Not unless you have money, power, and connections; then, you can buy your way out. That's not to say Ning is corrupted. It's a rather strict system and penalties are applied evenly for the most part. I've seen a beggar and a nobleman executed on the same day for similar crimes. They group people of different classes together purposefully for executions to show that no one is above the law."

"How did you end up here, Kang Lang? Han Bei said you failed at something. Is that why?"

He smiles sadly. "At the age of seven, I completed my first assassination. Over the years, my looks developed and became my greatest asset. I can infiltrate almost anywhere by simply dressing as a beautiful female. You can see why they sent me to the Circle as Mu Dan to kill He Pi."

"What did you say?!"

"Surprised? I thought it was too obvious. You really are dense!"

"How is that obvious? You're his fiancée!"

"Yes. He is an interesting man. When he called me to his chamber after our initial encounter, I was prepared to seduce him. He'd behaved so boorishly at the Peony Palace, I thought it wouldn't have taken any effort at all. Instead, he invited me to tea and requested that I teach him the preparation of proper disguises."

"He Pi knew?"

"Yes. No one's ever resisted my pretty face. I was so shocked, I didn't know what to do. So, I played along.

Anyway, we conversed for hours and by the end of it, he thanked me and asked if there was anything he could do for me in return. Before then, no one's ever asked me that. People always used me however they wanted as long as it was to their convenience."

"You mean, people like me." I feel ashamed again. I may resemble He Pi but I'm nothing like him.

"Don't start crying or you'll ruin your makeup."

"I'm not."

"Then don't look so sad. I didn't mean what I said. I always get something from you."

"What are you talking about? I've never done anything for you."

"Sure you have! You always let me torture you and it brings me so much joy! Not to mention, you did promise to assault Han Bei. I can't ask for more than that."

"I disagree, but continue. What did you ask for?"

"Nothing. I had no idea what to ask for. He then dubbed Mu Dan his fiancée so I could stay until I can discover what it is I want. That sly man! Of all the places to put me, he sent me to the Circle where all the pretty girls are. Needless to say that although His Highness left those harpies starved, I've always been the gentleman to fulfill their desires." He smirks at the recollection of each conquest.

This must be the reason he still has men's clothes despite having lived at the Circle. His male self is dashing and he can be manipulative and charming. If he claims to be a prince, no woman would question him. Still, how vulgar.

"I didn't need to know that last part."

"What? Are you jealous? Don't be. They were empty temptations and nothing more. Anyhow, I think His Highness merely went through all that trouble just so I wouldn't kill him. I don't know. Still, there's a magnetic charm to He Pi. I decided to stay my hand at the time and become his private council. It's been six years. We're still very good friends."

"Friends," I scoff. "It's so obvious you love him."

"I do, but not in the same manner that I love you."

Pain is coursing through Kang Lang's reflection in the mirror. He keeps saying he loves me and of course, I can't return the kind words. Surely, there must be something I can do for him.

"Kang Lang, I'll help you find happiness. I promise."

"Don't make promises you can't keep. You're the last person who should be saying that to me."

"I don't care. I want you by my side until I can find your happiness and then you'll realize how stupid you've been for thinking I'm anything special."

"That was almost a sweet thing to say if you hadn't called me stupid. Anyway, I'll stay by your side until the very end. I've already decided that. Now, look up and tell me what you think."

He skillfully wove my hair into a flower headdress. I can't believe a few layers of powder and accessories can cause such a transformation. It may sound vain, but I could rival the courtesans in Peony Palace.

"Is that really me? How did you do that?"

"Because I'm talented, darling. Now, let's go have some fun."

Chapter 27 – 3

During our escape, we snuck past several guards and even scaled a wall. I must admit, it's never boring when Kang Lang is near, even though half of the time, I just want to choke the life out of him.

As we waltz down the streets, leering eyes scrutinize from both sides. Everyone is seemingly staring at us. Kang Lang's boasted reputation must really be something!

The closer we walk to the market center, the denser the crowds of patrons become. Kang Lang holds tightly onto my hand and leads the way down several streets, until reaching the front of a large store.

"So, what do you want to do first? Eat or shop?"

"I don't have any money. Can we just sightsee?"

"An emperor without money? Ridiculous!" Kang Lang chuckles. "I didn't ask whether you had money. I asked what it is you want to do. I'm the son of a Ning lord, remember? Let me spoil you today."

"You really shouldn't."

"Don't be so dull!" He sighs exasperatedly. "It's a pretty girl's prerogative to be spoiled by her suitor. I've always been spoiled for that reason, but I've never had a chance to do the same. Humor me."

"If you insist."

"I do."

"Then, can we find a bookstore? I really like poetries by Mian Shi Fen. That was the only nonreligious book my master had at the temple and—"

"Boring! No books! Pretty girls don't read. It turns them ugly!"

"Does it?"

"Of course! The moment a woman knows more than me, I find her ugly. That's why I like you so much, because you'll always be oblivious."

"Bastard!" First, he calls me ugly and now, he calls me stupid.

"What's that, darling? You want a new bauble for your hair? Sure, I can buy you one!"

"I didn't say—"

Without allowing further protest, Kang Lang pulls me to a nearby stall full of trinkets and accessories. Colored glass, painted ceramics, and carved wooden items—everything is so beautiful. However, I'm confused.

"Kang Lang, what use can I have for these?"

"Is that a trick question?"

"What I mean is... you know I won't ever dress this way again once we return. It would be a waste."

"Stop being so tiresomely pragmatic! Just buy something! It's a gift! Throw it away, treasure it, wear it, sell it... do whatever you want. We're not leaving until you pick something."

This is uncomfortable. Wearing women's clothing is already a big step for me; shopping for trinkets and being spoiled is pushing it a little far. He's agitated by my stubbornness. I might as well play along.

"How about this?" The wooden comb is carved with patterns of flowers and leaves.

"Hmm. Simple but pretty. Reminds me of you."

He's calling me stupid again, isn't he? Of course he is! He's grinning from ear to ear. Kang Lang hands the comb over to the elderly shopkeeper, who wraps it in colored paper. I still can't believe how beautiful everything in this little stall is, and there are stalls and shops spanning as far as the eyes can see. This market really is amazing!

"Ack! What are you doing?" I was still entranced by the shop's display when Kang Lang abruptly slides an arm around my waist. Before I can push away, he's already making a scene.

"What are you doing staring at my lover like that, huh? Want me to poke your eyes out?!"

Oh, my goodness. Who is he yelling at?

"You got something to say?"

Kang Lang draws our bodies closer. In the abrupt swing, I finally realize the person he's challenging is none other than the frowning Demon General. If he recognizes me, I'll be in so much trouble!

"K-Knock it off! That's Bai Hu!"

Burying my face in his arm, I whisper desperately for relief. He pretends as though not having heard a word. Kang Lang continues goading the older man and drawing more attention from bystanders, until Bai Hu finally leaves. A victorious grin spreads across the cheeky face.

"What is wrong with you?! Was he even looking at me?"

"No. Something about him irked me. Anyway, I've just always wanted to do that."

"Do what?"

"Make a scene in public because another man is looking at my woman. Too bad he wouldn't fight me. That would have been fun."

"What kind of crazy fantasies do you have in that head of yours?"

"All kinds. In one version, I win and you become so enraptured that you immediately beg me to claim you.

Another version, I'm mortally wounded and you kill yourself to follow me in death."

I have no idea how to respond to his nonsense. Or maybe, I do. Abrupt laughter bursts without pause. My counterpart sulks.

"Real life is so boring," he mutters while reaching for his coin pouch to pay for the comb.

"There's not a romance novel written that could satisfy your particular dramatics, *Lord* Kang Lang."

Still pouting, the cheeky man shakes his head at me disappointedly. Once we start down the street to another vendor for steamed buns, his good mood suddenly returns.

The afternoon went by quickly. I was afraid our amusement would be cut short, but when night fell, the market came to life again. Lanterns light the entire district, giving off a warm and comforting glow while the chaos of commerce intensifies. The maddening scene of night markets is ever more exciting.

"Do you want to eat anything else?" Kang Lang looks down and smiles softly. I can't help notice how charming he appears in this light; more so than usual.

"No, I can't eat another thing. Could we walk a while longer? I don't remember going down that way to those distant glowing lanterns. They're pretty."

Kang Lang turns toward the direction I mentioned. Far away, faint glimmers of light can be seen in the darkened night.

"Are you sure you want to go down there? That's the Red Light District."

"Wha—!" No wonder all those lights are red! I feel so incredibly stupid.

"I mean, if you want to go, I'll gladly take you."

Without another word, he drags me down the path.

"Hey, stop! I-I didn't know!"

"Are you sure you didn't know or are you too embarrassed to admit you want to spend the night with me there?"

"Stop being so damn vulgar!"

"You're the one who asked me to take you to the Red Light District." He flicks my forehead and chuckles. I feel like a child when I'm with him. Maybe, that's not it. I just feel carefree.

We stroll around the market for a while longer before making our way back to the palace. Once inside, Kang Lang leans down and kisses my forehead to bid goodnight.

"Thanks for the fun day, Bao Lai. Let's go again sometime."

"I had fun, too. Thank you, for everything."

"Don't make that grateful face or I'll start getting naughty ideas. Go on, tell San An about Su Jian and then off to bed."

"Didn't you say I wasn't allowed to chase after San An today?"

"I changed my mind."

Curiosity wants to know the reason; logic dictates imparting news of the assassin to the Minister is more important right now. Despite the sweet smile, Kang Lang's not particularly happy with the notion of breaking our agreement while I run to his rival. He'd planned for us to spend the night having "girl talk," as he'd put it. That'll have to wait. I'll make it up to Kang Lang later. There's no time to waste.

"Thank you!"

Following an obeisance, I rush to San An's chamber. The embarrassing event from earlier in the day hasn't left me. Hopefully, San An has calmed.

Chapter 27 – 4

"San An, may I come in?"

Moments after my sheepish voice calls to him, the Minister opens the door. Immediately, he is frozen in place. The expression on the beet-red face is a mixture of shock and fear.

"What's wrong?"

"Bao... Lai?"

"Yes? San An, I have good news."

A short, uneasy pause ensues. Finally letting out a sigh, he steps aside and gestures for me to enter. Upon closing the door, San An's expression turns bitter.

"Why do you come to me this way? Was it not enough torment for me to witness you in another man's embrace; you must come to taunt me in succession?"

"What are you talking about?"

San An won't look at me, but then, I remember I'm not dressed as He Pi. This was no mistake. Kang Lang purposefully sent me here in this state. No, this is my fault. I should have known better.

"San An, I'm sorry. I had no intention to taunt you. I just forgot to change back."

"Change back? Did you go somewhere?"

Why do I keep saying the wrong thing? I can't take it back now!

"I..."

"You reek of the markets. Did you leave the palace?"

"Well, yes, but Kang Lang was with me. Everything was fine."

"You left the palace with Kang Lang?"

"Y-Yes."

"How long were you away?"

"Since this afternoon."

"This afternoon? Our esteemed guests, who graciously came to assist with Nan Rong's troubles, were deprived of civilities due to them. Your Highness was nowhere to be found and they took it as a slight. My efforts to assuage the situation were barely successful. I am certain Lord Han Bei saw through the excuses. If he chooses to withdraw Ning's support, I have no doubt Bei Ling will renege their agreement of the interim retreat. Were you simply spending the day with Kang Lang to further earn his favor, so that should war fall to Nan Rong, you may follow him to Ning?"

"How can you say that? I would never!"

"Your words are meaningless. Your actions have clearly shown me the person you really are."

"You're being cruel! It was a mistake. I didn't know—"

"What did you not know? That you are not allowed to leave the palace? That you have an important role to maintain—a role that could mean life or death for our people? Or, that I don't want to see another man touch you and for you to accept his advances so easily?"

"San An! Please, just listen to me! Kang Lang gave me the assassin's identity!"

"Why? Did you give him everything he asked?"

Resentment and boiling rage break his calm demeanor. He's doing everything to suppress an outburst.

"No!" To hear San An accuse me of such things is unbearable. Sharp pains radiating from my chest continue spreading. I can't breathe.

"Then why would he tell you?"

"That's not important! Just listen!"

"You expect me to listen to anything you have to say? After you blatantly disregard my affections and yet, allow Kang Lang to do whatever he desires without so much as a single act of resistance? Against my wishes, you left the palace with him, dressed in *that* manner, and then to come here and flaunt in front of me and tell me that it's not important how you coaxed the answers from him!"

The more he speaks, the more San An is unable to control his pain. His voice gradually increases in tremor and temper.

"How many times have you gone to him behind my back? How many times have you let him freely put his hands on you, to then come to me and look into my eyes with that same sweet innocence? How many lips have stained your mouth with tainted kisses?! How many men have you confessed your affections for and still sound so honest?! How much more disgrace must I suffer for worshipping an unfaithful woman?!"

"San An, please! Just stop!" No matter how I try to choke back the tears, they keep surging. Everything inside is falling apart. Where do I even begin to explain? Remorse and turmoil sap composure. The strength from my legs withers. I've collapsed to my knees.

"Stand up! Stand up and disappear from my sight! Go back to him and be happy!"

"No. I'm begging you. Just listen to me!"

"There is nothing more I need to hear."

Every fiber of my being is on fire. As much pain as I feel, he must be suffering a thousand times worse. Yet, why can't he understand? Why can't he understand that Kang Lang is not my lover? Why can't he understand that I want nothing more than to be by his side? Maybe, it's because I've never shown him a true ounce of affection. I've never told him how much he means to me; to bind him through my words. But, I can't tell him. It would be heartless. We can't be together as long as I'm He Pi. More importantly, I know I don't deserve him. He's been suffering in silence while I was away finding amusement. If I just let him hate me, then at least I can't ever hurt him again.

Suppressing anguish rising in my soul, I labor through the only message that still means anything to San An.

"Please, just tell the council that the assassin's name is Ying, a man with two different eye colors. He's employed by Su Jian of Bei Ling, who may have connections to you."

"Su Jian?" San An turns pale as though he'd seen a ghost. From shock, his mind is immediately directed elsewhere. The demeanor turns distant.

San An finally has the answer he's been searching. While he is distracted by this thought, I should take my leave. As I pass him on the way to the door, he remains unchanged. I feel happy bitterness knowing he's finally free of me.

Chapter 28: A Secret Revealed

Wen Meng forgave my rudeness from prior day. Han Bei was discontented. The emissary kept glaring in my direction during our meeting this morning. I don't know what to make of it. San An did not attend. I was worried but at the same time, relieved.

Upon my path to He Pi's quarters, Han Bei stops me. Visibly, his previous displeasure has deepened. Before I have a chance to begin, he pulls me into an empty room.

"Sire, it is with regret that I must return to Ning. I hope everything goes well with Bei Ling." As he speaks, Han Bei twirls the long red hair between his fingers as if to disregard and also to address me in tandem.

"Lord Han Bei, are you withdrawing Ning's support from Nan Rong? I apologize for my carelessness yesterday. It will not happen again!"

He makes no real effort to acknowledge my low bow.

"No. I couldn't care less for yesterday's lack of pleasantries."

"Then, tell me why. Have I slighted you in some way?"

"Not at all. You've slighted my blood and I find that deplorable. I do not think you are a trustworthy man."

Another person who thinks I'm not trustworthy. The recollection of San An's charges thoroughly pains my core.

"Please explain. How have I slighted your blood?"

"Don't play innocent, sire. You claim to be faithful to Kang Lang but yesterday, I clearly saw a courtesan in pink garb rushed into your chamber with tears streaming down her face. I suppose she came to you for comfort? She did not leave the entire night."

I made another mistake. Why didn't I exert more discretion? How can I explain it was me he saw? But then, that robe belongs to a very specific person.

"You are mistaken, Lord Han Bei. It was my fiancée who entered my quarters last night. Mu Dan can confirm that the robe belongs to him and that he was in fact, there."

"I am no fool, sire. I can recognize my own brother under any disguise. You continue with your attempts to deceive me, but it is futile. If I cannot trust your character, then I cannot trust you. If I cannot trust you, then there is no reason for Ning to bear the burden of an alliance that reaps no benefits."

"Our lands must stand together if we are to withstand Bei Ling's ploys. You said so yourself! Should Nan Rong fall, Ning is not far behind!"

My heart is beating out of my chest. No matter what, I need to convince him to stay. Nan Rong needs his help.

He's looking at me with the same disgust I saw on San An's face and I become paralyzed from shame.

"Ning is more than capable of destroying Bei Ling; just as Ning is more than capable of destroying Nan Rong. Farewell, Your Highness."

Without another word, Han Bei turns to leave. What should I do? I can't let him go!

Chapter 28 – 2

"Lord Han Bei! Wait! Just give me a moment of your time. I can explain!"

"I don't need to hear excuses, sire."

"Then, don't listen! See with your own eyes. Please, just come with me!"

Han Bei's path is barred. I've run in front and pressed my back against the door. The frowning emissary is contemplating whether to push me aside. Something keeps him and the blithe lord eventually decides to humor me. I lead Han Bei to my chamber and then, going behind the screen, change into the pink robe and let down my hair. He's completely baffled when I step out to present the result.

"It was me, Lord Han Bei. You saw me running to my room."

"He Pi is a woman?"

"No. He's missing. I've been attempting to fill his shoes for some time now. The irony of it is I became He Pi to deter a Ning invasion. Yet, here I am telling you, a representative of Ning, the one truth I wasn't allowed to divulge. You have no obligations here, I understand. I'm sorry for lying. Punishment should solely be against me; not my country. I'm begging you, please help Nan Rong!"

Kneeling down, I bow low to the floor. The room becomes silent for an exaggerated span of time. He might have left altogether, but I can't raise my head unless I'm certain. When I begin to lose hope, finally, hesitant hands lift me up. He's kneeled in front.

"Why were you crying?"

"Because I hate myself for my weaknesses and foolishness."

"I see. Another weak and foolish woman." He scoffs. "Who are you, really?"

"I'm a nobody by the name of Bao Lai."

"Bao Lai?" Repeating the words in a breathless whisper, his sharp eyes suddenly search every inch of my face. "From where do you hail?"

"I grew up as a student at Tian Mao Yi Temple in the south. My birth is unknown."

"Unknown?"

"Yes. Master Tai Hung was my guardian. He told me that I was left there without so much as a note."

Something in my reply triggers his fierce gaze to drill holes through me. What exactly is he looking for? I want to, but cannot look away. Focus must be kept to show him that I have nothing to hide.

After an indeterminable, agonizing span of time, Han Bei pulls me to my feet.

"Fate is a curious thing, isn't it?" He mutters. "I will guarantee Ning's support under one condition."

"Yes?"

"After everything settles, you will come with me to Ning."

"To Ning... with you? Why?"

"I'd prefer to not discuss the matter now."

"But... I'm not a man," the faint words fall nervously. I was afraid he would be offended. Instead, the emissary chuckles mirthfully.

"Yes, you are just another tiresome woman and not even close to the standard of women I'm accustomed to. You're safe from me, *sire*. What is your response?"

I have no desire to leave Nan Rong but there is nothing for me here. Jin's delayed his return; though, after everything I've done, I'm not worthy to even be near him. And San An, I can't think of the Minister without shuddering from guilt. It's too late for me to resume my previous reclusive life. I've been marred enough through my experiences these past several months that claiming ignorance is no longer a right. Kang Lang failed his task. He can't return to Ning. I'm fated for loneliness for all the pain I've caused and the mistakes I've made. This end is just.

"I will do as you ask, Lord Han Bei. When matters settle, I will follow you to Ning."

"A wise decision. Let us pretend last night's event never happened. As promised, I will continue supporting Nan Rong."

I bow deeply while Han Bei takes his leave. Just as he passes the threshold, Kang Lang enters. Without exchanging words, they glare in each other's direction like two vipers prepared to strike. Once Kang Lang and I are alone, he turns a steeled expression.

"Why was Han Bei in your room and why are you still wearing that?"

"He threatened to leave. This was the only thing I could do to convince him that it was me he saw running into He Pi's chamber last night. He was offended by His Highness's supposed fickleness toward Mu Dan."

"Why would Han Bei mind that He Pi is unfaithful?"

"Maybe your brother cares more for you than you think."

"*Preposterous.*" He relishes the word, almost languorously. "In any case, is he willing to help knowing you're not the *man* he thought you were?"

"Yes."

"Really? What does Han Bei expect in return?"

"Nothing."

"You're a terrible liar."

I can't tell Kang Lang my promise or he'll become upset and make things worse. Han Bei's support is integral.

"Really, he didn't ask for anything. Han Bei was just glad He Pi isn't unfaithful."

"You keep lying to me and I'll punish you." He grins cheerfully.

It's Kang Lang's nature to ignore boundaries. I like his playful demeanor at times. Yet, my indulgence of his ways has only come to cause me grief. His forefinger abruptly runs down my cheek. I step away.

"I was only kidding. What's wrong?"

"Kang Lang. I like you, I really do. It's only recent that I've realized how dear you are to me but..."

"But?"

Out of old habit, Kang Lang takes as many steps toward me as I'd taken back.

"You need to keep your hands to yourself."

He pauses. It's apparent that I've insulted him.

"Where is this coming from suddenly? Did San An finally claim you? Why are you so defensive?"

"I trust you and this is why I'm telling you. Stop being inappropriate and stop teasing me. It makes me uncomfortable."

After staring silently for a drawn moment, Kang Lang sighs and rubs his face. "I guess you were right. San An is not the typical man. If he were, he wouldn't have hurt you this way."

"What?"

"I can see the torment on your face. I take it he was angry and said some mean things? I really thought he would overreact and fight to win you; not push you away. I'll talk to him."

"No! Don't you dare!"

"Why?"

"He's finally free of me. Just let him be." My eyes are misting again. Why can't I exert some control? Why does my body keep disobeying me!

"You know as well as I do, he has not been freed. Anger and jealousy make men say stupid things. I wouldn't take anything he said seriously. Cheer up. Let's go talk to San An about Su Jian and get this mess solved all at once."

"No, please don't mention anything to him. Just leave things as they are."

"You are miserable with things the way they are, which makes me miserable."

"I'm not miserable! I'm just tired from lack of sleep! You've read me all wrong!"

Kang Lang's response to my weak smile is darkened temper. "Stop treating me like I'm an imbecile! What did San An do to you? Tell me or I'll rip out his heart for breaking yours after I slit his throat for hurting you with callous words!"

The violent wrath he carefully hides under the usual cheerful demeanor abruptly plasters on his face. Kang Lang turns toward the door to make good on his threat. Grabbing desperately onto his arm, I'm merely dragged along.

"Kang Lang, wait! Don't hurt San An! He didn't do anything! He didn't say anything that was wrong! It's my fault! It's my fault I've been nothing but a harlot!"

Kang Lang brusquely ceases. Slowly, a blank stare tilts down. Tremors quickly spread through his whole body until Kang Lang shakes with rage. *"Did he say that?! Did San An call you a harlot?!"*

I've never heard his voice raised so loud or the tone so piercing. The strength of his anger exerts into the air at a force so tremendous, it's almost tangible.

"N-No! He didn't! He should have! What else would you call someone who tells one man she loves him and then turns around and flaunts in front of his brother? A woman who allows yet another to put his hands all over her without retaliation whenever he finds it amusing, and then goes running back to face all three as though nothing's happened?!"

"Without retaliation? You've retaliated against me more times than I can remember! You've raised your hands, your feet, even your forehead, to abuse me countless times! It wasn't your fault I was relentless! Blame me! Don't blame yourself!"

"It was my fault! I knew anger goaded you to continue, so why did I keep defaulting to it?"

"Because you're a violent woman; it's in your disposition! That's why I like you! That's why I keep going back to you! You couldn't stop me, anyway. The more you've retaliated, the more force I've used. San An's wrong to think otherwise!"

"B-But, at times... I *enjoyed* your advances. What about that? Doesn't that make me a harlot?!"

"You've never known pleasure. You *should* be easily excited. It's human nature. Why do I even have to explain this to you? Are you really that confused?"

I don't know how to respond. Is it not my fault? Is the reason as simple as the fact that I'm human and I do stupid things because I lack experience to handle these situations? I grew up in a temple and dressed as a male all my life. Maybe these basic reasonings should have been learned from youth but I've missed all that. I'm just a child inside an adult's body.

"Listen, I don't know how you feel to tell you whether you really love Jin or not. The way I see it, Jin's a nice person and you like him. You've grown attached to him and that's normal. You've grown attached to me and that's normal, too. In all my years at the palace, San An's been cold toward everyone. He's practically obsessed with you. Whether you love him or not is your business. I'm sorry for having interfered. I never intended to hurt or confuse you with my reckless behaviors. So, don't beat yourself up."

It sounds so simple. I just can't do it. He's trying to spare me even though I have faults in this. Surprisingly, I think Kang Lang knows me better than I do myself.

"Didn't you say that you're younger than me, Kang Lang?"

"What's with *that* question? To be honest, I'm not sure. My guess is you're older. I'm twenty-three."

"You're right. I'm twenty-six." I feel silly for being older than him and yet, so behind in my years. He can be juvenile but he's much more experienced. In some ways, I feel guilty for my sheltered life and in others, jealous of his maturity.

"Yes, I'm younger than you, but just recently you've started living. I've been out in this world much longer. The reality is the way culture and society expect for anyone to behave compared to how a logical human react isn't always aligned. Most of the time, they're complete opposites. Rewards fall more often in the lap of the active callous, than the passive saint."

"What do you mean by that?"

"It's like talking to a wall!" He repeats the previous charges with a charming smile. "What I mean is... there's nothing wrong with being human—being a woman instead of a doll. You can be flawed. And, if you want something, don't sit around in perfect poses waiting for it to come to you. Regardless of what anyone says, don't doubt yourself. Fight for what you want no matter the consequences."

"Surely, there are some consequences that should never be breached."

"You keep talking like that and you'll never get anywhere. I don't understand you. You're active in others' causes but passive in your own desires. Why?"

"Am I? I don't see that."

"Sure! You promised to find happiness for me. Even though you won't admit it, I know you made a deal with Han Bei to keep Nan Rong safe. At the cost of your own happiness, you'd rather San An hate you than for him to be miserable. Stop thinking of what's best for others. If you desire Jin, then drag him back from Xiong. If you desire San An, then march to his room and force him to surrender his trifling jealousy. And, if you want me, just say the word."

The short wink accompanying his offer forces a smile to my face. Is he right? What do I want most? At the moment, I'm not certain of anything.

"Well, maybe, I don't know what I desire. Like you said, I'm gullible. Maybe this whole time, I've mistaken others' desires as my own. I can't satisfy everyone's happiness."

"For once, you don't sound like an imbecile."

"Thanks, I think. Well, no, just… thank you, Kang Lang. I'm going to break free from all these emotions and focus on the most important thing right now."

"Hold on there! I never said emotions are bad. Just ignore other people and do what *you* feel."

"You sound reckless as usual."

He makes me smile and he knows how to cheer me up. I feel pleasantly calm just from looking at his sweet face. Maybe I don't know what I want, but at the moment, I am sure of wanting one thing.

"Kang Lang, may I hug you?"

Emerald eyes sparkle in reverie. Clasping a hand to his mouth, he giggles. "Oh! Someone's falling for me! What? Stop frowning! Go ahead. You don't need to ask my permission."

His strong arms draw our embrace closer. Warmth floods over me and the nostalgic scent that drifts from his clothes puts my mind at ease. A thought comes to me: I cherish this person. I think I've come to cherish him in the same manner that Mu Dan cherishes He Pi.

Chapter 29: Progress

Wen Meng, Han Bei, Kang Lang, Bai Hu, Qing Hai, Zhen Yue, the council, and I gathered around noon in the war room. San An reviewed Kang Lang's report and Wen Meng confirmed that indeed the assailant from Mount Chou had mismatched colored eyes.

"Prime Minister, who is Su Jian?" Even though I've addressed him, I'm still nervous. He hasn't acknowledged me since the group gathered. Without Kang Lang sitting nearby, I wouldn't be able to keep composure.

San An glances quickly in my direction and then reverts attention to the large map on the table. "Kang Lang, your source believes this Su Jian has connections to me, is that correct?"

"Yes." Kang Lang replies.

"Then, I fear the past has come back to haunt us. In the last war at court, only three of Emperor Jin's children were thought to have survived. We can now confirm the report is incorrect."

Su Jian is San An's brother. I can't believe it was he who sent Ying to injure San An and descended Bei Ling's wrath upon Nan Rong.

In place of my silent disbelief, Han Bei poses doubt. "What makes you think this Su Jian is your brother, Prime Minister? With everything Empress Pai had accomplished, one must assume the list of men by that name with grudges against you is massive."

At the mention of Empress Pai, San An's countenance turns severe. Han Bei purposefully touched his nerves. A corner of his mouth lifts into a victorious smirk. I should keep silent to remain in Ning's favor but I'm too tempted to defend San An and thus, I can't keep thoughts bounded.

"Lord Han Bei, even an assassin of Ying's caliber would have difficulties making his way into our palace in broad daylight. No one saw him entered; meaning, whoever sent him must have secret knowledge of this palace's layouts. Additionally, he could have easily disposed of the Prime Minister and me at such close proximity. He merely provoked Nan Rong by directing our attention to the East. I think we should consider the Minister's premise that this Su Jian is his brother."

Han Bei glares whilst condescension flows. "*His* brother? Isn't Su Jian *your* brother too, Your Highness?"

"Well, yes—"

"If you will pretend to be He Pi, at least think before you speak!"

My breathing disrupts. Obviously, he's aware of my ruse but did he have to let everyone else know I've made a mess of things? The room is deafly silent. San An, sighing sharply, takes the lead and confronts Han Bei. When he speaks, the tone is tempered steel.

"What are you accusing His Highness of, Lord Han Bei?"

"That *he* is a woman named, Bao Lai. A woman who has divulged that He Pi is missing and that you've all kept me from the truth for fear of a Ning invasion."

I don't need to see his face to know San An is staring bitterly in my direction. Everyone else except for Kang Lang and Wen Meng despise me at the moment. The latter, only because of shock.

"Is this true?" Wen Meng starts up.

"Yes. She invited me to her chamber this morning and showed me her true self, then *begged* me to save Nan Rong. To instruct a common woman to beg anything of me is just insulting. The Southland truly is *pathetic*!"

"Han, shut up!"

"You think you can bark orders at me, little brother?"

Sparks of anger fly between the brothers, while everyone else becomes agitated. Side conversations erupt and then the room breaks to uproar. We are far off topic when threat is on the horizon. Once again, it's my fault.

"Lord Han Bei!" Without considering the room's sentiment, I'm on my feet staring at the emissary. "Regardless of everything I've said and done, you promised to assist Nan Rong. Are you a man of your word?"

"Of course."

"Then, please help us instead of causing disquiet with your derision and condescension!"

I pray he won't bring up the other piece of our bargain. He's contemplating whether to humiliate me further. Maybe it's my imagination, but I think Han Bei casted a glance at Kang Lang before ultimately rescinding.

"Very well." Han Bei resumes his former pose of sitting with arms crossed while tilting his head to the side, as though sleeping through a boring lecture.

With that matter settled, San An interposes, "Chief Wen Meng, I hope you will keep this revelation solely within current company."

Wen Meng stares at San An, then at me, and then to the Minister again. "I disagree with a woman sitting in the council. I will keep your secret but I won't indulge the nonsense of having her here."

What is his problem? Shouldn't he be more concerned by the fact that I'm an imposter instead of fussing over my gender? Undoubtedly, I want to stay, but my presence is stalling important discussions. Surely, Kang Lang will bring news. I might as well retreat. After a brisk bow, I march from the room and head to the gardens for fresh air.

Chapter 29 – 2

Crossing the short bridge leading to the lily garden, I meet someone carrying a basket of herbs coming in the opposite direction. He's surprised by the chance encounter; the sentiment is brief.

"Master Yu."

"Your Highness."

It's still awkward to see the court physician; mostly, because I thought the council had put him to death. I'm glad they didn't. I just hope he's no longer a threat to San An. The Minister's suffered enough. Why can't he and everyone else from Empress Pai's time just let the past be? Wait a minute. That's it!

"Master Yu. May I have a minute of your time?"

The physician, who wasted no time walking past me, turns about. After studying my expression to find the reason, he grudgingly complies.

In the lily garden, on the stone bench beneath one of the tall dove trees, the court physician is shuffling uncomfortably. So, am I. At the moment, feelings matter little. I need information.

"Master Yu. You've been at court for most of your life, haven't you?"

"Yes, since I was seventeen."

"You must know almost everything that's happened at court."

"What exactly do you want to know, Your Highness?" The exasperated way he speaks reminds me of my master whenever I'd vexed him.

"Su Jian, son of the late Emperor Jin—I mean, my brother. What can you tell me about him?"

"Why the sudden interest in a dead man, Your Highness?" He peers cautiously from a sidelong glance. It's evident he knows I'm an imposter.

"Curiosity. The name came up and I became curious."

Master Yu momentarily ponders the request and then, rolling up the sleeves of his long robe, settles into a stiffer pose. "Su Jian was second in line for succession, after the Prime Minister. His mother was the daughter of a nobleman from Bei Ling. He was rumored to have died near the end of the conflict through Empress Pai's mass poisoning."

"Why do you say, 'rumored?' Do you think he is alive?"

"For a time, Crown Prince San An was said to have perished. Empress Pai used the opportunity to rid of the competitions and then, he suddenly returned. Likewise, it is possible Prince Su Jian ran with his mother to Bei Ling."

"Why would he suddenly target San An?"

"Are you saying Su Jian is alive, Your Highness?"

"I think he is and he's threatening Nan Rong. If you know anything else, please tell me."

News are bound to spread soon. I might as well attempt to learn as much as I can before truths fade into one with rumors.

"I owe you no debt sire, to divulge anything I may know. However, since Miss Bao Lai convinced the Prime Minister to spare my life even after she'd suffered from my treachery, this message is for her. Bei Ling has a child emperor who's no more than a puppet. On the outside, the council keeps him as their charge. In actuality, Bei Ling's council has no authority. Prime Minister Wang Liang's coercion of Cai Pai is steering their policies."

"How does Wang Liang connect to Su Jian?"

"It is my supposition that Wang Liang was born the day Su Jian reportedly died."

Does he mean Bei Ling's prime minister is Su Jian?

"How? How do you know this?"

"I tried and failed to save all the children of the court brought to me during the conflict. I was young and inexperienced. Medicine is to treat injuries and illnesses. When something as unnatural as poison enters the systems, especially something as potent as sleeping nettle, there's a slim chance for an unskilled person to make the antidote in time. Miss Bao Lai is alive because I already had the antidote made. I don't keep any poison without the cure. The Prime Minister lived because the poison that inflicted him was weak. Forgive me, I'm rambling, sire.

Consort Wu brought Prince Su Jian, or a boy she claimed was Prince Su Jian, to the infirmary and left him to die in my care. Before his body was cold, she returned to Bei Ling. To confirm my suspicions, I visited the North some years later and a young man resembling the Su Jian that I knew received me at Consort Wu's door. It is a shame she passed before my arrival."

"You've never told anyone?"

"What would have been the point? I was happy to see him well. I thought this child was able to escape the chaos and deserved to live peacefully. For the world to know he lives, Su Jian would only come to know death. He introduced himself as Wang Liang. I never thought inside he was still Su Jian."

The more he speaks, the more Master Yu reminds me of Master Tai Hung. For a moment, I was back at the temple sitting under the magnolia trees with him. Nostalgia sweeps over as I fall to silent contemplation of what felt, another lifetime.

"If you will excuse me, sire, I must return inside and bring these herbs to Master Dui."

"Oh, certainly. I'm sorry for keeping you. Before you go, could you tell me who exactly is Master Dui?"

"He's a local physician and apothecary rumored to be some sort of genius at this craft. After my scandal, they brought him to replace me. He insisted otherwise. In short, I'm his assistant. Master Dui is the official court physician."

"Oh! I'm sorry."

"Don't apologize, sire. It's a small punishment for the much larger crime I've committed."

"But... you weren't really going to kill San An, were you? I poisoned myself; you didn't."

"Since when were you poisoned, Your Majesty? I thought I mentioned it was Miss Bao Lai who suffered from my treachery."

I didn't correct him prior, when he pointed at the real me. It doesn't matter since he knows everything. Giving Master Yu a nervous smile, I reply, "Bao Lai and I are so close; sometimes, I feel we are the same person. Truly, you don't seem the cruel type. You wouldn't have hurt San An."

"I don't know what I would have been capable of at the time."

"You don't intend to ever again, right?"

"I'm no different than Su Jian, sire. On the outside, I am a physician. On the inside, I'm still a resentful man.

I can't predict my own actions, just as I'm certain the Wang Liang I met those years ago never thought he would live to bring war to three countries."

He's right. In the last several months, I've done things I never thought myself capable—things I find deplorable—and I know I will continue to do so as long as I live. The future is never certain.

Not wanting to keep him any longer, I thank Master Yu and part ways.

Chapter 30: A Broken Heart

Now that the Peony Palace is vacant, I have no idea where to find Kang Lang. He still lives in the palace of course, so he must be hiding his things somewhere. I have to share everything I've learned and he undoubtedly has news from the council.

Why did I think walking around this massive place and checking every room was a good plan? I've been at this for an hour. Maybe, I should wait in my chamber. He's bound to come sooner or later.

Upon rounding a corner to my quarters, San An comes forthwith in the opposite direction. Happiness swells and then dampens under guilt. Seeing San An so unhappy feels like knives plunging deep into my chest. The same sentiment is reflected back from that face so dear to me. I don't want to be his misery but this is important. The Minister, pushing through lingering hesitation, beckons me to follow.

Once past the threshold, San An locks the chamber door and starts for the only seat in the room: his bed. He must be severely tired to take such a relaxed pose when it's obvious he's still upset. I linger diffidently near the door.

"Does Your Highness wish to tell me why it was necessary to exhibit your gender to Lord Han Bei this morning?"

I was hoping he wouldn't ask that and I certainly hope Han Bei kept his mouth shut about our agreement.

"He threatened to leave when he thought He Pi was unfaithful to Mu Dan. I had to do something."

"You did not think him leaving was better than Ning realizing our weakness?"

"I thought an alliance with Ning was crucial for Nan Rong. I wasn't thinking."

"I don't believe that. You always think but you never choose common sense."

He's still as cold and distant as when we last spoke. I long to hear his voice; yet, every jagged word ruptures another piece of my composure.

"I apologize. Everything is fine in the end. Ning will ally with us."

"For the duration of this conflict with Bei Ling. If He Pi does not return by then, do you think Ning will not pick up arms immediately?"

He's right. Our agreement did not specify perpetuity. If war with the North does come, Nan Rong will severely weaken and become an easy target for Ning. What have I done?

"I'm sorry." All I can do is mutter an apology; words change nothing.

San An remains silent for a time. Then, slowly, the Minister exhales his frustration. "What did you promise Han Bei for the alliance?"

"I did not promise anything."

"You continue to lie to me after everything that's transpired?"

His tone hardens. Still, I can't tell him the truth. I don't even know all the details of Han Bei's request. What is there to say? As upset as San An is, he'll likely overreact.

"Yes, I'm lying to you. All you have to know is that I will do everything I can to keep Nan Rong safe."

"Everything? You don't have anything to your name, Bao Lai. Have you promised yourself to him?"

"Don't be ridiculous. He's lost all interests since the moment he learned of my gender."

"And yet, you refuse to tell me the truth?"

"Yes."

My short answer forces the Minister to his feet. He comes hither and cups my chin in his hand. Raising my gaze into his, ardent agony pours from his eyes. His arm slightly trembles and then, reluctantly, quivering lips descend toward my own.

Why are you doing this to yourself, San An? Stop suffering because of me!

Panic abruptly invokes Kang Lang's advice. I must do as I feel, no matter what anyone else wants. I must do the right thing even when the wrong thing is so bitterly tempting. This is how I feel.

Withdrawing my face from his grasp, I march toward the window. San An is shocked by my refusal but it was enough to draw back his senses.

"San An, I've learned that Su Jian is Wang Liang, Bei Ling's prime minister. He's controlling Cai Pai. I see war as inevitability. What has the council decided?"

The Minister speedily turns around. "How were you able to learn this?"

"A certain court physician you were kind enough to spare told me everything he knew."

"I see. He told me nothing of the sort when I visited earlier. It's Bao Lai who has loosened his petty tongue."

"How long do you think it has been since he's known of Bao Lai?"

"I imagine from the moment He Pi stormed into the infirmary for my sake."

His sharp eyes soften. Our minds race to the same memory; the one event that led San An to change his perception of me, and likewise, my perception of him.

"I didn't really do anything except poisoned myself, you know that. No matter what he says or does, I doubt Master Yu would have let you died. I acted out of guilt, not courage. You shouldn't confuse obligations and gratefulness for affections."

He flinches and then the expression draws blank. During the ensuing long pause, San An carefully studies my apathetic face. Those words meant to cut through his delusions, cut through me deeper. The notion that his affections for me stemmed from unearned heroics makes me realize that I'll never deserve San An.

A soft, deep sigh escapes. San An's brows furrow. "This is your way of rejecting me?"

Swallowing a lump in my throat, I cast out a tremulous sigh. "This is my way of saying your affections are misguided for an untrustworthy woman."

"Misguided as they are, I still love you."

The soft voice falters. San An's pleading with me in his own way. Throbbing pain overcomes my heart, mirroring coursing suffering on his face. I can't stay anymore or I'll be too tempted to prolong his misery by encouraging him. Mustering all my nerves, a sardonic smile appears.

"Love me? I'm sorry to say this Minister, but you're wasting your time."

Suffering turns to despair. The ache of heartbreak clearly displays upon his gentle face. How I've marred his beautiful soul! The guilt of which will never leave me as long as I live. There's naught I can do but speedily pass out of the room without looking back.

Chapter 31: Jin's Return

The council met daily from early morning to after dusk. I wasn't able to take part; thus, Kang Lang brings news after each session. The sight of him coming and going from my quarters must grieve San An. I haven't spoken to the Minister since I broke his heart. I hope pain will make him despise me and then eventually, fade into indifference. Even if he never forgives me, I want him to be happy. There is no future for me in Nan Rong. Want as I may, we cannot be together. Mostly, he simply deserves better.

The door creaks open. Kang Lang saunters in, sporting a wide grin.

"You always look so happy when you come but you never bring any good news, Kang Lang."

"I'm just happy to see you, Your Highness." Walking to the bed, he settles beside me, and then leans over and presses the length of his arm against mine.

"What are you doing?"

"I'm keeping my hands to myself. I wanted to hug you. Is this inappropriate?"

"No, a little awkward though. You're more cheerful than usual. Should I be worried?"

"You're so mean, Your Highness! I bring good news this time!"

"Really?"

"Bei Ling is showing signs of movement. The assault on Mount Chou may resume any day now!"

"How is that good news?"

"I've killed countless people but assassinations are not romantic. If there is going to be full-fledged war... It'll be like something out of a novel! This is my chance to become a great hero or to die honorably in battle defending the woman I love!"

"What is wrong with you?" Ignoring my protest, the silly person is brimming with excitement. "You can't control yourself around death and blood. It's better to keep you from battle."

"Are you afraid of my true nature, Your Highness?" Rolling his eyes to the ceiling, faint flushes of fearful expectations curl over his cheeks.

"No. You're the silliest person I've ever met. That is your true nature. The version of you that was groomed to kill is just a subset. Ultimately, no matter how you are or what moods you're in, I'm not afraid because I trust you, Kang Lang."

Eyes, widened from surprise, turn nervous. He remains silent for a time before nervousness breaks away to a grin. "You keep saying things like that and then scold me for not keeping my hands to myself. I think you're more sadistic than I am."

"I've learned much from you, Kang Lang."

We can't help but turn to one another and laugh; though, the moment is cut short when the door unexpectedly opens. San An enters; stern as ever. Anxiety and guilt abruptly wash over me.

"Your Highness, please come with me. You too, Kang Lang."

Without waiting for reply, the Minister leaves the room. Kang Lang and I scuttle after San An.

Chapter 31 – 2

As the door to San An's quarters opens, a familiar face smiles shyly from across the room. I can't believe it's him.

"Jin!" On impulse, my feet start forward; hindered immediately by rising embarrassment. We did not part on good terms. Becoming too friendly now would not be prudent. He may misunderstand, whether for good or ill.

San An realizes my hesitation, and even though I've injured him, continues to place my feelings before his own. Subtly, he signals to Kang Lang. "There are other matters we must discuss. Come with me."

Kang Lang nudges my arm and gives a knowing smile before following the Minister in tow. Finally, Jin and I are alone. It's a moment I've dreamt of and feared at once.

"It's been a while," Jin smiles weakly. "Have you been well?"

"Yes. How are you?"

"Fine."

Jin shuffles uneasily. He must feel awkward due to our previous encounter. Maybe, he thinks I'm upset.

"I'm really happy to see you back, Jin. Did you have a pleasant time in Xiong?"

"Yes. I met His Majesty right before returning."

"What? He Pi is alive?!" Rushing forth, my hands tug at Jin's sleeve. His smile widens into a perfect grin. I've never seen him this happy.

"Yes! We didn't have long to speak. He wanted me to relay a message to you."

"T-To me?"

"He said to tell you that... Don't take this the wrong way; these are his words, not mine." Jin's face turns beet-red. Clearing his throat, he continues. "He said when he returns, he will make you his woman."

"What?! I'll pound his face in if he has the nerve to try!" Who does He Pi think he is to say something like that to... well, to Jin to say to me!

"You haven't changed a bit, have you?" That boyish laugh is so charming, it warms my heart. "His Highness teases every woman. I'm sorry he couldn't spare you."

"Wait, did he come? Is he here?"

Jin's demeanor stiffens. Whilst staring at the floor, a heavy sigh falls. "No. He's returned to Bei Ling."

"What's he doing in Bei Ling? Never mind. I don't want to keep asking pointless questions. Can you tell me everything, from the top?"

He signals for me to sit and then takes the seat across the tea table. Jin removes the cord binding his hair and runs a hand over the long dark strands draping over his handsome face. Something about that face reminds me of San An and suddenly, heat rises to my visage.

"His Highness did not go into details about the reason he left. Apparently, he caught wind of the assault in the capital and decided to investigate. Oh, he thanks you for substituting for him and he apologizes for putting you in danger. He promises to repay you once he comes back."

"He doesn't need to do that."

"His Highness intends to repay you by making you his woman."

"Well, that'll happen over Mu Dan's dead body."

Jin chuckles softy and then forces a smile. "Speaking of Mu Dan, I see you two are on friendlier terms."

"Yes. Kang Lang is my dear friend. He's decided to give up Mu Dan."

"I see."

I thought he would be gladdened by this revelation. Instead, the countenance turns solemn. "Is something the matter, Jin?"

"I'm surprised, that's all." Jin forces a smile. "When His Highness first left for Bei Ling, he met with an underground faction known as the White Cranes. He's staying with them for now. They are of the mindset that power must be reclaimed for Cai Pai without Wang Liang's influences. His Highness believes that once Wang Liang is removed, Nan Rong's safety will become certain."

"How did he meet these people? What exactly are they planning? Cai Pai is still a child. He'll just become a puppet under a new master."

"His Highness trusts that the White Cranes will put Cai Pai in capable hands. Apparently, ever since Wang Liang's grip around the child emperor deepened, Bei Ling's political, social, and economic struggles have increased tenfold. Everything he's done has pushed Bei Ling to prepare for war. He's confiscated supplies and funds from rich and poor, drafted every man available, even ripped children away from their families to join training regiments, and terrorized the other court members into submission. Bei Ling may look to Cai Pai, but Wang Liang holds all authorities. As to your first question, I really don't know. We did not have much time to converse. He knew I would be in Xiong at the time, which was the reason he came."

"Have you told San An?"

"Yes, the Prime Minister is aware."

"Did he tell you Wang Liang is Su Jian?"

"Su Jian?"

"Su Jian, Consort Wu's child with Emperor Jin. He's... your brother."

He leans back in the chair. Jin's startled reaction carries with it, fright. "My... brother."

"Yes. Unlike your brothers here at court, he's... well, actually, besides from the obvious reason, I'm not sure what he wishes to accomplish. If he's willing to raise a sword against his own blood—against you and San An—he must be removed."

Jin's eyes glaze over, lost in thoughts or perhaps, lost in time in recollection of old memories. I understand his dilemma. He doesn't want to see another brother die. I doubt it can be helped this time. Su Jian must have plotted this for years while making his way to power. He's not going to retreat over some kind words. As much as I am against causing Jin pain, if there is a chance, I would not hesitate to dispose of Wang Liang.

"Jin, does He Pi know?"

"He did not say. Whether that was due to ignorance or just to spare me from anxiety, I'm not certain. What else has happened since I've been gone?"

"Where to begin? Ning has promised to give Nan Rong support against Bei Ling and Wen Meng, the bandit of Mount Chou, has joined the council. Oh, and, San An disbanded the Circle."

"His Highness will be disappointed! What made the Prime Minister do that?"

"One of the courtesans from Bei Ling attempted to take my life after the assassin targeted Cai Pai. Wait! The assassin who injured San An was sent by Su Jian and Su Jian is Wang Liang. Cai Pai is under Wang Liang's protection. What if we find Ying and convince him to betray Su Jian? That'll prove that the prime minister of Bei Ling ordered the attack on Bei Ling's emperor. Surely, we can convince their generals and ministers to remove Wang Liang. Nan Rong will not have to endure war."

"Finding the assassin won't be easy. Plus, I'm afraid at this point, Wang Liang's hold over Bei Ling is too strong. We'd need more than the words of an assassin."

"I guess you're right. Besides, San An's probably considered that."

"Maybe. Tell me, an attempt was made on your life after I left?"

"Oh. Yes. I'm fine though, obviously. Kang Lang saved me."

"Kang Lang?" Solemnity returns and then slowly softens to something sweeter. Jin reaches across the table for my hand and squeezes tightly. "I'm sorry that I wasn't here to protect you. Twice now, your life was in danger and I couldn't do anything for you."

"Don't apologize. It was my fault for being careless. I should have known better. Anyway, you saved me the first time, remember?"

"I didn't do much of anything."

"That's not true, Jin. You've done a lot for me since my arrival. I'm glad we're friends. I hope we can continue to be friends long after everything is resolved."

"Why wouldn't we? You sound as though you plan to leave."

He smiles but I can't return the gesture. I have to leave; there's no doubt. Angst causes a brief withdrawal. His grip on my hand tautens.

"Bao Lai, *will* you leave when this is over?"

"With He Pi's return, I won't be needed. Not unless he wants to keep a body double."

"For everything you've accomplished, His Highness will not mind keeping you here."

"Well, I haven't done much of anything except cause problems for everyone. Besides, I don't belong here."

"What will you do? Return home, marry, and start a family?"

"Uh... I'm not sure. I haven't thought that far."

"It's not safe for a young woman to live alone. You should have someone with you. *I* would be..."

Faint colors emerge from deep within his cheeks just as a jolt erupts in my heart. He doesn't continue and his attention is cast to the table. I thought Jin doesn't see me that way. Is he actually proposing to come with me?

"I'm sorry," he mutters.

"Why are you apologizing? You did nothing wrong."

Jin glances up but finds it difficult to resume. Even though I'm terribly curious, conscience warns against pushing further.

Thankfully, San An and Kang Lang return to break the awkward moment. With other matters to discuss, San An and Jin stay in the room while Kang Lang and I depart. Once we are in the halls, his tongue clicks. Kang Lang turns to me.

"Hmm... I saw Jin holding your hand. Are you trying to kill poor San An?"

"Don't even joke like that! It wasn't anything serious."

"For you, maybe. Jin was adorable! He was fighting with himself to confess something. From the startled expression, I can easily guess."

"Don't be ridiculous. Jin doesn't see me that way."

"I can't tell whether you're naïve or in denial. I don't like it either way."

"We were discussing He Pi. He's been found. Well, more like, he found Jin. Did San An tell you? You aren't very excited. You should be. He might decide to make you empress after all."

"I only want the title while you are He Pi."

"Me? Why? I have no real authority."

"Because then *we'd* be married, silly! You're so dense!"

"Oh."

"What do you mean, 'Oh?' Anyway, I *am* happy he's alive. He's sure to have some exciting tales to tell. And, just to let you know, we'll be spending much more time together from now on."

"Why's that?"

"Can't you pretend to be a little more enthused?"

"Sorry. We're together every day. How much more time could we be spending?"

"I'm been given special permissions by the Prime Minister to sleep in your room, bathe you, feed you, dress you, and so forth. I'll be the first and last person you'll see every day."

"Really? Why would San An give you those permissions?"

Kang Lang returns my frown with a mischievous grin. "He's assigned me as your bodyguard. So, while I'm guarding you, your body is mine."

"You were doing so well, Kang Lang. Vulgarity is not appreciated. More importantly, why would the Minister assign you such a position?"

"If war comes, you'll need to make appearances on the battlefield to rally morale. No one wants to fight for a faceless leader. He Pi and the White Cranes will strike Bei Ling from the inside and you are expected to lead the charge from the frontline. No worries. I will protect you with my life."

"I see. What you mean to say is, San An's assigned you as my babysitter."

"Yes, you're my baby!" Kang Lang reaches over and pinches both my cheeks. "Stop frowning! You know I hate it when you frown. I see his motive though, don't you?"

"What do you mean? And stop pinching, my face is numb!" Jerking my head away, I smack his hands. Kang Lang then links our arms together and saunters down the hall.

"Assigning me to be by your side; he wants you to be happy. That is to say, he thinks we're in love. I suppose he's half right. If only one of us weren't too damn stubborn to fall for the handsome assassin!"

"San An needs to focus on San An instead of bothering with me."

"I can't believe after everything I've done, you choose Jin. And here I thought I knew you well."

"You're wrong. I'm not choosing anyone. When this is over, I'll take my leave."

"Why would you choose to live as a commoner when I know He Pi would not refuse to make you a princess? You're so boring sometimes. Oh well, I guess I don't have a choice. When you leave, I'll go with you. "

"You will? I thought you'd *rather die* than leave the palace!"

"Don't be sarcastic! You're telling me you won't choose anyone but I know you're really saying you choose me, since none of the others can follow. Wouldn't hurt for me to try living as a peasant for once."

"You're awfully presumptuous. Who said I'd let you come?"

"You know you can't resist me. I'm too beautiful."

His vain declarations flutter airily. A smile immediately breaks across my face.

"You sound exactly like Han Bei!"

Kang Lang gasps deeply in offense while my index finger digs into his cheek. Playfully grinning at the silly person, I run down the corridor and he gives chase.

Chapter 32: A Third Confession

Next door, Kang Lang has retired for the night. San An really did send him to guard me. I wonder whether it's because I'm He Pi or as Kang Lang said, he's pushing me into the arms of his believed rival. I want to tell San An the truth. I want him to know I can't stay in Nan Rong once this ordeal is over. The question remains, when will this conflict end? It could last months or even years. War means death and no one is above exception.

Life is short. Shouldn't I live recklessly and do whatever makes me happy? Yet, my happiness would only mean distraction and that's the last thing anyone needs right now. If I live by obligations, then I chance dying without ever having truly lived. Which is worse? What should I do? I thought I've decided but I'm in doubt of everything.

Despite these jumbled feelings, I keep seeing an obscured face in my mind. I cannot ascertain who it is that haunts me. More than anything in the world, I know he is the one I wish to stand by, the one I've been waiting to meet all my life, and the one I would not hesitate to give body and soul if he will have me. Whose reflection is this?

A soft knock at the door cuts short my anxiety. Jin quietly enters the room, appearing absolutely nervous.

"Sorry, I shouldn't disturb you at this hour but I saw light under the door."

"It's fine. Is something the matter?"

Lifting from the bed, I pay Jin full attention. His gaze averts. "No. We didn't quite finish our conversation earlier. I was going to bring your dinner but the Prime Minister insists that Kang Lang is your caretaker now."

"Yes, that's true. You don't need to look after me anymore, Jin. Thank you for everything you've done."

Inhaling sharply, he upturns a glance. The expression is of confusion, sadness, and frustration.

"Is this your response, Bao Lai? Do you want me to go away?"

"Of course not. You've just arrived."

"That's not what I meant." His voice trails away.

I'm such a dolt! It took a moment more to grasp the intention. He's wounded by my carelessness. Still, he rejected me. Why bring it up now?

"Jin. We're friends. I want us to always be friends."

"Friends… Is that all we are? I've only been away for a month and everything's changed. Was it how I left things between us that caused this spiral?"

"You didn't do anything wrong. I'm just… a bad person."

"No, you're not. I shouldn't have been a coward. All I could do was think of you after leaving, and then I realized I wanted nothing more than to have answered your confession. It was cruel to have just walked away. Even if you will not accept me now, I want you to know my reply."

"Jin, you don't have to do that. Don't tell me things you can't take back."

My stomach's in a knot and my heart wrenches in pain. I start up to stop him. I can't let him do this to himself. I can't let him suffer like San An!

"I forgive you for not having answered me. Really! Some things are better left unsaid."

"No, I must say this. I owe you this much."

"You don't owe me anything! And, you certainly shouldn't feel obligated to answer me favorably because it's in your nature to be kind."

"I would never mistake obligations for affections." He replies candidly.

"Just think it over! What could I possibly have done to make you happy? I've made you miserable since the day we've met! Isn't it possible you're just trying to be a gentleman to someone who's hardly a lady?"

"Bao Lai..." The tone signals that he couldn't care less for my protest. His mind is made up. The loving glance is one I've seen before. More than anything, I just want to erupt in tears.

"Don't say it!" Grabbing his arm, I beg with every part of my expression for him to relinquish the thought.

Jin is determined. "Bao Lai, I love you."

His words feel no less than knives plunging deep into my heart. Useless tears begin flowing, which merely begs the gentleman in him to offer a shoulder and a tender embrace. This isn't right! Gently, my arms push away. The embrace grows more ardent. Jin draws me in deeper. Nostalgia is becoming unbearable! I've dreamt of this moment for so long, that it's felt a lifetime ago. All I feel now when the dream has come true is sorrow and heartache.

"You're making a mistake!"

The more I plea for him to come to his senses, the more Jin loses himself in the moment. His lips flutter across my cheek. A part of me wishes to stay this way, enveloped in his loving arms forever. How selfish is the thought! He's been injured enough. I can't allow this to continue!

As I attempt to withdraw, his hold tightens. Softly, Jin whispers the words that make me grow cold. "You promised to love me however I want. Did you forget?"

I hadn't forgotten, but at the time of my oath, I did not consider for that love to exist beyond friendship. Yet, another promise I must break to someone undeserving of my mendacity.

"It was my fault for running away. I shouldn't have been a coward. If you no longer want my affections, say the word and I'll speak of it no more. However, I want to give you a promise as well, that I'll love you however you want me to and I will do so without question."

One last strong embrace and then Jin releases me. Though his face is flushed, he's smiling all the same. I know he's hiding sorrow. Satisfying my curiosity won't make things better for either of us. I might as well return the gesture and accept things as they are.

"Jin, first and foremost, we need to help He Pi remove Wang Liang. There's too much at stake right now to focus on wants and desires. I suppose what I mean is, don't wait for me. I won't lie and say I don't love you, but I am saying I can't be with you. I hate lying to you, Jin. This is the truth."

"I will respect your request. Just know that I come back to you now as a changed man. Until I hear the words, I won't give up."

Jin does not permit enough time to give a response before quitting the room. I think I made another mistake. Should I have just lied and said I don't want him? Is honesty a cruel thing to employ? Though Jin shouldn't love me in this manner; I still want him nearby. Selfish, selfish desires!

Chapter 33: For Lack of Reason

A few days pass by and the single person who comes to my side is Kang Lang. As much as I want to see San An and Jin, I don't have anything worth saying to them. This face of He Pi—or maybe, this face of mine—only serves to cause dissonance and nothing more.

As usual, Kang Lang saunters in after the council meeting with a wide grin. Before I can ask, he throws both arms around me.

"We're going to war!" He sings happily. Immediately, I dart up. Kang Lang pulls me back down. "Preparations are still being made. You can't just charge into Bei Ling by yourself, silly."

"Tell me what's happened!" I shake him severely. His sole reaction is to widen that irritating grin. I push again.

"I just did. We're going to war. Han Bei returned to Ning for reinforcements, Jin left days ago to join He Pi in Bei Ling, and Wen Meng is gathering his peons to act as first line defense on Mount Chou. Likely this time, they won't bother from that side. They'll probably take the Lan Yue Pass by way of Feng Jia. San An and the others are preparing to march any day now. So, as Nan Rong's substitute leader, you'll need to prepare."

"Jin left? When exactly did he leave? Why would San An prepare for the march? He's the prime minister.

He's not supposed to fight! And, what do you mean they're going through Feng Jia? I thought this was between Nan Rong and Bei Ling!"

"So many questions! Okay, I'll humor you." Kang Lang lies on the bed and tilts over a grin. His inability to take this seriously frustrates me to no end.

"Jin left in the mid of night after his love confession. Yes, I heard everything next door. Don't frown. It's not my fault. You people should learn to lower your voices. San An is prepared to do battle because of you, isn't that obvious? And lastly, knowing that Nan Rong earned Ning's alliance, Bei Ling has gathered support from Ye and Feng Jia. That is to say, those two lands will not participate in battle but through claiming neutrality, they're allowing Bei Ling to enter their territories and gain different access points to the South."

"How was Wang Liang able to manage that?"

"The same way he's able to accomplish anything: by bullying others. He truly was born in the wrong country. If he were in Ning, he might be emperor."

"You're impressed?"

"Of course. It takes a strong man to kill and a smart one to make others kill for his authority. It is unfortunate this Su Jian is clever. He will be that much more difficult to depose."

"I never thought *you* would know intimidation, Kang Lang."

"Don't be silly. I like a challenge. Still, I can't be reckless with you as my charge. I will protect you, Bao Lai."

"Stop saying that! I don't want you to protect me and I don't want San An to go to battle for my sake! What is wrong with all of you? Why are you in love with me? I don't grasp the reason and I can't stand it!"

As I bury my face in my hands, Kang Lang draws me tightly into his arms. The embrace is warm and comforting. Slowly, his hand strokes my head as though I were a child. For whatever reason, it calms me.

"Don't ask stupid questions. I won't assume why the others love you. I love you because I just do."

"That's a stupid reason!" Jerking back, I move to the edge of the bed.

"Why is that a stupid reason? Which reason would make my affections, or anyone's affections, valid?"

San An once asked me something similar. He's declared that love doesn't need to be based on any particular reason; else, it would be too mechanical. Maybe he's right. However, a reason is better than no reason at all, isn't it?

"Kang Lang, if there isn't a reason to love, does that mean falling out of love can happen just as quickly?"

He shrugs and sits up. Then, removing He Pi's crown from my head, begins braiding my hair. "If you need a reason to do something, then maybe you don't really want to do it. Just because there's a reason to love someone doesn't mean that you will or that you'll be in love with that person forever. Love and loyalty are two different things. Some people stay because of loyalty and not love. Some people have no loyalty and still love ardently. I like being with you for no reason at all. So, I want to be useful to you. That is *my* choice. Someday, when I don't want to remain by your side, then I'll leave. In the meantime, don't bother with reasons. Pedantic people are boring. If you bore me, I'll leave sooner."

"I thought two people fall in love because they support each other in ways no others can. Why would you love me when I can't do anything for you?"

Kang Lang bursts into delirious guffaws. Grabbing onto my shoulders, he gently shakes them while kissing the back of my head. "You're so silly! Where did you read that from? If you have to be useful for me to love you, that's no different from you trying to buy my affections. Contrary to what you may think, I'm not that kind of girl!"

Giggling, he flings both arms around my shoulders. "Besides, under the premise that you must find a particular someone to support you, then there's only one person in the world who would be capable. The fact is love is all about location. The nearest person with the closest qualifications, so to say."

"That's a sad notion, Kang Lang."

"Why? Do you think in the entire world, soul mates are born in the same villages or towns? Most people marry those in the same vicinity, whether out of love or loyalty, or maybe just convenience. When you can find someone who attracts your attention and keeps you wanting theirs, it's much more exhilarating than to search for reasons. Reasons are obligations; debts, perhaps. My mother used to say, people marry because they are fated this lifetime for debts owed in past lives. I say life is to build debts, not pay off accruements from another lifetime. Does that make sense?"

"I think so. I still don't understand why you're attracted to me. You've been in the Peony Palace with the most beautiful women of all five lands. Why aren't you attached to any of them?"

"You're still looking for reasons. Because they are beautiful, I *must* want them? I'm more beautiful than all those harpies!" Mu Dan surfaces in the resentful tone.

I can't help but smile. "Sometimes, I think you just like to tease me, Kang Lang."

"I do. Now, I like to be serious with you, as well. I won't tell you how to live your life. Just know that I'll stay with you until the end."

"You don't have to say it like that! I admit I'm no match for the likes of you and the generals, but I'm not *that* helpless. I can swing a weapon just fine! Don't risk your life for my sake! I'm not worth it. Save your strength for He Pi!"

"Your self-loathing is insufferable." Kang Lang whispers indolently. "If you don't stop, I'll have to give you a bit more courage."

"What is that supposed to mean?"

"You're being a silly girl. Allow me to turn you into a woman. Then, you'll release all your childish anxieties." His seductive tone is accompanied by kisses against the base of my neck. On impulse, I turn around and take hold of his cheeks. Tears mist over his pretty eyes.

"I'm sorry! I'm sorry! Let go!"

"Did you learn your lesson?"

"Yes, Your Highness!"

Kang Lang rubs his face as my grip softens. Soon after, he grins.

"I love it when you force me to obedience, Your Highness! I've never allowed a woman to dominate me but I'm willing to give you that right."

I have nothing to say to that. Not knowing how to respond, I leave the room frowning and Kang Lang saunters after.

Chapter 34: A Chance to be Useful

In the following week, Bei Ling sent a small group to Mount Chou in order to distract Nan Rong from the larger force, which was sent to Lan Yue Pass by way of Feng Jia. Wen Meng and his bandits easily routed the diversion and the first regiment, led by Bai Hu and Zhen Yue, pushed back Bei Ling's larger force.

Outside in the streets, the people rejoiced. Inside the palace, the atmosphere is somber. It has now been a week since the event. I was summoned to San An's quarters with Kang Lang. The Prime Minister is reviewing several documents when we arrive.

"Good, you're both here." San An shuffles the papers aside. Without pleasantries, the Minister begins. "There isn't much time, so I'll be brief. Bei Ling's first attempt was merely to test our preparedness. There's word that another march will likely occur through Ye's Tian Sheng Mountain Path. However, scouts have also seen activities from several other points. We don't have enough soldiers to divide our army and hope for victory. We must discern where their main forces lie.

Lord Han Bei has not returned from Ning. All the same, we cannot depend solely on our eastern ally for victory. I will attempt to persuade Ye's leaders to rescind the neutrality pact with Bei Ling. What that means is I will be away from the capital. The council is single-minded in their desire to charge directly into the northern territory. If it cannot be helped, Kang Lang, you must take Bao Lai to Ning. You have connections there to protect her, don't you? Do not put her in danger by sending our false He Pi to the front. I feel that the moment a direct attack begins, the only thing it will accomplish is to have our main forces surrounded. Our small army will scatter in an instant."

"San An, you can't enter Ye! It's too dangerous!" The way he speaks makes me think he doesn't expect to return and he's entrusting me to Kang Lang. I thought he was a careful man. Truly, he's reckless and he's putting me above himself again. It's infuriating!

"I must go. We need every advantage we can afford. Ye is complying with Bei Ling through fear. The greater fear they must realize is how expendable they will become once we fall. Neutrality is a joke before conquest."

"Bei Ling will not tolerate interference. They won't permit you to waltz into Ye without resistance."

"I'm not a man without some talents, Bao Lai. Through the previous wars at court, I was able to gain experience regarding infiltration and averting danger." San An forces a weak smile.

I can't accept it. "I won't let you go, San An. Even should you manage to sneak by their guards, Ye's leaders are more than likely under watch. How can you have any influence when fear is keeping them?"

"I will do what I must." The Prime Minister replies succinctly; signaling for no further contentions.

I hate it when he brushes me off and I hate it when he volunteers to put himself in danger without any guarantee of success! I trust him when he's thinking clearly. This time, I know he's pulling desperately at invisible strings.

"I will go, San An. Without He Pi, you are Nan Rong."

"You know I cannot allow that!" His brows furrow. Ardent pain stains every piece of composure. "It is less conspicuous for me to go. He Pi will be killed on sight; without hesitation."

Kang Lang, who has been sitting quietly for the duration of our conversation, suddenly rises and interjects on my behalf. "It is indeed troublesome to send He Pi. Bao Lai is insignificant. Why not send her?"

"That's right! I can do it, San An!"

"And I'll be near to protect her," Kang Lang grins.

The Minister glances in our direction. Clearly, he is displeased. "I thought you love her, Kang Lang. Why so quick to put the woman you love in danger?"

"I want her to be happy. She won't be if you die. As skilled as you are, Prime Minister, you won't succeed. There's one thing that remains to be true: men, no matter in which dire situations they are in and no matter their dispositions, cannot help but be swayed by beauty. Of the five lands, Ye has the largest Circle and yet, their leaders are never satisfied. We can easily pass for courtesans. I will use my connections to find our way in."

"She is not Mu Dan. I forbid her virtues to be tainted for the sake of compromise."

"You insult me, sir!" Kang Lang gripes irritably. "If you think I'll allow unwanted hands to touch her, you're wrong."

"Please, San An, let me do this! I trust Kang Lang!"

"And you do not trust me?"

I understand his frustration, but must he twist everything I say? Kang Lang is little bothered. Following a smirk, the blithe man replies with ease.

"You're an imbecile. Of course, she doesn't trust you when you're willingly throwing your life away for her. Live for Bao Lai, then, she might reconsider. She's just like you—so quick to depression and always wanting to be useful. You're both stubborn asses!"

"Kang Lang!"

He grins when I forcibly tug at his arm. How is insulting San An going to earn his compliance? Yet, as the thought crosses my mind, the Minister reenters conversation.

"Were I to permit this nonsense, Bao Lai is not the most eloquent diplomat we can send, while you are not much use except for seducing weak men."

"Do you hear how he insults us, Your Highness?" With both hands on his hips, Kang Lang pouts boyishly. "As ineloquent as she is, you couldn't help but fall for this commoner, *Prince San An*. Surely, she has some charms that even your cold nature can't resist. With my guidance, we'll succeed."

San An can't deny it. Following a moment of contemplation, he ventures a direct stare into my eyes. "Bao Lai. Is this your wish? I don't support this decision. You know I can't stand the thought of you in danger. If it is your will to trust Kang Lang, I won't deny you."

For once, he's actually agreed to let me help. Knowing that San An will be safe, I inadvertently smile though, it merely provokes him to further discontentment. Without allowing another word to be exchanged, Kang Lang drags me from the room.

Chapter 35: A Ploy for Diplomacy

Once we are alone in my chamber, I finally think it's safe to bring up the troubling subject.

"How exactly are we going to convince Ye to rescind their neutrality pact with Bei Ling? I understand we must infiltrate their palace, but what then?"

"I will clear the path for you to meet with Ye's emperor." Kang Lang replies factually.

"What am I supposed to say? 'Stop helping Bei Ling or I'll punch your face in?'"

"I'd pay good money to see that," Kang Lang guffaws. "Well, my idea is simpler. Everyone finds your androgynous version of He Pi attractive. When given the chance, present yourself as His Highness."

"Doesn't their leader prefer women? Han Bei's attraction was by pure chance. I don't think it'll have much effect on Emperor Neng Cao."

"Don't be dense. Ye is terrified of Bei Ling. What would Neng Cao think when He Pi himself traverses past all the guards to meet him in person? He'll have more faith in us or at least, less fear of Bei Ling. The rest is up to you. Turn that charm of yours on him."

"I don't know what charm you're talking about!"

"That charm! Randomly becoming angry, it's endearing!"

"To you, maybe."

"I'm a man, too." He raises an eyebrow. "No one likes a boring woman but one that's as cute as He Pi with an innocent disposition is naturally charming, especially when she confuses men who think she's their gender."

"That doesn't make any sense!"

"See? Randomly getting angry. So cute!"

He pinches my cheeks. I slap away his hands. "You're crazy. I guess it doesn't matter. I have to succeed. For Nan Rong."

"You mean for San An? This is to protect him, right?"

There's no point denying it. I'd do anything to stop San An from walking into trouble. Yet, at the same time, I'm putting Kang Lang in danger. I'm being selfish and I'm using him again.

"Kang Lang, just help me pass the border. I can do the rest alone."

Returning a sour look, Kang Lang lets out a scoff. "If you die, San An will kill me, anyway. I'll take my chances in Ye."

"Are you afraid of San An?"

"He doesn't look it but San An is quite the fencer. Besides that, you know I won't leave you, so save your breath.   It's not my first time infiltrating Ye and certainly not my first time in their palace. Last time, I killed one of their ministers. I forget which one."

He talks about assassinations as casually as one would recall taking a stroll. I keep overlooking that under his usual teasing self is a man of great skills; however frightening those skills may be. I do trust Kang Lang but I'm still anxious for him. Seeing my hesitation, he sighs deeply and falls onto the bed.

"Don't worry so much. I'm doing this because I want to. If anything happens, it's not your fault."

"That's not it at all! It's not a matter of faults! I don't want you to get hurt!"

"Why, do you love me?"   His usual grin is accompanied by sarcasm.   Why can't he take this seriously? Then again, maybe he's right.

"Yes, I do love you."

Eyes grow wide; Kang Lang darts up. However, realizing the meaning behind my words, Kang Lang frowns and pokes my forehead.

"You're evil!"

"Yes. I admit it. I love you dearly as my friend. I'm bound to be worried."

"I'm sick of that word... friend. Whatever." He grumbles noisily and then stretches down onto the bed. "Come over here and sleep, *friend*. We'll leave first thing tomorrow."

"Shouldn't you go back to your room?"

"Why? I'm already here. A girl doesn't work for free!" Patting the spot nearby, Mu Dan's voice invites me to join. Honestly, I don't mind as long as nothing strange happens. It is Kang Lang, so I may be too optimistic.

"You *know* you want to spend the night with me." The wink that follows his seductive voice makes me laugh. He's incredibly childish!

"Well, I would be lying to say that I've never wondered what a night with you would be like." In saying so, I lie next to Kang Lang.

Not liking my sarcasm, he sulks and turns his back to me. "If you're going to come into bed making jokes, don't expect anything from me."

I turn my back to him and pull up the covers. His usual warmth calms my anxiety. In due time, we fall into deep slumber.

Chapter 36: A Trip to Ye

Early in the morning, Kang Lang and I left the palace on one horse and headed west. At sundown the border village of Xi Mai came into view, and then under the cover of night, Kang Lang skillfully navigated safely inside Ye. It would take another day for us to reach Ye's capital of Liang Bi.

"Don't look so scared, you'll draw attention." Kang Lang whispers softly as we stroll down the market.

Tonight, his contact will help us infiltrate the palace. For now, we have some free time. I wanted to remain at the inn but my counterpart thought fresh air would help ease my tension and also give him a chance to survey our obstacles. As we stroll, I hold tightly onto his arm. Every so often, Kang Lang, in the borrowed disguise, would lean down and pretends to whisper words of love while inspecting the city's layout.

"I'm sorry. I didn't think Bei Ling would have this many guards here."

"Yes, we can expect that the number inside is far greater. Turn this way for a moment. I think that's a good route to use later."

Kang Lang slightly twists my position southwest and then same as before, leans down slowly whilst inspecting the scene from an angle. This time, a man in unique armors makes his way over. He doesn't appear a soldier but he is wearing Bei Ling's colors. The eyes on his narrow face are like those of a hawk. Upon viewing the colors, I realize his identity.

"Who are you?" The hard tone causes me to wince. Kang Lang frowns without the slightest intimidation. I pray this man doesn't recognize us. "You've been spying on the guards for a while now. Did you think I wouldn't notice?"

That sharp, piercing gaze of his infuriates me. This is the man who'd injured San An!

"I'm with my beautiful wife. It's our honeymoon. Why would I spy on your ugly guards?" Kang Lang answers in a voice different from his usual personas. I grasp he's concealing his identity; though, it may not be enough to fool the assassin, Ying.

Ying's expression tautens. His fingers slide ever so slightly toward the blade at his hip. "Don't take me for a fool, boy! You were looking at your wife but your attention was elsewhere."

My heart rate quickens. Ying's charges are drawing in the attention of other Bei Ling soldiers. I must do something!

Play along (Continue to page 385)

Defend Kang Lang (Continue to page 389)

Chapter 36 – 2

"You were doing it again?!" Throwing down Kang Lang's arm, I step between him and Ying. With both hands on my hips, the thought of Mu Dan takes over my persona. "You lecherous man! I told you to keep your eyes in your head! How many times do I have to say it? I'm *your wife*! You're only supposed to look at me, not these ugly harpies! You promised you'd stop once we are married! Did you lie to me?"

"I-I'm sorry, my dear." Kang Lang chuckles nervously while scratching the back of his head. "Old habits die hard. Forgive me?"

The boyish smile is charming and ostensibly sincere. His handsome face captivates my attention for a moment and then, giggles bursts in the manner I've heard him done so many times before. Throwing my arms around his body, I squeeze with all my strength. "I forgive you!"

Kang Lang smiles in relief. Just when I thought tension would end, the opportunist leans down and presses a kiss so severely that I feel warm all over. The display irks the other man. Ying, scoffing impatiently, leaves us while the remaining soldiers disperse. Following a long, passionate moment, my *husband* finally moves away. We stroll with arms linked back to the inn.

Once inside, Kang Lang sweeps me off my feet and lies down on the bed. The sweet embrace grows more fervent. He moves atop and pins down my hands.

"Did he follow us?" I whisper into his ear as Kang Lang leans down and runs burning lips over my neck.

"No," he replies gently.

"Then, what the hell are you doing?!"

"Calm down! What did you expect after *that* display? If you're going to call yourself my wife, I want my dues as your husband."

"You started it!"

This reminds me of our time together when we first met. Back then, I was so afraid of this silly person. If only I'd known then, I would have teased him into submission. Kang Lang glares back as though having read my thought. At once, we burst into laughter.

Lying down beside me, he draws my entirety into a loving embrace. San An would be angry by my lack of resistance. I just don't feel a need to retaliate. Perhaps, I'm so used to Kang Lang's arms that it's natural to stay with him this way.

"Do you think he still suspects us?"

"As long as he doesn't see us in the market again, there's no need to worry. I never thought Ying would be here instead of Bei Ling. Normally, at this point, Wang Liang should fear for his life and keep his best resource close. This Su Jian is either an idiot or he's overconfident. Either way, he's really troublesome." Sighing heavily, Kang Lang continues. "Anyway, quick thinking back there. After six years of living in the Circle, I've lost my touch. If it weren't for you, I might not be here right now."

"We make a good team! I've learned more from you than anyone. Besides, you've saved me plenty of times. I'm just glad I could be useful for once."

The room falls silent without his response. Kang Lang's countenance is utterly serious.

"Kang Lang, is something the matter?"

"No." The concise answer is somewhat cold. His eyes glide to my face but they lack the usual warmth.

"Did I say something wrong?"

"Don't be absurd." Taking a deep breath, he smiles sadly. "I wonder had I met you first, would you have loved me? Or, was it how we met that made you closed your mind to the idea of me?"

"Now is not the time to discuss this, considering our task at hand."

"I'm not as strong as I used to be and I've never been on these missions with another I want to protect so dearly. Should I happen to fail, you need to escape without me. But if things do come to that, I want you to know my affections."

"I'm not leaving Ye without you! And, I do know your affections!"

"You just don't take me seriously."

"I do! I just... can't return your feelings."

"You can't or you won't?"

Why must he keep pushing his love for me when it causes him so much pain? I feel terrible for hurting him. Maybe, he's right.   If we had met under different circumstances—in my old life as a recluse—there is no doubt I would give him everything. At current times, it's not possible. He's risking his life to make me happy and I can't do anything for him. Guilt overflows and still, I can't find the right words.

Pushing through heartache, a gentle hand strokes my face. He softly sighs. "Just stay with me this way until night comes."

His sweet touch twists my heart into a knot. A flush of emotions overwhelms conscience. I hold onto him desperately, praying that he'll never float away. What is this strange feeling taunting me in the back of my mind? I keep pushing away the horrid thought but it keeps coming back. I don't want to think it! I fear this may be the last time we are together this way.

Continue to page 390

Chapter 36 – 3

I step between Ying and Kang Lang.

"Where do you get off harassing us this way? He was looking at me! We were just taking a stroll, so mind your own business!"

Ying studies my face intently; his lips purse from discontentment. Around us, many civilians gather. They, too, are irritated by Bei Ling's overbearing intrusions and begin sneering at the foreign soldiers. Attention is the last thing an assassin wants. Ying's hand grudgingly absconds from the blade. Sharp eyes redirect toward Kang Lang.

"Keep your woman in line. If I catch you both here again, I won't be so kind."

Kang Lang and I link arms and stroll back to the inn.

Continue to page 398

Chapter 37: The Cowardly Emperor

We met Kang Lang's contact at the designated time and made our way inside to one of the empty rooms. Dressed as courtesans, Mu Dan and I started for Neng Cao's quarters. Though the path was littered with guards, we were able to pass through with ease due to Mu Dan's practiced charms. With a sweet smile, a flutter of lashes, and a light touch on the arm, every man who stopped us believed Mu Dan's story of our summons to comfort Neng Cao.

Upon reaching His Highness's chamber door, consternation turns my feet to stone when the last person I expected is standing as the lone guard. Without one fraction of doubt, Mu Dan charges forthwith, pulling me along.

"Who goes there?" Ying reaches for his blade.

"How rude!" Mu Dan steps forward to divide Ying from me. "We were sent to comfort His Majesty for the recent stress he's had to endure with you Bei Ling soldiers running rampant in our palace. Let us through!"

Ying frowns; his hand is still on the sword's hilt. "No one may enter. Go back to your Circle, woman."

Gasping from offense, Mu Dan's hands fly to his hips. "I will not! And, don't call me, 'woman!' I'm clearly a lady!"

"I see a harlot and nothing more. This is your last warning. Go back to the Circle now or I'll send you back in pieces." Ying begins drawing out the blade.

"Sir! Wait!" Pulling Mu Dan back, I step in between. "My friend is a little overzealous about meeting His Highness. I'm sorry for the trouble."

Despite his dangerous profession, Ying must have a sense of compassion because the nervous plea stalls his hand. For a long moment thereafter, Ying studies my face intently. Out of fear that he might recognize me from earlier in the market, my gaze lowers to the floor. His hand abruptly leaves the sword. Ying reaches out and lifts up my painted face.

"Do I know you?" Tilting his head, Ying scans me from different angles.

"N-No. I don't think so. I would never forget eyes as unique and beautiful as yours, sir."

A nervous smile returns his scrutiny. Suddenly, his narrow face turns marginally pink.

"You're just a girl. Why are you here with the likes of these *experienced* women?" He leers at Mu Dan. The latter pouts.

"I came to help those who matter to me, sir. I'm not a talented person. There's very little else I can do, and since I have nothing to my name, no man will want me. I would not have come to the Circle had life provided other opportunities."

The touch of his hand becomes increasingly warm; bony fingers linger on my face. I can't believe I'm practically flirting with this dangerous man and it's actually having an impact! When did I learn to become this person?

Pulling away shyly, I give a small smile and then stare at the floor. "I'm sorry. I shouldn't burden you with my troubles."

"Why do you keep looking down? Are you hiding something?" The hardened tone throws my breathing into variations.

"I'm... nervous. You're just so handsome and gallant, I thought maybe... No! Forgive my impertinence!"

Making a low bow, I spin around. He takes hold of my wrist. When I turn back, Ying withdraws and flusters. "I apologize! I would never casually put my hands on a lady... You're not being impertinent. What did you want to ask me?"

"I cannot ask it of you, sir! We've only just met. What rights do I have to *beg* you to save me from a courtesan's humiliation? I know a man with your honor would indeed, under different circumstances, defend mine. I only hope in the next life we can meet again. By any grace, I will have earned the privilege to serve you then."

Colors on his face deepen. Sharp eyes dart furiously as once more, I take my leave. After Mu Dan and I cross a short portion of the hall, I slightly turn back and cast a longing look. Taking the glance as encouragement, Ying marches forward and offers to play escort back to the Circle.

"There are too many ill-minded men in these halls. It's not safe to wander unprotected. Please, allow me."

I accept the offer and link our arms together. Not more than three steps are taken when Ying groans and falls to the floor. Mu Dan is standing behind, holding a tiny needle.

"Did-Did you...?"

"No, the cad and I have unfinished business. He'll be asleep for a while. This is precaution I brought. If they find a dead body, everyone will be alarmed. A sleeping soldier, they'll likely attribute to drinking. Anyway, there's no time to discuss but after we leave, there's much I want to say to you. Go on, I'll deal with Ying."

Once changed into He Pi's garment outside of the door, I slip into the chamber. At the unexpected visit, Neng Cao startles to his feet. I didn't think Ye's emperor is a young man, too. The lands are now truly in the hands of youths.

"Who are you?" A tremulous voice accompanies his tremulous disposition. He is so thin and frail, no wonder Wang Liang easily intimidated Ye.

"Please, forgive my intrusion, Your Highness. We must speak. He Pi of Nan Rong stands before you."

"He Pi?" Quickly skimming my garbs, Neng Cao rushes forward and grabs both my hands. "How did you evade Ying? Are you here to save us? Or... are you here to kill us? We didn't want this! We didn't want Bei Ling to have access of Tian Sheng but Wang Liang—"

"Calm down, Your Highness. I didn't come to hurt you. I understand your predicament but Nan Rong needs Ye to expel Bei Ling. This *is* in regards to Tian Sheng. Do not claim neutrality and allow Wang Liang to make you his puppet. You must know that once the Southland falls, Bei Ling will annex the smaller territories to prepare for war with Ning."

"Don't you think we know that?" Neng Cao throws down my hands and backs away. "What are we supposed to do? We are practically a prisoner inside our own palace. That assassin won't leave us be!"

"This is your land, Your Highness. If you will not defend it, then who will? You have soldiers and you have the authority to, with a word, throw out Bei Ling. Ally with Nan Rong and rid of Wang Liang. Cai Pai doesn't want this war any more than we do."

"Their soldiers are everywhere! Bei Ling is too strong! We fear instant retaliation, even from Feng Jia!"

"Numbers matter little, sire. I have come to you unharmed. This is the poor quality of soldiers they've employed. Do not let immediate fear take from you everything in the end."

"You make it sound so simple, but the moment you leave, we must deal with this burden alone."

Neng Cao walks to the bed and falls heavily upon the silk sheets. Placing a hand over his eyes, he disregards my endeavors. His attitude is vexing. Furthermore, he makes me appreciate He Pi's active role as a leader.

Marching forthwith, I crouch above and rip away his hand. He looks up startled and then annoyed. Neng Cao jerks back while glaring in dismay. "How dare you touch us in this manner?!"

"When push comes to shove, you *can* retaliate, can't you? What are you waiting for? Are you a coward or are you just too damn lazy to do anything?"

"You have no right!"

"The hell I don't! You're permitting Bei Ling to attack my territory through Ye; not because you agree with them but because you're afraid! I risked everything coming here to prove the strength of Nan Rong—to free you—but you're not willing to lift a finger for your country even knowing that Wang Liang will just take Ye in the end. If you think he'll let you live to claim authority, you're wrong! I'm giving you two choices. Live as a puppet until Bei Ling slaughters you or die by my hand now for being a coward. You're going to die anyway since you're not willing to save yourself by doing the right thing. You might as well let me take it from you. At least, I'll spare your people in the process."

Inching backward, Neng Cao flusters. I want to advance and strike further fear in him. Is this the power Kang Lang felt when he used to bully me? More and more, I think his personality is rubbing off on me. I really am susceptible to my surroundings.

Just as my thoughts trail toward Kang Lang, Mu Dan enters the room. Neng Cao runs from the bed and hides behind his figure.

"You're using a courtesan to shield yourself? Pathetic."

Mu Dan gawks on astonishingly. He looks over his shoulders at the cowering Neng Cao. Although he keeps it hidden, Kang Lang is amused.

"What are you doing to His Highness?" Mu Dan frets.

"His Highness is not willing to comply. Drastic measures are called for. Since Neng Cao has no interest in ruling Ye, then I will take it from him. It's better this way. I won't let Ye fall into destruction, as it undoubtedly would, in the hands of Bei Ling."

"Is this true, Your Highness?" Mu Dan turns around and crouches down toward Neng Cao. "Are you willing to give our land to Bei Ling? What would your father, the late Emperor Zhou, thinks? Isn't it true he's always respected the Southland for their policy of peace?"

"What do you expect from us? We told you, we cannot do this alone!"

Chapter 37: The Cowardly Emperor

Neng Cao is nearly in tears. Parts of me feel sad for him but pity is hardly enough to excuse his irresponsible leadership. He is not allowed to sit idle and let Bei Ling take Nan Rong!

"Where are your ministers and generals? How are you alone?!"

As I stomp forward, Mu Dan raises a hand to stop me. "Ye has been disorganized for some time now, even before Bei Ling's interference. I can see his dilemma."

"How can you defend him?"

"I'm not defending anyone, Your Highness. It's the simple truth. I think it's best that you return to Nan Rong and permit me to assist His Majesty Neng Cao with Bei Ling's expulsion. That is, if he's willing to accept my help."

The hard glare that follows forces Neng Cao's compliance. At the moment, I couldn't care less for Ye's response. My world is on the verge of collapsing. What is Kang Lang saying? He wants to stay here? The thought of us parting is not acceptable. I can't leave him not knowing what can happen. No, I won't allow it!

Shaking my head, I reach out for him. Barely do my arms encircle Kang Lang, a sharp pain touches my shoulder. Everything falters. The last thing I remember is the softness of his lips pressing against my forehead and then I wake in Nan Rong.

Continue to page 400

Chapter 37 – 2

We met Kang Lang's contact at the designated time and made our way inside to one of the empty rooms. Dressed as courtesans, Mu Dan and I started for Neng Cao's quarters. Though the path was littered with guards, we were able to pass through with ease due to Mu Dan's practiced charms. With a sweet smile, a flutter of lashes, and a light touch on the arm, every man who stopped us believed Mu Dan's story of our summons to comfort Neng Cao.

Upon reaching His Highness's chamber door, consternation turns my feet to stone when the last person I expected is standing as the lone guard. Without one fraction of doubt, Mu Dan charges forthwith, pulling me along.

"Who goes there?" Ying reaches for the blade at his hip.

"How rude!" Mu Dan steps forward to divide Ying from me. "We were sent to comfort His Majesty for the recent stress he's had to endure with you Bei Ling soldiers running rampant in our palace. Let us through!"

Ying frowns; his hand is still on the hilt of the sword. "No one may enter. Go back to your Circle, woman."

Gasping from offense, Mu Dan's hands fly to his hips. "I will not! And, don't call me, '*woman*!' I'm clearly a lady!"

"I see a harlot and nothing more. This is your last warning. Go back to the Circle now or I'll send you back in pieces." Ying begins drawing out the blade.

"Sir! Wait!" Pulling Mu Dan back, I step in between. "My friend is a little overzealous about meeting His Highness. I'm sorry for the trouble."

Despite his dangerous profession, Ying must have a sense of compassion because the nervous plea stalls his hand. For a long moment thereafter, Ying studies my face intently. He hasn't budged. Maybe everything will be all right.

"You! From the market!"

In one swift motion, the blade glides from the scabbard. My confrontation with Ying earlier allowed him to have closely examined my face. What have I done?

Regret echoes at light speed, though I have no time to react. Kang Lang moves to protect me as cold metal pierces through us both. I wish I could apologize. Our brief time together in life is cut short as we fall as one into the abyss.

The End.

Chapter 38: Startling Realizations

That bastard! Why did he prick me with the needle? What was he thinking? He promised to stay with me. How can he do this?

Tears well and then spread down my face. I jump off the bed and rush from the room. My vision is hazy, and in my careless state, I inadvertently run into San An. Strong arms pull me forward as I tumble back.

"You're finally awake, Bao Lai. Are you well?"

"San An... I'm sorry! I have to leave!"

"Don't be foolish. Kang Lang returned you for your own safety. Why waste his efforts?"

"But—"

"I understand your distress. Kang Lang is confident he will succeed. There is no need to worry. You trust him, don't you?"

"Yes, of course, but how can I not worry? He's there alone with that coward of an emperor! If Neng Cao turns on Kang Lang—"

"Neng Cao is constantly fearful of the closest threat. At this point, that threat is Kang Lang. You'll only serve to distract him. Stay and be of service to Nan Rong."

What service can I provide? So far, I've done nothing. My attempt to earn Ye's alliance resulted in

Kang Lang's absence. Without him, I feel lost. Every part of me yearns to see my friend again; to hear his boisterous giggles, laugh at his incessant teasing, speak to him about anything and everything without fear of scrutiny, and feel his warmth. The warmth of his arms, his body, and his words. The soft and sweetness of his kisses. The gentle touch of his hands on my face. I miss him.

I miss him so much, I can't stand it! I'd give anything to have him back! Oh, dear heaven. Why is this happening? Was he right? Am I truly that dense? After all this time of pushing him away, can it be I actually love that silly person, as much more than a friend? Is that why it hurts so much to be away from him? Why am I conscious of this fact now when he's so far away?

Here San An stands before me and I admit that I love him, too. Untrustworthy, disloyal, traitor! I can't stand being seen! I just want to crawl in a hole and hide my shame!

"What is the matter? You've gone pale."

San An reaches out and I recoil. Shaking my head, I start to retreat. Not more than a few steps are taken and then I find myself lodged in San An's loving arms.

"S-San An. Why?"

"You don't have to cry alone. I'm here for you."

The tender words make me want to burst into tears. After all the trouble I've caused, I don't deserve to cry. I don't want San An to worry. Mostly, I can't admit the reason to him. My mind races for a quick fib.

"I'm not crying. Kang Lang is doing his best. I need to prepare, too."

"What do you hope to accomplish?"

"I'm not sure. All this time, Wang Liang knew I'm an imposter. Why didn't he expose me before Ning allied with us? Nothing makes sense. He could have easily provoked Ning to march on Nan Rong with the revelation that He Pi is missing, let both our countries exhaust all resources, and then strike. Why take this longer route?"

"Perhaps, his ambition was Ning but when we did not order a march, turned his attention to Nan Rong."

"He threatened Ye and Feng Jia for access to Nan Rong just to ultimately conquer Ning. I can't understand his motive. Is it power or is it revenge?"

"If he can take Ning, Wang Liang will have both."

We both freeze in place from coming to the same conclusion. Everything Wang Liang has accomplished since Bei Ling became active was to direct open war at Nan Rong. Since we did not react as anticipated after Ying's assault, it was his expectation for Ning to ally with us, to send us resources and push all foci to the Southland. In turn, Ning would become exposed to certain weaknesses that Wang Liang can exploit. Once Ning is taken, Nan Rong will fall in succession.

"I'll go to Ning."

The Minister calls out when I pull away. "Your place is here, Your Highness. There are other matters I must discuss with Lord Han Bei. I will go."

"No, Han Bei made a deal with me. If by that agreement his territory is in danger, I won't allow you to absolve my negligence by substitution. Besides, He Pi is alive. My playing his part is rather pointless now. Our enemies are fully aware. You don't really need me here anymore, do you?"

With lips pressed together into a line, San An's attention averts. When he finally speaks, the tone is low and timid. "Must you ask me that? Even though I don't need you to stay as He Pi... I still need you."

Words that make me deliriously happy also erupt pains in my chest. My future is promised to Han Bei. There's nothing I can say in return and nothing I can do. On some level, San An must know there is no hope for us. Why must he keep doing this to himself?

As Ning's Grand General crosses my mind, he suddenly rounds a corner and approaches. With affection for He Pi dismissed, there merely lies condescension in his demeanor.

"Lord Han Bei. You're here!"

"That's plenty obvious, isn't it, Your Highness?"

He's so indifferent toward me, but in many ways Han Bei resembles Kang Lang, and that's enough for me to accept his sarcasm in good stride.

Clearing his throat, San An moves forward on my behalf. "Nan Rong welcomes your return, Lord Han Bei. I didn't receive word that you were coming. I hope your trip was pleasant. Will you accompany me to council—"

"With all due respect, Prime Minister, I'm here for *her*." Han Bei leers in my direction and scans me from head to toe. "We made a pact and unfortunately, I happen to be a man of my word. Therefore, I must tolerate coming to the Southland, but I refuse to suffer your false pleasantries. Come, girl, I have news for you."

Han Bei immediately makes for He Pi's quarters while dragging me along by the wrist. San An moves to stop the emissary. I signal for him to abstain.

Chapter 38 – 2

Once the chamber door opens, Han Bei flings me forward like a ragdoll. I nearly tip over. Before I can rebuff his rude behaviors, the emissary brusquely jerks my collar and throws me against the wall. Petal lips curl into a frown whilst green eyes bear into my soul with a vicious stare.

"I heard my dear little brother is alone in Ye because of you. Don't deny it. I know this was your doing." Scoffing from disgust, Han Bei takes hold of my collar.

"What does he see in you that would change him so? He used to be a pragmatist and now he lives as a fool! I took every good measure to help you for his sake and this is how you repay me? You sent my only brother into a tiger's den! As powerful as he is, do you honestly think he can defeat an entire nation? Did arrogance compel you to send him to his death?! Does it feel good to dominate someone to the extent that he's willing to die in your servitude?! *Do you have any idea what you've done?!* He is an heir to the Zhao line while you are just another piece of trash they picked off the streets! Tell me why I shouldn't take your life. Give me a reason to spare you when your conceit couldn't spare Kang Lang!"

The sarcastic tone gradually increases to violent fury. The hand clenched around my collar moves to my throat. The force of his thin fingers constricts all airflow. I'm on the verge of falling unconscious. I have no means by which to answer him.

"Stay awake! I'm not done with you! I want you to feel every pain I feel for having lost a brother!"

His fingers move away. My lungs desperately gasp for air. Everything in me is quaking from grief. My quaking knees falter. Han Bei, giving no quarters, tersely grabs my arm and drags across the floor.

"Untrustworthy filth! You used him to find favor with these nobles! Even now when his condition is unknown, I see you lusting after the Prime Minister! What is it about you? What makes you so special compared to all the other whores vying for power? Your face sickens me! A face without any charm! Is it your body? Is there something special on that body of yours worth dying for?!"

With little effort, Han Bei rips open the silk robe and exposes my bare skin. He stops my attempt at pulling the pieces over. One hard shove forces me to my back. A forearm lodges across my throat. His heavy body bears down.

"Lord Han Bei... please."

"Shut your mouth! I'm going to kill you and then I will destroy Nan Rong. Ye will fall. Feng Jia will *burn!* Bei Ling will be nothing but a pile of ash! But first... First, I will remove that innocence of yours so that no one else in this life or next can be deceived by your treachery! You should thank me. I won't let you die without knowing the true pain of pleasure!"

His teeth brutally sink into my shoulder. Fingers dig deep into my skin. It's taking everything in me to keep from crying out.

Han Bei is right. I deserve to die if I caused Kang Lang his life. However, more than just my life is at stake. I won't let him harm San An, Jin, and everyone else I've come to care for, including the people of Nan Rong. If Kang Lang is alive... No, I know he is! He won't let this transgression go. Kang Lang will never forgive Han Bei for my death. I can't permit brothers to kill each other over me!

Many cruel fates await unless I can calm this beast, Han Bei. Oxygen is in short supply; I can barely stay awake. Words won't reach him.

As his teeth sink a little deeper, a moan escapes and my arms fly around his neck. Han Bei, confused by my seeming arousal, looks up. His body slightly lifts off. A swift jerk of my knee into his sensitive area and the emissary falls over in pain. By assaulting his brother, I fulfilled my promise to Kang Lang.

Quickly rolling away, I stagger to my feet. Yet, fleeing is not an option; else, everyone will be in danger of this madman.

"Kang Lang is the greatest lover in the world, you will never come close!"

"What?" Han Bei glances up, still wincing from the offense.

"He told me to say that. If that makes you angry, let's go to Ye and confront him."

"You wretch! You dare say his name after your perfidy!"

"Kang Lang is alive. I know he is!"

"How would you know? You've used him and abused him! He can forgive you, but I won't!"

Han Bei charges forward like a wild animal. I complete the final of Kang Lang's three requests by slamming a fist squarely into the emissary's face. I can't believe my attack connected. Maybe, he never suspected that I'm naturally a brute. In a state of bewilderment, Han Bei stumbles back a step.

"Listen! Do you think you're the only one who loves Kang Lang? I love him, too, damn it! I don't want him in Ye any more than you do! Help me retrieve him if you have the nerves. Otherwise, at least let me try! Should I fail, then kill me in any manner you choose! Just... let me see him again!"

I miss you, Kang Lang. I miss you so much! Please come back to me safely!

The earth is quaking or maybe, it's my body trembling. Heavy tears blur my vision and I can't do else but collapse to my knees. Han Bei stands motionless before my pathetic state. Whatever is keeping him from exacting vengeance is marginally winning over rage.

Following a long moment of disquiet, a heavy scoff erupts through the silence. Without another word, the emissary parts from the room.

Chapter 39: Kang Lang's Ambition

Despite the unexpected confrontation, Han Bei had come to Nan Rong with reinforcements, as promised. However, with the revelation of Bei Ling's potential plot, the emissary returned to Ning and left Captain Xian in charge.

I could not bring myself to tell San An the truth about our private meet. All the same, Han Bei didn't say another word to me before leaving. Something in his demeanor changed. There lack the usual sarcastic and condescending air; replaced by somberness. I know it's due to Kang Lang. I've still not heard from him and my attempts to leave the palace were barred by San An.

Late one evening, I wander into the courtyard and find Captain Xian staring at the night sky. A young man with hazel eyes and dark hair, the Captain is seemingly a man of few words. Tonight, he chooses to forgo silence.

"You do not need to leave, Your Highness. I've finished admiring the stars."

His perception is admirable. Xian never turned his head and saw me nonetheless. My lack of civility and sudden retreat is very unlike He Pi. Even without this encounter, I fear he already knows the truth.

"One can never fully finish admiring the stars, can one?" I chuckle nervously. "Don't mind me. Please, enjoy the view of Nan Rong."

"You mean to say the sky is different in Nan Rong than in Ning? I'd like to think no matter where one resides, what lies above doesn't change."

"How so?"

"The heavens see all. Every crime a man commits and every lie he tells is recorded. Justice is dealt as the heavens deem fit. Do you think, had it not been for the Prime Minister and Empress Pai, would Prince Su Jian threaten the Southland in current time?"

"Are you implying that Nan Rong deserves to be destroyed? The Southland is not a lone target. This war will not spare the other countries."

"So you assume, sire. If the other lands do not deserve punishment, then Bei Ling will not claim them. Surely, as the Son of Heaven, you believe in Heaven's will."

"Don't quote divine rights to me! Heaven may deal punishment where Heaven sees fit but mankind is corrupt and impure. Vengeances and desires drive political hands while innocent people are forced to suffer! What say you, Captain? Would you sit idle for one to slay many in the name of Heaven, or take the sin of killing one to save many and in the process incur Heaven's wrath? If you do not wish to stand with Nan

411

Rong, then I implore you to take leave, but do not stand there and tell me Wang Liang has the right to do as he pleases!"

How dare he speak ill of San An and Nan Rong? A slight against the Prime Minister is no less than spitting in my face. It's unlike me not to retaliate; that much hasn't changed.

My hands are balled into fists. Xian remains absurdly still despite the piercing gaze. In due time, a soft laugh escapes and then his countenance relaxes. "I see why Kang Lang didn't slay you now, sire. He's always been the type to like a person of passion."

Why Kang Lang did not slay me? He means the task Kang Lang failed, which keeps him from returning to Ning. Then, that means Xian still believes I'm He Pi.

"Yes, well, Kang Lang is an enigma, isn't he?"

"You must not know him well, sire. Kang Lang is as simple as a man can be. The only reason he's still alive is due pure luck. Born into nobility, lived like a prince, and then threw it all away because he's jealous of his elder brother. He betrayed Ning in exchange for hiding in the Southland, where he feels special. He's just a lucky simpleton."

"Don't speak ill of Kang Lang! He is a great man! Courageous, talented, and intelligent! Ning doesn't deserve him. That's why he's joined Nan Rong!"

Xian laughs shortly. "Since he's such a great asset, why don't you fetch him from Ye?"

"I... trust Kang Lang. Besides, I cannot leave the palace. Unless... you're willing to help me. Are you? I'll reward you handsomely."

"That's brash. How pathetic must this land be for its emperor to bribe a mere soldier! What makes you think I'm a man who seeks rewards, sire? If you want my help, I expect help in return."

"Anything!"

"Very well. When you see the lucky simpleton, tell him that Hua Ye still waits for him. She's tired of raising the boy on her own."

"What did you say? Kang Lang has a son?!"

I'm going to kill him. What an irresponsible jerk! And then to make me fall for him! I can't breathe. I'll find Kang Lang and then I will kill him!

"Why are you distraught, *Your Highness*? What does this have to do with you?"

"I... feel guilty for putting him in danger when he has a child waiting at home."

Xian smirks as though seeing through my lie. "If you'll tell him, I'll escort you across Ye's border."

"Y-Yes, yes I will! But... what should I tell San An?"

"Are you afraid of the Prime Minister, sire?"

"No. I don't want him to worry. He's my elder brother, after all. You know how brothers are."

"I truly don't, sire. I only have sisters. I keep hoping to find the house empty when I return but I'm always disappointed."

"That's just mean!"

"You sound like my sisters, sire." Xian chortles loudly while scratching his face. "Tell the Prime Minister you're to accompany me to the Xiong Nu Barracks outside of the capital to survey Ning's regiment training. I should hope a week is enough time to fetch your Kang Lang?"

"Yes. Thank you. I'll go now!"

Chapter 39 – 2

I ran to San An's quarters but he'd already left court. It was probably for the best since I doubt he'd have let me accompany Xian. Instead, I left a note.

The next day, Xian and I rode west to Xi Mai. The Captain used the cover of night to traverse through the borders safely; after which, he departed for Nan Rong. I changed into my old clothes and traveled to Liang Bi as a man without trouble. However, once I arrived in Ye's capital, there are still signs of Bei Ling's influences.

Without Kang Lang's contact, entering the palace unnoticed would be impossible. I don't have Kang Lang's skills to disguise as a courtesan. I'm not talented enough to scale walls alone and I can't approach the guards dressed as a man without raising suspicions. That leaves the most obvious disguise. I should try being myself.

Dressed as an ordinary woman, I approach two guards at the front and plea for passage.

"And why the hell should we do that, girl?" The ugly guard on the left chortles.

"My sister is a courtesan for His Majesty. I've received word she is ill. Please, let me see her! I beg you! This is all the money I have, in this pouch here. Allow me a few minutes with Mu Dan and you can have it, along with my eternal gratitude!"

415

"Absolutely not! We've been given strict orders!" The young man on the right interjects. He seems new to the post and takes his position seriously.

Upon reviewing his demeanor, there lies that same innocent air I felt when last in Ying's company. Money's not going to distort his views. A bleeding heart plea might. The one on the left is contemplating money. Whom should I attempt to exploit?

Use a bleeding heart plea (Continue to page 417)

Use money (Continue to page 424)

Chapter 39 – 3

I can't bribe the greedy one without the decent one causing commotion. I might as well put on a good show. With quivering lips and crinkled brows, I turn to the younger man and reach for his arm. He flusters and turns pale.

"Please, sir! She's my only family! Mu Dan gave up her freedom to support me. If she hadn't, we'd both be working in the Red Light District! Can't you understand the shame and dishonor she's saved me from? How can I turn away now when she's ill? She's all I have! Don't you have siblings of your own? Wouldn't you do anything for them? Just take this, please!"

I shove the pouch in his hand but the young man refuses. However, the troubled expression signals that his will is dwindling.

"Only for a moment! I must see my sister! Please, just take this! It's everything I have! There's nothing else I can give! But... if there's anything at all, say the word and... I won't deny you."

The insinuation makes him blush from ear-to-ear. He doesn't respond. Hence, his counterpart replies on his behalf.

"All this just to see her sister. Well, that sounds like a good deal, Rui. I'll take the money and you can have the girl. She's being awfully fair, don't you think?" The ugly one smiles while baring yellow teeth.

Rui battles with himself to relinquish duties over emotions. In the end, Kang Lang was right; favor often falls in the lap of the active callous than of the passive saint. The young man concedes and without allowing his counterpart to my meager fortune, takes my hand and leads the way toward the Circle. Oddly enough, this Circle isn't guarded.

"Be quick. If anyone catches you, we'll both be in trouble."

After giving Rui an appreciative bow, I slip inside. As excessive as I thought Nan Rong's Circle seemed, Ye's Circle makes the former looks insignificant. There are enough women here to form an army. How am I supposed to find Kang Lang?

The women grow curious that someone so plain is suddenly amongst them. Curiosity brings the courtesans to inspect and break down my confidence with demeaning comments and tactful ridicule. I haven't even said a word. I suppose this is the game women in the Circle play. They really are harpies!

"Mu-Mu Dan! Mu Dan, where are you?!"

Shoving the harpies aside, I run deeper into the palace and yell for Mu Dan. There is no response. If not here, he's likely with Neng Cao. However, I can't enter His Highness's quarters with Rui guarding me. I know better than to put a good man in such a bad position, but it can't be helped. Taking one of the courtesan robes, I slip out the other side of the Circle and make my way to the main palace.

Guards impede the path to Neng Cao's quarters. Most are reluctant to believe my story. A courtesan would never approach His Majesty without headdress and powder. I may not have Mu Dan's practiced charms but there are other natural charms to which men are fallible. Upon drawing the neck of the robe lower to demonstrate the size of my particular area, all doubts vanish.

Just as I reach the door to Neng Cao's chamber, someone jerks my collar and cold steel suddenly presses against my throat.

"Move and die. Who sent you?" The hard, icy tone threatens to end me without hesitation. Still, I know this voice.

"Kang Lang?"

Lowering the blade, he spins me around. I'm so happy to see him! Instantaneously, I leap into his arms.

"What—how—"

His adorable expressions of confusion and surprise urge my hold to tighten. The familiar scent and loving warmth hasn't changed. I've missed him so much!

"What are you doing here?" Kang Lang finally murmurs.

"I came to find you, of course. I'm glad you're safe!"

"Of course, I'm safe! Didn't I tell you to trust me? It's not safe for you though. Go back to Nan Rong!"

"Why are you angry? I thought you'd be happy to see me."

He frowns and turns away. Is it just my imagination or is he indifferent? Maybe, even cold and agitated. This isn't the same man I remember. Surely, he has a lot on his mind.

"Hey, Captain Xian said to deliver a message: Hua Ye wants you to return."

"Why would she want that?" He turns back and gives an impatient stare.

"She doesn't want to raise her son alone. Does that make any sense?"

"Hua gave birth? That's great news!"

A smile curls over his mouth while the expression softens. My heart sinks and a knot forms in my stomach. So, it's true.

"I guess this means you'll be returning to Ning."

"Hmph! You couldn't drag me back there in chains!"

"What about Hua Ye?"

"What about her? She gave birth. The boy is her responsibility, not mine."

"You heartless bastard! How can you say that?"

"Why are you yelling at me?"

"You're a father! Don't you feel any obligation at all to your child?"

"Are you nuts? Hua Ye is my cousin!"

"You impregnated your cousin?!"

"What are you talking about?!"

The dumbfounded look on his face turns mine beet-red. I'm an idiot!

"You really are dense!" Kang Lang sighs exasperatedly. "Xian is her husband."

"Oh... He knew I'm not He Pi and he was just toying with me?"

"Doesn't take much to fool you," he scoffs. "Do I look like I'm anyone's father? Sure, I've bedded plenty of women but I didn't impregnate anyone, all right?"

"Is that supposed to make me feel better? You think I want to hear about your excursions with other women?"

"What are you getting mad for? Why would you even care?"

"Because..."

"Because what?"

Heat rising inside seeks to burn every inch of me. My heart is beating viciously. I can't say it! I'm bound to Han Bei and Kang Lang can't return to Ning. What would be the point of getting both our hopes up? I imagined this moment over and over in my mind. Here we are, and my lips must remain sealed. My lack of a response triggers his agitation.

"If that's all you have to say, then leave. I have things to do."

His words are like slaps across my face. How can he be so cold? He did change, but why? Is he mad at me? Without thinking, I clutch onto his robe.

Neng Cao's door suddenly opens and His Highness emerges, though he appears completely different. There's no mistaking it. The coward of an emperor is a woman. Her long hair is let down and her chest is unbound. She gawks at me and then pulls Kang Lang into her arms as though he were her property.

"Who is this?" Neng Cao scans me up and down. A nasty, condescending sneer follows.

"She's nobody," is the cold, succinct response. Draping his arms over her shoulders, Kang Lang pulls Neng Cao close, in the fashion he once held me.

Chapter 39: Kang Lang's Ambition

Pain radiates over my entirety. I want to scream at him but I can't breathe. I don't believe this! How could he? All the things he said, did he lie to me? I should be happy for him. I should be happy he's found someone to make him whole when obviously, there's no future for us. I just can't stand it!

Everything in me is shaking violently. I refuse to cry and give her the satisfaction of seeing me defeated. How dare she take my precious Kang Lang! Why does he love her? What's so great about Neng Cao? What does she have that I don't? Power, title, wealth?

Didn't Kang Lang ask this once when confessing his love and I brutally brushed him aside? Is this the pain I caused him, then? This bitter agony of wanting; only for the heart to be ripped to shreds. I'm so sorry, Kang Lang! If this is the misery I've caused you, then I don't deserve your attention!

Neng Cao grimaces. Hungry lips arch upward while Kang Lang leisurely leans down. She's purposefully taunting me by flaunting his obedient affections. I can't look! I don't want to see it! My feet move on their own and I flee from the horrid scene.

Continue to page 436

Chapter 39 – 4

It takes less effort to corrupt someone beyond corruption. Facing the greedy guard, the pouch of coins once more provides temptation.

"This is all the money I have. Please, there's nothing else I can give you except the shoes off my feet. You can take them, too, if you want! Just let me see my sister one last time. I swear I won't bother you again!"

The instant his fat fingers reach for the pouch, the younger man protests. He threatens to report the extortion and then angry conversations ensue. This was not my intention. They're making a scene and drawing in attention from Bei Ling soldiers. Things will likely escalate. I should make myself scarce.

My feet twist around but before I can contemplate retreat, a hard voice ends the hectic scene. A man, covered from head to toe in heavy armors, exits the gate. His intimidating figure immediately puts everyone to silence. After chastising the two guards for the commotion, he drags me inside by the arm. As I run to keep up, he bellows, "You dare bribe my guards? An unforgivable offense! You will be *punished!*"

Why am I not afraid? I don't know this person and yet, I feel complacent. Wait, did he just say he's going to *punish* me?

"Kang Lang?"

The stranger momentarily glances over his shoulder and then continues leading the way. However his voice and demeanor may change, I know it's him. I'm so elated; an ample smile breaks across my face.

"Where are we going?"

"Quite, girl! Don't make a fuss!"

He's afraid someone might see. I best play along for now. Finally, we reach an empty room located in one of the secluded corridors. After locking the door, Kang Lang takes off the helmet and gently pushes me against the door.

"So, how do I look? Am I dashing in this armor?"

"It's very becoming."

I've missed his charming grin and I've missed him. Here he is at last. My arms fly around his neck and with all my strength, pull him close. The familiar scent and loving warmth haven't changed; neither have his handsome physique, dramatic emerald eyes, and pretty petal lips. I can't take my eyes away lest this moment fades into dream. He's finally in my arms. I never knew how much I needed him.

To my surprise, the inappropriate person who constantly teased me is blushing ear-to-ear from becoming the center of my longing gaze.

"Why are you so shy, Kang Lang?"

"Did you hit your head?" He snaps.

Placing a hand to my forehead, Kang Lang inspects the depths of my gaze for signs of madness. I am deliriously happy.

"Did I? You're the one who pricked me with that needle. I don't remember anything."

"Oh, I did. Sorry. Why exactly are you here?"

"To find you, of course. I'm so glad you're safe!"

"Stubborn woman! Do you know how difficult it was to send you back to Nan Rong in that state? How did you find your way back here?"

"Captain Xian helped me in exchange for delivering this message: Hua Ye wants you to return."

"Why would she want that?"

"She doesn't want to raise her son alone. Does that make any sense?"

"Hua gave birth? That's great news!"

A smile curls over his mouth while the expression softens. My heart sinks and a knot forms in my stomach. So, it's true.

"I guess this means you'll be returning to Ning."

"Hmph! You couldn't drag me back there in chains!"

"What about Hua Ye?"

"What about her? She gave birth. The boy is her responsibility, not mine."

"You heartless bastard! How can you say that?"

"Why are you yelling at me?"

"You're a father! Don't you feel any obligations at all to your child?"

"Are you nuts? Hua Ye is my cousin!"

"You impregnated your cousin?!"

"What are you talking about?!"

The dumbfounded look on his face turns mine beet-red. I'm an idiot!

"You really are dense!" Kang Lang sighs exasperatedly. "Xian is her husband."

"Oh... He knew I'm not He Pi and he was just toying with me?"

"Doesn't take much to fool you," he scoffs. "Do I look like I'm anyone's father? Sure, I've bedded plenty of women but I didn't impregnate anyone, all right?"

"Is that supposed to make me feel better? You think I want to hear about your excursions with other women?"

"What are you getting mad for? Why would you even care?"

"Because…"

"Because what?"

Heat rising inside seeks to burn every inch of me. My heart is beating viciously. Obligations abruptly nag at my conscience. I'm bound to Han Bei and Kang Lang can't return to Ning. What would be the point of getting both our hopes up? I imagined this moment over and over in my mind. Here we are, and my resolve is dwindling.

Maybe, I'm not certain of my desires. I do love Kang Lang, but is this love what I think it is? The desire to be in each other's company; how is that different from the close friendship we currently share? If I merely love him as my friend and nothing more, then the words should not be said. However, part of me yearns for his touch. I can't deny that.

These conflicting emotions are driving me mad. Deep inside, I know the answer is apparent. Taking a deep breath, I decide that

I do love Kang Lang. (Continue to page 429)

I still don't know. (Continue to page 434)

Chapter 39 – 5

I came all this way for him and then foolishly let reasons and doubts obscure conviction. I'm excited and also frightened by the prospect. However, I know this to be true: I do love Kang Lang. I love him dearly. There are no words to convey my affections thoroughly. Even if I were to confess that I love him a million times, words aren't enough. I would rather show him my affections in ways he can't misinterpret.

Without another thought, I press against his body and plant a burning kiss on his mouth. His initial reaction to withdraw is overwhelmed by calling passion. Unable to deny temptation, Kang Lang pushes back against the door and begins a barrage of kisses from my lips to my neck and then my chest. Yet, when my mind becomes clouded with excitement, he pulls away. His body is trembling.

"What's wrong?" I reach out and unexpectedly, he moves farther away.

"You have to go," Kang Lang mutters through shortened breaths.

"Why?"

"I'm... doing something I'm not proud of. I'm seducing Neng Cao so that she'll withdraw support for Bei Ling." Kang Lang timidly looks away.

"What? But Neng Cao is... a woman?"

"Yes. That's partially the reason Ye is in shambles. Her ministers know the truth and they don't respect her authority. You saw how she is. She can't command anyone without help. I... can't bear the idea of hurting you. It's best that we part ways. Otherwise, seducing her will be impossible."

"Then, don't seduce her! Come back to Nan Rong! We'll find another way! Don't do this because of me. This isn't what I want. I want you! Why else would I come back here? I love you, Kang Lang!"

"You would choose to tell me this now?" His wry chuckle can't overshadow inner discord he tries so hard to suppress.

"I'm sorry I didn't realize it sooner. I refuse to return without you and... I sure as hell won't let you bed another woman! You do it and I'll kill you!"

"Stop getting angry. You're making me hot and bothered! Look, I promise I won't bed her, but that's all I can promise. Once this is over, I'll return to your side and then we'll have the rest of our lives for you to scream and yell at me. It's not just Tian Sheng at stake anymore. If I stay in Ye, I might be able to gain some intelligence on Bei Ling's movements. I want to do this, not just for you or He Pi, but also for Nan Rong. It's my home now. I want to protect it, too."

"But... I don't want you to."

"For once, I'm not selfish and you're against it?"

"You're never selfish! I am. I don't want you in danger and I can't stand the idea of you with anyone else. You promised you'd stay with me!"

"Don't make this harder than it already is. I've made up my mind."

He moves farther away in the attempt to distance himself physically and emotionally. I can't accept that. This pain within won't subside. There's so much that can keep us apart. I want proof to bind us forever; to ensure he'll come back to me. Even now when we are so close, I feel a deep longing for us to be closer.

"Kang Lang, can I... spend the night with you?"

This is what I want. No matter what anyone thinks, I should throw caution to the wind. Kang Lang taught this to me. I'd rather be an active callous than a passive saint.

"If you will tease me, Your Highness, put a little more effort into it. Besides, this is neither the time nor place for boorish jokes."

Kang Lang rolls his eyes and makes for the door. My hands clutch at his armor and another kiss is pressed against his mouth. The fervent heat and ardor signal to him that my request is hardly a joke. He's so shocked and confused that every attempt to provide a retort is unsuccessful; words are locked in his throat. Anger and frustration seize his countenance and then the painful looks of longing overcome his convictions.

"Do you even know what you're saying?!" He cries bitterly to object; all the while, his body grudgingly complies.

Lips overlap lips, hands overlap hands, and then his entire being compresses against mine. Lost in wonder of love and desire, Kang Lang throws away all discretion. Once we remove all pieces of fabrics and armors separating bare skin, bind each other in eternal oath as our bodies intertwine.

Lost in a daze of ecstasy, unbearable coursing waves of pain and pleasure threaten to drown me beneath his love. Kang Lang never releases his embrace. Whenever I fear the feeling would end, another immeasurable surge follows until every ounce of strength is relinquished and every breath empties from my lungs.

By the time we're lying still in each other's arms, night has descended over the horizon. This is what it must mean to be happy. I close my eyes to record the moment but there is nothing that can capture this feeling in its entirety.

"I love you, Kang Lang. Don't forget me." A breathless whisper flows as I desperately clutch at his broad shoulders.

"I won't forget you in any lifetime," he replies while stroking my hair. "I swear I'll come back to you. Wait for me a little longer."

"I will. Just remember, if you bed her, I'll kill you."

"Stop talking like that or I won't let you go!"

A soft chuckle flows and then a small kiss plants on his lips. "Seriously, though. It's fine to give her council but hurting her with your charms is cruel. I'm not asking this out of jealousy. I'm asking as someone who now knows love and the pain it can cause. Don't seduce her."

"It's all I know how to do," my beloved scoffs. "Although... I won't be able to use my charms on any woman from now on or I'll feel too guilty. So, you win."

"Good. Should things go awry, I want you to return to Nan Rong. Do you hear me?"

"Yes, my love. I do. You know how much I hate tears. I vow to never make you cry again."

Another bout of loving kisses with a force that makes every part of me quivers, and then we part. As painful as it is to leave, I know we'll be together again.

Continue to page 451

Chapter 39 – 6

My lack of a response triggers his agitation.

"If that's all you have to say, then leave. It's not safe here. Go back to Nan Rong." The tone grows increasingly cold and distant.

I don't know what to say in return; neither do I have the chance to sort my thoughts. Kang Lang navigates past me out of the door and makes his way down the hall. Someone turns a corner and then quickly flies into his arms.

"My love!" She cries.

The sight that follows makes me turn cold. Kang Lang embraces her as though it were only too natural. What does he think he's doing? Is this the reason he wanted me to leave?

The overzealous girl eventually notices me and in turn, I recognize her. There's no mistaking it. The coward of an emperor, Neng Cao, is a woman. Her long hair is let down and her chest is unbound. She gawks at me and then pulls Kang Lang into her arms as though he were her property.

"Who is that?" Neng Cao scans me up and down. A nasty, condescending sneer follows.

"She's nobody," is the cold, succinct response. Draping his arms over her shoulders, Kang Lang pulls Neng Cao close, in the fashion he once held me.

Pain radiates over my entirety. I want to scream at him but I can't breathe. I don't believe this! How could he? All the things he said, did he lie to me? I should be happy for him. I should be happy he's found someone to make him whole when obviously, there's no future for us.

Everything in me is shaking violently. I refuse to cry and give her the satisfaction of seeing me defeated. How dare she take my precious Kang Lang! Why does he love her? What's so great about Neng Cao? What does she have that I don't? Power, title, wealth?

Didn't Kang Lang ask this once when confessing his love and I brutally brushed him aside? Is this the pain I caused him, then? This bitter agony of wanting; only for the heart to be ripped to shreds. I'm so sorry, Kang Lang! If this is the misery I've caused you, then I don't deserve your attention!

Neng Cao grimaces. Hungry lips arch upward while Kang Lang leisurely leans down. She's purposefully taunting me by flaunting his obedient affections. I can't look! I don't want to see it! My feet move on their own and I flee from the horrid scene.

Chapter 40: Calloused Hands

San An left for Ning prior to my venture to Ye and still has not returned. Part of me is glad that is the case. In my state of distress over Kang Lang, I would have undoubtedly done something foolish; nothing less than throwing myself at San An.

Since my arrival, I've kept trying to see the objective and brush aside the notions of love and affection. It's been futile. This feeling of loneliness will not subside. Jin is in Bei Ling, Kang Lang in Ye, and San An in Ning. The generals don't care to address me and the council despises me. I truly can't do anything; I shouldn't be in the palace.

Dressed in my old clothes, I take to the streets. The busy scene helps calm my nerves. The more I observe, the more I realize that no matter what happens outside of Nan Rong, things have not changed. The markets are bustling and people still go about their daily lives. I want to keep Nan Rong from war so that the happy faces I see will never be stained with tears. If only He Pi were here. All I have are ambitions; it's he who holds the talents.

Time passes by in a blur. Of all the places, I'm suddenly upon the stall where Kang Lang had purchased the comb for me. Memories of our time together fill my heart with joy; yet, almost instantly, despair overtakes the sensation. Jealousy is an ugly color on anyone's face. I've attempted to bury the feeling deep inside. At the moment, the surge can't be contained.

Kang Lang is happy. I should be happy for him. He's told me all along that he didn't have any reason to love me; that once interest is lost, he would leave. I can't be angry with him. As experienced as he must be, he's never been unfaithful. While he loved me, I know he did not lie with another. Now that he loves Neng Cao, Kang Lang treats me with indifference. Unlike me, he is not cruel. I hold more than one heart in my hands.

At first, I thought my resemblance to He Pi put me into awkward situations with these men. Now, I know it's me. I have no resolve. Am I capable of actually loving anyone? Or, as Kang Lang said, I'm too gullible. I've let my surroundings sway opinions instead of the contrary. One thing is true: I do care for all three. Where caring, friendship, love, and intimacy overlap and diverge is still a mystery. This is something I've yet to learn.

"Get back here!"

From afar, screams erupt left and right. Down the street, Bai Hu is chasing a young man. Hu is fast but his heavy armor and broad stature make it difficult to traverse the narrow streets filled with pedestrians. The man he's chasing is lanky and able to freely move. Abruptly, the culprit makes a sharp turn hoping to lose Hu in the crowd. Oh, no. He's running right at me! I don't understand what's happening but I might as well give Hu the benefit of the doubt.

The young man closes in. My foot immediately rises at an opportune moment and sends him reeling to the ground. The man briefly turns to me and grimaces before attempting another escape. It is too late. As he struggles to his feet, Bai Hu takes hold and rips a purse from his hand.

"Thieving idiot! Did you think I'd let you get away?" Baring his fangs, Bai Hu hands the thief over to the approaching guards.

By this time, I had endeavored to slip away lest he recognizes me. The crowd eventually blocks his view, and then I thought all is well. Of course, I shouldn't have let my guard down. Just as I breathe a sigh of relief, Hu jerks at my collar and spins me around.

"Hey, you. Good work back there."

"T-Thanks." My head is down to avoid eye contact.

The tactless man nudges up my chin. Immediately, a heavy frown covers his face. "You! What the hell are you doing out here?"

"That's none of your business!" I slap his hand away and move back.

"You're really a pain, you know that? The Minister's been looking for you. At a time like this, can't you be a little more useful?"

"San An's returned? I'll go back right away!"

"Like hell I trust you!"

Hu grabs my wrist and drags me to the palace. There's no point protesting his rough conduct. I had every intention of returning. After tossing me in San An's quarters, he mumbles inaudibly and then leaves. Upon scanning my attire, San An's brows furrow from displeasure. As usual, I've done the wrong thing.

"Were you trying to run away?" San An lifts off the chair and draws near.

"No. I needed to clear my mind. I thought a change of view would be nice."

"I see. And, you did not think it was important to tell anyone?"

"You were away. Who else would care if I leave? Besides, you didn't tell me when you left for Ning. Don't get mad at me when you've done the exact same!"

He studies my expression with great care. "When have you become so impertinent?"

Am I being impertinent? I didn't realize until now that my personality shifts when I'm speaking to different people. With Kang Lang, I'm always careless and casual. With San An, I typically choose my words better and most of the time, seem to stand on ceremony. Has San An never seen the real me? Could I drive him away too if he knew the truth? Then again, who is the real me? I don't know anymore.

"I'm not being impertinent. You keep doing as you please, while I feel to be in your favor, I must put on a mask. I'm not perfect and I have enough flaws to make you cringe. You want the truth? Here it is. I missed Kang Lang. I realized I love him, so I went to Ye, but things have changed between us. He's discarded his affections for me. I was frustrated and angry, so I left for the market to distract myself. It's no one's business.

Don't tell me that I'm endangering Nan Rong. By now, I think my disguise has worn off. I'm not He Pi. The real emperor is alive. I don't know why I'm here. If it's to raise morale for the troops on the frontline, then I'll do just that. However, we both know that's hardly imperative. Ning's alliance, He Pi's safety, and your guidance are all that Nan Rong needs. Those three pieces are secured."

San An listens silently through a blank expression. I want to look away, but can't. Trying to hide anything is pointless. Had I told Kang Lang that I love him, regardless of consequences, and he had outright rejected me, it would hurt much less than to never have confessed at all. This thought continues eating at my core. It's the only thing I've regret from my recent trip to Ye. I'm tired of regrets and I'm tired of secrets. From now on, I will be brutally honest. I don't want to live or die wearing someone else's mask.

"I never intended for you to feel that you must be perfect for me," San An returns. "If I did, then I apologize. I'm not perfect either. Forgive me for having injured you with my cruel accusations."

Chapter 40: Calloused Hands

"Don't apologize. It's my fault. You're someone so above me—at first, I would never dare dream that I'd mean anything to you. It validated my ego to know you cared. I tried harder to keep composure near you than anyone else. Sometimes, I do rush to your quarters just to see you—even taunt you, as you've said—and then I feel terrible afterwards. You know my faults. You were right to say all those things. But, I'm leaving Nan Rong when this is over. I promised Han Bei. I don't know his true intentions but it doesn't change the fact that I have to leave."

The Prime Minister steps forward. I feel no need to retreat. Peering deeply into my eyes, San An reaches for my hands. A small smile appears as his thumbs smooth over my skin.

"Do you remember how shy you were when I first touched your hands? You tried to hide your rough skin. Why are you comfortable now? Have your skin softened or have you learned to rid of your shyness?"

"I don't care to hide anymore, San An. You've seen and touched my rough skin. If they do not bother you, maybe they shouldn't bother me."

A bright chuckle bursts from San An. The smile becomes a grin. "You see? By showing me the truth, we are able to become closer. Don't hide from me. I want to see all your flaws and I want to feel every inch exposed."

His lips flutter to my hands, kissing every curve and crevice. Then, from my hands, soft lips move to my wrists. My heart is beating furiously. After everything that's happened between us, I can't believe I'm still this nervous just to be near him. Lifting his gaze, San An's face closes in. Before our lips meet, instincts draw back.

"You shouldn't."

"Why?"

"You know I can't stay in Nan Rong and that I love Kang Lang."

"Why would any of that concern me? Don't stop me unless that's what you want. Everything else and everyone else is inconsequential."

"You sound so reckless!"

"Yes. This is the real me. I've been hiding calloused hands from you, as well. That is why no matter how my desires for you overwhelmed me, there was little chance for us to be close. Show me your everything and I'll bare to you my soul."

He leans in closer. What should I do?

I don't know what I want (Continue to page 443)

Accept his affections (Continue to page 444)

Chapter 40 – 2

"Please don't." Jerking back, I move away.

"This is your final answer? You will never accept me?"

"I don't know what I want, San An. I'm lost in this sea of emotions. I'll only end up hurting you! I love Jin and I also love Kang Lang. There's no reason for you to suffer my treachery. Through it all, I've already decided to follow Han Bei. I can't seem to keep any promises but should I live through this conflict, I'll at least keep one."

San An contemplates for a drawn moment. Bitterness sweeps over his demeanor and then suddenly, washes away as though reaching new revelation. Unfeeling eyes stare deeply into my soul.

"If this is your desire, then I will trouble you no more."

Through the single declaration, my heart suddenly shatters. This is everything I wanted, for San An to be free, so why does it feel as though I've lost a part of me? Once he disappears from the room, my quaking knees buckle and endless tears stream uncontrollably.

Continue to page 453

Chapter 40 – 3

The kiss that follows makes my knees buckle. He's kissed me before but never in this manner. This kiss is unreserved. The full force of his passion thrusts through every stroke of his lips. I can't tell who this person is dominating every part of my will. The touch of his hands running down my body makes me quiver. Abruptly, San An recoils. He's blushing from ear-to-ear; though, I imagine my expression is no different.

"We must stop here; else, I won't be able to retain control. I'm not a dishonorable man. You must become my wife before I take you as my lover."

"But, Han Bei..."

"Han Bei doesn't frighten me, Bao Lai. Say the word and I will ensure you'll never leave my side. If you wish to follow him, I cannot stop you."

I have no desire to follow Han Bei. It's just that, I promised and promises should not be broken. At the moment, I couldn't care less about that. I want to be near San An.

Reaching for his hand, I lead him to the tea table and take the seat across. "Why were you in Ning, San An? Did something happen?"

"You wish to discuss court matters now? Is this your way of rejecting me?"

"Had I wanted to reject you, San An, your advances would have met my fist instead of my lips."

His posture stiffens. I can't blame him for being surprised. "Have you always been such a brute?"

"Always. At the temple where I grew up, a famous general often came to teach the students self-defense. We also had a massive training field. Monks from other temples often came to train and spar with one another. In the old days, tournaments were held for fun. You would think holy men would be reserved, but they're actually quite crude. I learned a few things here and there. Master Tai Hung used to smack my head for constant use of profanity!"

It's hard not to laugh at the fond memories. San An, likewise, returns the sentiment. His reaction is contrary to expectations, though, I'm glad.

"What about you, San An? What were you like before?"

"Before what? Before I became an old man?"

"You're not old!"

"I am too old for you, perhaps? I am thirty-two, so I must be at least ten years your senior."

"I'm twenty-six, San An! Almost twenty-seven!"

Squinting, he peers closely at my face. "I don't believe you."

"Oh, I see! When you said age behind innocence, which *age* were you implying? You must have thought I was a kid. After realizing I'm old, you don't *want* to believe it? I guess you're disappointed. You shouldn't have disbanded the Circle. There were plenty of young women there!"

San An is startled when I leap to my feet. I've never seen him so out of character; to fluster and blush with youthful naïveté. It's difficult to believe this is the same San An.

"W-Wait! Don't go! I didn't mean it that way!"

Sauntering around the table, my arms drape over his shoulders. Heat rising to his face is apparent; I can feel the fervor of his anxiety.

"Are you... actually teasing me?"

"Yes, San An. I don't care how old you are. Tell me everything."

"That could very well take all night. Will you spend the night here with me?" Though he tries to return my jest, the attempt is executed clumsily. For that, I find him utterly adorable.

"Don't tease me, San An, or I might take it seriously."

A boyish grin appears. The cheeky man draws me onto his lap and then begins. "What can I tell you about me? Hmm. I was raised to succeed the crown. There was very little room for childhood. I've been forced to be serious from the day I was born. Even if the real me isn't this person, I can't break from this role. It makes me very boring, I think."

"I don't think so. I like men who can be serious and the way you are has always drawn me to you. Although, there were times you can be forceful which is very unlike your usual gentle nature. You bewilder me sometimes, San An."

"Yes, sometimes too forceful. I was to become emperor. I traded my youth to prepare for a title that will never be mine. I'm still human, Bao Lai. The ordeal made me resentful. I want obedience to prove I still have authority; to prove it wasn't all for naught. For that reason, I've been cruel to many, including you. I'm sorry."

"Don't apologize. I haven't been kind to you. My lack of loyalty must hurt you dearly."

"You can't be disloyal when you were never mine. Simply because I desire you doesn't mean you've been claimed, Bao Lai. I'm possessive and easily jealous. That's no fault of yours. I shouldn't have allowed my misery to pain you. The shame of it mars me, even now."

"And why do you want me? I'm not special anymore and I really didn't save your life."

"Whatever reasons first made me look upon you do not matter. That I cannot take my eyes away is the result of everything that has happened. I tried, Bao Lai. I tried to rid myself of this feeling but I cannot. Your being is imprinted deep into my soul. I'll never be free."

Hidden suffering courses to the surface and floods over San An's face. There's more to be said but words aren't needed. I understand now. In some ways, it was the same for me. San An pushed his affections and caught my attention. No—even before that—from the first moment I laid eyes on him, he had my consideration. I couldn't look away, then. Now that we are so close, I never will. My lips press lightly against San An's to convey unspoken reciprocation. He returns a kiss so deep that my whole body tingles.

"What are you doing to me?" He whispers fearfully.

"It is my desire to torment you for as long as I can, San An."

He laughs happily at my mischievous grin. While locked in each other's tender embrace, conversations of anything and everything pour forth. Now and again, he'd give reminders of his affections through warm loving kisses.

When we part for the night, suddenly it becomes clear that this is the person I've been waiting to meet all my life. Emptiness and confusion subside. I truly love San An, in every way possible. I have for a long time but I was too preoccupied with doubts and obligations to evidently see the truth. Without hesitation, I march to his chamber and enter unannounced.

"Is something the matter?" San An darts up.

"No. I just... wanted to torment you a little longer. Is that all right?"

He doesn't quite know how to reply, or maybe, he doesn't understand my intention.

San An flushes thoroughly when I pull him onto the bed and lie down adjacent. My arms wrap tightly around his back. Slowly, he returns the embrace. For someone who can be so forceful, his hesitant reaction is endearing.

"Are you very innocent San An or do you not want me to stay?"

"I've never slept next to a woman. You'll have to excuse my awkwardness."

"You mean, you've never..."

"No." The reply is soft and timid. He must feel completely embarrassed. Was it mean to make him admit it? I just wanted to know everything.

"Good," I whisper in return. "I don't want another to have any part of you."

"And, what of you?"

"I've never... either. But, I've slept next to Kang Lang and Jin. At the temple, sometimes, heavy storms leaked rainwater through the roofs and flooded the dorms. Then, all the students slept in the common room. The others were all males of course. Also, when I was little, I was afraid of the dark and often slept next to Master Tai Hung. So, sleeping next to a man doesn't trouble me."

"I see."

"Does that bother you?"

"Yes. I thought you were innocent but I was wrong."

Sharp pains shoot over my chest. When my gaze arches upward to gauge his expression, San An is smiling. I can't believe I fell for it! He's just being cheeky. Agitated by my inability to think of a quip, my face buries in his chest to hide embarrassment.

"How do you expect me to sleep when you're so brazen, Bao Lai?"

"Do you want me to leave?"

"After tempting me this way, you couldn't if you tried."

San An chuckles while increasing the strength of his embrace. Warmth steadily spreads throughout my entirety. I hope someday I can make him as happy as he makes me.

Continue to page 456

Chapter 41: An Honest Admission

When I enter the palace, San An immediately comes to fetch me. After the Minister closes the door to his quarters, turns to me with distress on his brows.

"Why did you leave, Bao Lai? I know your note was insincere. Do you know how worried I was?"

I don't grasp the reason, but for once, I'm not fearful of disappointing San An. "I'm sorry. The truth is I was in Ye. I had to see Kang Lang again."

San An studies my face as pain swells over his. Slowly, he releases a deep sigh. "I see. You have made your decision. I'd always known but I didn't truly believe it, until now. He has *changed* you, hasn't he?"

"Yes. I'm sorry. You are dear to me, San An, and I will always consider you a friend. However, I love Kang Lang."

Choking back a lump in his throat, San An stares directly into my eyes. Even though he's accepted my refusal, there are still words he needs to hear to fully relinquish the attachment. I feel horrible for causing his pain but he deserves my honesty, even if it, too, will only bring more torment.

"Tell me," he begins. "Have you ever... *considered* loving me?"

"Yes." The confession forces a wave of undeniable guilt to wash over me. "I loved you, but my love merely caused your misery and that's not what love should bring. Love should convey happiness. I've come to realize the elation of that happiness when love is presented to and from the person who understands and accepts me despite my flaws. I want that for you, San An. There is someone wonderful worthy of you; whom you can love for every charm and every defect. That woman is not me."

The room falls excruciatingly silent. Anguish surges over the Minister and with passing time, steadily dissipates to indifference. His unfeeling eyes then bear into my soul.

"You have not given me the opportunity and yet, you dismiss me for being shallow. Had you told me of your affections, I could accept every flaw in the world. I am prone to jealousy and I do overreact, but my affections are true. However, you have made my decision for me and in the end, it is you who cannot accept me or my faults. Therefore, I shall trouble you no more, my lady."

San An immediately quits the room. For my assumptions, I've again marred his gentle soul. I regret causing him pain but I don't regret my decision. Another fault of mine was clearly shown; another of my imperfections that Kang Lang can accept. As my love looks upon me to absolve his past sins, I, too, look upon him to absolve mine.

Continue to page 461

Chapter 42: Bei Ling's Invasion

A few days later, news of battle at Tian Sheng Mountain Path reached the capital. Both sides suffered mass casualties but Nan Rong was able to repel Bei Ling's forces. At the same time, there were reports of scuttles throughout multiple points on the northern borders, as well as along the borders of Feng Jia and Ye. The ministers, excluding San An, pushed for a direct march into Bei Ling. Ultimately, Nan Rong's generals had no choice but to obey. As San An expected, the direct march resulted in Nan Rong's forces scattering and only half of the men returned. Had it not been for Ning's reinforcements and Captain Xian's military prowess, all would have been lost.

Immediately, Bei Ling sent another group south. This time, Wen Meng and his bandits intercepted the lot and were able to hold the advancing army until imperial forces regrouped and resumed defense. Noticeably, the number of scuttles along Ye's borders diminished. I know in my heart that Kang Lang's interference played no small part. I pray that he is safe.

On the fifth day of the month, He Pi's armors were sent to my chamber. Morale has dwindled greatly and the faceless leader was called to the frontline. Even from the palace, I can feel the atmosphere of the empire change. The oppressive air is filled with somberness. So many lives were lost and so much happiness wiped away. All due to one man who cannot be satisfied with

453

the power he's been bestowed. My intent for battle is one objective: I will make Su Jian pay for his crimes.

"Your Highness, are you prepared?" San An comes into my chamber dressed in armor. He looks so natural in them.

"San An, are you going too?"

"Yes. I am a servant of Nan Rong. If I can be of use to my country, then I will take on any task."

"Aren't you more suited here to direct the forces? The council's last mistake nearly cost us the war. You're the single voice of reason."

"The council has no regards for my advice. I am better suited for the battlefield."

He's agitated by my attempt to interfere with resolve. I'm just really worried for him. I don't doubt that San An can defend himself in any fight. War is a different matter. The idea of him hurt or worse tears at my heart. If any god out there can hear my prayers, please protect San An!

"San An, how much time is left?"

"We leave at dawn. You should prepare yourself for the days ahead. Should you show any weakness or fear, your presence will only serve to vanquish the troops' low morale. It's best you don't go unless you are certain."

"I will go. If this is the only use Nan Rong will have for me, then like you, I will take on any task."

The Minister's lips press together. There's more he wants to say but ultimately, he chooses silence. After San An leaves my chamber, I fall to silent prayers for everyone who must endure this conflict.

Continue to page 464

Chapter 42 – 2

A few days later, news of battle at Tian Sheng Mountain Path reached the capital. Both sides suffered mass casualties but Nan Rong was able to repel Bei Ling's forces. At the same time, there were reports of scuttles throughout multiple points on the northern borders, as well as along the borders of Feng Jia and Ye. The ministers, excluding San An, pushed for a direct march into Bei Ling. Ultimately, Nan Rong's generals had no choice but to obey. As San An expected, the direct march resulted in Nan Rong's forces scattering and only half of the men returned. Had it not been for Ning's reinforcements and Captain Xian's military prowess, all would have been lost.

Immediately, Bei Ling sent another group south. This time, Wen Meng and his bandits intercepted the lot and were able to hold the advancing army until imperial forces regrouped and resumed defense. Noticeably, the number of scuttles along Ye's borders diminished. I know in my heart that Kang Lang's interference played no small part. I pray that he is safe.

On the fifth day of the month, He Pi's armors were sent to my chamber. Morale has dwindled greatly and the faceless leader was called to the frontline. Even from the palace, I can feel the atmosphere of the empire change. The oppressive air is filled with somberness. So many lives were lost and so much happiness wiped away. All due to one man who cannot be satisfied with

the power he's been bestowed. My intent for battle is one objective: I will make Su Jian pay for his crimes.

"Your Highness, are you prepared?" San An comes into my chamber dressed in armor. He looks so natural in them.

"San An, are you going, too?"

"Yes. I won't ever leave your side."

As he kisses me, a deep ache echoes in my heart. I know it's pointless to contend but I have to try. "Please, don't go. Stay here where it's safe! Nan Rong needs you!"

"I've spent my whole life coveting Nan Rong. Now, I only covet you, Bao Lai. I will protect you, my everything."

"Don't say that! Don't protect me! Just protect yourself, that's all I ask!"

Clutching at his breastplate, I kiss San An over and over again but it doesn't feel enough. I don't want to lose him. I'd rather die a million deaths than to see one hair on his head displaced! But, I know he'll protect me and I'm bound to run into trouble. I love San An too much to see harm come to him. Yet, no matter how I plead, he won't listen.

"As you would do anything to protect me, Bao Lai, I would do no less for you. Let us go to battle together as proud servants of Nan Rong. Live for me, as I live for you, and we'll see this war to the end."

San An's kisses rain on my eyelids, cheeks, and mouth. Despite the confident words, his lips quiver while feverishly imprinting passion onto me. Deep inside, he fears this may be the last time we are together. That fear, too, eats away at my soul.

"San An, how much time is left before we march?"

"Until dawn breaks, Bao Lai."

"Then, until dawn break, will you stay with me?"

"Yes," his whisper is hoarse and low.

Our embrace grows stronger while his kisses rain softy. He doesn't grasp my intention. When I reach to unbuckle his armor, San An steps back, startled.

"Are you... implying..."

"Yes. I want to be honest with myself and with you. This is what I want. Should we die, at least let us leave this world having known each other's touch. Bind my soul to yours so that I may find you next life. Should we prevail, then this will be the first of many happy moments to come."

He hesitates. Perhaps, it is inappropriate to say such things at a time like this. I feel no shame for wanting to offer my body and soul. If he refuses, I'll still love him. If he is willing, I'm determined to give him everything.

"Is this truly your desire, Bao Lai?"

Why is pain coursing over his expression? Maybe, his answer is clear.

"I won't force this on you, Minister. Just know that I am yours whenever you will have me."

I reach to buckle the strap of his armor. San An abruptly seizes my hands. In one swift motion, strong arms sweep me off my feet. San An carries me to the bed; each step, a mixture of excitement and pain.

"This is not good-bye, do you understand me?!" San An grits through the manifestation of his tortures. His forehead presses again mine. "I will never let you go!"

Words won't come. My response is a short nod. It's all he needs to surrender doubts and apprehensions. Caught in the whims of desire, our armors quickly scatter to the floor. The many pieces overlap; same as our bodies. His gentle soul erupts in flames, pouring forth every agony and sadness he's kept inside for so long. No matter how many times I cry out his name, the words are forever tempting and seductive. San An... I never want to stop saying your name.

More and more, the assaults of his love make me grow weak until there is nothing left to take and then somehow, he manages to steal another piece of me. When I reach up to push back the sweat-drenched hair from his handsome face, San An thrusts a feverish kiss against my mouth and then claims the last piece of my soul.

Continue to page 471

Chapter 42 – 3

A few days later, news of battle at Tian Sheng Mountain Path reached the capital. Both sides suffered mass casualties but Nan Rong was able to repel Bei Ling's forces. At the same time, there were reports of scuttles throughout multiple points on the northern borders, as well as along the borders of Feng Jia and Ye. The ministers, excluding San An, pushed for a direct march into Bei Ling. Ultimately, Nan Rong's generals had no choice but to obey. As San An expected, the direct march resulted in Nan Rong's forces scattering and only half of the men returned. Had it not been for Ning's reinforcements and Captain Xian's military prowess, all would have been lost.

Immediately, Bei Ling sent another group south. This time, Wen Meng and his bandits intercepted the lot and were able to hold the advancing army until imperial forces regrouped and resumed defense. Noticeably, the number of scuttles along Ye's borders diminished. I know in my heart that Kang Lang's interference played no small part. I pray that he is safe.

On the fifth day of the month, He Pi's armors were sent to my chamber. Morale has dwindled greatly and the faceless leader was called to the frontline. Even from the palace, I can feel the atmosphere of the empire change. The oppressive air is filled with somberness. So many lives were lost and so much happiness wiped away. All due to one man who cannot be satisfied with

the power he's been bestowed. My intent for battle is one objective: I will make Su Jian pay for his crimes.

"Your Highness, are you prepared?" San An comes into my chamber dressed in armor. He looks so natural in them.

"San An, are you going too?"

"Yes. I am a servant of Nan Rong. If I can be of use to my country, then I will take on any task."

"Aren't you more suited here to direct the forces? The council's last mistake nearly cost us the war. You're the single voice of reason."

"The council has no regards for my advice. I am better suited for the battlefield."

He's agitated by my attempt to interfere with resolve. I'm just really worried for him. I don't doubt that San An can defend himself in any fight. War is a different matter. The idea of him hurt or worse tears at my heart. If any god out there can hear my prayers, please protect San An!

"San An, how much time is left?"

"We leave at dawn. You should prepare yourself for the days ahead. Should you show any weakness or fear, your presence will only serve to vanquish the troops' low morale. It's best you don't go unless you are certain."

"I will go. If this is the only use Nan Rong will have for me, then like you, I will take on any task."

The Minister's lips press together. There's more he wants to say but ultimately, he chooses silence. After San An leaves my chamber, I fall to silent prayers for everyone who must endure this conflict.

Continue to page 478

Chapter 43: My Council

Qing Hai, Bai Hu, Zhen Yue, San An, and I were gathered in the main tent of the northern base, Zhong Ren, when a messenger rushed in. After tossing the letter he was tasked to deliver onto the table, the man immediately collapsed from fatigue. Qing Hai and I took him to Master Dui. Eventually, Hai stayed to assist the physician while I returned to San An.

When I enter the tent, the Minister is frantically studying the large map on the desk. Bai Hu and Zhen Yue are in no better moods.

"San An, what happened?"

"Kang Lang sent words that Feng Jia has withdrawn the neutrality pact. They've outright sided with Bei Ling. Currently, their entire force is marching to Nan Rong. With Bei Ling's reinforcements, their small army has grown five times the size. We don't have enough soldiers to keep this front and defend against a northwest invasion."

"What of Ye? They've ejected Bei Ling. Can't we convince them to intercept Feng Jia?"

"Ye's army is weak and few. However, their territory has major access points to Nan Rong. I fear that although Feng Jia will be coming for the Southland, Bei Ling will march to Ye. Should we choose to abandon

this base, we can only intercept one of the other two fronts."

This is absurd! If we repel Feng Jia, then Ye will fall to Bei Ling, which doesn't bode well for Nan Rong. Then again, why is it assumed that Ye's army will fail without our interference? Once our forces quash Feng Jia, we can still assist the West.

"San An, we need to trust Kang Lang."

"What are you mumbling about? Stop wasting time!" Bai Hu sneers.

Ignoring the Demon General, I approach the map and review the markers. "In Ye, we have Kang Lang. He's not a man to be underestimated. To the east is Ning; that front is secured. Mount Chou has Wen Meng. He's proven himself capable. Why don't we allow him and the other generals to hold Bei Ling? That gives us enough leverage to meet with Feng Jia."

"We don't have enough troops to divide our strength and still be able to fend off Feng Jia." San An replies.

"San An, what if we don't fend them off? What if we feign retreat?"

"Are you deaf?" Bai Hu growls. "He said we don't have enough troops. You won't be *feigning* retreat. You'll *actually* be running away once they've scattered the lines!"

"But—"

"Why are you even talking when you're so oblivious—"

"Shut up, Bai Hu!"

He's such a loudmouth! I hate his condescension! Why doesn't he ever give me a chance before brushing me off? And yet, the tent is now silent. Hu's face is slightly red. Was that all I had to do?

Quickly pulling together remaining composure, I turn back to San An. "When the council sent Nan Rong directly to Bei Ling, the North surrounded us because of their multiple vantage points. Once Feng Jia marches too far into Nan Rong, can't we do the same? Ye may be weak, but if they can flank Feng Jia, it might throw enemy lines into disarray.

Plus, we still have Captain Xian's support. Ning's soldiers are widely feared; enough to impact morale. If we can make their numbers seem overwhelming, it might give us an advantage. Also, even though I've never met He Pi, I know he is not a passive man. Surely, he's been waiting for an opportune moment to strike from inside Bei Ling. That is to say, the farther we can draw out Bei Ling's forces, the weaker Wang Liang's internal line of defense will become."

I hold my breath during the deafening silence that ensues. When I thought my lungs would burst, Zhen Yue steps forward.

"Considering our resources, feigning retreat is a dangerous strategy. Unless there is no other recourse, we should avoid this at all costs."

Depression takes me. Why do I bother? I don't know anything about war! It's less embarrassing to simply apologize than to make a fuss. As I begin to do just that, Zhen Yue moves abreast.

"However, I don't see any other recourse."

"Yes, we are in desperate times." San An sighs. "This will require precise coordination and collaboration. Let us move forward with this endeavor."

Did I hear that right? Are they actually going with *my* plan? I wanted them to, but now it scares me a little. San An calls for Qing Hai and prepares letters for the parties involved. Everyone then move out to their designated positions.

Yue and Hu, along with several other generals, gather their men to intercept Feng Jia. Qing Hai leaves for Ye to assist Kang Lang and messengers are sent to Ning as well as our capital. San An and I remain at the northern base with the remaining officers.

Once everything settled, San An calls me to his tent.

"Your Majesty can wield knowledge effectively when given the basics."

"I'm glad you think so. If I am of any use, it's all thanks to you and Kang Lang. You taught me policies and tactics, while Kang Lang taught me true human nature."

San An gives no reply. His mind is preoccupied by the ordeal.

"San An, you never told me why you left for Ning the last time. Does Han Bei intend to send more reinforcements?"

San An sighs heavily. "No. Han Bei's primary concern is Ning. Their scouts reported movements near Ying Ling's borders, so our conjectures were correct. This is the reason we haven't had a direct confrontation with Bei Ling's main forces. They've been keeping us busy with decoys, hoping to lure resources from Ning. Though, I never thought Feng Jia would march under their banners."

"Bei Ling's forces should be at par with Nan Rong but with the way things turned out, they could have taken the Southland with ease. Why then, focus on the more arduous task of conquering Ning?"

"Su Jian's actions indicate to me that he's approaching this from an emotional position. By comparison to you and Kang Lang, I'm not as well versed in human nature. My books and scrolls serve as the basis for my judgment. Perhaps, you can shed some light on the subject from the natural perspective."

"Well, Kang Lang would see this more clearly. From the emotional perspective, my guess is Su Jian wants to relish Nan Rong's destruction. He is not able to do that while living in fear of retaliation from Ning. The East would never allow another country to have an army that could rival theirs, since their primary source of power lies within military might. Ning can bully every other nation when they are divided; Ning can't win against all four united. Although, why send Feng Jia south if Su Jian wants Nan Rong to fall last? He's so confusing!"

"Just another decoy, Your Highness. It is fortunate Su Jian has little expectations for Feng Jia to succeed."

"Do you really think so, San An?"

"Yes. Though there will be casualties, Feng Jia will not take Nan Rong."

The idea of casualties mars my conscience. So many deaths. So much suffering. Every time a soldier moves out is another chance for him to die. Life is fickle and also precious. For love of country or family, everyone around is risking their lives. Even though we're stationed near Bei Ling, I'm in the safest position possible. This façade of He Pi guarantees my protection. I just want to be useful. I want this war to end and I want everyone to be safe.

"San An... Could I go to Bei Ling?"

He shoots over such a hard glare, I feel tremors.

"What purpose would that serve?"

"Kang Lang's taught me enough. I could try to close my distance to Wang Liang."

"Su Jian is too careful a man, especially during this time of conflict. He is not foolish enough to chase after courtesans."

"Blood cannot despise blood, as you've said. His hands will stay for He Pi."

"He knows you are an imposter. I understand your desire to assist but you can best serve Nan Rong by staying here."

Without allowing the chance for protests, San An leaves the tent.

Continue to page 485

Chapter 43 – 2

Qing Hai, Bai Hu, Zhen Yue, San An, and I were gathered in the main tent of the northern base, Zhong Ren, when a messenger rushed in. After tossing the letter he was tasked to deliver onto the table, the man immediately collapsed from fatigue. Qing Hai and I took him to Master Dui. Eventually, Hai stayed to assist the physician while I returned to San An.

When I enter the tent, the Minister is frantically studying the large map on the desk. Bai Hu and Zhen Yue are in no better moods.

"San An, what happened?"

"Kang Lang sent words that Feng Jia has withdrawn the neutrality pact. They've outright sided with Bei Ling. Currently, their entire force is marching to Nan Rong. With Bei Ling's reinforcements, their small army has grown five times the size. We don't have enough soldiers to keep this front and defend against a northwest invasion."

"What of Ye? They've ejected Bei Ling. Can't we convince them to intercept Feng Jia?"

"Ye's army is weak and few. However, their territory has major access points to Nan Rong. I fear that although Feng Jia will be coming for the Southland, Bei Ling will march to Ye. Should we choose to abandon

this base, we can only intercept one of the other two fronts."

This is absurd! If we repel Feng Jia, then Ye will fall to Bei Ling, which doesn't bode well for Nan Rong. Then again, why is it assumed that Ye's army will fail without our interference? Once our forces quash Feng Jia, we can still assist the West.

"San An, we need to trust Kang Lang."

"What are you mumbling about? Stop wasting time!" Bai Hu sneers.

Ignoring the Demon General, I approach the map and review the markers. "In Ye, we have Kang Lang. He's not a man to be underestimated. To the east is Ning; that front is secured. Mount Chou has Wen Meng. He's proven himself capable. Why don't we allow him and the other generals to hold Bei Ling? That gives us enough leverage to meet with Feng Jia."

"We don't have enough troops to divide our strength and still be able to fend off Feng Jia." San An replies.

"San An, what if we don't fend them off? What if we feign retreat?"

"Are you deaf? He said we don't have enough troops. You won't be *feigning* retreat, you'll *actually* be running away once they've scattered the lines!"

"But—"

"Why are you even talking when you're so oblivious—"

"Let her speak, General. Bao Lai's words carry my authority and I refuse to tolerate insubordination."

San An's grimace puts the Demon General to silence. Through the Minister's encouraging nod, composure is gathered and then I continue.

"When the council sent Nan Rong directly to Bei Ling, the North surrounded us because of their multiple vantage points. Once Feng Jia marches too far into Nan Rong, can't we do the same? Ye may be weak, but if they can flank Feng Jia, it might throw enemy lines into disarray.

Plus, we still have Captain Xian's support. Ning's soldiers are widely feared; enough to impact morale. If we can make their numbers seem overwhelming, it might give us an advantage. Also, even though I've never met He Pi, I know he is not a passive man. Surely, he's been waiting for an opportune moment to strike from inside Bei Ling. That is to say, the farther we can draw out Bei Ling's forces, the weaker Wang Liang's internal line of defense will become."

I hold my breath during the deafening silence that ensues. When I thought my lungs would burst, Zhen Yue steps forward.

"Considering our resources, feigning retreat is a dangerous strategy. Unless there is no other recourse, we should avoid this at all costs."

Depression takes me. Why do I bother? I don't know anything about war! It's less embarrassing to simply apologize than to make a fuss. As I begin to do just that, Zhen Yue moves abreast.

"However, I don't see any other recourse."

"Yes, we are in desperate times." San An sighs. "This will require precise coordination and collaboration. Let us move forward with this endeavor."

Did I hear that right? Are they actually going with *my* plan? I wanted them to, but now it scares me a little. San An calls for Qing Hai and prepares letters for the parties involved. Everyone then move out to their designated positions.

Yue and Hu, along with several other generals, gather their men to intercept Feng Jia. Qing Hai leaves for Ye to assist Kang Lang and messengers are sent to Ning as well as our capital. San An and I remain at the northern base with the remaining officers.

When only we remain in the tent, San An draws me into an embrace.

"Your Majesty can wield knowledge effectively when given the basics."

"I'm glad you think so. If I am of any use, it's all thanks to you and Kang Lang. You taught me policies and tactics, while Kang Lang taught me true human nature."

San An gives no reply. His mind is preoccupied by the ordeal.

"San An, you never told me why you left for Ning the last time. Does Han Bei intend to send more reinforcements?"

San An sighs heavily. "No. Han Bei's primary concern is Ning. Their scouts reported movements near Ying Ling's borders, so our conjectures were correct. This is the reason we haven't had a direct confrontation with Bei Ling's main forces. They've been keeping us busy with decoys, hoping to lure resources from Ning. Though, I never thought Feng Jia would march under their banners."

"Bei Ling's forces should be at par with Nan Rong but with the way things turned out, they could have taken the Southland with ease. Why then, focus on the more arduous task of conquering Ning?"

"Su Jian's actions indicate to me that he's approaching this from an emotional position. By comparison to you and Kang Lang, I'm not as well versed in human nature. My books and scrolls serve as the basis for my judgment. Perhaps, you can shed some light on the subject from the natural perspective."

"Well, Kang Lang would see this more clearly. From the emotional perspective, my guess is Su Jian wants to relish Nan Rong's destruction. He is not able to do that while living in fear of retaliation from Ning. The East would never allow another country to have an army that could rival theirs, since their primary source of power lies within military might. Ning can bully every other nation when they are divided; Ning can't win against all four united. Although, why send Feng Jia south if Su Jian wants Nan Rong to fall last? He's so confusing!"

"Just another decoy, Your Highness. It is fortunate Su Jian has little expectations for Feng Jia to succeed."

"Do you really think so, San An?"

"Yes. Though there will be casualties, Feng Jia will not take Nan Rong."

The idea of casualties mars my conscience. So many deaths. So much suffering. Every time a soldier moves out is another chance for him to die. Life is fickle and also precious. For love of country or family, everyone around is risking their lives. Even though we're stationed near Bei Ling, I'm in the safest position possible. This façade of He Pi guarantees my protection. I just want to be useful. I want this war to end and I want San An to be safe.

"San An... could I go to Bei Ling?"

"Absolutely not."

"Kang Lang's taught me enough. I could try closing my distance to Wang Liang."

"Su Jian is too careful a man, especially during this time of conflict. He is not foolish enough to chase after courtesans."

"Blood cannot despise blood, as you've said. His hands will stay for He Pi."

"He knows you are an imposter. I understand your desire to assist but you can best serve Nan Rong by staying here."

San An's right. For the time being, I should have faith in our allies. Whether it is due confidence or intuition, at heart, I believe our endeavors will be successful.

Following a short pause, his embrace strengthens. San An whispers, "You are never to leave my side!"

His sudden affection brings ardent elation. Whatever happens, I won't ever let you go either, San An.

Continue to page 487

Chapter 43 – 3

Qing Hai, Bai Hu, Zhen Yue, San An, and I were gathered in the main tent of the northern base, Zhong Ren, when a messenger rushed in. After tossing the letter he was tasked to deliver onto the table, the man immediately collapsed from fatigue. Qing Hai and I took him to Master Dui. Eventually, Hai stayed to assist the physician while I returned to San An.

When I enter the tent, the Minister is frantically studying the large map on the desk. Bai Hu and Zhen Yue are in no better moods.

"San An, what happened?"

"Kang Lang sent words that Feng Jia has withdrawn the neutrality pact. They've outright sided with Bei Ling. Currently, their entire force is marching to Nan Rong. With Bei Ling's reinforcements, their small army has grown five times the size. We don't have enough soldiers to keep this front and defend against a northwest invasion."

"What of Ye? They've ejected Bei Ling. Can't we convince them to intercept Feng Jia?"

"Ye's army is weak and few. However, their territory has major access points to Nan Rong. I fear that although Feng Jia will be coming for the Southland, Bei Ling will march to Ye. Should we choose to abandon

this base, we can only intercept one of the other two fronts."

This is absurd! If we repel Feng Jia, then Ye will fall to Bei Ling, which doesn't bode well for Nan Rong. Then again, why is it assumed that Ye's army will fail without our interference? Once our forces quash Feng Jia, we can still assist the West.

"San An, we need to trust Kang Lang."

"What are you mumbling about? Stop wasting time!" Bai Hu sneers.

Ignoring the Demon General, I approach the map and review the markers. "In Ye, we have Kang Lang. He's not a man to be underestimated. To the east is Ning; that front is secured. Mount Chou has Wen Meng. He's proven himself capable. Why don't we allow him and the other generals to hold Bei Ling? That gives us enough leverage to meet with Feng Jia."

"We don't have enough troops to divide our strength and still be able to fend off Feng Jia." San An replies.

"San An, what if we don't fend them off? What if we feign retreat?"

"Are you deaf? He said we don't have enough troops. You won't be *feigning* retreat, you'll *actually* be running away once they've scattered the lines!"

"But—"

"Why are you even talking when you're so oblivious—"

"Shut up, Bai Hu!"

He's such a loudmouth! I hate his condescension! Why doesn't he ever give me a chance before brushing me off? And yet, the tent is now silent. Hu's face is slightly red. Was that all I had to do?

Quickly pulling together remaining composure, I turn back to San An. "When the council sent Nan Rong directly to Bei Ling, the North surrounded us because of their multiple vantage points. Once Feng Jia marches too far into Nan Rong, can't we do the same? Ye may be weak, but if they can flank Feng Jia, it might throw enemy lines into disarray.

Plus, we still have Captain Xian's support. Ning's soldiers are widely feared; enough to impact morale. If we can make their numbers seem overwhelming, it might give us an advantage. Also, even though I've never met He Pi, I know he is not a passive man. Surely, he's been waiting for an opportune moment to strike from inside Bei Ling. That is to say, the farther we can draw out Bei Ling's forces, the weaker Wang Liang's internal line of defense will become."

I hold my breath during the deafening silence that ensues. When I thought my lungs would burst, Zhen Yue steps forward.

"Considering our resources, feigning retreat is a dangerous strategy. Unless there is no other recourse, we should avoid this at all costs."

Depression takes me. Why do I bother? I don't know anything about war! It's less embarrassing to simply apologize than to make a fuss. As I begin to do just that, Zhen Yue moves abreast.

"However, I don't see any other recourse."

"Yes, we are in desperate times." San An sighs. "This will require precise coordination and collaboration. Let us move forward with this endeavor."

Did I hear that right? Are they actually going with *my* plan? I wanted them to, but now it scares me a little. San An calls for Qing Hai and prepares letters for the parties involved. Everyone then move out to their designated positions.

Yue and Hu, along with several other generals, gather their men to intercept Feng Jia. Qing Hai leaves for Ye to assist Kang Lang and messengers are sent to Ning as well as our capital. San An and I remain at the northern base with the remaining officers.

Once everything settled, San An calls me to his tent.

"Your Majesty can wield knowledge effectively when given the basics."

"I'm glad you think so. If I am of any use, it's all thanks to you and Kang Lang. You taught me policies and tactics, while Kang Lang taught me true human nature."

San An gives no reply. His mind is preoccupied by the ordeal.

"San An, you never told me why you left for Ning the last time. Does Han Bei intend to send more reinforcements?"

San An sighs heavily. "No. Han Bei's primary concern is Ning. Their scouts reported movements near Ying Ling's borders, so our conjectures were correct. This is the reason we haven't had a direct confrontation with Bei Ling's main forces. They've been keeping us busy with decoys, hoping to lure resources from Ning. Though, I never thought Feng Jia would march under their banners."

"Bei Ling's forces should be at par with Nan Rong but with the way things turned out, they could have taken the Southland with ease. Why then, focus on the more arduous task of conquering Ning?"

"Su Jian's actions indicate to me that he's approaching this from an emotional position. By comparison to you and Kang Lang, I'm not as well versed in human nature. My books and scrolls serve as the basis for my judgment. Perhaps, you can shed some light on the subject from the natural perspective."

"Well, Kang Lang would see this more clearly. From the emotional perspective, my guess is Su Jian wants to relish Nan Rong's destruction. He is not able to do that while living in fear of retaliation from Ning. The East would never allow another country to have an army that could rival theirs, since their primary source of power lies within military might. Ning can bully every other nation when they are divided; Ning can't win against all four united. Although, why send Feng Jia south if Su Jian wants Nan Rong to fall last? He's so confusing!"

"Just another decoy, Your Highness. It is fortunate Su Jian has little expectations for Feng Jia to succeed."

"Do you really think so, San An?"

"Yes. Though there will be casualties, Feng Jia will not take Nan Rong."

The idea of casualties mars my conscience. So many deaths. So much suffering. Every time a soldier moves out is another chance for him to die. Life is fickle and also precious. For love of country or family, everyone around is risking their lives. Even though we're stationed near Bei Ling, I'm in the safest position possible. This façade of He Pi guarantees my protection. I just want to be useful. I want this war to end and I want Kang Lang to return.

"San An... Could I go to Bei Ling?"

He shoots over such a hard glare, I feel tremors.

"What purpose would that serve?"

"Kang Lang's taught me enough. I could try to close my distance to Wang Liang."

"Su Jian is too careful a man, especially during this time of conflict. He is not foolish enough to chase after courtesans."

"Blood cannot despise blood, as you've said. His hands will stay for He Pi."

"He knows you are an imposter. I understand your desire to assist but you can best serve Nan Rong by staying here."

Without allowing the chance for protests, San An leaves the tent.

Continue to page 489

Chapter 44: Turn of Tides

Nan Rong's forces met Feng Jia at Lan Yue Pass. A short melee ensued and then Nan Rong fell back. The enemy gave chase for several days to as far as Ping. After rallying with Captain Xian's reinforcements, the Southern army turned the battle against Feng Jia; the latter fled from the field when Ning's colors seemingly flooded behind Nan Rong's confident forces. The East's threatening black and silver armors signaled to Feng Jia the large casualties they would undoubtedly incur. If only they knew the majority of those armors were worn by farmers, craftsmen, and other civilians who came to assist their beloved Nan Rong. The back of the lines were merely painted straw puppets.

Feng Jia's retreat was thwarted by Kang Lang, who marched under Ye's banners and flanked the fleeing army. Fear and confusion caused generals and peons alike to leave ranks and scatter. The rest were either slain or captured. To this end, Ye invaded Feng Jia and removed Bei Ling's influences. Kang Lang, having led the assault, was established as the Grand Commander of Ye's newly captured territory, renamed Bao Dan.

When news of the East's massive reinforcements in the Southland reached Bei Ling, Wang Liang ordered the North's main forces to enter Ning. To their surprise, Han Bei, who had withdrawn his men from Ying Ling by San An's instructions, marched forth to meet the North's

generals with five hundred thousand Ning soldiers and cleared the battlefield with ease.

His main forces scattered, Wang Liang's last attempt to take Nan Rong will soon come upon us. That is San An's expectation.

Continue to page 491

Chapter 44 – 2

Nan Rong's forces met Feng Jia at Lan Yue Pass. A short melee ensued and then Nan Rong fell back. The enemy gave chase for several days to as far as Ping. After rallying with Captain Xian's reinforcements, the Southern army turned the battle against Feng Jia; the latter fled from the field when Ning's colors seemingly flooded behind Nan Rong's confident forces. The East's threatening black and silver armors signaled to Feng Jia the large casualties they would undoubtedly incur. If only they knew the majority of those armors were worn by farmers, craftsmen, and other civilians who came to assist their beloved Nan Rong. The back of the lines were merely painted straw puppets.

Feng Jia's retreat was thwarted by Kang Lang, who marched under Ye's banners and flanked the fleeing army. Fear and confusion caused generals and peons alike to leave ranks and scatter. The rest were either slain or captured. To this end, Ye invaded Feng Jia and removed Bei Ling's influences. Kang Lang, having led the assault, was established as the Grand Commander of Ye's newly captured territory, renamed Bao Dan.

When news of the East's massive reinforcements in the Southland reached Bei Ling, Wang Liang ordered the North's main forces to enter Ning. To their surprise, Han Bei, who had withdrawn his men from Ying Ling by San An's instructions, marched forth to meet the North's

generals with five hundred thousand Ning soldiers and cleared the battlefield with ease.

His main forces scattered, Wang Liang's last attempt to take Nan Rong will soon come upon us. That is San An's expectation.

Continue to page 498

Chapter 44 – 3

Nan Rong's forces met Feng Jia at Lan Yue Pass. A short melee ensued and then Nan Rong fell back. The enemy gave chase for several days to as far as Ping. After rallying with Captain Xian's reinforcements, the Southern army turned the battle against Feng Jia; the latter fled from the field when Ning's colors seemingly flooded behind Nan Rong's confident forces. The East's threatening black and silver armors signaled to Feng Jia the large casualties they would undoubtedly incur. If only they knew the majority of those armors were worn by farmers, craftsmen, and other civilians who came to assist their beloved Nan Rong. The back of the lines were merely painted straw puppets.

Feng Jia's retreat was thwarted by Kang Lang, who marched under Ye's banners and flanked the fleeing army. Fear and confusion caused generals and peons alike to leave ranks and scatter. The rest were either slain or captured. To this end, Ye invaded Feng Jia and removed Bei Ling's influences. Kang Lang, having led the assault, was established as the Grand Commander of Ye's newly captured territory, renamed Bao Dan.

When news of the East's massive reinforcements in the Southland reached Bei Ling, Wang Liang ordered the North's main forces to enter Ning. To their surprise, Han Bei, who had withdrawn his men from Ying Ling by San An's instructions, marched forth to meet the North's

generals with five hundred thousand Ning soldiers and cleared the battlefield with ease.

His main forces scattered, Wang Liang's last attempt to take Nan Rong will soon come upon us. That is San An's expectation.

Continue to page 502

Chapter 45: Brothers United

Sentinels kept close watch from our towers while a handful of Wen Meng's bandits advanced farther out to scout for signs of movements from the north.

In the east, Han Bei is making his way through Ying Ling and in the west, Kang Lang is preparing to advance forth into Bei Ling. The remainder of Nan Rong's military leaders not currently at the northern base was making their way here. However, their march was impeded by sudden illness that swept over the ranks.

"Ye and Bao Dan are reporting similar cases. I imagine Bei Ling, before taking leave of Feng Jia, tainted the water supply of the River Huan, which flows through all three territories." San An explains.

Master Yu was sent to treat the soldiers but the situation remains grim. Bodies are piling daily from this ailment that appears neither poison nor disease. Although the affliction is seemingly incurable, if the person is strong enough to withstand the assaults after three days, then there is a chance for survival. We've been careful with our water supply but fear is causing morale to dwindle. Many soldiers have family members who have fallen ill. It's natural that they want to leave ranks. However, duties bind them, and soon, there erupts discord all around.

While we contemplate the next move, drums signal movements from the north. San An and I run to the gate

to meet a lone rider galloping toward the base at full speed whilst kicking large amounts of dust into the air. The sentinels ready their weapons. However, there's no mistaking him.

Despite the Minister's protest, I rush outside while flailing my arms in the air for the sentinels to yield. The rider comes to an abrupt halt and leaps off the mare. Disregarding my disguise, his arms fly around me.

"Jin! What are you doing here? Why did you come alone? That's dangerous!"

"I had no choice. I was afraid you might have... Let's go inside."

In the large tent, Jin takes three pieces of paper from his breast pocket. I scan them over and realize his reason for coming.

"It is poison! How did you find the antidote?"

"You can thank the White Cranes for the instructions. Su Jian's last resort before giving up Feng Jia was to poison San An. He's used a slow-reacting toxin, which is why so many have been afflicted. Had everyone been on immediate guard, there would have been significantly less casualties. Not only that, by allowing the toxin to wash from the body in three days, he aimed to fool our physicians into believing the cause is more likely ailment."

San An is disheartened. No matter how many years have gone by, troubles from his past will not relinquish.

Why can't Su Jian understand that it was not the Minister's fault? He was simply another victim.

"San An, we'll stop him."

My attempt to provide succor is met with disregard. In my stead, Jin steps forward and places a hand on the Minister's shoulder.

"San An... Brother. Don't endure this pain alone. He Pi and I are with you and so is Bao Lai. Enough is enough. Su Jian may be our brother, but his actions are unforgivable. Whatever happened long ago was not our fault. We were children then. As men now, we are responsible for our actions. Soon enough, we three will unite to guide Nan Rong into a proper future. We only ask that you continue the fight a while longer."

The Minister's expression changed the moment Jin called him, "Brother." From taut apprehension, he now appears calm. This is everything San An needed to hear all along; that he still has family who cares for him.

Curiously, San An is not the only one who's had a change in demeanor. "Jin, does that mean—"

"Yes. I've come to terms with my blood and my life. He Pi and I will rejoin Nan Rong when the ordeal is over, and with San An, establish our dynasty anew. We each have our weaknesses and strengths. Together, we can lead the Southland effectively. And you, Bao Lai, will remain in our council."

"Who, me? Council? Are you nuts?"

Jin laughs and touches his fingers to my cheek. The same loving warm smile I remember is still there. However, his sense of self and confidence are new aspects I've not experienced. I'm so glad they've come to an understanding at last.

"Now is not the time to dawdle," San An interrupts brusquely. "We must distribute this list to every physician in the three territories."

"You are right, Brother. There is no time to waste. I will continue south and deliver instructions to Master Yu. Send messengers to the other territories quickly. We'll meet again soon."

Jin immediately parts from the tent. As I start after him to call for messengers, San An stops my effort.

"What is it, San An? We don't have time to lose."

"Bao Lai, I must apologize. Another note arrived yesterday. Kang Lang was poisoned. I feared a foolhardy response, so I've kept this from you."

San An's grievous eyes beg for my forgiveness.

"What...?" I feel numb. How could this happen! Kang Lang went to Ye for my sake! He's been suffering and I couldn't do anything for him!

Trepidation threatens to suffocate me. Out of panic, I grab one of the copies and dash for the exit. The moment sunlight peeks through the tent, a hard voice cries out as arms surround my body and I'm knocked to the ground. The world spirals while dread turns my entire being cold.

"S-San An!"

An arrow is lodged in his back. San An's fallen unconscious on top of me. Why is this horrible nightmare repeating?

The assailant takes the opportunity of our immobile states and charges with sword drawn. The guards are closing in but they won't be able to stop him in time. My arms attempt to shield San An. I know it's not enough. Someone, anyone, please save San An!

As the assailant brings down his blade, a sharp echo of metal striking metal erupts. The man who saves us is ironically, the same man who previously injured San An. With little effort, Ying slays the attacker. Before I can say anything, he flees from the base.

Kang Lang didn't kill him after all. Was this his way of repaying the debt? At the moment, who really cares!

"Master Dui!"

When fighting erupted, the court physician was already making his way over with a box of supplies. Once I move from underneath San An, Dui frantically treats his wound. Blood keeps pooling.

"Was he poisoned?! Why won't he stop bleeding?! San An! Please, wake up!"

"Your Highness! The arrow's not poisoned but the wound is deep. I may need to cut inside and find the source to stop the bleeding. Please, have one of the guards boil some water to disinfect the equipments. I also need to fetch a few items."

"Surgery? Water? No... no water!"

"Sire..."

"No water, it's poisoned!" The arrow is clean. In case the assassin failed, the water we'd use to treat the wound is enough to finish the rest. I'm glad the assailant was careless and overconfident, but it doesn't change the current dire situation.

"But, Your Highness!"

"Don't argue! Just save him! I'll start a fire for you. Cauterize the source if you must. The heat will disinfect all your tools. Hurry!"

Master Dui refocuses attention to San An whilst I rush to the closest torch and begin a fire outside of the tent.

"Everyone! Did you hear me? Don't drink the water until it's been tested. Find another clean source. In the meantime, send out messengers to Bao Dan and Ye with the antidote instructions. Lieutenant Zheng, I'm entrusting these efforts onto you."

Zheng promptly replies a confirmation and proceeds gathering his men.

Returning to San An's side, minutes feel like eternity. Once more, the Minister saved me after every pain and injury I've dealt.

I thought you've been freed from me, San An. Why must you keep doing this to yourself?

__Continue to page 512__

Chapter 45 – 2

Sentinels kept close watch from our towers while a handful of Wen Meng's bandits advanced farther out to scout for signs of movements from the north.

In the east, Han Bei is making his way through Ying Ling and in the west, Kang Lang is preparing to advance forth into Bei Ling. The remainder of Nan Rong's military leaders not currently at the northern base was making their way here. However, their march was impeded by sudden illness that swept over the ranks.

"Ye and Bao Dan are reporting similar cases. I imagine Bei Ling, before taking leave of Feng Jia, tainted the water supply of the River Huan, which flows through all three territories." San An explains.

Master Yu was sent to treat the soldiers but the situation remains grim. Bodies are piling daily from this ailment that appears neither poison nor disease. Although the affliction is seemingly incurable, if the person is strong enough to withstand the assaults after three days, then there is a chance for survival. We've been careful with our water supply but fear is causing morale to dwindle. Many soldiers have family members who have fallen ill. It's natural that they want to leave ranks. However, duties bind them, and soon, there erupts discord all around.

While we contemplate the next move, drums signal movements from the north. San An and I run to the gate

to meet a lone rider galloping toward the base at full speed whilst kicking large amounts of dust into the air. The sentinels ready their weapons. However, there's no mistaking him.

Despite the Minister's protest, I rush outside while flailing my arms in the air for the sentinels to yield. The rider comes to an abrupt halt and leaps off the mare. Disregarding my disguise, his arms fly around me.

"Jin! What are you doing here? Why did you come alone? That's dangerous!"

"I had no choice. I was afraid you might have... Let's go inside."

In the large tent, Jin takes three pieces of paper from his breast pocket. I scan them over and realize his reason for coming.

"It is poison! How did you find the antidote?"

"You can thank the White Cranes for the instructions. Su Jian's last resort before giving up Feng Jia was to poison San An. He's used a slow-reacting toxin, which is why so many have been afflicted. Had everyone been on immediate guard, there would have been significantly less casualties. Not only that, by allowing the toxin to wash from the body in three days, he aimed to fool our physicians into believing the cause is more likely ailment."

San An is disheartened. No matter how many years have gone by, troubles from his past will not relinquish.

Why can't Su Jian understand that it was not the Minister's fault? He was simply another victim.

"San An, we'll stop him."

My attempt to provide succor is met with disregard. In my stead, Jin steps forward and places a hand on the Minister's shoulder.

"San An... Brother. Don't endure this pain alone. He Pi and I are with you and so is Bao Lai. Enough is enough. Su Jian may be our brother, but his actions are unforgivable. Whatever happened long ago was not our fault. We were children then. As men now, we are responsible for our actions. Soon enough, we three will unite to guide Nan Rong into a proper future. We only ask that you continue the fight a while longer."

The Minister's expression changed the moment Jin called him, "Brother." From taut apprehension, he now appears calm. This is everything San An needed to hear all along; that he still has family who cares for him.

Curiously, San An is not the only one who's had a change in demeanor. "Jin, does that mean—"

"Yes. I've come to terms with my blood and my life. He Pi and I will rejoin Nan Rong when the ordeal is over, and with San An, establish our dynasty anew. We each have our weaknesses and strengths. Together, we can lead the Southland effectively. And you, Bao Lai, will remain in our council."

"Who, me? Council? Are you nuts?"

Jin laughs and touches his fingers to my cheek. The same loving warm smile I remember is still there. However, his sense of self and confidence are new aspects I've not experienced. I'm so glad they've come to an understanding at last.

"Now is not the time to dawdle," San An remarks. "We must distribute this list to every physician in the three territories. Also, Bao Lai, I must apologize. Another note arrived yesterday. Kang Lang was poisoned. I feared a foolhardy response, so I've kept this from you."

"What? K-Kang Lang was... San An, I have to go now!"

"Yes. I know you worry for him. Now that there is hope, I'll have a messenger escort you to Bao Dan. Hurry. Come back to me soon."

San An trusts me and that makes me happy. After embracing my love, Jin and I leave the base together with two messengers and eventually part ways. Jin goes south to Master Yu, a messenger rides to Ye, and yet another escorts me to Mu Lai, the capital of Bao Dan.

Continue to page 546

Chapter 45 – 3

Sentinels kept close watch from our towers while a handful of Wen Meng's bandits advanced farther out to scout for signs of movements from the north.

In the east, Han Bei is making his way through Ying Ling and in the west, Kang Lang is preparing to advance forth into Bei Ling. The remainder of Nan Rong's military leaders not currently at the northern base was making their way here. However, their march was impeded by sudden illness that swept over the ranks.

"Ye and Bao Dan are reporting similar cases. I imagine Bei Ling, before taking leave of Feng Jia, tainted the water supply of the River Huan, which flows through all three territories." San An explains.

Master Yu was sent to treat the soldiers but the situation remains grim. Bodies are piling daily from this ailment that appears neither poison nor disease. Although the affliction is seemingly incurable, if the person is strong enough to withstand the assaults after three days, then there is a chance for survival. We've been careful with our water supply but fear is causing morale to dwindle. Many soldiers have family members who have fallen ill. It's natural that they want to leave ranks. However, duties bind them, and soon, there erupts discord all around.

While we contemplate the next move, drums signal movements from the north. San An and I run to the gate

to meet a lone rider galloping toward the base at full speed whilst kicking large amounts of dust into the air. The sentinels ready their weapons. However, there's no mistaking him.

Despite the Minister's protest, I rush outside while flailing my arms in the air for the sentinels to yield. The rider comes to an abrupt halt and leaps off the mare. Disregarding my disguise, his arms fly around me.

"Jin! What are you doing here? Why did you come alone? That's dangerous!"

"I had no choice. I was afraid you might have... Let's go inside."

In the large tent, Jin takes three pieces of paper from his breast pocket. I scan them over and realize his reason for coming.

"It is poison! How did you find the antidote?"

"You can thank the White Cranes for the instructions. Su Jian's last resort before giving up Feng Jia was to poison San An. He's used a slow-reacting toxin, which is why so many have been afflicted. Had everyone been on immediate guard, there would have been significantly less casualties. Not only that, by allowing the toxin to wash from the body in three days, he aimed to fool our physicians into believing the cause is more likely ailment."

San An is disheartened. No matter how many years have gone by, troubles from his past will not relinquish.

Why can't Su Jian understand that it was not the Minister's fault? He was simply another victim.

"San An, we'll stop him."

My attempt to provide succor is met with disregard. In my stead, Jin steps forward and places a hand on the Minister's shoulder.

"San An... Brother. Don't endure this pain alone. He Pi and I are with you and so is Bao Lai. Enough is enough. Su Jian may be our brother, but his actions are unforgivable. Whatever happened long ago was not our fault. We were children then. As men now, we are responsible for our actions. Soon enough, we three will unite to guide Nan Rong into a proper future. We only ask that you continue the fight a while longer."

The Minister's expression changed the moment Jin called him, "Brother." From taut apprehension, he now appears calm. This is everything San An needed to hear all along; that he still has family who cares for him.

Curiously, San An is not the only one who's had a change in demeanor. "Jin, does that mean—"

"Yes. I've come to terms with my blood and my life. He Pi and I will rejoin Nan Rong when the ordeal is over, and with San An, establish our dynasty anew. We each have our weaknesses and strengths. Together, we can lead the Southland effectively. And you, Bao Lai, will remain in our council."

"Who, me? Council? Are you nuts?"

Jin laughs and touches his fingers to my cheek. The same loving warm smile I remember is still there. However, his sense of self and confidence are new aspects I've not experienced. I'm so glad they've come to an understanding at last.

"Now is not the time to dawdle," San An interrupts brusquely. "We must distribute this list to every physician in the three territories. Also, Bao Lai, I must apologize. Another note arrived yesterday. Kang Lang was poisoned. I feared a foolhardy response, so I've kept this from you."

"What...?" I feel numb. Kang Lang. My Kang Lang! How could this happen? How could I have let you suffered alone all this time in Bao Dan!

Trepidation threatens to suffocate me. Out of panic, I grab one of the copies and dash for the exit. The moment sunlight peeks through the tent, a hard voice cries out as arms surround my body and I'm knocked to the ground. The world spirals while dread turns my entire being cold.

"J-Jin!"

An arrow is lodged in his back. Jin's fallen unconscious on top of me.

The assailant charges. San An draws his blade and storms forward. Soldiers rush to defend the Minister though San An's skills are far better than any man present. The assailant never had a chance.

"Jin! Jin!" What am I yelling at Jin for? *"Master Dui!"*

When fighting erupted, the court physician was already making his way over with a box of supplies. Once Jin is moved inside San An's tent, Dui frantically treats his wound. Blood keeps pooling.

"Was he poisoned?! Why won't he stop bleeding?! Jin! Please, wake up!"

"Your Highness! The arrow's not poisoned but the wound is deep. I may need to cut inside and find the source to stop the bleeding. Please, have one of the guards boil some water to disinfect the equipments. I also need to fetch a few items."

"Surgery? Water? No... no water!"

"Sire..."

"No water, it's poisoned!" The arrow is clean. In case the assassin failed, the water we'd use to treat the wound is enough to finish the rest. I'm glad the assailant was careless and overconfident, but it doesn't change the current dire situation.

"But, Your Highness!"

"Don't argue! Just save him! I'll start a fire for you. Cauterize the source if you must. The heat will disinfect all your tools. Hurry!"

Master Dui refocuses attention to Jin whilst I rush to the closest torch and begin a fire outside of the tent.

Chapter 45: Brothers United

San An heard our conversation and immediately takes necessary precautions.

Minutes feel like eternity. Everything seems a horrid nightmare that won't end. Jin is hurt because of my recklessness and there's nothing I can do.

Please Jin, wake up. Kang Lang, please wait for me.

Chapter 46: Bao Dan

Blurry night descended over the horizon. Dui and San An were tending to Jin and didn't need interruption. I've been sitting in silence, gawking at the darkened skies.

Above, a bright star seemingly vies for my attention. It glimmers and twinkles in an attempt to comfort my troubles. I know this star. Master Tai Hung once said it is meant for me, because my name is Bao Lai, the same as this star, Polaris.

Polaris. Can you hear me? Please, Heaven above, spare Jin and Kang Lang. Keep them safe. I'll gladly trade my life for theirs.

"Bao Lai." The soft whisper echoes. For a moment, I thought Polaris answered my prayers. As my eyes reopen, San An stands before me. His demeanor is solemn.

"San An, is Jin... How is Jin?"

"He'll live."

Relief escapes in a sharp exhale before tears again flow.

"I hope your tears are happy ones." San An removes a kerchief from his breast pocket and, kneeling down, wipes my face.

"They are. I'm so sorry. I didn't mean to hurt Jin!"

"It was not your fault. We were targeted. This unfortunate incident could not have been avoided. Thanks to you, Jin and everyone else here were saved. We tested the water supply and as you've warned, it was poisoned."

San An's kind words put me into further shame. My head lowers to keep him from witnessing more tears. Immediately, San An places a warm hand on my cheek.

"Look up, Bao Lai. There's no point for us both to be miserable. Take to Bao Dan."

His warm, albeit wounded eyes stare back gently. Each time I've thought he's been freed, invisible shackles continue binding the Minister. San An always employ every fashion to guarantee my happiness at the cost of his own. After all the insults I've dealt, he still wants to comfort me. I truly hope this wonderful man will be loved by someone more deserving.

"San An, I don't want to see you miserable because of me. What must I do to free you?"

He smiles and then shyly glances at the sky. "It is a prison I've made for myself. You cannot free me, Bao Lai. Though, maybe with time, all will resolve."

"Please don't withdraw from love because of my faults. You must find happiness!"

I reach for his hands and squeeze tightly. Following a pause, he returns the gesture.

"An arduous task, but if you will ask this of me, then I won't deny you. I would never deny you of anything." A delicate hint of sadness is hidden behind amity.

"I do! I wish you happiness, San An! All the happiness in the world!"

"Then, by your blessing, I'm certain I will find that happiness. Now, I've arranged an escort for you."

"But, Jin..."

"Jin will be fine. I will tend to my brother. You have done everything I've asked and more; therefore, I release you of this duty. You are no longer He Pi."

Jin saved me and I'm still worried for him. I shouldn't leave. Be that as it may, Kang Lang is far away and suffering alone. I'm too conflicted to choose. Hence, San An makes the final decision.

"As you are no longer He Pi, you don't belong here. If you will not leave of your own accord, then I must remove you by force."

"When you put it that way... Thank you, San An, for everything. Please believe me when I say I am grateful for having known you. And, please tell Jin that I'm sorry. I hope we'll meet again."

"I am grateful for our chance meeting as well, Bao Lai. Through you, I have come to look outside of myself and learned to love another. I have known the sorrows of love. Now, I also wish to see the joy that it can bring, as it has for you and Kang Lang. We will all certainly meet again."

Removing He Pi's crown, I return my title to the man who first bestowed it to me. Following a warm embrace, San An sends me with one of the lieutenants across the borders to Bao Dan. From there, I make my way to find Grand Commander Kang Lang in the capital of Mu Lai.

Continue to page 588

Chapter 47: A Choice from the Heart

Blurry night descended over the horizon. Dui was tending to San An and didn't need interruption. I've been sitting in silence, gawking at the darkened skies.

Above, a bright star seemingly vies for my attention. It glimmers and twinkles in an attempt to comfort my troubles. I know this star. Master Tai Hung once said it is meant for me, because my name is Bao Lai, the same as this star, Polaris.

Polaris. Can you hear me? Please, Heaven above, spare my beloveds. Keep Kang Lang and San An safe. I'll gladly trade my life for theirs.

"Your Highness," a distant voice calls out.

For a moment, I thought Polaris answered my silent prayers. As my eyes reopen, Dui is standing before me. His demeanor is solemn and he's excessively fatigued. It's possible he may fall over at any moment.

"Master Dui! How is San An?"

"He's stable for now."

Relief escapes in a sharp exhale before tears again flow.

"You sure cry a lot, sire." Dui remarks. "Anyway, the Minister is resting and you were right, Your Highness, the water supply was poisoned. Lieutenant Zheng and his men found a clean spring in one of the caves nearby. For now, things are secured."

"Thank you, Master Dui."

"No need to thank me."

I thought he'd said all he'd wanted. Yet, Dui hesitates.

"Is something the matter, Master Dui?"

"Well, I know this isn't my business but..." Pausing, Dui shuffles in place. "Your fiancé, Your Highness, is the Grand Commander of Bao Dan, isn't he?"

Why do I even bother wearing this disguise? Does everyone know I'm a fraud?

"Y-Yes. Is there a point?"

"I'm not judging you, of course. It's just that if you're worried, then now's the time to leave. I'll watch over the Prime Minister. At this point, there's nothing else to be done."

He's giving me a chance to escape to Bao Dan. Should I go? San An is stable and I have no idea what's become of Kang Lang. I don't want to leave San An but I also want to see Kang Lang, even if he doesn't care to see me.

How they've both suffered—are still suffering— because of me! Kang Lang left for Ye to protect my happiness. San An, once more, protected my life.

Should anything happen to either of them, I don't know what I'd do. It's an undeniable fact: I love them both. Yet, the reality is, I can't be in two places at once, and likewise, I cannot continue holding two hearts in my hands. I must make the decision now.

While uncertainty causes panic, sudden throbbing pain in my heart forces the realization that within the depths of my soul, I do know who matters most to me.

Stay with San An (Continue to page 515)

Go to Bao Dan (Continue to page 562)

Chapter 48: My Sweet Minister

I trust you, Kang Lang. If I doubt you for even a moment, you'll only sulk. I hope you're in Neng Cao's care and I hope you're safe. You've always been strong, so stay strong for the one you love.

"I will stay with San An. May I see him?"

"Yes. I gave him a draught for the pain. The Minister won't likely wake up until tomorrow. All the same, try not to wake him."

Master Dui takes the lead into the tent, and after inspecting San An's condition once more with great care, quietly leaves.

Taking to the chair at his bedside, my hands reach for his hand. San An is so pale. His breathing is low and his body is nearly still. It's killing me to see him this way. Everything hurts, inside and out; from my heart to my soul, my mind and body—all at once.

I'm afraid... terrified of losing you, San An! I love you. I love you so much! Please, don't leave me!

Tears rain endlessly and the world around become obscured. I can't see his face through the haze clouding my eyes. I can't see his face... a world without San An... is too cruel a world. A world where my existence is meaningless. Why did it take so long to realize he's the person I've been waiting to meet all my life? All my

515

doubts are vanquished and through the haze, everything becomes clear.

I love you, San An! I will spend my life making up for every pain I've caused and every injury I've dealt. Stay with me. Please, don't go.

"I love you. Stay with me." The words fall repetitiously in prayer until becoming a wish. Somewhere in the midst of distress, reality blurs into dreams. In them, we are together. Once San An wakes, I'll do anything to make his dreams come true.

Chapter 48 – 2

A gentle hand stroking my hair induces overflowing nostalgia. This intoxicating scent is one I've come to adore. The source is within reach and still, I can't grasp it. Somewhere in the floating darkness, a soft voice calls out my name.

Sharp pain swells the instant eyelids fling open. I can barely see through swollen eyes. Rubbing through dried rheum, his pale face finally comes into view. He's awake!

"San An! I'm so glad! Are you okay? Do you need anything? Are you hurting?"

Apathetic eyes direct back. San An doesn't respond.

"Try to contain your excitement, Your Highness. The Prime Minister needs rest."

"Hmphf! D-Doctor!" I had no idea Dui was in the tent. Shock nearly sent me to the floor.

"Yes, Your Highness." He ignores my foolishness and examines San An. Then, taking a small wooden bowl from a nearby table, presents it to me.

"Well, since you're here, Highness, maybe you can convince the Minister to take his medicine. I've tried. He's in no state for me to force it down his throat."

The physician places the bowl in my hands and then leaves the tent. Once Dui's out of ear's reach, I turn to the Minister.

"Why do you refuse this medicine, San An?"

His attention suddenly averts, leaving the tent to deafening silence. San An's utterly aloof. I know he's still wounded by my previous indifference. He has every right to snub me. I just refuse to let him push me away. I love this man more than anything in the world. Even if he never loves me again, I'll stay. This is what I want and I'll be damned before I give up San An!

"I'm sorry, San An. You're injured because of me. I know you must not want to see this face that's caused you so much sorrow or waste your breath on someone who's ignored your pleading for so long. Well, you don't have to speak another word to me as long as I live. Just let me tend to you. San An, I know you're in pain so please, take the medicine."

Excruciating silence won't abscond. My heart is on the verge of bursting. I took his affections for granted and now that it's gone, I've lost half of me.

Why do I keep crying when he's the one who's hurt? It's not fair to him. I haven't been fair to San An. The shame of which beckons me to turn from his grace. Yet, San An, as forgiving as ever, softly relieves my anguish through his words. "It's bitter."

Spinning back hastily, the bowl in my hand nearly slips to the floor. "That's why you won't take it?!"

Tilting his gaze, displeasure sets a frown on his mouth. The injury pains him; still, he continues. "Why are you here, Bao Lai? Didn't Dui send you to Bao Dan?"

I thought Dui saw through my disguise when he told me to leave for my fiancé in Bao Dan. He did it through San An's instructions. Though in a life threatening state, San An was thinking of *my* happiness, again. Then, he must still love me. I'm so happy! And yet, he attempted to send me away—to assume I'm heartless enough to let him suffer alone. How dare he!

"You... you... you jerk! Did you think I would leave when your life was in danger?!"

Emotions rise in torrents; I don't know what more to say. Words won't come. All the same, there are no words to express how I feel. Confusion pouring from the expression peering back abruptly returns to apathy. Slowly, his attention shifts to utter disregard.

Sharp shooting pains radiate from my chest. My lungs feel tight. The torment merely increases as time goes by. This is the same pain I've caused him. San An's tried to be freed of me so many times before. Was this last attempt to send me away due to his love or was it merely for himself? Maybe, he's found resolve to relinquish me just as I've found resolve to never let him go. We're both stubborn. Between his wants and mine, I choose to be selfish.

"Mmmh!"

A muffled moan escapes from San An's lips when my own press against them with as much passion as I can muster. My trembling hand reaches for his face. This beautiful face of the man I love, why have I never before touched it? His beautiful hands, beautiful body, beautiful mind, and beautiful soul; I won't accept any less than to have them all to myself. San An shirks away and my hold draws him back. I've tasted every part of his sweet lips and still, I want more. Time and time again, passion imprint onto San An until my face turns numb. If this kiss is the only medium to convey my affections, then let it never end.

Light wind rustles against the tent, followed by a strong gale that bursts inside. Shock manages to pull back my senses. I shouldn't be so rough. The Minister *is* injured. Our lips finally part. San An's beet-red face gawks on in bewilderment.

"Bao... Lai."

"Yes, San An?"

"Why...?"

"Because I wanted to and, I'm not leaving you. You shouldn't have confessed that you loved me, San An. You'll never be rid of me."

The Minister is too shocked to return neither words nor gestures; though, soon after, the distance between us grows. He's resumed the indifferent pose.

"San An, please take the medicine and then sleep. You'll heal faster this way."

"What special concern is it of yours for my state of affairs? Leave me."

His contempt crushes my heart; misery courses through and through. He can hate me forever. I am by his side and that is enough.

"Yes. Please, give me more of your callous disdain, San An. Scorn me. Hurt me as I've hurt you until you can learn to look upon me again. Until then, allow me to stay as your servant, forever by your side."

The clenched jaw serves to conceal his suffering. I don't want him to suffer; but, rather he suffers by chiding me than to suffer in silence. I await his rebuke though none comes. In place of anger, concern floods his countenance.

"It isn't safe here. Our allies are far away and this base's defenses are meager. Wang Liang will likely come for me now that his assassin's perished. If you are my servant, then follow my command: take to Bao Dan and seek refuge."

"Is that the only reason you want me to leave?"

"Why must you question me to soothe your ego yet again? Your dear Kang Lang will protect you. I am in no state to promise your safety."

"Yes! Soothe my ego. Say you love me and don't let me go! With you, I'll gladly face any danger. For a short time, I saw the world without you, San An. It is not a world I wish to live in."

"What do you hope to accomplish by torturing me? I cannot have you but still, you want my regards? You would take from me my last drop of dignity to validate your esteem?" A heavy scoff falls and then his expression peers into mine. "I promised myself once to never deny you of anything, Your Highness. If vindication will soothe your ego, then you will have it. I love you. I love you so much, I've lost all reason! How many times more will you have me repeat the words until you are satisfied? I love you, Bao Lai!"

"And I love you, San An."

"An egregious lie!" Bitterness erupts. A single tear wells in the corner of his eyes. I've made San An cry but I have no regrets. Show me everything. Don't suffer in silence.

"Your servant would not dare." Taking his gentle hand in mine, I loosen the collar of my robe and slip it underneath. His hand trembles at the touch of the bounded rises on my chest.

"Even if you will not have me now, San An, I am yours."

"Why?" The hoarse whisper forces a few more tears to surge.

"Love doesn't need any particular reason, San An; else, it would be too mechanical. If reasons will soothe *your* ego, then let it be known that you have dominated every part of my will. Through kindness, or otherwise, derision, I've come to realize you are all I need in this world. So, live for me. I beg this of you."

Slowly withdrawing his tremulous hand from beneath my robe, San An turns away. Whether he believes or doubts my affections, I won't run. For my boldness, I may appear a disgrace. Still, I'd rather he look upon me with ridicule than for him to never look upon me again.

"It's too bitter," he finally responds shyly. I thought he meant our love, until his eyes fall on the bowl of medicine.

He's afraid of a little bitter taste but it was fine to take an arrow to the back? The childish nonsense!

"Then, allow your servant to add something sweet."

Sipping a small amount of the bitter liquid, my mouth presses against his to pass the concoction through. San An momentarily withdraws from the taste, and then immediately, his lips seek to take every trace from mine.

His adorable blushing urges me to continue. In little time, the bowl of medicine is empty. He falls asleep soon after. Lying beside San An, I eventually follow suit.

Chapter 48 – 3

In the week that followed, San An and I spent endless days together. Though still emotionally reserved, his guard loosened daily, and then it felt as though we met again for the first time. We spoke of anything and everything, and allowed each other into the deepest parts of our souls.

Between Dui's examinations, I snuck kisses to San An. The Minister continued griping about bitter medicine, which merely resulted in even more kisses. I never want to stop kissing those lips. When He Pi's disguise can finally be removed, I never will.

"San An, a letter came today. Kang Lang has recovered. He's resumed Bao Dan's assault against Bei Ling. Hu and Yue arrived last night. The troops are resting but they'll move out soon. Hopefully, it won't be long until this war is over and He Pi returns."

"That is wonderful news! Now that our generals have come, I can feel relieved. I've been so worried for your safety."

"And I was worried for yours; for different reasons. Not long ago, I felt you had retreated; resigned all your will. I'm happy that your eyes are livelier now."

"If they are livelier, it is because of you."

"But, *I* caused your dejection. Please, forgive me."

"I will not." Pausing, his tone turns sheepish. "However, were you to become my wife, I would not dare hold grudges. Even the mightiest of villains and the greatest of heroes submit to their wives."

The thought sets my cheeks on fire. Wife! Yes, I want to become San An's wife! No other will have him but me. Though he smirks at my ridiculous reaction, his face isn't less red.

"How you tease me, Minister! A crown prince married to a servant? You must share Kang Lang's dramatics."

The mention of his believed rival turns San An's expression sour. I haven't changed. I always say the wrong thing. He becomes quiet.

"San An, Kang Lang is my friend. I will speak of him from time to time, but that doesn't diminish my affections for you."

"Is he simply your friend? As I recall, he is your beloved."

"He is my friend and I do love him. I also love Jin. However, I've come to understand that the love I have for them is based purely on familiarity and friendship. I was too excited by the prospect of love that I've confused dependency and amiability for intimacy, desire, and ardent adoration. After all I've done, you don't have to believe me. Maybe someday soon, I can prove to you everything. Until then, please don't be sad; just be angry with me."

A gentle hand caresses my cheek; soft fingers linger a moment more. I cling tightly onto his arm, kiss his fingertips, and then trace my lips on the curves on his palm. It then occurs to me, I've seen this palm before. After examining every line and crevice with care, an impertinent grin crosses my mouth.

"Must I ask the reason?" San An's head tilts due confusion.

Kneeling beside the bed, I present my left palm. San An understands and holds up his right. Every line is a match from beginning to end. Every nook, crevice, divergence and convergence, and every curve to every turn are in perfect proportions. Pressing our palms together, a deep kiss ensues which courses a new wondrous sensation throughout. My soul mate is beside me, but then, I never needed lines on a palm to validate that.

While drawing back to catch our breaths, a thought occurs to me: I want more from San An. As close as we are, I still feel worlds apart. Disappointedly, my desire is not possible in our predicament. Just as I decide to steal another kiss, Bai Hu storms into the tent, followed by Zhen Yue.

"Prime Minister! You look terrible!"

"It's a pleasure to see you, too, Bai Hu." San An replies dryly. "Haven't you any manners to first announce yourself before disrupting others?"

"I have no manners, Minister. Anyway, we need to borrow her." Hu points my way. "We're heading to Bei Ling and she's the *fearless leader*. Even though they've recovered, the men's morale is low. This will probably be the final push. Everything counts."

"Absolutely not!" San An, frowning, grips my hand tightly.

"San An, it's okay. I should go."

"After your promises to stay by me, you wish to leave my side, Bao Lai?"

"Of course not! It's just... if I can be of service, I should go. I'll come back soon. Right, Hu?"

"Yeah, yeah. We'll protect her." Bai Hu mumbles.

The Minister stares at my pleading eyes and then heaves a sigh of concession. "Tell the men to rest for today. We'll depart for Bei Ling tomorrow."

"What do you mean, 'we?' You can't go San An!"

"Either I accompany you or you're to stay here."

"Stubborn, stubborn man! You can barely sit up without wincing and you want to ride to battle?"

"Is... something going on between you two?" Hu rolls his eyes from me to the Minister. There is no response aside for our frustrated and flustered faces. Both soldiers glance curiously at one another and then, shrugging, part from the tent.

"San An. I know you're worried, but so am I. Maybe my presence will mean nothing. However, if there is at least a chance I can help bring this conflict to a quick end, then I should. Would you do otherwise were you in my shoes?"

Biting his lips, San An looks away. "I'm not discounting your efforts. Your safety is everything to me."

"And your safety is everything to me! This is why I must go. San An, frankly, you can't stop me. I just don't want you to hate me."

"I could never hate you," the pained whisper is almost inaudible.

Tumults swell in my chest. I want to provide an oath; a promise that my words are true. Climbing onto the bed, I crouch over San An. He's startled by my impulsiveness. Still, his attention is mine.

"Take from me anything you wish; whether it is my body or my soul. I promise everything to you."

The crimson face stares back in dismay. At first shocked by my boldness, his fingers then gently touch my cheek.

"I am not a dishonorable man, Bao Lai. Until your heart and soul is bound to mine on the day of our nuptial, I dare not. Hurry and save Nan Rong, and then return to my side."

"Thank you, San An!" Soft kisses rain. All my will exerts an everlasting imprint onto his lips.

With San An entrusted to Dui's care, I take my leave with the generals. Just a while longer and then this conflict will be over. When I return, our lives can begin. There is no greater happiness I can dream than to become San An's wife.

Chapter 48 – 4

Bao Dan and Ning continued their advances. With Nan Rong's generals, I accompanied our forces north. Our troops were disheartened at first, but knowing that victory is on the horizon, morale increased the closer we came to Bei Ling. On the day before Nan Rong's forces would undoubtedly meet the opposition in battle, the best news we've received since this conflict began spread like wildfire: He Pi and the White Cranes stormed the palace and claimed Emperor Cai Pai under their protection. The remaining guards who served Wang Liang either surrendered or were put to death and the North's defenses withdrew from the front line.

Bei Ling was no longer a threat. However, Wang Liang was nowhere to be found. Some claimed he perished during the raid, though that supposition is yet confirmed. My intuition signaled that he is alive. Whether he will become a threat in the future remains to be seen.

In place of Wang Liang's authority, a new council comprising of White Crane members formed. At present, representatives from all the lands are gathered in Sai Mi's—Bei Ling's capital—courtyard to discuss matters of diplomacy and the potential danger Su Jian may pose.

Those in attendant are familiar faces I had anticipated to see again, and also a new face that is hardly unfamiliar: He Pi's. I hope he doesn't notice my

inappropriate gawking. It's strange to see my face on someone else's body; though, he must feel the same.

After matters settle, Kang Lang, Jin, and He Pi approach. The first to address me is He Pi; though, not in the manner I'd expected. His Highness reaches for my shoulders and brings his face close. I thought he was joking, but when it becomes apparent he would not stop, my hand instinctively flies across his face. Rubbing his cheek, He Pi stares on with wounded eyes.

"You're mean!" He scolds me. "Didn't Jin deliver my message? You're my woman, right?"

"Your Highness is an idiot. I am to become your sister, so do not joke that way."

"My sister?"

Kang Lang and Jin turn solemn. My answer is clear; I've chosen San An. In time, Jin forces an amiable smile while Kang Lang frowns bitterly.

"That's too bad!" He Pi sings. "Oh, well. Before I go, I'll give you a boon—anything you want for having subbed in my stead."

"That's not necessary, Your Highness. Well, wait, I suppose there is one thing. Please return Consort En's titles and give Empress Pai the respect she deserves. I don't know what must be done but if you can restore them... well, actually, all the women from court during the conflict... to grace, that is all I ask."

He Pi throws a short grin and complies. The elation in Jin's expression gladdens my heart. I just hope that with time, he will come to forgive my previous transgressions.

Before returning with Jin to Nan Rong, His Highness presented a letter that by his request, I had to promise not to read until I've left Bei Ling. I don't know whether He Pi is an enigma or that he's the most childish person I've ever met. Though, that same childishness is sometimes exerted by San An and Jin. It must run in the bloodline.

Kang Lang, alternatively, remained silent until we are alone. Both arms are crossed and his back is to the wall. This silly person has never been more serious. In exchange for my friendly smile, I receive a frown.

"I'm happy you're well, Kang Lang."

"Are you? How well can I possibly be, knowing you've chosen the Minister? Just so I can clear this from my mind, when you last returned to Ye, there was something you wanted to tell me, wasn't there?"

"Y-Yes."

"I hope you realize my affections for Neng Cao were pretense to earn her support for Nan Rong. Was it enough to drive you into San An's arms?"

Everything Kang Lang endured was for me, I know that. His injuries from the poison, his conquest of Feng Jia, to the seduction of Neng Cao were to bring about my happiness. Still, I've not been able to do a thing for him. Guilt surges within, but I owe him the truth.

"No. Maybe, I've always known San An is the one, but I was too stubborn. When I thought you loved Neng Cao, I understood the pain you felt for my rejections. I'm sorry. You mean more to me than you'll ever know. Is there nothing I can do for you, my dearest friend?"

The bitter frown lingers. His piercing stare continues scrutinizing me. For a time, the world around grows still. Then, like a fading flame, inner turmoil slowly dissipates and the frown releases into a perfect grin. Patting my head, Kang Lang guffaws.

"Good girl! You finally grew up! If you want to make it up to me, come to my wedding. I expect *nice* gifts."

"You-You're getting married?!"

"Don't sound so jealous! At first, I seduced her because of you but, what can I say? That timid cross-dressing wallflower reminded me of a certain fake He Pi. I became fond of her. Unlike you, she's so in love with me that I almost feel bad for taking advantage. Anyway, like I said, bring *nice* gifts. The Emperor of Ye and Bao Dan commands thee!"

Without the proper response, I merely nod in compliance. His authoritative air provokes a burst of laughter. After his usual griping, Kang Lang joins in. I'm truly happy he's found someone deserving of his devotion. And, I haven't forgotten Jin. It is my ambition to find his happiness, however many years more that may take.

Following our extended pleasantries, Kang Lang leaves for Bao Dan while I prepare for my return to San An. Upon reaching the entrance of the courtyard, another familiar face emerges from the shadows to impede the path. This one, however, makes me shudder.

"Lord Han Bei, what—"

"Enough small talk. Are you ready to fulfill your part of our agreement?"

"Right now? Could I—"

"No. I kept my promise and delivered reinforcements promptly. Will you return my honor with disrespect through stall tactics? Had I done the same, this happy day would not exist for Nan Rong. Ungrateful woman! If you will keep your words, come with me now!"

Why is he such a bully? I must keep my promise but every part of me is screaming for San An. Before I can plead for an extension, Han Bei storms off. I have no choice but to follow him. Never did I dream doing so would change everything.

Chapter 48 – 5

"Your Highness, the caravan from Nan Rong will reach our capital this afternoon. Will you allow me an audience at this time?"

I've been looking out the massive window from my study while waiting for Nan Rong's emissary to arrive. After leaving with Han Bei, my life changed drastically and obligations kept me from returning to San An. As it happens, the late Empress Dong Xing did have a younger sister who was taken to safety during the previous wars at court. That infant was Bao Lai, Princess of Fan Fa. Han Bei saw the resemblance in our faces and thus proposed the agreement that brought me to Ning. The letter which He Pi presented in Bei Ling also proved my birthright. How he came across this document, I do not know. There's very little chance he would tell me.

Yet, I didn't want this authority. My nephew, Emperor Yuan, abdicated on my behalf, and against my wishes. He's young and wants the freedom to travel. I envy that. Still, with this authority, there are changes in Ning's laws I intend to make so that the East will retain friendship with Nan Rong. I've also pardoned Kang Lang. He returned home to visit his parents and present his new bride. Han Bei, whose demeanor has softened toward me, remains my private council.

"Of course, Lord Han Bei. What can I do for you?"

"Does Your Highness intend to forge an alliance with Nan Rong through marriage?"

"You're forward as usual, Lord Han Bei. Yes, if San An will have me."

"Then, allow me to speak my mind before it is too late. I am the better candidate. For a long time, I was your sister's council and then your nephew's. In short, for a very long time, I was Ning. Despite your opinion, the country's welfare should be placed first and foremost, in the hands of a true Ning citizen. Everything I do, I do for Ning. For the sake of the Eastern Empire and perhaps, for my sake, give your hand to me."

"Lord Han Bei, I don't doubt your love for Ning but this is a matter of the heart. Even though you find it selfish, I trust San An. He is a capable and trustworthy man."

"If it is a matter of the heart, then certainly you cannot be that blind! From the first moment we've met, I've desired you, regardless of your gender! Would I have placed Ning in danger to support the Southland for an agreement that didn't benefit me, if not for you? My derision was a farce. Surely, you knew!"

"I-I'm sorry, I had no idea. I'm flattered, really. That makes little difference, I love San An."

Where is this coming from? I truly thought he hated me the moment he learned of my gender.

Han Bei's hardened tone quickly concedes to the sarcastic manner to which I've grown accustomed. His serious demeanor turns indolent.

"As you will, Your Highness." He returns airily before taking leave from the room.

Without knowing how to proceed, my attention returns to the window.

Chapter 48 – 6

Shortly after lunch, Nan Rong's emissary and the large caravan arrive. Unable to contain excitement, I rush to receive San An at the gate. In front of the nobles, composure and formality are kept. It feels like an eternity before the Minister and I finally take to the gardens for a stroll. Immediately, my arms fly around the man I dearly love. The gesture is not returned.

"San An?"

"Your Highness."

"You mustn't call me that. I'm still Bao Lai. Is everything all right?"

"I could not be happier. Nan Rong was invited to this peace summit by our feared adversary. The Southland is grateful to Your Highness for entertaining the idea."

Why is he so aloof? Is he putting on airs because of my title or is he angry that I did not return to Nan Rong after the assembly in Bei Ling? I clutch him tightly, but my dear minister relinquishes me.

"Your Highness, that is highly inappropriate."

"I've done much more inappropriate things than hold you, San An. Are you bashful?"

Without response, he continues the stroll. I move to match his pace while the emotional distance between us grows. As I contemplate for the right words, San An rehearses prepared discussions he's once used when Han Bei came to Nan Rong. I listen intently, only to realize he has no other desire than for the Southland's safety.

Afternoon turned to evening and a feast was prepared. San An, our guest of honor, retreated to his provided quarters shortly before celebrations began. Han Bei, too agitated by my disregard or perhaps, too agitated by my refusal to make him Ning's emperor, declined the invitation. Once more, I'm alone at a table set for three.

I can't imagine San An's withdrawn because of my title. He loved me while I was a peasant. Why hate me when I can do so much for him? Surely, he understood the reason we had to be apart until now. Or, has he decided against me altogether? Absence makes the heart grow fonder, but absence also equates to forgetfulness. If he's forgotten his affections for me, then maybe, I should also... No, I refuse concession! I've waited for him all my life. If I must wait a while longer for San An to love me again, then I will.

Chapter 48 – 7

The doors of his chamber burst open. I march in unannounced. San An, who has been watching the night sky from the window, abruptly directs attention to my fury.

"San An!"

"Your Highness?"

"It's Bao Lai! Address me as anything else and I won't have Ning ally with Nan Rong!"

Momentarily turning grim, he frowns. "Are you threatening me, Empress of Ning?"

"That I am! I'll let *that one* slide, but you must not do so again! Minister, why are you avoiding me?"

"I do not dare."

"Then, why must I dine alone tonight? You are my guest but you refuse to humor me for one meal. Even if your affections are lost, you can afford civility, can you not?"

His brows crinkle severely. San An moves to close the doors. I face him with every ounce of impertinence my courage can offer.

"Do not mention my affections so easily. Due affections, I did not wish to make Your Highness uncomfortable. Never would I dream of disrupting your time with Lord Han Bei."

"Han Bei? What does Han Bei have to do with you avoiding me?"

"You've come to me in sought of my attention and sweet words. Are you taunting me, Your Highness? Does my misery bring you joy?"

"Do you think so poorly of me that anytime I'm in the company of another man, I must lose my favor for you? I've confessed my ardent affections and promised myself to you! Why is that not enough? What must I do, San An, for you to accept me?"

"Have you no loyalty to anyone, Your Highness? Your future is promised to Lord Han Bei. How can you take your engagement so lightly? How much salt will you rub in my wounds?"

"Engagement? You... insolent man! If I were engaged, I never would have sent for you nor would I have had to endure the pain of being without you these many months! Who has told you such a heinous lie? Was it Han Bei?"

"Your dearest Kang Lang personally brought the *joyous* news to me. Are you saying that is not true?

"Yes, it's not true. For you to believe his words is nothing short of a slap across my face."

"I... don't understand. Why would Kang Lang lie?" Remorse fills every part of his expression but I know he's still not convinced.

"Kang Lang is dramatic. Against my protest, he's still not learned that you are not that type of man."

"What type of man, am I not?"

"The type to become jealous with passion. I suppose he thought the news would rush you to my side at once. He's mistaken. Kang Lang has been trying to taunt you into an overreaction for some time now; however, that is not within your character."

Recollections of that silly person force a smile to my face. I must send a letter to complain.

"I am... not a man of passion? Is that why he openly showed his vulgar lust for you in my quarters? And... I insulted your honor when you came to me after! Bao Lai—"

"I don't want to hear anymore, San An. Just listen. If you doubt me, then freely take your leave until you can learn to trust me. I'll wait for you. Forever, if I must."

This deep, echoing pain inside won't leave me. I fear my lack of resolve in the past has come to cost my future. His blank expression is unreadable; hence, my soul is drawn into a void.

"I love you." These words are all I can muster through a faint whisper.

Abruptly, San An's jaw clenches. His eyes sharpen. Hidden suffering courses to the surface and floods over his countenance.

Rushing hither, his arms encircle my entirety. San An presses a kiss so fervent that I can't breathe. Bouts and bouts of deep, loving kisses continue sapping my will. I fall against San An, who lifts me onto the bed and proceeds until I've drowned beneath his passion.

Once San An draws back shortly to catch our breaths, I can't help but laugh upon seeing his mouth stained by my lip balm.

"That's not the reaction I was hoping, Bao Lai."

"No, your lips are red." As I pull up a sleeve to wipe away the colors, he grabs my wrist and continues bombarding kisses until my face becomes numb.

"I'm sorry," he whispers while pulling away and resting his head on my chest. As I gently stroke his hair, San An's breathing calms and regains normalcy.

"We must stop apologizing to each other, San An. If you can forgive me, then know that I forgive you."

A short silence ensues and then San An pushes off the bed. Leaning over me, his gentle hand nudges up my chin to draw our two gazes into one. "Then, let us speak no more of the past. If you love me, truly and ardently, tell me at once."

My eyes burrow deeply into the beautiful brown stars looking back. "I love you with every part of me."

"Then, every part of you belongs to me."

San An unfastens the sash around my waist, reaches for the collars of my robe, and lifts them open.

"San An! Wait!"

"I have waited and I can wait no longer. Does Bao Lai refuse me?"

"Never! But first, accept my request."

"Anything."

"Stay beside me and become my lord. I can't give you Nan Rong, Minister, but I will make you emperor of Ning."

"Are you proposing to me, Bao Lai? You have become too bold!"

"Yes. You will see boldness in my every passion once you accept me."

"I have no other ambition than to make you mine. Though, I do feel cheated at this moment. It was my privilege to propose. For this offense, I may never forgive you."

"I shall gladly spend my life by your side to make amends."

San An smiles bright, and with one final confession of his love, begins claiming every part of me.

The End.

Chapter 49: My Dearest Friend

Master Huai, the physician of Mu Lai, made quick work of the instructions. Kang Lang and others, who were afflicted, were promptly treated. Copies of the instructions, along with completed batches of the antidotes, were distributed to other cities in Bao Dan.

Currently, the Grand Commander is resting quietly in his chamber. How innocent he appears for someone so foulmouthed! I can't help but smile while watching him sleep. No matter what happens between us, I'll always be grateful that we met and he'll always have a special place in my heart.

Late in the evening, my dear friend stirs. Kang Lang lifts up and yawns lazily like a child woken from a nap. He then peers sleepily while stretching both arms in the air.

"Hmm? When did you arrive, Your Majesty?"

"Earlier today. How do you feel, Kang Lang?"

It's a simple enough question and yet, he pouts. "How do I feel? I leave you alone for a moment and your innocence is lost. How do you think I feel?"

"What is that supposed to mean?"

"Do you deny it, Your Highness? You are a woman now, aren't you?"

"Yes. I am San An's woman."

I feel no shame to admit those words. If anything, I am proud. Kang Lang giggles and then frowns.

"How ironic. My efforts to have San An claim you were fruitful and yet, now, I'm terribly jealous. Did you know I seduced Neng Cao for her compliance? She's proposed to me. I've put off answering in hopes I could win you. Maybe, I'll answer her now."

"I pushed San An to claim me, so there's no need to feel envious. Still, that is cruel, Kang Lang. Did you truly seduce her?"

"Oh! It was *your* idea? I've read you all wrong, Your Highness! Not so innocent after all!" He giggles. "Well, what can I say? That timid cross-dressing wallflower reminds me of a certain fake He Pi. I've grown fond of her. Of course, she's nothing compared to the real imposter, but she'll do. Why are you frowning? She's delighted by my company and I could do a lot worse."

"Uh... huh. Well, I wish every happiness in the world for you, Kang Lang."

"If my happiness truly matters, Your Highness, then ditch San An and let's elope." He gives a familiar grin.

"Are you certain about that? I'm no longer pure."

"So? Neither am I."

"You do have a point."

While exchanging awkward stares, laughter suddenly bursts in the fashion we'd grown accustomed. I really missed having these silly conversations with him. As I take a seat on his bed, I'm reminded of our bond. Although I've come to realize my love for him stops at friendship, it doesn't change the fact that this person is dear to me. He is my dearest friend.

"I'm sorry, Kang Lang, for having put you in danger."

"Don't be, Your Highness. At first, everything was for you. I now do this for Nan Rong. I guess you can say I've come to love the Southland and also Bao Dan."

"Quite the obvious name choices: Bao Dan and Mu Lai. Oh, by the way, Kang Lang, about our promise... I fulfilled all three parts."

"What promise? Oh, you mean—you did not!"

"I did!"

"Why would you tell me that? I'll only fall deeper in love with you!"

Kang Lang, laughing, draws me into his arms. The days we spent together at Nan Rong's palace have ended. Be that as it may, I feel the same affable friendship as when we were Mu Dan and He Pi. Life will take us down different paths. In some ways, I'm saddened by this fact; in many others, happy and excited for whatever the future has in store for us.

"So, how did Han Bei react? Did he cry?"

"I can't imagine Lord Han Bei crying. No, he was confused and then, annoyed. You really should give him a chance. Beyond all doubts, your brother loves you."

"I don't want anyone's love except yours, Bao Lai." Kang Lang whispers while resting his chin on my shoulder.

"And, you have it. I love you very much, Kang Lang."

"Yes, I know. I love you, too."

Although I cannot stay by his side in the manner he desires, I have every intention for us to remain close. Someday, he will love Neng Cao ardently and live in blissful felicity. This is the future I pray for him.

We sit together until sunrise and recount our time apart. Then, taking leave of Kang Lang, I return to my beloved's side.

Chapter 50: San An's Temptation

San An's kisses rain on my face when I enter the tent. I've missed his touch and it's clear the pain of desire has also inflicted him.

"Just a while longer, San An, and this war will end. I'll have you all to myself."

"Don't tempt me, Bao Lai, or I will have you here and now."

Grinning impishly, we lean in closer to steal another kiss. Barely do our lips touch, Zhen Yue and Bai Hu abruptly storm into the tent. The pair arrived the day prior.

"Are we going now, Prime Minister?"

"Patience, Bai Hu. Make the final preparations. I'll join soon enough."

The Demon General starts to say more but at once, turns silent from taking notice of my gawking. Grumbling inaudibly, he signals to Yue and leaves the tent. I have no idea what that was about.

"Are we marching to Bei Ling, San An?"

"I will march with our generals. You must stay here with Qing Hai."

"No! We must stay together! Isn't that why I came? He Pi's appearance provides morale."

"I couldn't live with myself if something were to happen to you."

"And I cannot live without you, San An! Don't make my decisions for me!"

Staring back defiantly, almost impudently, every inch of me wishes to convey that I won't take no for an answer. At first troubled, a smile eventually appears on his gentle face, and then a kiss so exceedingly fervent is pressed against my lips that I grow weak.

Is he refuting my protest by sealing my lips? The nerve of him! I wish he'd never stop.

"You know I'm stubborn, Minister." The words fall tremulously as our lips part. My hands clutch tightly at his armor.

"I know. We are one and the same, Bao Lai. You will stay by my side and I will protect you."

Another kiss to form our agreement and then together, we leave the tent.

Chapter 50 – 2

Bao Dan, Ning, and Nan Rong continued the advance. Our troops were disheartened at first, but knowing that victory is on the horizon, morale increased the closer we came to Bei Ling. On the day before Nan Rong's forces would undoubtedly meet the opposition in battle, the best news we've received since this conflict began spread like wildfire: He Pi and the White Cranes stormed the palace and claimed Emperor Cai Pai under their protection. The remaining guards who served Wang Liang either surrendered or were put to death and the North's defenses withdrew from the front line.

Bei Ling was no longer a threat. However, Wang Liang was nowhere to be found. Some claimed he perished during the raid, though that supposition is yet confirmed. My intuition signaled that he is alive. Whether he will become a threat in the future remains to be seen.

In place of Wang Liang's authority, a new council comprising of White Crane members formed. At present, representatives from all the lands are gathered in Sai Mi's—Bei Ling's capital—courtyard to discuss matters of diplomacy and the potential danger Su Jian may pose.

Those in attendant are familiar faces I had anticipated to see again, and also a new face that is hardly unfamiliar: He Pi's. I hope he doesn't notice my

inappropriate gawking. It's strange to see my face on someone else's body; though, he must feel the same.

After matters settle, Jin and He Pi approach. The first to address me is He Pi; though, not in the manner I'd expected. His Highness reaches for my shoulders and brings his face close.

"Your Majesty, you have taken my crown and I will allow that, but do not think you may take my lady without retaliation."

He Pi immediately withdraws at San An's threatening tone. Sulking, he sticks out his tongue at the Minister.

"Oh, well. Since you won't let me have any fun, I'll return to Nan Rong. Before I go, is there anything I can grant you, *San An's lady*, for having subbed in my stead?"

"Anything?" Undoubtedly, one request comes to mind. "Please return Consort En's titles and give Empress Pai the respect she deserves. I don't know what must be done but if you can restore them... well, actually, all the women from court during the conflict... to grace, that is all I ask."

He Pi throws a short grin and complies. Standing behind His Highness, Jin looks up and smiles. His elation gladdens my heart. I hope that with time, he will come to forgive my previous transgressions.

Without delay, San An places a loving hand on my shoulder and moves forward to address He Pi. "Your Majesty. Will you also grant me one request for my services to Nan Rong?"

"No. You disbanded the Circle, Brother. I can't forgive that."

Though his words are harsh, the tone is teasing. He Pi grins childishly and urges the Minister to continue.

"Forgive me for resigning from my post. I wish to live as an ordinary man beside Bao Lai. Authority and power are meaningless to me, now. To have the respect and love of the woman I adore is everything."

He Pi, frowning, turns to me. "You have broken my brother, Miss Bao Lai! Will you apologize?"

"I am not sorry," is my reply.

His Highness, grinning, abruptly turns serious. "Where will you go, San An? I will surely require your council in the future. You must tell me."

"Somewhere far away, where Bao Lai and I can live peacefully."

Reverting to his childish persona, He Pi frets. "And where exactly is, *'far away,'* Brother? Oh! I know! Take the Summer Palace! It's sitting bare. Make it your home. I command it!"

"Well, if His Highness commands it." San An smirks.

Chapter 50: San An's Temptation

Jin was right. He Pi is very childish but what makes me glad is how childish he now appears before San An. As I recall, Jin noted His Highness is sarcastic and indolent in front of everyone except for the former and women. For him to extend that childishness toward his eldest brother must mean they are on good terms. San An, likewise, is less stern in front of his kin. I hope someday we can all sit together at the same table for repast and recount our time apart during the conflict.

A few pleasantries are exchanged and then He Pi and Jin prepare the caravan for departure. Once San An and I are alone in the courtyard, my beloved steals a kiss from me. While we share longing looks, our peace is once more disrupted.

"Your open display of affection makes me sick."

We turn to meet Kang Lang and Han Bei coming forthwith. My cheeky friend grins mischievously while rushing to embrace me. I return the gesture.

"Are you jealous, San An?"

"Not at all, Kang Lang. Ever since I discovered your secret fancy for me, I've come to understand why you've used Bao Lai to coerce my envy."

Colors erupt over his cheeks. Kang Lang turns away and scoffs. His bashful reaction is too endearing; San An and I can't help but laugh.

"Actually, I apologize for my rudeness." San An places a hand on his former rival's shoulder. "I know of everything you've done for Bao Lai and Nan Rong. You have my eternal gratitude."

"That so? Then, treat her well. I love her, too, you know!"

"Yes, I know, and I will." San An bows low.

"Fine, fine. Just to set the records straight, I don't *fancy* you, Minister! I respect the man that you are. No matter what His Highness says, He Pi looks up to you and I, too... whatever. You're both to come to my wedding and I expect *nice* gifts!"

"Congratulations! Kang Lang, Emperor of Bao Dan and Ye!"

"That's right!" He returns my grin.

After landing a peck on my forehead, Kang Lang runs to the gate. Neng Cao came for him. I'm delighted to see that while she looks upon my dear friend, ardent love pours from her eyes. He will come to love her, I know it. One day, Jin, too, will find someone deserving of his adoration.

As I'm lost in this thought, Han Bei's hard tone draws my wandering mind back to reality. I still have one more promise to fulfill.

"Lord Han Bei—"

"I hate false pleasantries." Han Bei sighs. "So, the Prime Minister has chosen an ordinary life. Tell me, Bao Lai, is this also your ambition?"

"Yes. I wish to live beside San An."

Scoffing, Han Bei rolls his eyes. "Tiresome woman! So be it. Your debt is cleared. If only you knew the future that waits in Ning."

I've not a chance to reply when Han Bei retreats from the courtyard. The Grand General may be brusque and mostly confusing, but I know he's a good man and a caring elder brother. He aided Nan Rong for Kang Lang's sake and just now, forgave my debt so that I may stay with San An.

"Is something the matter? You look troubled."

Startled by San An's hand squeezing mine, I jump a little before looking up with a nervous smile.

"No, I'm not troubled. Just curious. What do you think he meant when he mentioned Ning? What could possibly await me there?"

"Shall we find out?" San An's grip tightens. He attempts to follow Han Bei. Immediately, I pull back.

"N-No. That's okay. I'd rather we begin our lives now, San An. Will you take me to the Summer Palace?"

"It would be my pleasure."

With a loving smile, San An and I walk hand-in-hand from the courtyard. In due time, the Southern caravan starts for Nan Rong. At the crossroad to the capital, San An and I part ways with He Pi and Jin, and then continue our route south to the Summer Palace in Tiao.

Chapter 50 – 3

Tall trees, gardens, and lakes abound; the entire sensation of the area can only be compared to a luxurious scene from a prized silk scroll.

I've heard stories of the Summer Palace but never imagined the grandeur so excessive. There are at least three hundred rooms; each equal to or larger than He Pi's chamber. Furthermore, even though the structure has been underutilized by His Highness, guards and servants are plentiful.

Our abrupt presence caused quite the commotion. While everyone who came to welcome us were severely kind, I wanted San An all to myself. It wasn't until nightfall that we are able to be alone in each other's company.

The chamber door closes. San An checks the lock for the third time.

"Are you worried someone might interrupt, my dear?"

My beloved is not amused by the teasing grin. Settling on the bed beside me, San An threads long fingers through my hair.

"No. I am worried that you will attempt to leave."

"Nonsense, I would never!"

"Oh, but I fear you might. You have teased me long enough, temptress. I'm afraid you'll not be able to withstand my passion and will be forced to flee. Know that it is impossible. This room was chosen as our chamber, for it is in the most secluded part of the palace. Your sense of direction is also horrid. Don't think you can escape."

As serious as he sounds, San An is blushing from ear-to-ear. He's never been more adorable. In response to his teasing, I move away and take to a nearby wall.

"I refuse you, San An."

"Why is my temptress so cruel?" Starting to his feet, my beloved comes hither.

"If I cannot withstand your passion, then let us not begin. Or, do you wish to drive me away?"

At a loss for words, San An falls silent. Pain surfacing toward his eyes forces my retraction from the game. Immediately, my arms reach out to embrace him. Yet, barely have I touched his back, my feet are swept off the floor.

"San An?"

"You will pay dearly for toying with me!"

The hardened frown slowly transforms into a grin. San An plants a deep, loving kiss while laying me gently on the bed.

To his astonishment, my hands reach for his collar and begin undressing him. He makes no attempt to refuse my brazenness; though, confusion and anxiety flood.

"What's wrong, San An? Do you not want to?"

"My endeavors to tease you have only resulted in my embarrassment. You have defeated me, Bao Lai."

"My dearest love, you aimed to tease me using the premise that I would withdraw. However, I love you too much to ever deny you of anything. Hardly is age still hiding behind innocence."

"You will never let those words go, will you?"

"Never! How could I ever forget that event? It was the first time you kissed me and it was my first kiss. If only I had known how much I would come to love you, I would have made you blushed from head to toe!"

San An chuckles and begins loosening my robe. I think he might actually be blushing from head to toe.

"Are you shy, San An? You must be hiding age behind innocence."

His face is crimson. My love arches up a tender gaze. "I will suffer your teasing no more, temptress!"

San An silences my impertinence with a kiss. His passion flows endlessly, from gentle reminders of his adoration to powerful confessions of his desires. All my will relinquishes and I submit to his every whim.

The End.

Chapter 51: The Better Woman

San An is safe. Kang Lang's condition is unknown. I must go to Bao Dan and support him however I can. More than that, I really miss him. Since the day we parted in Ye—despite how we left things—I wanted nothing more than to resume his side.

Though it may have taken too long to realize my affections, I know I love Kang Lang. I don't need reasons to justify how I feel. That's something he taught me. It may be a small chance, but as long as there is a chance, I'll prove my adoration and win back Kang Lang.

"Master Dui. Please, look after San An with the greatest of care. Anything he needs—anything at all— don't hesitate to keep him safe. I'm leaving to join my fiancé in Bao Dan."

"I understand, Your Highness." Dui bows deeply.

Once authority is conferred to Lieutenant Zheng in my absence, a scout accompanied me across the borders to Bao Dan and then to the capital of Mu Lai. Thank goodness, Grand Commander Kang Lang was treated with Jin's antidote.

When I enter the chamber, he's sleeping so peacefully that I don't dare wake him. Long eyelashes flutter from a sweet dream. His chest rises and lowers in succeeding rhythm. Silky, light brown hair drape over the boyish face that somehow also seems mature.

Chapter 51: The Better Woman

He is quite a sight. I've always known he was beautiful. I didn't appreciate just how beautiful he is to me, until now. Never have I felt happier than to just stay by his side.

From his eyes to his nose, attention traces down to his petal mouth. What a lovely mouth it is. The very one that filled me with desires when he kissed me and gave comfort when I was troubled. The same mouth told me to accept my flaws because they make me human and teased me incessantly so that I'd smile.

One glance at that lovely mouth and an overwhelming flood of unbridled emotions swell. Desire is suffocating. Leaning over, I steal a kiss from his pretty lips.

Kang Lang stirs. As dramatic as it would be to wake my handsome prince from slumber, it's better that he sleeps and recovers. Instead, I reach for his hand and cradle it between my own.

I've only been at his bedside for fifteen minutes when the doors creak open and Neng Cao enters. A cold chill runs through me when our eyes lock. This is the woman he loves and the reason for my misery. What was I expecting? I came to Bao Dan for Kang Lang, all the while, he loves her. I must respect that.

Neng Cao beckons me into the halls where unspoken rivalry renders the atmosphere to disquiet. We're both shuffling apprehensively. However, nothing will be solved through silence. The first to speak is Neng Cao.

"You are not He Pi, are you?"

"No. I am Bao Lai, His Highness's body double. And, you're a woman... Well, obviously, you are."

Neng Cao, frowning, immediately lifts sharpened eyes to my face. "So, you're Bao Lai. We knew it!"

"Knew what?"

"You are the woman Kang Lang calls for in his sleep. He gives us excuses after excuses. He swears he loves us, but we are not convinced. We offered him everything; yet, he continues withholding affections. It's all because of you. Tell us, do you love him?"

"Yes. Without a doubt."

"Is that so? What can you do for him?"

"Do? I love Kang Lang. There isn't anything I would *not* do for him."

"Anyone can love and anyone can promise to do everything for the person they love. The matter becomes whether one is capable. Are you someone of authority to give Kang Lang the life he deserves? We have two countries to offer him. What have you?"

Words are stuck in my throat. I don't know how to respond. I don't have properties or titles. I have nothing to my name. Han Bei's charges suddenly ring loudly in my mind; Kang Lang is an heir to the Zhao line, a prestigious noble family in Ning, while I'm just trash they picked off the streets. What could I possibly do for Kang Lang that Neng Cao couldn't?

Without my reply, Neng Cao continues. "If you truly love him and are willing to do anything for him, then leave. No one could love him more than us and we will ensure he'll never be in want. Is that not something you'd wish for your beloved?"

Kang Lang said that if I have to be useful for him to love me, then that's no different from trying to buy his affections. He's not that type of person. I know he meant it. Although, if he loves me, then why did he slight me for her? He's been deceptive. I don't know who is the fool here, Neng Cao or I?

Panic lures attention toward the room where he's sleeping. It may not be grand, but it is the best Mu Lai can offer. If he weren't the Grand Commander of Bao Dan, Kang Lang might not be alive. It's no secret that people of power are treated with the best the world can offer. When the antidote was made, he surely received the first dosage and he's been kept safe due to his position—a position which Neng Cao bestowed. A life with me would not be beneficial. Even if he could be happy, I can't guarantee comfort or safety; not in the manner that this empress can.

I thought Kang Lang chose for me. It's my turn to choose for him. My greatest wish is for his safety and happiness. Though I want to be in his arms, conscience takes me away from Bao Dan without looking back.

Chapter 51 – 2

As I enter Nan Rong's northern base, Bai Hu, Zhen Yue, and Qing Hai are preparing their men for the march to Bei Ling. I glance over at the tent where San An is resting and decide he doesn't need to be disturbed. I am sorry to have caused him so much anguish; both emotionally and physically. Hopefully, someday, he can forgive me and find happiness beside the person deserving of his attention.

At the moment, I can't deny that a selfish thought is surfacing, but I refuse to be swayed by foolish temptations. Even though I cannot have Kang Lang, I won't be so fickle as to throw myself at the Minister. How droll. Resolve has finally been formed and it doesn't bring me happiness.

The choice has been made and there's no going back. I might not be able to give Kang Lang the life he deserves, but while I'm He Pi, I'll ensure that peace will return soon so that his new life can begin.

"General, may I ride with you to Bei Ling?" The question is directed at Bai Hu.

Hu turns back and nods. "I was wondering where you went. Yeah, we need you, *fearless leader*. You'll ride with Qing Hai."

Chapter 51 – 3

Bao Dan and Ning continued their advances. With Nan Rong's generals, I accompanied our forces north. Our troops were disheartened at first, but knowing that victory is on the horizon, morale increased the closer we came to Bei Ling. On the day before Nan Rong's forces would undoubtedly meet the opposition in battle, the best news we've received since this conflict began spread like wildfire: He Pi and the White Cranes stormed the palace and claimed Emperor Cai Pai under their protection. The remaining guards who served Wang Liang either surrendered or were put to death and the North's defenses withdrew from the front line.

Bei Ling was no longer a threat. However, Wang Liang was nowhere to be found. Some claimed he perished during the raid, though that supposition is yet confirmed. My intuition signaled that he is alive. Whether he will become a threat in the future remains to be seen.

In place of Wang Liang's authority, a new council comprising of White Crane members formed. At present, representatives from all the lands are gathered in Sai Mi's—Bei Ling's capital—courtyard to discuss matters of diplomacy and the potential danger Su Jian may pose.

Those in attendant are familiar faces I had anticipated to see again, and also a new face that is hardly unfamiliar: He Pi's. I hope he doesn't notice my

inappropriate gawking. It's strange to see my face on someone else's body; though, he must feel the same.

While scanning the courtyard, excitement grows when Kang Lang's figure walks into view. Hopes dash high just when I think he's turning to meet my shameless staring. Instead, he turns to greet Neng Cao, whose hands wrap around his arm as she comes near. He smiles the same sweet smile I once thought was reserved for me. The sight is tearing my heart to pieces. I know anger is baseless since I've made my choice and entrusted him to Neng Cao. Still, I can't bear to see it. Running away is all I've done. It's the cowardly reaction to which my feet default.

"If you are willing to give him up, then don't cry. It's pathetic." Han Bei scoffs curtly.

I thought I was finally alone in this secluded area. Suspended tears were falling like rain until the familiar condescending tone brusquely cuts off my wretched sniveling. Red hair flutters like wildfire. Green eyes cut through me like sharpened glass.

"Lord Han Bei. I... No, you're right. Have you come for our arrangement?"

Han Bei nods and then turns to leave without invoking further conversations. I follow him not knowing what the future holds. Never did I realize doing so would change everything.

Chapter 51 – 4

The weather's grown chilly lately and although the trees still carry vestiges of colored leaves, the air signals that winter is near. I wonder if I'll ever become used to this region's climate.

After leaving with Han Bei, my life changed drastically. As it happens, the late Empress Dong Xing did have a younger sister who was taken to safety during the previous wars at court. That infant was Bao Lai, Princess of Fan Fa. Han Bei saw the resemblance in our faces and thus proposed the agreement that brought me to Ning.

A few days after our arrival, the Grand General received a letter from He Pi, which proved my birthright. I am disappointed that I couldn't speak to His Highness in person. I wonder how great of a man he truly is. Apparently, while I pretended to be him, he pretended to be me at the old temple and somehow, found the edict in Master Tai Hung's study. It's unclear whether the old man had inadvertently forgotten about the edict before he passed or that he thought I was better suited for life away from court. Parts of me are saddened for having been robbed of my past. The other parts are glad for my previous life at temple. Those were pleasant days, to be sure.

Yet, I didn't want this authority. My nephew, Emperor Yuan, abdicated on my behalf, and against my wishes. He's young and wants the freedom to travel. I envy that. Still, with this authority, there are changes in Ning's laws I intend to make so that the East will retain friendship with Nan Rong.

A cold wind rushes past and whistles noisily through the trees. Ning's weather has been dreary and on days like this, I feel so alone. How ironic! After relinquishing pursuit of Kang Lang due to my inability to provide for him, I'm now the empress of this most powerful country and yet, I've lost every right to approach my beloved. His engagement to Neng Cao is widely known. An invitation was sent to Ning out of goodwill; though, I know my presence is not expected. What could I say to him that would not be a lie, while holding the one truth I cannot divulge?

Neng Cao may be a cowardly leader but I am a coward of a woman. I love Kang Lang and that should have been enough. Power and authority mean nothing when happiness is absent. Maybe, the greater fear I have is his happiness after all. If he is happy in her arms, who am I to cause disquiet? At the core of it all, I regret not having thrown caution to the wind and confronted him in Ye and Bao Dan. Consequences seem negligible in the end. Once nuptial vows are taken, Kang Lang will eternally be bound to Neng Cao.

"If only I could have..."

Wait, what am I thinking? What foolish logic! He's not married and I do have something more to offer! Rewards fall more often in the laps of the active callous, than of the passive saint! Neng Cao used her authority to push me away from Kang Lang. My authority now exceeds hers. Two can play at this game! I will fight for Kang Lang until he outright rejects me!

Quickly turning to quit my stroll and call for Han Bei, my feet are abruptly frozen to the spot. Two guards and the Grand General are coming hither with another man in chains. The sight of the prisoner makes my heart leap into my throat.

"Kang Lang! Lord Han Bei, what have you done?"

"Your Majesty," Han Bei bows. "This intruder was caught sneaking into your quarters. He is known as Zhao Kang Lang, a deserter who allied with Nan Rong after failing his assignment. The law calls for his immediate execution. You must give the orders."

"Absolutely not! Let him go!"

"The law should not be waived so easily, Your Highness. Stability cannot be maintained through favoritism."

Why is Han Bei doing this? I know he loves his brother, so why must he force my hands? He can't expect me to give the ruthless decree, or any decree for that matter, that would hurt Kang Lang. However, he does expect a rebuttal.

"Lord Han Bei, this man is the Grand Commander of Bao Dan and future emperor of Ye. We cannot treat our esteemed guest so poorly."

"Titles bestowed by worthless countries are worthless in Ning, Your Highness. Unless he is someone of import to the East—someone indispensable—his crimes should not be overlooked."

Han Bei's long, agonizing stare burrows deeply into my own. It takes a long while to fully grasp his intentions. Lord Han Bei is right. I must stop being so pathetic. Kang Lang is the most important, most indispensable person to me. It's clear that importance should extend to Ning.

Taking a firm stance, my answer is given. "This man is the future emperor of Ning. He is my fiancé. I pardon all of his crimes, which were hardly crimes to begin with, since they've brought Ning valuable allies. Let him go."

Smirking, Han Bei orders the guards to release Kang Lang. The former parties then retreat.

For the duration of the unexpected event that passed, my love did not once acknowledge me through words or gestures. Now that we are finally alone, he finds the ground more entertaining to watch. His inattentiveness worries me. Though my heart is beating out of my chest, I muster every ounce of courage and reach for his hand. Glancing up, his face reddens.

"Are you okay, Kang Lang?"

"Your Highness..."

"I'm still Bao Lai," a smile flows across my face. His returned expression is taut. I bet he's angry. "Kang Lang, I... I'm sorry."

"What for?"

"For leaving Bao Dan. For giving you up. I didn't have anything to offer you then, but now, I do. I offer you all of Ning! So please, stay with me!"

"When were you in Bao Dan? What are you talking about, giving me up? We were never together."

"She didn't tell you? Then... why have you come?"

"You mean, Neng Cao? What did she not tell me?"

Embarrassment seizes my tongue. Kang Lang's hand squeezes mine encouragingly. We've come this far; I need to tell him the truth.

"After you were poisoned, I went to Bao Dan. I was by your side when Neng Cao called me away. She declared that with her title and power, she could give you what I couldn't. I... just wanted you to have everything you deserve and the safety of authority that I couldn't promise. That's why I don't understand. If she didn't tell you, then did you come because you love me again?"

Hope flies high and then burns asunder when a resentful frown crosses him. Kang Lang gives a hard stare and then abruptly, his composure weakens. His arms fly around me.

"You *were* in Bao Dan! I thought I dreamt your touch. When I woke, you weren't there, I..."

His shoulders tremble. However much he tries to suppress the reaction, the anguish he felt then is clearly displayed to me now. My arms hold him tight with as much vigor as I can summon while warmth from his body seeks me for comfort, and I in turn, urge my heat onto him until those broad shoulders cease their tremors.

"Imbecile." He whispers. His tone is hoarse and low, as though repressing sobs. It's not like him to cry. If he refuses to let sadness fall, then I shall shed them for him. With my face pressed against his chest, his clothes become stained with my tears.

The strong grip strengthens. Kang Lang sighs deprecatingly. "Do you know how close I came to making the biggest mistake of my life? Didn't I tell you that it doesn't matter what you can do for me? I only want you!"

"I thought you loved her." Proclaiming the thought forces another surge of sharp pain to claw at my chest. I want to say more but words won't come.

"Are you that dense? I was using her to gain control of Ye, so they'd expel Bei Ling. I'm... sorry you had to see the disgraceful act; but it was just that—an act."

Looking up to gauge his expression, emerald stars gazing back convey honesty he so desperately wants me to understand.

"You mean you seduced her? Kang Lang, that's cruel! Besides, the war's been over for some time now and you *are* engaged to her, aren't you?"

"I thought—I thought you chose San An. After having been so happy by your side, I couldn't stand the idea of being alone. In some ways, she reminded me of you, so I tried to make the best of things. I was still miserable. In the end, I couldn't do it! I broke the engagement and returned to Nan Rong to win you from San An, but the Minister revealed something even more troubling. When did you become Ning's empress?"

"I'm still as surprised as you are. Wait, you went to Nan Rong to win me from San An? I was moments away from leaving for Bao Dan to win you from Neng Cao."

Kang Lang's rather astonished. We stare at one another and burst into laughter.

"Would you really have fought for me, Your Highness?" Kang Lang kisses my forehead gently. The bauble in my hair suddenly catches his eyes and Kang Lang's fingers trace over the carvings. My most prized possession: the comb Kang Lang purchased for me in Nan Rong. I've adorned it every day since coming to Ning and began dressing as a woman.

"Yes, and if I had to descend Ning upon Bao Dan to retrieve you, I would have. I've let childish fears and obligations kept me. I won't anymore. Please, believe me. I say this with all my sincerity. Kang Lang, I love you."

"You've said those words to me before. Has the meaning behind them changed or am I still only your friend?"

"You are still my dearest friend but I refuse to have our bond end there. I stole a kiss from you in Bao Dan, and I intend to keep stealing kisses from you for as long as I live."

In saying so, I steal a short kiss. Surprised, Kang Lang looks away to conceal blushing cheeks.

"Why so bashful, my love?"

The teasing smile lights his face crimson. In time, shy tremors on his lips form into a frown.

His thumb then traces the outline of my lower lip, coursing heat throughout my body in hopeful expectations. Yet, when my heart is beating furiously, he gives a pained smile and removes his touch.

"Dare I even ask why you no longer desire me?"

"I desire you too much, Your Highness." Kang Lang releases me and moves away.

"Really? You once said there isn't a better way to convey desire than to put your hands all over someone.

If I'm not mistaken, this means you've grown bored of me, right?"

My attempt to coax a smile from Kang Lang instead, turns his expression sour. He moves toward a maple tree, whose red and orange leaves saunter playfully with every gust of wind. I don't understand the reason he's seemingly avoiding me but I won't let him go; that much, I've decided. Thus, I follow him under the shade.

"Kang Lang! You've never aspired to return to Ning. Yet, here you are. You came for me, didn't you?"

"Of course, I did."

"Why are you tortured for having to endure my company? If I've done anything to displease you—"

After all this time, I still can't control myself. Tears are welling in the corners of my eyes. I feel so pathetic. Kang Lang, startled by the flood of his most hated thing in the world, quickly lifts his sleeves and wipes them from my face.

"Hey, don't cry! It's not you I'm angry at. It's me!"

"You don't have to lie."

"I'm not!"

The more I push for a reason, the more his attention averts. Without recourse, my arms wrap around him. Kang Lang hesitates for a long time. Ultimately, he humors me and lets out a deep sigh.

"It's just... I came here with all these expectations of some grand scenes, I guess, of love and confession. I was prepared to win you, somehow, but to know that you loved me while I was with another is... I feel guilty. How can I kiss you freely when only days ago, my lips were pressed against another's?"

"That's what you're worried about?!"

For someone who claimed he's been in the company of countless women, he's troubled over something as simple as a kiss? I find his guilt too adorable. An unexpected chortle escapes. Hands fly over my mouth to muffle the sound, but it's too late. He's noticed.

"Hey, don't laugh at me!"

"How can I not? While you loved me, my lips were not pure either. San An's kissed me—"

"Right. San An kissed you. Did you ever kiss him?"

"Well... that's not really the point."

"That is entirely the point!"

Embarrassment and frustration flood his expression. More than anything, he truly does appear to be tormented by guilt. Words clearly won't calm him. Instead, I steal another kiss—a true kiss to express my affections and forgiveness, and not the prior teasing peck. Kang Lang retreats a step, and in turn, I push him against the tree trunk. His hesitant lips, too tempted by passion, slowly return my ardor. When I finally withdraw, his flustering has only increased.

"Days ago, you didn't know that I love you. So, I'll forgive you. Now that you know, there are no excuses. If you ever leave me again, if I see you tease another woman, if I even hear you mention Neng Cao, I *will* kill you. Understood?"

The wide-eyed stare lingers for a time. Gradually, a corner of his mouth rises to a smirk.

"You're so romantic, Your Highness!" His eyes dazzle from my threat. I thought he'd appreciate that.

"Good. I've decided that within the week, Mu Dan will become my empress and Kang Lang, you will become my lord. That is to say, I will spend my life in the pursuit of your happiness if you will accept me. What do you think of that?"

"You wish to make an honest woman out of me, Your Highness?" Mu Dan giggles.

How I've missed that giggle! I return a smile. Immediately, his arm links around mine. Kang Lang escorts me down the path of my previous stroll.

"You didn't answer me, Kang Lang. Do you find my proposal agreeable?"

"Why don't you put the ceremony together and see whether I attend, Your Highness."

"If you don't want to…"

"Now, now. Don't cry again. You won't coerce me into marriage that easily."

"I wasn't. What I meant was if you don't want to, I'll inform Lord Han Bei that I've changed my mind. I'll accept his proposal. You may remain here as my consort, if you wish."

His pace comes to a complete halt. Kang Lang, grimacing, draws me into his arms and plants kiss after kiss on every inch of my face.

"Don't try so hard, Kang Lang! It's too late. Offer's gone! A girl can't wait forever! I'm marrying Han Bei."

Contrary to expectations, he is neither amused nor vexed by the crude jests. A pained look plasters on his face; similar to the one he carried that day I rejected his confession in Nan Rong. Hurriedly, I grab onto his shoulders.

"I was joking, Kang Lang. To me, there isn't anyone else. I've loved you for some time now, but this is all news to you so, I understand. It's too sudden, right? I won't push the subject again until you find it appropriate."

"You misunderstand. I accepted Neng Cao's proposal because I felt lonely. You're saying Han Bei proposed and you declined, even though you were lonely, too? What were you planning to do?"

"Well, I *was* planning to win you from her. If that endeavor was unsuccessful then, I guess... nothing. I don't know what you expect me to say."

He's turned silent. Guilt is once more apparent in the woeful expression. This is hardly the same man I remember; the one who teased me unrestrained. His newfound self-loathing is insufferable! Just when I've become him, he's become me. I finally understand the vexation I've caused him.

"I told you not to mention Neng Cao or I'd kill you. Did you not think me honest? Maybe for a first offense, I will only punish you instead."

The sun has set. Around us, the air is becoming exceedingly chilly. My arm links around the frozen man and escorts him inside. Kang Lang remains quiet the entire trek. The glazed look signals that he's hardly listened to a word I've said and completely oblivious to where I've led him.

It's not until I shove him forcibly onto my bed does he wake from the self-induced trance of guilt. Flustering, Kang Lang attempts to sit up. I lean over to keep him from succeeding. The scene is all too familiar. We are posed in the same manner he used to taunt me in Nan Rong.

"Listen to me! Stop blaming yourself for my faults. If I weren't a coward—if I'd told you how I felt in Ye— we would have been together these many lonely months. And yes, I was lonely; *devastated* when I heard of your engagement. It doesn't matter what might have happened because what's happening now is more important. Now, we are together, so stop ignoring me!"

The returned blank stare is tearing at my composure. I understand his baseless guilt but anger in me won't subside. He did not love Neng Cao and still, he accepted her proposal and put on a good show of his affections. He claims to love me and yet, can't do either. Maybe all it took was this reunion for him to be conscious of the truth: he doesn't love me after all.

"How can you even think that?! Of course I love you!" Kang Lang shouts wrathfully.

I'd forgotten he can read my mind. I don't really care. The thought needed to be conveyed one way or another.

"Fine. Take all the time you need. Come find me in the study when you want my company."

As I attempt to move off, Kang Lang draws me beside him and cradles my body tightly. I feel slightly crushed. His fiery heat warms me thoroughly. The room falls silent and then it feels like time is standing still.

Little by little and with great care, his hold relaxes. The soft hand touches my cheek. Glancing down is a familiar, amiable face I've longed to see.

"First, you rejected me," he begins. "And then, you attacked me in Bao Dan while I slept. Just now, you took me to bed and accused me of not loving you because I'm not willing to offer my body? You ought to be ashamed!"

"I'm... sorry?"

"You should be. The nerve! How dare you propose when obviously, I've planned a thousand ways for the moment to be perfect? I will never accept your proposal, so you might as well concede and accept mine."

"Are you... asking me?"

"Not at all. At this point, you don't have a choice. You are mine and mine alone, Your Highness."

How possessive! I expected nothing less and I also feel the same. I'll never give Kang Lang to another. He understands my sentiment, and though no words are exchanged, it becomes apparent that our engagement is set. While lying quietly in his warmth, something troubling comes to mind.

"Kang Lang, you said that you met San An in Nan Rong. How is he and how is Jin?"

"They're both well. The Minister is unhappy for the obvious reason, but he's also less cold than I remember. Jin and He Pi are with him. I've never seen those three get along so charmingly. Anyway, don't worry. With time, I'm sure everything will be fine."

"I hope so. They're all wonderful men and they deserve to be happy."

"What about me, Your Highness?" The familiar pouting returns. I've truly missed his silly expressions.

"Are you not happy, Kang Lang?"

"Of course! Your Highness is my happiness. Yet, I can't help but find our circumstance severely awkward. You've rejected me multitudes of times and now we're engaged. Again, I'm too happy to fully express how I feel. Maybe for that reason, a part of me also can't accept that this is real."

"The delusion could be yours or mine. That doesn't matter, does it?"

"No, I guess not." Kang Lang sends a sultry whisper into my ear while playful fingers caress the length of my arm, down to my waist, and then my thigh.

The teasing man never learns. It's high time revenge is mine. Pushing off the bed, I move atop and then leisurely, reach down to undo his robe. Kang Lang stares back wide-eyed before quickly stopping me.

"Bao Lai, what are you—"

"I've never known your touch in this manner. Though I have dreamt of it, the feeling was fleeting. If you wish to know whether I am real or fantasy, then this is the way. Show me your passion and I'll validate our existences."

His face grows increasingly hot from my crooked smile. Kang Lang does his best to muster a grin. Shyly, strong arms lift up my body with ease and exchange our positions.

My beloved, looking down, is blushing from ear-to-ear. He's never been more adorable. I relinquish his apprehensions by placing a soft peck on his lips. For that, he returns my affection with a deep, loving kiss.

Yet, once more when my heart beats furiously from expectations, he withdraws. Lying down adjacent, his comforting arms hold me tightly while sultry lips caress my cheek.

"I believe you," he whispers. "After our nuptial, I will take everything from you. For now, tell me what's happened since we parted in Ye."

"Are you rejecting my advances, Kang Lang?"

"Yes, Your Highness. I'm not that type of girl!"

The cheerful giggles make me burst into laughter. It's not like him to deny what he wants, especially given the opportunity. He's doing this for me. To preserve my honor until we are married. How noble he's become.

"You are, indeed, not that type of girl. You are a gentleman, after all. Kang Lang, I love you."

"Yes, I know. I'm sure someday I will grow fond of you, too."

The mischievous grin makes me want to punish him. Maybe, he hasn't changed much after all. I wouldn't want him any other way.

Lying in each other's embrace, we recount our time apart until slumber eventually lulls reality into dreams.

I will always be grateful for my time at Nan Rong's palace, where I met so many wonderful people, including my beloved Kang Lang. It is my ambition to find happiness for San An and Jin, however many years that may take.

At the moment, I am happy. For most of my life, I was without a past and had no prospect for a future. Now, I have both. I will live in the present and take pleasure in every joy I can find. Once Kang Lang is eternally bound to me on the day of our nuptial, I will ensure for him all the happiness in the world.

The End.

Chapter 52: The Handsome Assassin

A pretty servant girl directed me to Kang Lang's quarters. San An might have He Pi's crown, but I still wear his armor. It was easy enough to bluff my way inside.

Currently, the Grand Commander is resting quietly in his chamber. How innocent he appears for someone so foulmouthed. I can't keep from smiling while watching him sleep. We've only been away from each other for a short time and yet, it's felt an eternity. I love him. There's nothing I want more than to stay by his side and bring a smile to that sweet face each day that we are together.

Relief mixed with happiness calm my soul and weariness eventually lulls consciousness to slumber. In my dream are blissful days. We are beside each other, just the two of us, somewhere far away without the slightest notion of war, suffering, pain, or grief. A small house with a beautiful garden and wide-open spaces under an endless sky. My beloved takes my hand and leisurely, we stroll through a field of flowers while speaking of anything and everything.

Kang Lang smiles while glancing over, and then a soft hum of a song I've heard somewhere before drapes over the beautiful scene. The hum that began as a soft echo gradually grows louder. As the volume increases, a strange sensation comes over me. Inadvertently, a moan escapes.

Immediately, eyes burst open and panic shakes my very core.

"I like it when you make that noise. Do it again."

The seductive whisper throws me into a rage. I'm lying in Kang Lang's arms while he fondles my bare breasts.

"You bastard! What are you doing?"

I turn to punch his arm with my usual fury and then quickly withdraw upon recalling his condition.

"I'm-I'm sorry. Are you okay?"

His reply is boisterous, obnoxious laughter. I reach for the covers but he rips them off.

"Are you seriously trying to hide what I've already seen and touched... and tasted?" He grins.

"You! Shut up! I hate you so damn much!"

"Hey! You're the one who *begged* me to take you after I sent you back to Nan Rong."

"And what a mistake that was! If I'm just a joke to you then... then I'll—"

"Then, you'll what?" He smirks amusedly with a cheek in his palm as if to challenge me. I love him so much and it makes me want to hurt him!

"Then, I'll punish you!"

At my threat, his eyes immediately light up. Kang Lang reaches forward but I slap away his hands.

"You're just like Han Bei!"

He gasps deeply in offense while bulging eyes stare back vehemently. In the end, Kang Lang simply sulks. I'm still irritated by his vulgarity. Thus, I push the subject further.

"If you'll recall, I had an agreement with Han Bei. For his alliance, I promised to join him in Ning after this conflict is over. Since I'm just a joke to you, Kang Lang, I'll gladly take Han Bei."

"You wouldn't dare!"

"Why wouldn't I? He's strong, smart, and handsome. I hear he's a great lover, too."

The wistful tone puts Kang Lang in a rage. Growling furiously, he lunges forward and pushes me onto the bed. Clasping his hands over mine, kiss after kiss rain down until his chest heaves. As he pulls away shortly, my beloved pouts.

"Is it true? Did you promise him that?"

"Yes, but Han Bei despises me. There's no need to worry. I'm sure it's nothing."

"He lives only to take everything I have. My freedom, my life, and now, you!"

"You're wrong. Han Bei cares for you. He allied with Nan Rong because of you, and when he thought you wouldn't return from Ye, he..."

What am I doing? I can't tell him that. If Kang Lang finds out Han Bei assaulted me, he'd—

"I'll kill him!" His jaw clenches tightly.

"What?"

"How dare he put his hands on you?! I'll kill that bastard!"

"Stop reading my mind!"

Kang Lang attempts to move off the bed while I clutch onto his body desperately. For fear of hurting me, he holds back his strength; else, I'd be dragged to the floor.

"Why didn't you tell me?!" He bellows.

"Because I knew you'd react this way! Just calm down!"

"I'll calm after I slit that bastard's throat!"

"I already made him pay for the transgression! I promised you, remember? I fulfilled all three parts!"

He freezes to recollect the memory. A daunting moment passes, and then a smug smile curls over his pretty lips, followed by a burst of laughter. Kang Lang leans down and playfully kisses my cheek. Teasingly, he whispers, "Good girl!"

"Stop saying that! I'm older than you!"

"Then, it's time to grow up."

"What is that supposed to m—"

A fervent kiss removes my ability to protest. I attempt to pull free but cannot. Eventually, his passion soothes my rage.

Every time we come together feels like the first time. Just when I think this indescribable sensation can be grasped, the experience is anew and I'm pulled under his waves of unending passion. Kang Lang once promised such pain that I can't ever forget him. He's never once broken that promise. With great certainty, he never will.

Chapter 52 – 2

"I love you." The soft confession falls as a reminder of my affections. While lying in each other's arms, cool night air that slowly trickles in through the windows brings serenity to the wistful scene.

"Yes, I know. You keep saying the words and I always believe you." He replies flatly.

"You won't say them back?"

"Why? I have taken what I've wanted. What reasons would I have to lie?"

His tone is calm and cool. Kang Lang continues stroking my hair as if nothing unpleasant was exchanged. I know he's only teasing, but that doesn't alter resentment building within. Still, this moment with him is precious. I best not ruin it with my outburst. My response is to fall deeper into his embrace while both hands clutch his back with greater force. After some time, Kang Lang shifts uncomfortably.

"What's wrong, Kang Lang?"

"I... I... lo you," he mutters shyly.

"You 'lo' me? You mean to say you loath me?"

"Don't be a smartass. You know what I mean."

"I really don't. You've never had trouble saying the words before. Did you only say them to seduce me away from San An? And, as you've said, I've given you what you've wanted, why should you lie?"

"Troublesome woman! Where are you going?" He sighs exasperatedly when I pull away.

"You've taken the only thing I had to offer. Where I go from here is none of your concern."

Kang Lang grabs my hand, which tersely jerks back, while I dart off the bed. He storms from the other side and moves to bar my path.

"Bao Lai! You know I was joking!"

"I know."

"Then, why..."

"Because there's some truth to what you've said, but you will not be honest with me. What are you hiding?"

"I'm not hiding anything," he frowns.

Since my arrival, an invisible barrier seems to be separating us. Kang Lang is his usual teasing self. Undeniably, I feel he's holding a secret or withholding guilt. The possibilities are limitless and they continue nagging at my psyche.

"I have better things to do than to be in the company of a liar. If you have any regards for me, then tell the truth. Something is troubling you, isn't it?"

Chapter 52: The Handsome Assassin

Letting out a heavy sigh, Kang Lang wraps his arms around my waist and buries his face in my hair. I know he's attempting to hide from me, so I pull back and force a hard stare into his eyes. Succinctly, he turns away.

"Bao Lai, I... I'm not good at this."

"I disagree. You're a great liar."

"Enough of your derisions, woman!" Kang Lang tugs at my cheeks tersely. I slap his hands away. He gently draws me onto the bed and crouches atop.

"I'm not lying," he presses again.

"I don't believe you. Did you take Neng Cao?"

"Is that how you think of me?!"

He's always been able to take my insults in good stride. However, fierce pain and displeasure crossing his expression make me realize how much I've hurt him with the accusation of infidelity. I know Kang Lang would never be so callous. Remorse rises in my chest for even mentioning it.

"I'm sorry but I don't know what to think! We've always been so close, Kang Lang. Now that we are beyond friends, something is awry. I love you and I have attempted to share with you every part of me. Somehow, I feel that you've pulled away. Am I imagining things?"

His teeth grind and emerald eyes waver. It's almost as though he's pleading for me to let the subject subside.

I can't. In return, a determined stare pushes back. Following a long moment of hesitation, he timidly admits the truth. "No, you're not imagining things. The truth is... I'm afraid."

"Afraid of what?"

"You."

"Me? Why? If you don't want me, Kang Lang—"

"That's not what I... Tsk, ah! Stubborn woman! I'm afraid of loving you!"

What does he mean? I thought he's loved me all this time. Is he only now telling the truth? My chest tightens. Tears won't stop dripping from the corners of my eyes. Kang Lang quickly kisses them away.

"Don't cry! And stop jumping to conclusions! I do love you. I just never thought you'd return my affections. I prayed that you would, but when you finally did, I don't... I don't know what to do! How do I keep you? All it takes is one stupid word or action from me and this dream may end. I love you and it scares me senseless! Even if I could keep you, what future could we have together? I'm not good for anything except killing. Worse, I've been pretending to be a woman longer than I've been a man. Frankly, I don't know what it means to be a man anymore. And, if I can't be the man you think I am, will you hate me? What if I lose control and hurt you again? What if I can't provide for you?

Will you look at me the same once you realize how weak I really am?!"

He rambles like a madman. For once, I see ardent fear in his eyes. To know that the same man who once said he would leave me when his interests subside has now considered a future for us, force indescribable elation to well in my chest. I love him. There's no reason for his anxieties. My fingers reach for his face; Kang Lang stares back in bewilderment.

"I am not worried, Kang Lang. For most of my life, I've dressed as a man for one reason or other and I've always felt inferior to other women because I didn't know what it meant to be one. You were forced to dress as a woman for one reason or other, but that doesn't change who you are.

You accepted me as I am and taught me to accept myself for my shortcomings. I will never see you as anything else but the man I dearly adore. You're young and I'm naïve. We still have much to learn. Certainly, we can learn life together. When you're afraid, tell me your fears. When you're uncertain, tell me your doubts. In the road ahead, I may come to depend on you more than you will depend on me, but I still want you to depend on me. No matter what, I trust you and I want you to need me, too. "

Emerald eyes continue wavering. His shoulders tremble. I grasp his hand and Kang Lang kisses deeply in return.

I want to see his weaknesses, as he had seen mine, and come to love every part of him. There's nothing he can do to erase my affections and nothing he can say that will keep me away. I have been childish but I want to mature, so that I may support him to my best abilities.

Kang Lang lies down and draws us closer together. I glance up to present a smile, only to see that his face is flushed.

"What's wrong, Kang Lang?"

"Nothing. Well, I-I love you. After this conflict is over, I will make you my bride."

My heart jumps at his seeming proposal. Even though I refuted childishness, my desire to taunt him will never wane. "That's presumptuous. Who said I agreed?"

"Don't mock me after I've bared my soul to you. My heart can't take it." He mutters.

"I'm sorry!" Embarrassed, my face buries in his chest.

Kang Lang strokes my hair and whispers tenderly, "After everything we've done, you don't have a choice. I'm going to make an honest woman out of you."

"Same to you!"

Kang Lang returns a familiar giggle. As his embrace tightens, together, we drift into deep slumber.

Chapter 53: The March to Bei Ling

In the morning, I dress in He Pi's armors and then take to the main gates. Kang Lang was against it, but I've convinced him to let me take part in the campaign. I think he only agreed due fear of losing my approval. Even so, I'm glad he's willing to entertain my wishes.

"So, how do I look?" The Grand Commander of Bao Dan grins as he nears.

"Very dashing, indeed."

"Hmm. You look refined in that armor, too. What do you say we find a secluded area, rip off each other's armors, and make love until night comes?" Kang Lang whispers gingerly into my ear.

"I wonder whether your fantasy is really of He Pi instead of me," I frown.

"You know it is, Your Highness!" Kang Lang shouts loudly, drawing in the attention of his men.

With so many spectators nearby, I can't retaliate in the desired manner, to which Kang Lang smiles victoriously. Why am I in love with this person who finds joy in mocking me?

As he stares into my eyes with a wide grin spread across his face, I finally realize my method to exact vengeance. For whatever reason, Kang Lang can read my thoughts. Thus, I return the stare with a single thought in mind: *"You're just like Han Bei!"*

Immediately, his eyes widen. The grin twists into a bitter frown. I smile knowingly at my beloved and then saunters out of the large gates.

By noon, Bao Dan's army departs from Mu Lai. I never learned to ride a horse. Though Kang Lang insists that we ride together, I fear his impulsive, indiscreet taunting. It would seem strange enough for He Pi to ride in Kang Lang's lap; it would be worse for His Highness to constantly blush, too. Instead, I choose to march beside Kang Lang.

Still, he doesn't quit. Knowing the reason for my choice, Kang Lang throws seductive glances now and again from atop the steed. Whenever I roll my eyes, he would smile. Whenever I convey the one thought that irks him, my beloved would frown huffily. Ultimately, his silent teasing continues.

Near sunset, the army makes camp, and then soon, night falls over the horizon. Kang Lang's busy directing the soldiers. I thought it was best to remain inconspicuous and thus, have been gazing at the dark sky from behind his tent. The star that shares my name twinkles happily as though reflecting my joy. During my time at temple, I used to gaze upon this star and wondered if I'd followed the path north, would my destiny be revealed. I now march toward Polaris with my destiny.

"Are you thinking of me?" Kang Lang, grinning cheekily, slides an arm around my waist.

"Yes, actually. Although, should you be so bold? We all have images to keep. In my case, He Pi's image."

"It's more exciting to do bad things in public," he whispers. Soft lips brush against my cheek while his sweet breath tickles my ear.

"You're incorrigible, Kang Lang."

"And?"

"And, I love you for it."

That wasn't the answer he expected. Heat rises to the boyish face. Kang Lang looks away, embarrassed. "You've changed too much, Your Highness. At least, attempt to fluster at my teasing instead of turning it on me."

"If I'm pedantic, you'll leave sooner, right?"

"No! I won't ever!" Kang Lang turns back apprehensively. My response of a grin forces his frown. "I'll punish you later for that, Your Highness."

"I look forward to it." My hand reaches for Kang Lang's. Warm fingers squeeze tightly in return.

"Bao Lai, I agreed for you to march with us but tomorrow, we'll likely face Bei Ling's defense. You should stay here. I won't be able to do my best if I'm constantly worrying about you."

"Then don't worry about me. I learned to fight at temple. My skills are nothing compared to yours, but I can defend myself."

"I don't doubt that you can, but war is to kill. If you merely seek to play defense, then you might as well stay here. Listen, I didn't have a choice to become what I am. I don't want blood on your hands. It's something you can't ever wash away, no matter how little amount of blood is spilled or how hard you scrub at the taint."

"Fine. I won't kill but I will fight."

"Why are you so stubborn? You're making this harder for me."

"I've chosen to stand by you and I will continue to do so under all circumstances. You once told me to do whatever I feel is right. To me, this is right."

Kang Lang sends over a sidelong glare. I know he disagrees and maybe, he's right. I'll just be a hindrance. That doesn't mean I'll let him walk into danger alone. He left me behind once. I was so afraid for him in Bao Dan. I'd give anything to never be apart again.

My defiant stare pushes back. Tension between us mounts.

Chapter 53 – 2

"Ambush! It's an ambush! Everyone to arms. Now!"

Without warning, shouts erupt left and right. A barrage of fire arrows flies into the camp. Sudden reverberations of metal striking metal echo in the night; muffled solely by cries of death. Kang Lang immediately draws his weapon but my presence is keeping him from advancing.

"Go! I'll be fine!"

Hesitantly, he runs to direct the soldiers against the ambush. I draw He Pi's blade and follow at a distance as to not distract him.

Flames are bursting from the tents. No matter which way I turn, more arrows fly into the camp. Bei Ling has us surrounded!

"Hold formation. Don't break the line!"

Kang Lang furiously cuts down soldier after soldier to make way for Bao Dan's advance. His strikes are swift and powerful, so that he doesn't need more than one to dispatch any man; and at times, several men in one strike. However, more serves to bar our forces from both retreat and advancement. At this rate, the fire will consume everything. We'll be done for!

Terror is stripping away at composure. This nightmare has to end. Life isn't worth living without my love. Whatever it takes, I must save Kang Lang!

"Get down!"

Someone calls a warning just as another barrage of arrows flies into the camp. One arrow barely misses me and lands by my feet, after which, a small patch of short dry grass on the ground catches fire and then extinguishes into the earth. That's it! Kang Lang chose this area to set camp since it's away from the dry, grassy plains. Caution was taken to avoid a possible fire attack. Though our scouts failed to spot the threat, I see no reason why Bei Ling's ploy can't be used in our favor. The soldiers who are descending upon us are standing exactly where we feared to position ourselves.

Taking the arrow, I rush to fetch the first bow I can find. Sadly, it's taken from a Bao Dan soldier whose body now lies still. I hope he is at peace. If he can hear my prayers, please guide my hand.

The arrow is relit. With the string pulled back as far as my strength can muster, I let the arrow fly. As many arrows as I can find, the process is repeated. Soon after, those around follow my lead. Each shot is a prayer sent into the darkness. Eventually, my prayers are answered when flames from far beyond the camp ignite, causing disruption in enemy lines. I run toward the drums and begin beating furiously with all my might.

Bei Ling soldiers barring our escape misconstrue the fire from behind them and the sudden burst of drums for Bao Dan reinforcements. Doubts cause some of the men to flee. They in turn either trample fellow soldiers or frighten the men behind to withdraw.

A small break in their line is all that Kang Lang needs to advance his men. His ferocity forces the small break into a large fissure. Remaining Bao Dan soldiers rally and storm forward to cut down as many Bei Ling soldiers as they can before retreating to safety. In time, I follow them out.

Chapter 53 – 3

Although glad for their lives, the weary men are disgruntled. At least one third of Bao Dan's soldiers were lost in the ambush. The rest are trying to find someone to place faults. Naturally, anger is cast toward the scouts, sentinels, and Kang Lang.

Commander Ru is the first to voice his anger. "We are without supplies, manpower, and most importantly, a capable leader. Why should we continue risking our lives for the Southland? This is their war, not ours. Let them deal with it!"

Kang Lang steps forward to offer rebuttal. "Emperor Neng Cao entrusted us with this task—"

"Neng Cao is a woman!" Ru retorts. "We are not fools, *Grand Commander*. We know exactly what she is and what you've done to gain her favor. Out of respect for her father, we have kept silent on her pathetic attempts at concealing her gender. I, for one, have had enough! Empress or otherwise, a woman should have no say in military strategies!"

"Would you prefer to instead, serve Bei Ling?"

"Bei Ling is no longer a threat to Ye or Bao Dan, Your Highness." Ru responds to my snarl. "We have ejected them. Their target remains Nan Rong. I don't know the reason you came to our camp, sire, but you merely serve to mock us and the men who have died for your cause."

Guilt silences my contention. The soldiers who died in the ambush didn't deserve their end. Those faces I saw mere hours ago no longer walk on this earth. What was it all for? The war is not over. I don't want to see another man here perish. Once we advance again, casualties will be unavoidable.

While I hang my head, another voice enters conversation. "His Highness, He Pi, is the reason we are still alive and Grand Commander Kang Lang is the reason we're no longer Bei Ling's pawns. I will continue to fight along their side even if you won't, Commander Ru."

The elder who steps forward throws a smile in my direction. The crimson bow on his shoulder is unmistakable. He was the first man to help me return fire at Bei Ling. I give an appreciative bow and he does the same.

"Despite truth in your words, who here wants to risk his life for a woman playing war? Neng Cao is weak. She will forfeit Ye to this stranger from Nan Rong. The Southland is devious. We can't trust them. Isn't it obvious they sent a puppet to seduce Neng Cao just to annex our territory?"

Commander Ru turns to me and scowls. He can say whatever he wants about me but no one is allowed to insult Kang Lang. That's my job.

"Grand Commander Kang Lang could have simply fled and let everyone perished. Instead, he risked his life for you! That is hardly the actions of someone as self-serving as you've described!"

"I still refuse to serve a woman who wants to play war!" Ru bellows.

Others who share Ru's sentiment chime in. Soon, discussions become a riot. Is her gender truly that important? Would everything that transpired have been more bearable were she a man? I turn to Kang Lang but his response is clear. He's defeated. Yet, for everything he's done to protect the men, Kang Lang deserves reverence. Without recourse, I approach Commander Ru.

"Do you respect me in the least, Commander?"

The others fall silent while Ru gawks at my defiance. "I have no love for Nan Rong. Since you helped us during the retreat, you have my thanks, sire."

"Then, do you agree that I know a thing or two about war?"

Ru's lips purse. Ultimately, his head nods.

"Were I to be a woman, would my merits diminish?"

"That's not the point, sire. Were you a woman, you could not have accomplished everything you have as a man."

"I am very glad you said that." An unruly smile crawls over my mouth. Quickly, my hair is let down.

"I am not He Pi of Nan Rong. I am His Highness's substitute and Kang Lang's lover. If you think I would consent to have my lover seduce another woman, you are naïve. And, as you are also wrong in your charges of women knowing nothing about war, I suggest everyone here give Neng Cao a bit more credit. She's assigned you the best grand commander you'll ever have. Either show him some damn respect or leave!"

My hands are tightened fists. Though my words are filled with fury, my voice is shaking. Ru falls silent while the others stare in disbelief. What was I thinking? Is letting down my hair the single proof? After all, I'm still wearing He Pi's armor. To quash all doubts, I march toward Kang Lang and pull him into a deep, passionate kiss. Shock forces the latter from dejection.

"Bao Lai," Kang Lang whispers fearfully as our lips part. I return a smile. Immediately, his arms fly around me. Kang Lang returns kiss after kiss until the crowd grumbles and relinquishes the quarrel.

With the truth exposed, Ru reluctantly stayed even though ultimately, a number of soldiers left. Camp was remade with the materials we could salvage, a messenger was deployed to Bao Dan for supplies, and several men were sent to scout the area. The rest are recovering from the ordeal. When things seemingly settled, Kang Lang calls me aside.

I don't have the chance to speak when his strong arms embrace me with a familiar bone-crushing fervor.

I now welcome that pain. Realizing his folly, Kang Lang draws back.

"Bao Lai, I'm... so sorry." Kang Lang lowers his head.

"For what? You didn't do anything wrong."

"I made such a fuss about protecting you and then you... if it hadn't been for you... but you were in danger, I was so afraid!"

"You were in danger and I was afraid, too. I understand how you feel now, Kang Lang. I am a distraction and I'll only become more of a burden once I follow you to battle."

"No, don't say that. I don't want you away from me for even a moment. When we were separated in the base and I didn't know whether you were safe, I nearly lost my mind. I kept thinking that if you were next to me, we could flee somewhere far away. Just the two of us. Even now, I still feel that way."

"As wonderful as that sounds, I'm not leaving until this ordeal is over."

"Yes, you are a stubborn woman. Now that the others know your gender, you must stay close to me."

"Are you worried or jealous?"

"Both!" Kang Lang wraps both arms around my back and cradles me in the fashion a miser would his gold. I return the sentiment and press my face against his chest, inhaling the scent I never want to forget.

"Mind telling me where your sudden *strategy* came from, Your Highness? Was it San An?"

"Actually, one of the masters at the temple always came on Thursdays to recount his time in the army. His tales were often fantastic; I never knew whether any of them were true. The strategies he employed made perfect sense though. It's a good thing I used to skip studies to visit the training halls."

"Skipping studies to be in the company of brutes? I see why you're naturally attracted to me." He smiles. "Well, it wasn't just this time that one of your strategies saved lives. It was because of you that Feng Jia faltered and Han Bei was able to route Bei Ling's main forces in Ying Ling, wasn't it?"

"You give me too much credit. I copied a strategy heard long ago from temple and vaguely outlined an idea which San An put to good use. That was all."

"Don't be modest. Anyway, I won't lie. At first, Su Jian worried me. Who'd have thought Bao Lai was more dangerous?"

"You think so? You love danger; no wonder you're naturally attracted to me. Anyhow, Kang Lang, what happened back there? Why didn't our scouts see the ambush?"

"Ye's army sat idle for years. Most of their soldiers were untrained. Given the time constraints, this was the best I could do to prepare them. If anything, it was my fault. I am the grand commander. I should have sensed the danger."

"That's preposterous! It was not your fault! You saved them. Well... I must admit I think my presence lowered your guard. It's my fault."

"Don't be dense! If my guard lowered because of you, it's still my fault. What's done is done. You helped saved the men. When new supplies come, we'll make Bei Ling pay for this. In the meantime, stay vigilant. We're vulnerable right now. There's no telling what our enemies may do."

Nodding, I follow Kang Lang back to the camp and take our posts as sentinels.

Chapter 54: The Zhaos of Bao Dan

Ning continued advancing from the east. The remainder of Nan Rong's army resumed marching from the center. Once supplies arrived, Bao Dan's forces set out from the west. Soon enough, Bei Ling's defenses blocked our path.

As impressive as I thought he was during the ambush, Kang Lang was too distracted then by the thought of my condition to show his true prowess. In the open battlefield with me by his side, there were no reservations. His skills are—for lack of a better word—inhuman.

My role was to defend. That is to say, I promised Kang Lang that I would not spill blood. To my best abilities, I knocked unconscious as many men as possible and provided unskilled Bao Dan soldiers with an extra pair of hands. The battles were frightening but with Kang Lang nearby, I was not afraid. Each time opposition is met, Northern forces retreated with their tails between their legs.

On the day before Bao Dan's final march to Bei Ling's gates, the North's defenses withdrew. A short time later, we received news that He Pi and the White Cranes stormed the palace and claimed Emperor Cai Pai under their protection. The remaining guards who served Wang Liang either surrendered or were put to death.

Bei Ling was no longer a threat. However, Wang Liang was nowhere to be found. Some claimed he perished during the raid, though that supposition is yet confirmed. My intuition signaled that he is alive. Whether he will become a threat in the future remains to be seen.

In place of Wang Liang's authority, a new council comprising of White Crane members formed. At present, representatives from all the lands are gathered in Sai Mi's—Bei Ling's capital—courtyard to discuss matters of diplomacy and the potential danger Su Jian may pose.

Those in attendant are familiar faces I had anticipated to see again, and also a new face that is hardly unfamiliar: He Pi's. I hope he doesn't notice my inappropriate gawking. It's strange to see my face on someone else's body; though, he must feel the same.

"There is no need for concern. Wang Liang is a coward. He won't show his face again after this disgrace." Neng Cao speaks proudly. She's changed much since our first meeting. I'm glad to see that she's become a confident monarch. However, parts of me still dislike her for having been in Kang Lang's attention during our time apart.

"Considering that he's willing to poison civilians and abuse his own people, we can't take that chance. The shameless coward will likely return for another attempt. If he attacks our water supplies again, we will all be done for. I say, we must be proactive. We must deploy more men and bring him to justice!" This suggestion comes from a White Crane member by the name of Zhang Tang.

Despite the White Crane's efforts at ending the mass poisoning and freeing Cai Pai from Wang Liang's grasp, very few noblemen take them seriously. Though frustrated by this indifference, every member keeps composure and speaks with politeness and civility.

Yet, what started out as a peaceful discussion eventually turns into an uproar of side conversations. This ordeal is all too familiar; mostly, it's becoming intolerable. I'm hardly listening anymore. Kang Lang, seeing my dissatisfaction, leisurely assists me away from the chaos.

Once we are finally alone, he slips an arm around my waist and kisses each part of my face.

"Did you pull me away just for this, Kang Lang?"

"Are you refusing me?"

"Not at all. If someone were to walk by, it would be terribly embarrassing."

"Like I care what anyone thinks! Want me to prove it? Shall we continue this at the meeting?"

He takes my hand and starts toward the summit. I draw him back.

"You know you can't do that. You have an image to keep now, *Grand Commander Kang Lang*."

Turning to me, he pouts. "How many times are you going to call me that? You know I hate it."

"Me, too, especially since Neng Cao gave you that title."

"Oh! You're jealous! That's what that face was!"

"What face?"

"You frowned every time she spoke. I just thought you disagreed. It was jealousy all along! Did I tell you that she proposed to me? It would have been Kang Lang, *Emperor of Bao Dan and Ye*, had I wanted."

"Well, it's not like we're married! You can still tell her, yes!"

Jerking away my hand, I start for the courtyard. Kang Lang, flustering, pulls back. Out of habit, so that I can't misconstrue his affection, Kang Lang pushes me against a wall. His body presses hard against mine. His lips rob my lungs of air. I can't help but laugh when he, at long last, moves away.

"You find this funny?" He frowns.

"No, not funny. I feel nostalgic. Do you remember the first time Mu Dan took me outside and, well, nearly broke my arm? Who knew the scene of our first kiss would come to repeat and I'd still hate you, but in a much different way."

Regret surges. Kang Lang reaches for my right arm and run his lips over every curve and corner.

"It's okay, Kang Lang. Despite everything that happened, I'm glad we met. I'm lucky to know you and I'm happy to be loved by you. Let's take everything unpleasant from our pasts in good humor. They'll make good stories to reminisce in the future."

His cheeks flush soft pink. I reach out and touch his face while he ventures a nervous gaze into my eyes. Those emerald stars are as beautiful to me now as the day I first saw them, if not more so.

Still troubled by guilt, he remains silent, though there hints an apology in his stare. I urge him once more to release the senseless remorse by kissing his forehead gently. After some consideration, he gives a slight nod. Kang Lang continues the barrage of affectionate kisses.

Chapter 54 – 2

Prior to the summit's dismissal, Kang Lang and I snuck back into the courtyard. It was He Pi who ultimately called for the meeting to end.

Afterwards, some parties tarry in small groups to continue their griping. Neng Cao immediately parts from the scene. While Her Highness walks by, an angry glare shoots in my direction. I know she desires him. I am sorry for her pain, but I'm not giving Kang Lang to anyone. Once more, he reads my thoughts. My beloved tightly squeezes my hand.

Eventually, only He Pi, San An, Han Bei, Jin, Kang Lang, and I are left. He Pi briskly approaches with a grin and wraps his arms around my shoulders.

"Keep your hands off my woman, Your Highness!" Kang Lang quickly draws me into his arms.

He Pi's head tilts curiously. With an expression resembling that of a somnambulist, he responds, "That's my face—my reflection—if anything, this creature belongs to me."

His Highness leans in for a kiss. My hand instinctively flies across his face. Rubbing his cheek, He Pi stares on with wounded eyes.

"Didn't Jin deliver my message? You're mine, right?"

"Are you... out of your mind?! How can you talk like that and sound so innocent?" I scuttle farther back into Kang Lang's arms.

He Pi's response is a wry chuckle. Turning to Kang Lang, he frets like a little boy. "So, you don't want to play with me anymore, Mu Dan?"

"Play? No. Although, if you're willing to dress as a woman, Your Highness, I would gladly give my love to you both at once. It's not every day one can experience the joy of twin pleasures."

"Hmm, I'd rather Bao Lai dressed as He Pi and come to me instead. I finally realize the person I've been searching for my whole life, is me."

His Highness's hand reaches for my face. Immediately, I hide behind Kang Lang. "What is wrong with you? You're the great He Pi? I was supposed to model myself after you?!"

He Pi grins boyishly. I feel unnerved.

"Where have you been, anyway? Why did you leave Nan Rong?"

"That is a question I also have," San An steps forward to join the conversation.

He Pi shrugs. "I didn't leave Nan Rong. Not until Ying injured San An. I was perusing the market when a monk by the name of Lo Han offered to take me back to Tian Mao Yi Temple."

"Master Lo Han? Wait, he mistook you for me, so you left?"

"I wanted to know more about the person I was mistaken for. Can't help curiosity."

"You jerk! I can't believe how irresponsible you are! You let everything fall to chaos because of curiosity?!"

"Bao Lai... you shouldn't." Jin shakes his head and I realize my mistake. I've been He Pi for some time now, but the real He Pi, emperor of Nan Rong, deserves some respect.   Though, I fail to feel that respect at the moment.

His Highness chuckles. Then, through a sweet smile, declares, "It's okay, Jin. She can yell at me. After all, I ruined her reputation at the temple."

My heart stops. What did he mean by that? He didn't dare!   Then again, why should I take him seriously? He's learned everything from Mu Dan. For my apathetic reaction, He Pi grins. He then draws a letter from his shirt pocket to present as a peace offering.

"Here, I found this. I think Master Tai Hung meant to give it to you. Well, I must return to Nan Rong. Before I go, I'll give you a boon—anything you want for having subbed in my stead."

"I didn't do a very good job," the apology comes out as muffles. I've pressed my face against Kang Lang's back.

He Pi laughs boisterously. "She's almost as cute as me, Kang Lang! I'm jealous! Anyway, that I still have a country to call home is good enough for me. Pick something. I'll gladly make the decree to have you become my empress."

"Why, so you can use me as your body double when you leave the palace?"

"She's too smart, Kang Lang. I don't like her anymore."

Kang Lang smiles but makes no reply. While staring at the grinning He Pi, San An's figure catches my eyes. He's withdrawn from conversation. The pain of loneliness is ardently clear. Jin is also disappointed but forces his usual amiability. They've done so much for me. I want to repay them somehow.

"Your Highness." Stepping forth from behind my beloved, I continue. "I do have one request. Please return Consort En's titles and give Empress Pai the respect she deserves. I don't know what must be done but if you can restore them... well, actually, all the women from court during the conflict... to grace, that is all I ask."

He Pi throws a short grin and complies. San An glances over and Jin looks up. Crooked smiles form over their faces, which eventually shift to contentment. I know it's not enough. I just hope that with time, they will come to forgive my previous transgressions.

Following a few more pleasantries, He Pi and the Nan Rong princes prepare for the caravan home.

Han Bei, who has been waiting patiently, now comes forthwith. At the sight of his piercing green eyes, my breathing grows short. I was ready to begin my life with Kang Lang. One more obligation still keeps me.

"Are you ready to fulfill your promise?"

Without delay, Kang Lang chains both arms around me. "What do you want with her, Han?"

"Give me some credit, little brother. I am not interested in this girl in your perverse manner. I can do better."

"Then leave her be! Undo your agreement!"

"That entirely depends on her. I won't drag her to Ning kicking and screaming but if she's a woman of her word, she'll come with me by choice."

"Kang Lang, I'll go."

I had to break my promise to Jin. I don't want to break another which I'm capable of keeping. Refuting my decision, Kang Lang's hold increases in fervor.

"The hell you will! I'm not letting you out of my sight!"

"I'll come back. Won't I, Lord Han Bei?"

Han Bei shrugs and turns to the direction of the main gate; calling over his shoulder while leaving. "If you will come, then now is the time."

"Kang Lang…"

"No! If you go with him, I won't wait for you!" Kang Lang's voice disrupts into deep bitterness. His arms bind tighter.

What is he saying? Once I leave with Han Bei, he'll in turn, leave me? Is that how easily he can discard his affections? I refuse to believe that. Kang Lang must be testing me, but this is not a matter of love.

"Kang Lang, I don't love Han Bei."

"If you go with him, I won't forgive you. No matter the reason. Bao Lai, stay with me!"

"Why are you so insecure?"

I turn back but he won't look at me. Does he not trust me? Kang Lang mentioned that he never thought I would ever return his adoration. The fear in his eyes when confessing doubts prior is present tenfold. I don't want to break another promise, but I'd rather have a troubled conscience than to see him this way.

"Kang Lang, I'm leaving."

Wrath surges. Kang Lang grits his jaw. He gazes back intently for a short moment and then turns away. As he storms off, I grab onto his hand.

"Aren't you coming? Kang Lang?"

He whips around. From witnessing my cheeky grin, his body grows tremulous. In time, strength gives out and Kang Lang falls to his knees. I kneel down and wrap my arms around his back. The gesture is not returned.

"I was joking. Are you mad?"

No response. He stares back blankly as though consciousness is somewhere distant. Maybe, I went too far. My attempts to draw him back with kisses are futile and then the chills of panic turn everything cold. I'm shaking him but he won't respond. He's not blinking. I don't know if he's even breathing.

"Kang Lang! Please, say something! I'm sorry! Come back! Don't leave me! I'll do anything you want!"

My face buries in his chest to validate the heart that belongs to me is still beating. For a long time, there is only silence. I don't know else to do except increase the strength of my embrace and call out his name. When dread nearly suffocates me under its weight, slowly, his head lowers. Leaning close to my ear, my love whispers, "You will be punished."

My lips part but I don't have the chance to reply. Both my cheeks are trapped in severe grips. My eyes are watering; yet, I must endure the pain. I deserve this. I deserve to be punished.

He bursts into delirious laughter as though having read my thoughts. "I'm a bad influence on you, Bao Lai! Anyhow, will you break your promise to Han Bei?"

"Yes. From now on, I will only make promises to you and I intend to keep every single one. Although, were you serious? Would you have left me had I kept my promise to Han Bei?"

"No. I was leaving to fetch some rope so I could drag you back to Bao Dan." He grins. "Actually, I knew you were joking but, um... you wouldn't ever leave me, right?"

Though he says he knew, fear and doubt linger in troubled eyes. There's nothing I can do at the moment to fully wash away his apprehensions. With time, I know he will come to feel assured.

"Never! You won't ever be freed of me!"

Kang Lang's demeanor relaxes. His arms hold me tightly.

I never thought I would come to know love and certainly, never dreamed that I could earn love from this wonderful man. We may not have met on the best of terms, and he's driven me crazy from time to time, but I don't regret anything that's happened. Whichever path he chooses to walk, I will always remain beside him. This is my silent promise and I swear to never break it.

Chapter 54 – 3

Although Neng Cao still claims Bao Dan under Ye's authority, Kang Lang remains the Grand Commander. For his valiant accomplishments during the conflict, the people revere him as their true leader. He doesn't care for authority, and even though he gripes of his position daily, I know he's grown fond of the people.

After the assembly in Bei Ling, Kang Lang took me as his wife. I'm still not used to the idea of being called, Madam Zhao; though, my beloved finds it amusing and addresses me so whenever I vex him. I, in turn, refer to him as Mister Zhao.

"Madam Zhao!" Kang Lang cries while storming through the chamber door. "Did you think you could hide it from me?"

"Hide what, Mister Zhao?"

"Your clumsiness. Did you or did you not scrape your knee on the pavement outside earlier, Madam Zhao, and when I looked over, you ran away?"

"You saw that, did you?" I smile. "I had to hide it, Mister Zhao. You always overreact, even to the slightest of cuts. I've bandaged the scrape."

Kang Lang kneels by the bed, lifts up my robe's hem to survey the bandaging, and then slowly takes it apart.

"What are you doing? I've just put that on!"

Ignoring my objection, he looks over the wound and frowns. Though I've cleaned the scrape, the bandages are slightly stained red. Somehow, in the course of his campaign against Bei Ling, he's learned to suppress excitement at the sight of blood. Actually, he's changed dramatically since the day we met. This must be the real Kang Lang, the man hidden behind Mu Dan. He's the most loving husband a woman could ask for.

"Why exactly were you running in the first place? Did you forget you aren't wearing men's clothes anymore?"

"Well, that and I have exciting news."

"What? Are you pregnant?" He pouts.

"Yes. But since you sound so disappointed, just ignore what I've said."

His eyes broaden. Kang Lang grabs both my hands. "Bao Lai, are you?!"

Reflecting my grin, a wide smile breaks across his face. Though his expression is pure joy, Kang Lang's feared this day for some time now, of this I am certain. I am afraid, too. Just recently, I've come to see myself as a true woman. In spite of this, the idea of motherhood is still frightening. We're both still naïve in many ways but I know we always can depend on each other. Kang Lang reads my thoughts and smiles knowingly.

"You must be more careful, Bao Lai. You can't afford to fall with our child in your belly."

"Yes, I'm sorry. I won't run anymore. I promise. What about you, Kang Lang, are you happy?"

"Of course! I'm scared but I'm also happy. Don't worry, I promise to be the best father to our child."

"I know you will."

He sighs softly in relief and then slowly raises a hand to caress my belly.

"My dear, is that letter from He Pi still in the study?"

"Yes. Why?" Apprehension manifests over his eyes. My hand cups around his cheek to reassure Kang Lang.

"Well, I don't plan to use it to claim any authority. I would like our child to know of his or her past. I grew up without it and felt lost for a long time, until I met you and found a place by your side."

"I understand." He reaches up to kiss my cheek. Then, leisurely whispers, "Your secret is safe with me, Empress of Ning."

While the letter proved my birthright as the missing daughter of Empress Piao, we've chosen to stay in Bao Dan. Maybe someday, we will return to Ning. For now, this is our home.

Kang Lang kisses my forehead and then together, we leave the house for a stroll down the path which leads to a beautiful field of flowers under wide-open skies. In one way other another, my dream came true.

The End.

www.ingramcontent.com/pod-product-compliance
Lightning Source LLC
Chambersburg PA
CBHW051927020726
47501CB00001B/18